CAUSE FOR CONCERN

By

Linda Kistler

This book is a work of fiction. Places, events, and situations in this story are purely fictional. Any resemblance to actual persons, living or dead, is coincidental.

ISBN: 1-4107-7570-4 (e-book)
ISBN: 1-4107-7569-0 (Paperback)

Library of Congress Control Number: 2003095066

This book is printed on acid free paper.

Printed in the United States of America
Bloomington, IN

1stBooks - rev. 08/06/03

For my husband, Jim,
and in memory of my mother, Alice Miller

For Liz,

Enjoy,

Linda Kutter

12-16-03

Prologue

She reached for the cell phone, interrupting the second ring.

"Nancy, the limo is here. We'll come by for you and Dick in a few minutes."

"I'm ready, Ruth, but Dick isn't here. Apparently, he and Hillary went to the Center for some sort of emergency meeting early this morning. At least that's the gist of the note he left on the kitchen counter. He promised to meet me in front of Old Main at 10:45. That should be plenty of time."

"Fine. But it seems a bit odd they would go off to the hospital knowing they've got to come back in a couple of hours."

"I know," Nancy sighed. "Something urgent must have come up. When I awoke around 3 o'clock Dick still hadn't come to bed, and the light was on in the study. I assume he was working on his remarks for today."

"I dread the next few hours," Ruth confessed. "It won't be easy for any of us, especially Dick. But for the students' sake, we've got to present a strong public face."

Despite the pain in her friend's voice, Nancy was confident that Ruth Borovski's natural dignity would not abandon her. There would be no public display of emotion from Ruth, not today. She was far less confident of her own ability to control her emotions before impressionable students and an interested public.

"I'll meet you at the end of the driveway."

She switched off the phone, rinsed and stored her empty mug in the dishwasher and walked into the foyer for a final inspection. The hall mirror reflected a tall, slim woman with stylishly cut short black hair, noticeably graying. Brushing a bit of lint from her long-sleeved black silk dress, she checked the safety clasp of her antique gold necklace, a treasured gift from her ailing mother. She was as ready as she'd ever be. Retrieving her black shoulder bag, she slipped the cell phone into the bag and touched the supply of Kleenex stashed in the bottom. Closing the front door, she emerged into the warm sunshine of a brilliant spring morning.

As she walked along the curved brick path to the street, a black stretch limousine drew up to the curb. The driver quickly moved around the car, opened the rear passenger door and helped her inside. Greeting her friend with a brief hug, she settled into the rear seat and exchanged greetings with Ruth's sons, Paul and Anton, who occupied the facing seats.

Ruth Borovski, a petite woman in her late fifties, wore a navy blue sheath dress set off by a single strand of pearls. Fastidiously groomed, her calm demeanor and innate old world charm were evident. A pair of oversized dark glasses nested in her thick light hair. Her reading glasses,

v

usually suspended around her neck on a gold chain, were missing. Only the dark smudges beneath her hazel eyes betrayed the trauma of the past few weeks, hinting of the ordeal that lay ahead.

Anton Borovski, seated opposite Nancy, greeted affectionately the woman he considered his surrogate mother. Tall and lean, he had inherited his father's unruly thick dark hair and piercing brown eyes. In his black pinstripe suit and dark paisley tie, he could have been a Wall Street investment banker. In fact, he was a tenured Associate Professor at the University of California at Berkeley where he already had demonstrated promise as a world-class research chemist. Following in the footsteps of both parents, the son exuded a quiet confidence and inner control.

Paul Borovski resembled a younger male version of his mother. Of medium height, he had a marathoner's lean body and his mother's fair complexion and blond hair. A marathoner since his high school days, he continued to indulge his passion for running despite the demands of graduate work at Stanford. Both sons had arrived in Hillsdale three weeks ago to be with their parents.

"We're really getting the VIP treatment today," Nancy remarked, glancing around the interior of the limousine. "I can't remember the last time I rode in a limo that wasn't going to or from an airport."

"Larry Northrop insisted on this arrangement. It's a bit overdone," said Ruth. "He even planned to deliver us home after the service and lunch. I put my foot down. The limo won't be taking us home. The boys and I will spend some time together in the lab this afternoon going over our current research projects and mapping out how to proceed from here. Besides, I really need to get back to my students."

The limousine glided to a stop at the end of the quiet residential street, made a wide left turn onto Shawnee Hill Road and headed down the mountain toward the river bridge and the town beyond.

"You're seriously planning to stay on campus after the service and lunch?" Nancy asked. "Your classes and labs are already covered by others. Surely no one expects you to meet students today. Why put that additional pressure on yourself?"

"It's not pressure, Nancy, it's therapy," Ruth smiled. "Being in the lab with my students and the boys is infinitely better than coming back to an empty house. Jacob and I have jointly taught the doctoral lab in polymer science for years," she went on. "It meets this afternoon, and I've already missed the past three weeks. If it becomes too difficult to deal with, Paul and Anton can take over and finish up with the lab assistants."

Nancy knew enough not to argue further. She changed the subject. "Larry Northrop's reception last evening was lovely wasn't it? For everyone—faculty, students, administrators and our visitors—it was a very special occasion. People had a chance to relax, renew old acquaintances and meet new people. Larry is a master at providing the right setting for occasions like this. There was a lot of genuine warmth and hospitality at Cabot University last night.

"Jacob would have been delighted to see so many of his friends and colleagues assembled in one place," she observed. "It's an extraordinary tribute to his memory that people from around the country and even his colleagues from France managed to be here today."

"Dad would have been especially pleased that his friends didn't dwell on the purpose for the gathering," remarked Anton. "Clearly, some people used the occasion to network and catch up on news. The reception reminded me of an old fashioned class reunion."

"Did you notice Senator Harris bending the ear of Dr. Wensberg, the President's Science Advisor?" asked Paul Borovski. "I wonder what that was all about. And that wasn't the only conversation I would have liked to overhear," he laughed.

"This is probably the first visit to Cabot University for some guests," said Nancy. "I understand Dr. Wensberg and rest of the politicians from Washington flew into Hillsdale Regional Airport on a government jet. That doubtless made a big impression on Hillsdale's town fathers.

"The Hillsdale Chronicle reported this morning that more than three hundred people attended President Northrop's reception. And perhaps nine hundred people are expected for the memorial service this morning."

"Yes." Ruth's thoughts were clearly elsewhere.

"One positive outcome of this gathering," observed Anton, "may be to persuade the politicians to increase support for basic research in the sciences. We're really feeling the pinch of federal budget cuts even in my lab. I assume you and Dad have scrambled for research funds like everybody else."

"We're in good shape, thanks to several multi-year grants that still have another year to run," his mother responded.

She turned to Nancy. "In the turmoil of the last couple of weeks, did Paul tell you he's nearly finished his dissertation at Stanford?"

"Congratulations, Paul," Nancy said warmly, reaching over and grabbing his hand. "Finally. You must be relieved to finish and get on with your life. When will you defend your dissertation? And then what are your plans?"

"Hopefully, I'll be a newly minted Ph.D. by the end of the summer," Paul said, a touch of quiet pride in his voice. "I've been offered an assistant professorship at MIT, subject to completing my doctorate, of course. Although I want to discuss the options a little more with Mom and Anton, chances are pretty good that I'll move back east this fall. It's hard to pass up a faculty position at MIT, although the weather will take some getting used to after four years in California."

He paused for a moment. "My one regret is that the dissertation took so long to finish and Dad won't be here to celebrate with the rest of us."

The group was silent as the limousine slowly navigated the thickening traffic along Market Avenue. The majestic oaks that arched across the wide boulevard displayed the chartreuse leaves of early spring on this bright mid-May morning. Showy azaleas and mountain laurel, brilliant with blossoms, set off the delicate flowering dogwood trees and presented a blaze of color in the wide median strip separating the lanes of Hillsdale's principal residential avenue.

Traffic slowed to a crawl as the limousine approached Monument Square. After some delay, the car merged with others proceeding in a single line up University Avenue, a quarter-mile from their destination. The avenue was nearly impassable, clogged with throngs of people heading toward the university.

A flock of in-line skaters, bare-chested and arms flailing, careened among the cars, and hurtled toward the intersection of University Avenue and Main Street. Ignoring the traffic cop's shrill whistles, intent on beating the yellow light, they flew through the crowded intersection and disappeared down Market Avenue.

"There's an accident waiting to happen," Ruth observed.

A lone cyclist in black Speedo shorts and brilliant yellow top appeared alongside the limo, weaving carefully among the stalled vehicles. The group watched as he drew up to a bike rack near the campus entrance and locked his bike in an empty slot. The young man removed his helmet, worked his fingers through a mass of frizzy blond hair and joined the throngs slowly making their way through the wrought iron gates guarding the entrance to Cabot University.

The mass of humanity overflowed the sidewalks and blocked the driveway approaching Old Main, the university's oldest building and site of the eleven o'clock memorial service. Hundreds of students, many clad in scanty tank tops, cutoffs and sandals, mingled with townspeople and guests slowly moving toward the auditorium.

The silence deepened as each passenger braced for the ordeal that lay ahead. Reaching the university's main entrance at last, the crowd parted and the limousine glided between ornate wrought-iron gates and along the tree-lined semi-circular driveway. It slowed smoothly to a stop near the broad steps at the entrance to the building.

A campus security officer in formal dark blue dress uniform, complete with white gloves, opened both rear doors on the passenger side.

"Good morning, Professor Borovski," the officer removed his hat and greeted Ruth. He smiled toward Nancy and nodded to Anton and Paul Borovski. As they emerged into the brilliant sunshine, Ruth and Nancy quickly donned dark glasses.

"My instructions are to escort you directly upstairs to the President's suite," said the officer, clearing a path through the crowd. "President Northrop is already here along with a lot of visitors. Because of the crowd in the lobby, we'll use the side entrance." He led them along the side of the building.

Anton and Paul Borovski, guiding each woman by the elbow, followed the guard as throngs of people politely gave way for the party. Nancy nodded briefly to a few students and faculty colleagues she recognized. The group finally reached the side entrance and entered the building.

The security guard paused before the back stairway to the second floor. He turned awkwardly toward Ruth. "Professor Borovski, all of us in campus security extend our sympathy to you and your sons on the loss of Dr. Jacob. He was the heart and soul of this campus, and we will miss him greatly." He paused, unable to continue.

"Thank you, Henry," Ruth reached out and touched his arm. "And please tell the others I appreciate their thoughtfulness.

"Now, let's go upstairs," she said firmly.

They climbed the narrow stairway in silence. Opening the door to the second floor, they entered a spacious foyer outside the suite of offices occupied by the President of Cabot University. The area was overflowing with men and women engaged in muted conversation, some balancing pastries and cups of coffee.

Nancy recognized many of the dignitaries, senior faculty and administrators who had attended the reception the evening before. Ruth moved quickly to greet a man she and her husband considered both a close personal friend and professional colleague. Today he headed the contingent from Ecole Polytechnic in Paris. Exchanging brief comments in French, Ruth re-introduced her sons and Nancy to the visitors from France.

Larry Northrop, white-haired and distinguished, looking every inch the successful university President, stood near the door to his office. Seeing their arrival, he excused himself and quietly pushed through the crowd toward them. Kissing both women on the cheek, he shook hands with Anton and Paul and ushered them into his private office.

"Where's Dick?" The President turned to Nancy, an eyebrow raised.

"He'll be here shortly, Larry. He and Hillary Gardner went to Essex Medical Center early this morning. He promised to be here by 10:45. That's plenty of time."

Nancy glanced at her watch. "We agreed to meet outside on the front steps. I'd better get down there right now."

She worked her way across the crowded foyer, this time descending the wide front stairway to the main lobby. Pushing through the crush of people entering the first floor auditorium, she reached the ornate entrance doors and front steps. Nancy was stunned by the size of the crowd converging on Old Main. Squinting in the bright sunshine, she faced the oncoming throng, searching for her husband.

With a sigh of relief, she spotted Dick Atherton and Hillary Gardner, her childhood friend and Dick's colleague at Essex Medical Center, entering the main gate to the campus and moving with the crowd along the driveway toward the building. She waved and motioned toward the side entrance, working her way down the wide front steps. She greeted them at the guarded side entrance.

"Today, of all days, I can't believe you two felt you had to go to work for a couple of hours," she groused. "What was so important it couldn't wait until after the service?"

"Sorry, Nancy," said Dick, not at all apologetic. "We had to review some blood and tissue test results. The report was faxed from Philadelphia early this morning. I'll tell you about it later."

"It was my fault," Hillary interjected. "I got a phone call late last night that the test results were coming shortly. We both wanted to see if they confirmed our preliminary analysis."

"Tell me about it later." Nancy led them upstairs, across the crowded foyer and into the President's office. Larry Northrop, visibly relieved at their appearance, offered the newcomers coffee or tea.

"Here are copies of the printed program," Larry said, distributing copies to each person. "Let me review it with you briefly. It's almost time to move downstairs."

"I'll open the service with welcoming remarks, including recognizing our guests from Washington and around the country and from Europe. After the welcome, Rabbi Stein will offer a prayer. Then I'll give a brief personal reminiscence summarizing Jacob's influence on the students and faculty and his contribution to the university." The group read through the program as he reviewed it.

"Next, Dr. Wensberg, the President's Science Advisor, will recognize Jacob's national and international contributions to science," Northrop said. "Following his remarks, Kevin Parks, the graduate student that Ruth has personally selected, will speak on behalf of the students and alumni who worked with Jacob over the years."

He turned to Dick. "You're the last speaker. After your comments, I'll close the ceremony, thank everyone for coming and invite them to the reception. Our special guests already know they are invited to lunch.

"Any questions?" He glanced around the group.

"I'm as ready as I'll ever be," Dick said. "My eulogy is right here." He patted his jacket pocket.

"As far as seating arrangements are concerned," Larry continued, "Ruth, Paul and Anton will join me in the front row next to Dick, Rabbi Stein, Dr. Wensberg, and Kevin Parks. Nancy, you and Hillary will join some of our guests from Paris and around the country in the second row.

"We'll use the back stairway and enter the auditorium through the side door near the stage and take seats in the reserved section at the front of the auditorium."

"Larry, thank you for handling all of these details," said Ruth.

"This is the least I could do under the circumstances," he said. He glanced at his watch as the Old Main clock in the tower directly above them tolled the hour.

"It's eleven o'clock. If you're ready, Ruth, we should begin."

The party left the President's office and descended the side stairs to the first floor, followed by the guests assembled in the foyer. Passing through a short hallway, they entered Old Main auditorium. Larry leaned over and whispered a few words to Ruth. Taking her arm, he led her to her seat in the front row. Dick Atherton and Paul and Anton Borovski and the others took their places beside her. Nancy and Hillary seated themselves in the second row as student ushers escorted the other guests to seats in the reserved section.

Nancy settled into her chair and glanced around the auditorium. The room was filled beyond capacity. Faculty, staff, the Mayor, assorted town officials and others occupied all the seats on the auditorium's main floor. A few people milled around the rear of the hall, searching in vain for a vacant seat. The balcony was filled to overflowing, occupied mostly by students, many blocking the aisles and standing along the rear wall.

Last year, the exterior and interior of Old Main, including the auditorium and the handsome front stairway leading to the second floor, had been completely renovated and restored to its original splendor. The oldest building on the Cabot University campus, it was originally constructed in the 1860s. The region's finest example of Georgian architecture, the mellow red brick exterior was trimmed in white wood. Although the building was not the largest on campus, it was the landmark that defined the campus. Old Main's beautiful clock tower was clearly visible throughout the town, its bell tolling the hours throughout the day and night.

In the renovated interior, the auditorium and a fine museum of local artifacts occupied most of the first floor, with senior administrative offices housed on the second floor. Painted in a soft colonial white, the auditorium featured beautifully carved cornices around the ceilings and Palladium windows. Except for the carpeted aisles, the auditorium displayed the original wide-planked oak floor, restored to a mellow, rich luster. Comfortable new cushioned seats replaced the 1930s wooden seats that students and faculty had long detested.

Bright sunlight streamed through the two-story Palladium windows lining the east wall of the auditorium. Several windows were open to catch the gentle morning breeze. A half-dozen gleaming antique brass and crystal chandeliers cast a warm glow in the three-story room. For many years, Old Main auditorium had served as the traditional center for campus gatherings. The newly renovated room was the perfect setting for the memorial service that was about to begin.

The audience grew silent as Larry Northrop ascended the few steps to the stage and walked to the podium. The stage itself was unadorned except for a long bank of spring flowers in the front, and the heavy beige curtain at the rear on which was displayed the large blue and gold seal of Cabot University. Flags of the United States and Pennsylvania flanked the stage.

Adjusting the microphone, Larry began to speak. "On behalf of Ruth, Anton and Paul Borovski and the entire Cabot University family, welcome to this memorial service for Dr. Jacob Borovski, our colleague, world renowned academician, spouse, parent and friend."

Acknowledging the presence of the politicians from Washington and Harrisburg along with distinguished faculty from Harvard, Stanford, Berkeley, the Ecole Polytechnic in Paris and elsewhere, he began his prepared remarks.

Glancing around the crowded auditorium, Nancy recognized several prominent corporate executives, including the President and Chairman of Capital Chemicals, who were seated near Jacob Borovski's professional colleagues on the Chemistry Department faculty.

As Larry finished his opening remarks and introduced Rabbi Stein, Nancy's thoughts wandered back to the September afternoon nearly thirty-five years ago, to her first encounter with Jacob Borovski. Jacob, Nancy and thirteen other new faculty members had assembled in the Old Main auditorium for an orientation session with the President and other administrators. The group later would jokingly dub itself the Class of '65, marking the year they joined the faculty of Cabot University.

Jacob's commanding presence and natural leadership qualities were evident from the beginning. Nancy vividly recalled his wiry six foot three inch frame, the thick head of dark brown hair that defied control, his piercing, wide-set brown eyes, strong Semitic features and heavily accented baritone voice. Although he was fluent in four languages, one of Jacob's few linguistic failures was his inability to speak unaccented, fluent English, even after many years as an American citizen. She smiled to herself, recalling his habit of unconsciously lapsing without warning into Polish, German or French in the middle of an otherwise sensible conversation in English.

Her reverie ended abruptly. Rabbi Stein's prayer and Larry Northrop's personal reminiscence had already concluded. Dr. Robert Wensberg, the President's Science Advisor, offered greetings and read a personal condolence from the President, then launched into a eloquent summary of Jacob Borovski's scientific contributions and professional honors over the past quarter century. Jacob's stature as a research chemist and his collaboration with Ruth as his co-principal researcher were well known in academic circles. Nancy suspected, however, that many townspeople in the audience did not fully appreciate the international stature of the Borovskis, nor the luster their presence brought to the university.

Kevin Parks, one of Jacob and Ruth's doctoral students, mounted the stage and walked to the podium. Nancy was surprised that Ruth had selected him to represent Jacob's students and alumni. Apparently a brilliant graduate student in chemistry, Parks was a campus hanger-on, viewed by most faculty as a social misfit. He spent countless hours hanging around Jacob's office, working in his lab, even napping on an empty workbench or sleeping in a library carrel. A loner, his fellow graduate students ignored him.

Typically attired in filthy jeans, sneakers and a smelly T-shirt or sweatshirt, depending upon the season, his appalling personal hygiene was legendary among students and faculty. During the past year, he had grown a full, untrimmed beard. He looked more like one of Hillsdale's homeless than a brilliant graduate student of the famous Professor Borovski. Nancy considered him a minor nuisance, a perennial student, unable or unwilling to complete his thesis and move beyond the relatively sheltered campus environment. She had concluded long ago that his constant presence around Ruth and Jacob comprised his only social interaction at Cabot University.

Today, Nancy scarcely recognized Kevin Parks. Clad in a dress shirt and tie, clean khakis and a wool sport jacket despite the warmth of the day, he had shaved his beard and drawn back his long hair into a relatively neat ponytail. Kevin was transformed. A low murmur of recognition swept through the audience as he began to speak.

Kevin delivered his eulogy in a clear voice, his eloquence a stunning surprise to everyone who knew him. The audience listened intently to his remarks, delivered flawlessly and with extraordinary feeling. A brief ripple of applause erupted and quickly died as he left the podium.

Ruth had chosen well. Kevin Parks was indeed an appropriate representative of the students and alumni. Glancing down at her printed program, she realized that her husband would be the next and final speaker.

It was fitting that Dick Atherton, Jacob's closest personal friend, would deliver the principal eulogy. Dick had spent hours laboring over his remarks, a task that Nancy carefully refrained from discussing before the service. She felt a surge of intense affection for the tall slim man who had been her husband for more than thirty-five years. His erect bearing, thick head of silver hair and handsome, unlined features presented a commanding presence.

He climbed the few steps to the stage and walked to the podium. Adjusting the microphone, he reached into his jacket, pulled out his prepared notes and placed them on the lectern. Calmly, he glanced around the quiet auditorium, smiled down at Ruth and her sons and looked up at the students overflowing the balcony.

"We buried Jacob Borovski two weeks ago," he began. "It was a miserable day—raw and windy, with an unremitting downpour—a day that perfectly reflected the spirits of those gathered together at the graveside." He paused briefly. Nancy, startled, realized that he was struggling for control.

"We honored one of Jacob's last requests that his funeral be private and limited to members of his family and a few close friends. He wanted to spare Ruth, Paul and Anton the ordeal of a very public funeral. He also expressed his desire that there should be no public memorial service to mark his passing. I believe that the painkillers he was taking had clouded his judgment; for that reason, his request has been disregarded today. I will acknowledge my role in this gathering the next time I see him.

"However, I am confident he wouldn't object to my sharing a few details of the funeral with you. The ceremony was conducted in the Jewish tradition, with Anton and Paul reading the Khaddish, the traditional Hebrew prayers for the dead. Rabbi Stein of Temple Beth El here in Hillside spoke briefly and movingly of Jacob and what his life has meant to his family, to his temple, to the university and to the community at large. The simple ceremony and the words of Rabbi Stein were enormously comforting to those of us who were privileged to attend.

"Ruth, Paul and Anton have asked me to thank you for coming today," Dick continued. "They also want you to know that the community's outpouring of sympathy and kindness during the last difficult six months have eased immeasurably the pain of their loss." Dick glanced toward Ruth and the boys in the front row.

He began to read from his prepared remarks. "Today the students, faculty and staff of Cabot University and Jacob's friends and associates from here and abroad have gathered to bid farewell to a man whose influence and achievements extend far beyond the boundaries of this quiet university. I believe that Jacob would want any public memorial service to celebrate his life and not dwell on the last difficult months of his illness.

"Let me share with you some of his triumphs along with a few of his miscues. You already are aware of his professional accomplishments as a research scientist. I suspect that everyone here understands his devotion to teaching and his genuine affection for his students, not only those in this audience, but also the thousands of students whose lives he influenced over more than three decades. We need not dwell on the countless ways in which his spirit will live on in their memories and ours.

"I think you'll agree with me that Kevin Parks, one of Jacob's most promising current graduate students, has just delivered a superb remembrance of Jacob's contribution to his students and to student life here at Cabot University. Jacob not only prepared his students for professional careers in science, he prepared them for life.

"The President's Science Advisor has eloquently described Jacob's scientific contributions. His professional accomplishments are known throughout the world, and his presence brought international recognition to Cabot University. The many doctoral students nurtured under the demanding and watchful tutelage of Jacob (and Ruth) Borovski are eagerly sought after by the most prestigious universities and corporations around the country. The university was blessed to have a scientist of his intellect and stature as a faculty member for so many years."

He paused.

"This morning, I want to remember perhaps his most enduring achievements—those as a husband and father. In the two weeks since Ruth asked me to speak to this gathering, I have felt an overwhelming sense of inadequacy. How can I, in a few moments, summarize the essence of Jacob Borovski—his awesome intellect, his humanity, his courage, the essential experiences of a lifetime cut short?" Dick asked.

"I'd like to mention a few of his human qualities as I came to know them during our long friendship. Most of you know that Jacob joined the faculty of Cabot University in the autumn of 1965. As a young man, he abandoned a promising research career at Capital Chemicals Company, one of this country's premier corporations, to become a teacher. Jacob wanted to work with young people, to infuse in them the excitement he felt for science and the intellectual challenge of basic research.

"Let me go back a few years. Both Jacob and Ruth joined the research laboratory at the Oakton Division of Capital Chemicals in the early 1960s.

Ruth remained at Capital Chemicals for several years after Jacob came to Cabot. When she joined him on the faculty, they formed a teaching and research team in polymer chemistry that is known around the world.

"My wife, Nancy, also joined the faculty in 1965," he continued. "She came home the evening after her first day on campus, speaking enthusiastically about a new colleague—one Jacob Borovski, a chemistry professor. Having been married for only a year, I was a bit jealous of this unknown character that had so impressed her. Later that evening, we received a phone call from Jacob and Ruth inviting us to a get-acquainted dinner the following Saturday night. Thus began a friendship that has shaped and enriched our lives."

Dick smiled at the audience.

"Jacob and Ruth Borovski's hospitality is legendary. Since their arrival in Hillsdale, they have opened their home on countless occasions to students, faculty and professional associates from here and abroad. More than one foreign student arriving in Hillsdale without a dorm room and short on cash received food and shelter at their home, sometimes for several months, until they settled in.

"The often spontaneous gatherings of students, faculty and friends in Jacob and Ruth's living room are among my lasting memories of Jacob. None of us will forget the countless occasions when, sprawled on the living room floor, we debated the most serious issues of the day. And over the years, we never lacked controversial topics. The civil rights movement. The Vietnam War. Sex discrimination and affirmative action. The pro-choice, pro-life issue. More recently, the drug culture. Now, the lack of civility in our everyday encounters and the ugly increase in violence, whether on city streets or in quiet towns like Hillsdale.

"Those topics and more consumed us all. Inevitably, the discussions became more heated as the evening wore on, perhaps influenced by Jacob's extensive selection of fine French wines." Laughter rippled across the room. The audience relaxed.

"Jacob had strong convictions on every issue, bringing his awesome intellect to bear, usually on the liberal side. We all know it was almost impossible to win an argument with him. I'll always remember his emotional and intellectual stand against the Vietnam War. I recall vividly even now his leadership of the protest march through downtown Hillsdale following the deaths of the students at Kent State University. For many students, I suspect those faculty-student gatherings at the Borovski home were the most memorable part of their college experience."

Dick smiled ruefully. "It's ironic that I, an unrepentant conservative, should count as my best friend a man whose liberal views consistently put us on opposite sides of political issues. The fact is, Jacob and I rarely agreed on anything in the political arena. Still, in the midst of the most heated exchanges, we respected each other's views. Jacob was an intellectual, a Renaissance man. Respect for different views was one of his most memorable qualities.

"The Borovski's hospitality extended to many of the distinguished visitors with us here today. Many townspeople never realized that a number of Nobel Prize winners visited Hillsdale regularly as guests of Jacob and Ruth. Their home was always open to others, and most of us never failed to accept an invitation to join them. It's fair to say that their home has been the focal point of the faculty's social life on this campus.

"Jacob and Ruth's hospitality is just one reflection of their genuine affection for students, which was also displayed in other ways. For example, Jacob spent countless hours with his students in the classroom and laboratory. A master teacher and researcher, he demonstrated by example the joys and challenges of an endless search for knowledge.

"Some of you may not be aware that Jacob insisted on teaching one course in freshman chemistry each year. He said the best place to find future scientists was in the basic courses in chemistry, physics and mathematics. Hundreds of Cabot students first experienced the excitement and stimulation of science in general, and chemistry in particular, during those freshman chemistry lectures.

"Today, many of his former students carry on his legacy of excellence in the classroom and laboratory. They serve as professors at universities around the country and as research chemists in major companies here and abroad.

"Finally, let me relate an incident that took place a few years ago. I believe it helps to explain his optimistic sense of life, his boundless enthusiasm—the essence of his character. Many of you know that one of Jacob's passions was mountain climbing. Over the years he and I, along with Paul and Anton, shared many hiking and climbing adventures. Two years ago, Jacob and I, along with a very experienced mountain guide, reached the summit of the Matterhorn in Switzerland.

"That was one tough climb," Dick said ruefully, "and we were both exhausted and exhilarated at the same time. We were relaxing and enjoying magnificent views of the Swiss Alps before tackling the long descent to the village of Zermatt.

"As we rested, I jokingly asked him why he put himself through the physical torture of climbing a mountain, expecting to hear the usual reasons most of us give for climbing. I was wrong. Jacob simply said that he considered each day a gift. And climbing a mountain was the best way he knew to experience life to the fullest outside his laboratory.

"His answer surprised me. It concealed more than it revealed, unusual for Jacob. I didn't pursue the subject at the time. Although it was only ten o'clock in the morning, storm clouds were gathering in the west, and we hastily moved off the summit to lower ground and returned to the village."

Dick paused, leafing through several pages of his notes.

"You know that Jacob was born in Poland," he resumed. "A simple calculation would reveal that he was a child during the Holocaust. In fact, he was a Holocaust survivor. While I am tempted to describe, however inadequately, Jacob's experiences during the war years, that was a very private part of his life, one that he discussed with Nancy and me on only one occasion—the evening after we conquered the Matterhorn. Although I will not violate his confidence about those years, I am certain they profoundly shaped his view of life."

A surprised murmur swept through the audience.

"This quiet campus and the peaceful town of Hillsdale were far removed from the horrors that marked Jacob's early years in rural Poland during the Holocaust. There is no question in my mind that Jacob's philosophy, his respect for human life and his essential character were forged during those horrendous years in hiding. He savored the value of freedom and the priceless gift of life itself more than anyone I know.

"Despite his young age, the years between 1939 and 1945 molded his character and shaped his philosophy. During the endless hours his family spent in hiding from the Nazis, he told me that he constructed elaborate fantasies about how he would spend the rest of his life—if he survived the day. No experience, no challenge since the war, could possibly compare to the relentless trauma of that period. During the most dangerous times, he vowed that if his family were spared, he would treat each day of his life as a precious gift—a bonus, if you will. He kept that vow to the very end.

"I think you will agree that his spirit—the quiet confidence, the intellectual curiosity, the boundless enthusiasm, optimism and energy with which he greeted every challenge—will live on in each of us who knew him."

Dick paused. The audience was silent, the only sound the faint shuffling of papers picked up by the podium microphone. "Jacob Borovski lived an extraordinarily productive and meaningful life. Near the end, as his illness progressed and he knew the battle was lost, he was neither depressed nor disheartened. His concern was not for his own mortality. He was determined to prepare Ruth and his sons for the future."

Dick removed his glasses, folded his notes and put them in his pocket.

"Undoubtedly, my remarks have not done justice to the man we knew and loved. Jacob was my surrogate brother. During our years together, we literally shared the best of times and more recently, the worst of times.

"As a physician, my professional life is dedicated to healing the sick. Despite our best efforts, my colleagues and I at Essex Medical Center could not extend Jacob's life. We stood by as an especially lethal form of cancer attacked and destroyed his body. Medical experts here and around the country couldn't contain the spread of the disease.

"However, the disease never touched his mind and spirit. Until the very end, he was actively involved in the evaluation and treatment of his illness. Given his scientific training and intellectual curiosity, he examined the progress of his own illness with remarkable objectivity. His humor, courage and awesome intellect never failed him. Those of us who treated him will not forget his courage. He taught us how to die."

Dick looked out over the audience, his hands gripping the podium.

"His suffering has ended and he is no longer with us. His spirit will live on as long as each of us remembers him—his humanity, wisdom, his intellect and his devotion to his family, his students, this university and the town of Hillsdale.

"Thank you."

He walked across the stage toward the steps. Then he stopped abruptly and returned to the podium. He touched the microphone and waited for the audience to quiet.

"I know Jacob would want me to dwell on the good times. But these past few weeks since his death have been a time of questioning for me, and I suspect, for some of you in this audience.

"Many questions remain unanswered, and I am not referring to cosmic questions on the meaning of life and death. I'm referring to the medical questions that Jacob Borovski's illness raised in my mind. I believe there is, indeed, cause for concern."

His voice deepened.

"Why," he asked, "was a vigorous man in the prime of life suddenly struck down by cancer? Jacob was in excellent physical condition and he monitored his health through regular medical checkups. He survived the darkest years of human history during the Holocaust, abandoned Poland in the early postwar years, earned a doctorate in France, immigrated to this country and established an international reputation in his profession.

"During the last five years Jacob, who had spent a lifetime hiking and climbing in this country and abroad, conquered the Jungfrau and the Matterhorn in Switzerland, Mt. Hood in Washington, McKinley in Alaska, Kilimanjaro in Africa and several 14,000 foot peaks in the Rockies. In fact, we had begun preliminary planning for a two month trek to the Base Camp of Mt. Everest, an adventure we intended to pursue this summer.

"I have to ask *why*," his voice rose, tortured. "Why did an untreatable cancer suddenly strike down a man in extraordinarily good health, in the prime of life? For that matter, why have *at least twelve*—I repeat *twelve*—Cabot University faculty members been struck down by fatal cancers, many of them at an early age?

"They were your colleagues, friends and neighbors. They grew up and were educated all across this country. The only common thread in their lives and deaths is that all of them came to Cabot University between 1965 and 1970. They taught here, lived here and died here."

He threw up his hands.

"Think about it. Many of you in this room know who your fallen colleagues are. Let me remind you that these faculty and staff professionals died too soon, and in numbers possibly too large to be attributable to random deaths. But the total I can personally recall is twelve. There may be others. At least twelve of your colleagues—so far—who came to Cabot University in the late 1960s, have died of various forms of cancer. Except for Jacob Borovski, these victims were in their thirties or forties—statistically too young to die from cancer in such large numbers."

Anguished, he continued. *"Why are they dying? What's going on here? Is there a cancer hot spot on this campus?"* His fists pounding the podium, he pleaded for an answer from a stunned and silent audience.

"I am a physician—a pathologist—who cannot answer my own questions," he cried, "but I am convinced there is cause for concern. Was Jacob's death simply a tragedy, or is there something more sinister at work here? Could his death be part of a pattern? Should we investigate Jacob's death and the others as well, seeking a common cause? Or should we continue on our way, waiting for the next victim to be identified? The life of Jacob Borovski and the others who have died will be dishonored if we do not search for answers." His hands gripped the podium as he struggled for control.

"One final question. Have you noticed that practically no one dies of heart disease at this university? Yet cardiovascular diseases kill twice as many people as cancer in this country. Cancer, not heart disease, is the killer at Cabot University; and it strikes the relatively young."

A buzz erupted as the audience suddenly found its voice.

Dick stopped, unable to continue, suddenly appalled that his outburst cast a shadow over what he had intended to be a warm farewell to his friend. Too late, he realized that this was not the proper forum to voice his concerns.

"Let me leave you with this final thought," he began again, his voice ringing out across the auditorium, clear and strong once again. "Jacob Borovski, my best friend and a man admired and yes, loved, by everyone in this audience, is no longer with us. His death deprives Ruth, Anton and Paul of his companionship and love as a husband and father. His countless friends have lost a man of great humanity, intellect, loyalty and kindness. Students and colleagues will no longer benefit from his rigorous analytical gifts, nor be able to seek his guidance in their daily lives.

"I know that Jacob Borovski's spirit lives on in the minds and hearts of all who knew and admired him. I promise you he will not be forgotten.

"Let me repeat, however, there is cause for concern. I believe his life would be dishonored if we do not search for answers. And that search might as well begin here and now."

He strode rapidly from the stage and returned to his seat.

Ruth smiled gently through shining eyes. She leaned over and kissed his cheek.

The memorial service ended quickly with an invitation by the President to personally greet the Borovski family at a reception following the service.

The crowd rose and slowly filed out through the open doors at the rear of the auditorium. Nancy and Hillary joined the dignitaries at the side door as Larry Northrop, pointedly ignoring Dick, focused his attention on his foreign guests. Nancy squeezed her husband's hand as they climbed the narrow stairs to the second floor.

"Your eulogy was beautiful. No one could have done it better. But what were you talking about at the end?" she whispered to him.

"I'll explain later. Right now, I've got to apologize to Ruth and the boys. I really blew it."

In the reception area, Nancy made small talk with several colleagues while Dick took Ruth and the boys aside, speaking intensely for several moments. Ruth nodded and whispered something before she turned to speak to a cluster of foreign visitors. Dick and Nancy spoke casually to a few friends, then made their way down the broad main staircase. They joined Ruth, Paul and Anton who had formed a small reception line in the university museum next to the auditorium. Throngs of mourners quickly formed a line that extended the length of the museum's main exhibit area and into the lobby.

For the next hour, students, faculty and friends made their way among exhibits of Indian artifacts and other local memorabilia, chatting quietly, waiting patiently to extend personal condolences to the Borovski family. Finally Nancy, standing beside Anton and Dick, glanced toward Ruth. Alarmed to see her friend's usual steely composure visibly ebbing, she raised an eyebrow toward Dick, who quickly closed off the line.

During the luncheon gathering that followed, Nancy sought out Kevin Parks, the only student present. Looking painfully ill at ease in the unfamiliar setting, she sought to console him.

"Kevin, Dr. Jacob would have been very proud of you this morning. You did a wonderful job representing the students."

"Thanks, Professor Atherton. That's the first and hopefully the last time I ever have to deliver a eulogy." He smiled sadly, dark eyes gleaming.

"Come and sit with Dick and me," she led him to a table for eight which was only half occupied. Perhaps, she thought, the trauma of the past six months had matured Kevin. More important, the loss of his mentor might provide an incentive to finish his research and finally graduate. The risk, however, was that he might be unable to function without Jacob's direct guidance and encouragement.

Without formal good byes, Ruth, Anton and Paul slipped away shortly after one o'clock. Walking three abreast along the broad sidewalk, they cut diagonally across the Commons toward Starrett Science Center, the large classroom and laboratory complex that housed the Chemistry Department.

"Are you sure you want to deal with students in your lab today?" Paul eyed his mother.

"Positive," she said firmly. "It'll be good therapy. In fact, I feel better already. I haven't seen my doctoral students in weeks and they need my attention. Hopefully, a few hours in the lab will help me focus on my work instead of the loss of your father.

"Besides, I really need your help in evaluating the status of our current research. Jacob and I have been joint principal investigators on a major federal grant that extends through next year. It would have stretched us to complete the work with both of us putting in our normal sixty-hour weeks. Frankly, I don't see how I can finish the research and prepare the final report without Jacob, even if I bring in several more post doctoral students. I need a seasoned researcher to help me now."

Paul glanced over his mother's head to Anton. Clearly, she alone could not complete the $10 million National Science Foundation grant that was the linchpin of his parents' recent research.

"This afternoon, while I deal with my doctoral students and the post docs in the lab, would you two take a look at our most recent notes? See if you can suggest ways to proceed that give me a reasonable chance to complete the research on time."

She turned to her older son. "Anton, your dissertation work at Berkeley is really a spin-off of our work here. You and Jacob constantly discussed your research during the past year. I've got the phone bills and e-mails to prove it."

As they climbed the broad granite steps and entered Starrett Science Center, Ruth became more animated, displaying the enthusiasm that made her one of the most respected and popular professors on campus. During the elevator ride to the fourth floor, she summarized the general outlines of their current research. She led them down the hall to her office, unlocked the door and settled her two sons in Jacob's office, which adjoined her own.

Moments later, she grabbed two lab notebooks and returned to the polymer chemistry lab where she joined her doctoral students already at work.

Initially shocked at her unexpected appearance in the lab, after a brief flurry the students quietly resumed their work. Eager to bring her up to date on their research, they captured her undivided attention. The familiar lab routines and the intellectual give and take with her students cheered her. She focused on the problems at hand, confident, engaged and patient with her students' questions. The sadness and loss that threatened to overwhelm her earlier faded as the afternoon hours flew by in a blur. She could deal with any problems in this environment.

Paul and Anton settled down in Jacob's office, pouring over the pile of lab notes and computer printouts that covered the top of his desk. Several hours of intense study and debate later, they had evaluated the current status of their father's final work and compared it to the original joint research proposal. A plan began to take shape that would enable Ruth to finish the grant on time.

*   *   *   *

Nancy and Dick Atherton continued to circulate among the luncheon guests as the visiting dignitaries and politicians prepared to leave for the airport. Half an hour later they signaled Hillary Gardner, nodded toward the door and left the dwindling gathering.

Dick's late model Porsche was parked illegally near the main gate where he had hastily abandoned it that morning. It hadn't been towed despite the parking prohibition, probably because campus security recognized the car and its MD vanity plate.

"I can't believe you paid $90,000 for a car with a back seat designed for babies under the age of three," Hillary complained as she reluctantly shoehorned her ample frame onto the tiny rear bench seat.

Nancy crawled into the front passenger seat and fastened her seatbelt. She regarded her friend over her shoulder. "I gave up criticizing Dick's passion for fast cars and expensive airplanes years ago. You can't win that battle," she warned as Dick slid behind the wheel.

"All right, you two," Nancy continued, "you've kept me in suspense for the last three hours. It's time to tell me what you've been up to." She turned to her husband as the car sped down University Avenue toward the business district. The earlier crowds had dispersed, and pedestrian and auto traffic had returned to normal.

"The last twenty-four hours have been really strange," she regarded Dick and began to count on her fingers. "First, you didn't bother to come to bed last night. Not exactly our usual routine. Then you two go charging off to the Center before breakfast for some sort of emergency meeting. Next, you're almost late for the memorial service."

She eyed his profile as he expertly navigated the light afternoon traffic. "Finally, you throw out those really weird remarks about the nature of Jacob's illness in front of a thousand people.

"Mind telling me what's going on?" Nancy would not be put off any longer.

"If you'll calm down, I'll be glad to tell you," he retorted, downshifting and speeding through the intersection of University and Main.

"We just got the final pathology report on some of Jacob's tissue samples that I sent to Philadelphia. I wanted a second analysis to confirm my work, and Hillary also wanted verification of some hematology studies that puzzled her. I wanted to see whether the General Hospital pathologists in Philly reached the same conclusions we came up with two weeks ago.

"The report was faxed to the hospital late last night. At six o'clock this morning I got a call they were here."

Hillary took up the story. "That's why we went to the hospital before the service."

"So, what were the results?" Nancy asked.

"Both of our findings were confirmed by the people at General. They've been consulting with us on Jacob's case since his initial diagnosis," said Hillary.

Crossing the river bridge, Dick down shifted to third gear, and with a low growl, the Porsche responded, accelerating up the steep road to the crest of Shawnee Hill. He turned right onto Schmidt Farm Road and braked to a stop at the end of his driveway.

"We can talk more about this at dinner," Dick cut off discussion. "Hillary, can you drop by this evening after dinner? Nancy, would you ask Ruth and the boys to come over as well? Anton and Paul are scheduled to fly back to California tomorrow. I think we should review the test results together before they go," said Dick, anxious to get back to the hospital.

"Right. Consider it done," Nancy replied, subdued. She climbed from the car and helped Hillary crawl out of the rear seat. With a sigh of relief, Hillary settled into the passenger seat. The two physicians waved as Dick gunned the Porsche toward Essex Medical Center.

*   *   *   *

Nancy jogged along the bike path that linked Shawnee Hill and the town of Oakton, ten miles to the south along the river. The path traversed a high ridge overlooking the river on her right and the town of Hillsdale beyond. The brilliant morning sunshine had been replaced by an overcast sky, and the heavy, humid air signaled an evening rain. In the far distance, the clock tower atop Old Main caught a few anemic rays of sun low on the western horizon. The distant hum of commuter traffic was barely audible above the slap of her jogging shoes and the rhythmic sounds of her heavy breathing.

A mile from home she spotted a dozen Canada geese soaring overhead, honking furiously, searching for water. Slowly, the leader brought the flock into a shallow descent. They landed gracefully on Homer Schmidt's pond, safe for the evening. They would rise with the dawn and continue their flight north for the summer. She paused and watched as Homer, seated high on his tractor, plowed the broad field bordering the crest of the hill, preparing the soil for late summer corn. She waved and he responded with a tip of his Phillies baseball cap.

Homer Schmidt and his wife owned the mountain and hundreds of acres along its crest. The Schmidt Farm development, a cluster of expensive homes overlooking the river, was his sole concession to the economics of the recent real estate boom. Under strict zoning controls, he had been persuaded to sell forty acres of prime land to a developer. The sale had made him rich. Rather than spending his later years vacationing in Florida, he chose to continue the only lifestyle he had ever known, that of farmer and cattleman.

The low stone wall and ornate wrought iron gates that marked the entrance to Memorial Cemetery came into view on her left. She jogged along the wall, painfully aware that Jacob's fresh grave lay within the gates near the graves of five of her colleagues.

A trio of cyclists interrupted her reverie as she jumped aside to let them pass. Startled, she watched them continue south as the path branched a quarter-mile ahead. Hunched over their bikes, they pedaled furiously, oblivious to the beauty around them, intent only on reaching some distant finish line.

Maintaining her normal jogging pace, she reached the fork that led south toward Oakton. Glancing at her watch, she turned and began the uphill trek home, unwilling to impose the demands of a longer run on her already exhausted body.

She would deal with Dick and Hillary's unanswered questions later. For now, it was enough to savor the solitude, to eye the river far below, to glance upward at the gathering clouds and feel the moist wind in her hair, to feel her body respond to the demands she placed on it. The nightmare of the last six months that engulfed her life and dampened her spirit was finally ending. Today's memorial service marked both an end and a beginning. Her burden of grief began to lift.

*　*　*　*

They gathered at the Atherton home that evening, exhausted, depressed, relieved that the long day was finally coming to a close.

"No more stalling, Dick." Nancy passed coffee and dessert to her guests and her husband before serving herself. "You haven't explained the meaning of your outburst at the end of your eulogy. We all wonder why some of our colleagues have died of cancer. That's nothing new. But the issue has been investigated in the past and nothing came of it. Is there something about Jacob's cancer that sets it apart from all the others?"

"No. Nothing definitive—nothing we can point to with any confidence." He glanced at Hillary for confirmation.

"Then why the outburst?" asked Nancy, failing to conceal her frustration.

"We thought the analysis from Philadelphia would help us understand what precipitated Jacob's cancer," Hillary interrupted Dick. "Unfortunately, when we looked at the data more closely this afternoon, we found nothing really new. It's disappointing because we initially thought we were going to gain some new insights."

Dick looked across the coffee table at his wife. "Sorry to mislead you this afternoon. I really thought we had found something unique in the data we reviewed early this morning. I was wrong," he said.

"Our objective was to gain some new insights into the course of Jacob's disease—his cancer was an extraordinarily virulent form that metastasized so quickly we couldn't eliminate it or even put it into remission. We're trying to find ways to treat others. It's too late to help Jacob, but we hoped to improve treatment for others."

He turned to Ruth, Paul and Anton. "I over reacted this morning at the memorial service. Those comments were not in my notes, of course. Blame it on tension, on my own frustration at not being able to get Jacob into remission, to give him a few more years."

"Don't blame yourself," Ruth said gently. "You and Hillary and the entire medical staff at Essex did all that was humanly possible. Jacob gave it all he had; he was a fighter all his life. But like thousands of other cancer victims, the disease destroyed his body. It didn't destroy his spirit, I am certain of that."

"Yes, Ruth. Still I wonder whether his cancer could have been prevented."

"What do you mean?" Paul Borovski leaned forward and set his coffee cup on the table. "Cancer can't be prevented, at least in the sense you seem to be implying."

"During the last few weeks before he died, Jacob and I discussed cancer in general and what conditions may trigger the onset of the disease," Dick said. "He was fascinated by the subject intellectually. And he was quite dispassionate about his own situation. He examined his own condition very objectively in our discussions; he seemed to view his illness as a complex scientific puzzle that somehow we could solve.

"Maybe in the next few years some of the puzzle will be solved, and we can begin to develop successful treatments for many types of cancer. For example, the work being done in genetics is very promising. Gene therapy may ultimately help us prevent or delay certain types of cancer in people with genetic markers that predispose them to higher risk.

"We've known for some time that environmental factors may contribute to the development of certain cancers. Toxic chemicals, long exposure to radiation and other environmental factors may play a more important role than we understand now.

"Jacob and I had our last discussion on this topic a few days before he died. He brought up the issue, and had obviously been thinking about it. He mentioned Joe Santi, a young chemistry professor, who died twenty years ago of cancer. According to Jacob, at least a dozen faculty and staff have died of particularly virulent forms of cancer, mostly soft tissue cancers. He remembered that he had led a committee to examine the possibility of toxic contamination in the Chemistry Department after Joe died. Obviously, chemists use a lot of chemicals, some of them quite toxic."

"I recall that incident, now that you bring it up," said Ruth. "Of course, we searched the area, tested the air and water and conducted a very thorough analysis. We found no evidence linking cancer to the chemicals used in our research and teaching activities at the university. Cabot got a clean bill of health.

"It's interesting that Jacob should have been thinking about that," she mused. "I can understand his interest in those earlier cancer deaths given his own situation, which we all knew was hopeless. Is that what prompted you to make those remarks today?"

"Yes, and I apologize again, Ruth. I thought about it last night when I was working on the eulogy. It was stupid of me to lose control like that."

"You've already apologized enough, Dick. Let's just move on."

"Yes, of course," he said. "We should focus on our good times together."

"Like the summer before last, when we stayed in Zermatt and you and Jacob climbed the Matterhorn with Felix Schneider as your guide," Ruth smiled. "We four had a wonderful vacation in the Alps. Although Jacob had many interests outside of chemistry and his research, I think he was most passionate about his climbing; and the Matterhorn was one of his most satisfying climbs.

The evening was winding down.

"It's almost midnight," Anton noted, checking his watch. "Mother, even though you don't have to teach tomorrow, you'll probably want to spend a few hours in the lab. You need to get some rest," He glanced across the room at Paul and together they rose to leave.

"Thanks for everything," said Paul huskily, embracing Nancy in a bear hug. "And Dick, your eulogy for Dad was excellent—something I'll remember the rest of my life."

They walked to the door. Wordlessly, Nancy embraced Ruth and kissed her on the cheek.

"Get some rest. We'll see you tomorrow."

Part I

The Past

Chapter 1

They hiked in single file, their breathing labored. Slowly, they climbed the narrow path through the dense spruce forest. The warm morning sun cast deep shadows behind them as they emerged from the woods into a high mountain meadow. Masses of brilliant wildflowers cascaded across the meadow in the blinding sunlight, the colors spreading before them like a vast patchwork quilt. To the right, the land dropped steeply away toward the tiny Swiss village two miles below. Neatly stacked stone cairns marked the trail that rose ever more steeply into the distance, finally disappearing beyond a rock scree. Two miles to the west, the Matterhorn loomed above, its stark peak a brilliant silhouette in a nearly cloudless sky.

Gasping for breath in the thin mountain air, the two women collapsed onto a flat boulder. Shrugging out of their heavy packs, they propped them against their backs. Unclipping their water bottles, they savored deep cool draughts of pure mountain spring water. They rested, waiting patiently for their bodies to recover.

The women pushed their sunglasses into their hair, wiped the sweat from their eyes and gazed at the visual feast spread before them. Luminous sunlight transformed the ice fields on the south face of the Matterhorn into enormous slabs of gold. The massive lower flanks of the great mountain presented huge vertical slabs of granite ledge reaching into the blue sky.

The snow-clad peak provided a perfect backdrop for the delicate hues of the blue, red and yellow wildflowers hidden among the rocks and spread in all their glory across the mountain meadow. Although it was only eleven o'clock, in a few hours clouds would obscure the peak and surrender their moisture, feeding the eternal snowfields high on the mountain, then move across the valley, drenching the village of Zermatt in late afternoon showers.

Ruth dug through her pack and pulled out a pair of powerful binoculars while Nancy prepared to photograph the scene. Scanning the flanks and peak in the distance, she searched for signs of life.

"Those glasses probably aren't strong enough to pick up anyone on the peak," Nancy warned.

"I know. I can't help looking anyway."

Ruth glanced at her watch. "If the climb went as planned, they should have reached the summit by eight o'clock. That would put them well down from the peak by now. With a little luck, they'll be back by early evening."

"You're not really worried about them are you?" asked Nancy, surprised that her normally unemotional friend was displaying unmistakable signs of anxiety.

3

"With Felix Schneider as their guide, it's a foregone conclusion that they made it to the summit safely and are on their way down. Granted, the Matterhorn is a demanding climb. But they're in excellent shape. We both know how hard they trained. This climb is all they talked about for the past six months. And even the weather cooperated. It couldn't be more ideal given the time of year.

"We'll be listening to their war stories for the next year. And it'll give Jacob bragging rights around the university for at least six months," she chuckled.

Nancy checked her light meter and moved into the meadow, stooping to capture some close-up photos of the wildflowers displayed near an outcropping of granite.

"There's another benefit, too," she remarked, replacing her camera in its case.

"Maybe we'll finally regain control of our family rooms. No more piles of heavy clothing, boots, ropes, ice gear, maps and the assorted paraphernalia they used up there today," she pointed toward the mountain.

"With a little luck, this will be their last climb for a while," said Nancy. "We can stash their gear in the garage."

"Don't count on that," Ruth warned. "Didn't Dick tell you they plan to climb Mt. McKinley in Alaska next summer?"

Nancy groaned.

"Face it. They're addicted to climbing," said Ruth.

"At least we get to travel with them and go hiking on our own. I don't mind vacationing in Zermatt and vicariously sharing their adventures. If they decide to visit Alaska next summer, I'm ready."

Half an hour later they hoisted their daypacks onto their backs and continued their trek through the meadows and forests on the lower slopes of the Matterhorn.

*   *   *   *

Five hours later, exhausted and covered with dust from the dry mountain trail, they entered the chalet of Hannah and Felix Schneider, an elegant guesthouse surrounded by meadows three kilometers from the bustling tourist center of Zermatt. Many vacations, summer and winter, had earned the two couples status as part of the extended family of the prominent mountain guide and his wife.

A hour later, after a refreshing hot shower and a change into soft cotton sweaters and summer slacks, the two women gathered on the flower-laden patio, sipping a light May wine and watching the sunlight caress the distant peaks.

4

The narrow paved road from the village ended in the small parking area. Beyond the fenced pasture, a wide trail disappeared into a dense spruce forest, eventually leading to the lower slopes of the Matterhorn.

Hannah Schneider joined the two women, bearing a tray laden with freshly baked pastries and herb teas. They ate and drank, conversing quietly, savoring the peaceful scene, awaiting the first signs of the returning climbing party.

Nancy spotted them first. Jacob Borovski, Dick Atherton and Felix Schneider emerged from the dark forest, climbing ropes draped across their shoulders, heavy backpacks still in place.

There could be no doubt that the boisterous group had achieved their goal. The women grabbed the half empty bottle of wine and ran to greet them.

"We did it!" shouted Jacob, sweeping his diminutive wife into his arms in a giant bear hug.

"Never a doubt," exclaimed Dick, embracing his wife with equal enthusiasm.

Their Swiss hosts stood aside, smiling, enjoying their guests' celebration. Laughing and interrupting each other, they quickly emptied the wine bottle as they walked together through the gathering twilight, saluting the massive mountain they had conquered.

Chapter 2

They celebrated long into the night. Hannah Schneider's gourmet feast, complemented by Felix's selection of fine wines from the family's extensive cellar, provided a fitting victory dinner, one the two couples would never forget. At last, well after midnight, the Schneiders bade their guests goodnight and retired.

"One more round?" Jacob asked. He added a splash of cognac to Dick's brandy snifter and replenished his own. The four friends settled down once again near the massive stone fireplace. Facing each other in deep leather sofas, they gazed into the bed of glowing embers, all that remained of a blazing fire that took the edge off the evening chill.

"I remember as a teenager growing up in Hillsdale, dreaming of serious climbing adventures," said Dick. "But climbing the Matterhorn was not one of my goals. I dreamed of hikes in the White Mountains of New Hampshire and perhaps later conquering a few fourteen thousand foot peaks in the Rockies. Never the Alps. Certainly not the Matterhorn. Too high, too far away, too tough. Then, when I was stationed in Germany after I finished medical school, I took some rock climbing lessons and was bitten by the climbing bug. Still, I never expected to climb the Matterhorn, or any of the other major peaks we've climbed together."

"That's probably why I'll never forget the moment we finally reached the summit today. It's what I call a peak life experience," he laughed.

"Seriously, I couldn't have done this without you, Jacob. You provided the incentive, not to mention goading me into our training regimen and sharing the technical preparations." He raised his brandy snifter and saluted his friend.

Jacob Borovski regarded his friend pensively.

"Who would have predicted that a poor Polish Jew, one who barely survived the Holocaust, would one day conquer the Matterhorn? We never know where life will lead us. Perhaps we should keep the momentum going, begin planning another climb right now. This was really not such an impossible climb, you know."

"A climb always seems less challenging in retrospect," interrupted Dick.

Jacob would not be deterred.

"I suspect that climbing in Alaska—Mt. McKinley, for example—would be a lot tougher. However, we wouldn't enjoy the Schneiders' hospitality or these luxurious surroundings."

"And you certainly wouldn't have your wives waiting for you with wine and a gourmet feast to celebrate," Nancy said.

"Jacob," she continued, returning to his earlier comment. "Do you realize that you never talk about your early life in Poland? With the Cold War over, do you ever consider going back to visit your village in Poland? It shouldn't be that difficult," she observed. "Travel is virtually unrestricted. Why haven't you and Ruth ever returned to your childhood homes?" she asked.

"The reason is really quite simple, my dear. And painful, I must admit.

"There's nothing left for us to return to," he continued. "Our families are dead. My parents survived the war, but both of them died before I graduated from university in France.

"We don't discuss those years because they are painful, especially for Ruth." He reached for his wife's hand.

Ruth stared into the dying fire, her face deeply shadowed, her eyes clouded and sad, lost in the distant past.

"Many Holocaust survivors find it very painful to discuss their experiences during the Hitler regime. Although we don't speak of those days, they are not forgotten," he continued.

"In fact, virtually every day I recall those years and the lessons I learned in the midst of that unspeakable horror. This morning, when we reached the summit, for the first time in years, I felt the physical presence of my father and brother. How they would have loved to conquer the Matterhorn!" A sad smile deepened the creases of his craggy face.

"Dick, I suppose that experience would be viewed by a physician as a hallucination, or at least a manifestation of oxygen depravation at the high altitude."

His friend regarded him silently.

"You and Nancy are the closest friends we have. Yet neither of us have related to you those early years during the war.

"Make no mistake," he gestured toward his two listeners, "the years from 1941 when Hitler turned on Stalin and the Russians until 1945 and victory in Europe were the most important years of my life. I not only learned how to survive. Those years shaped the rules I live by—my personal philosophy.

"My education after the war, the graduate years in France, coming to the United States, professional success as a scientist and a teacher—were profoundly influenced by those early years. Although I was a young child during the Holocaust, I remember the period as though it happened only yesterday."

The dying embers deepened the shadows across Jacob's strong features. His piercing brown eyes somberly regarded his two friends.

"Would you like to know what it was like growing up in Poland during the war?"

7

"I'm sorry. Not if it's painful for you. Tonight is our night to celebrate, not to dredge up painful memories," said Dick.

"It's late," Nancy reminded them. "We probably all should go to bed," she glanced at her watch.

"Don't apologize, either of you," said Jacob, relaxed now. He stretched his long legs toward the fire and folded his arms. "I want you to know the story," he insisted. "Those years help to explain certain things—like why my religion is so important to me." Perhaps you should know the whole story. With our victory over the mountain today, I'm ready to talk about that part of my life.

"But first, let me take care of Ruth."

Leaning over his wife, he gently pulled her to her feet. "Time for bed, Ruth. It's been a long day for all of us. I'll be along shortly." He kissed her and waited at the bottom of the wide stairway until she closed the door to their bedroom.

Chapter 3

Nancy went to the sideboard and poured a glass of sparkling mineral water, adding a wedge of lime and fresh ice. She settled back in the leather sofa and curled her legs under her. Dick Atherton swirled the cognac in his goblet.

Jacob began to speak, his deep voice controlled and dispassionate. He might have been offering a lecture to his students.

"Although I was very young during the war, I matured quickly, of necessity. In retrospect, I really didn't have a childhood because of the war. We lived in Piotance, a small city of 25,000 people about 100 miles east of Warsaw. My father was a physician with a busy general practice. My older brother, Anton, often helped in his office after school. When allowed, I would watch them treat patients in the clinic near our home. From my earliest childhood, I dreamed of becoming a physician like my father. He treated everyone without regard to their faith. He and my mother were very well known and widely respected throughout the region. Ours was one of the most prominent Jewish families in town.

"Anton was twelve years older than I, and he was preparing to enter university in Paris when the war broke out. He planned to study medicine. Anton and my father were my heroes—they still are. In retrospect, I must have been a pest—always hanging out in Father's clinic, looking after patients like my brother," Jacob smiled.

"My earliest recollection of what was to come occurred during the summer of 1939. My Uncle Joseph—my mother's brother who lived in Warsaw—returned from a business trip to Paris and came to visit us in Piotance. That was unusual since he seldom came to our town. Rather, we periodically took a train to Warsaw to visit him and other relatives, usually during the high holy days. He arrived after dark, talked through the night with my parents, then climbed back into his car and left early the next morning. Anton and I had been ordered to bed, but we sneaked downstairs and listened to the conversation.

"Uncle Joseph had such horrendous news that my parents refused to believe him. Rumors were rife in Paris that thousands of German Jews were being forced from their homes and sent to so-called work camps. The Nazis confiscated their property—homes, businesses and personal property. Worse, however, were stories that the work camps were, in fact, death camps. Uncle Joseph claimed to have reliable information that German Jews were being put to death.

"Remember, this was years before anyone took seriously the few stories that had leaked out about death camps. Unfortunately, he couldn't convince my parents that such atrocities were occurring. They became embroiled in a huge shouting match over the news. The argument lasted through the night.

"My uncle told them he was in the process of selling his business. He planned to move his family to Palestine in late fall. My father still refused to take him seriously. In the very early morning, Uncle Joseph begged my parents to leave Poland and offered to make arrangements to move our family to Palestine along with his own.

"Not surprisingly, my father absolutely refused to even consider such a plan. He would never abandon his home and his patients. He believed that war with Germany would be avoided, and he called my uncle a crazy fool.

"However, he agreed to accompany Anton when he enrolled at university in Paris in October. He would decide for himself whether the story had any substance. Meanwhile, we would not leave Piotance.

"When they parted just before dawn, Father refused to embrace my uncle. They shook hands formally. Mother was in tears. Anton and I watched from behind the curtains of our second floor bedroom as Uncle Joseph climbed into his car and drove away. I never saw him again."

Jacob sat silently for a few moments.

"After the war, I tried to trace Uncle Joseph's family. I'm fairly confident that they never left Warsaw—they died in the final siege of the ghetto along with thousands of others.

"Less than a month after that visit, Germany invaded Poland, their tanks and artillery sweeping through the countryside like a scythe, destroying everything in their path. Father realized too late that Uncle Joseph was right. He desperately tried to contact him in Warsaw, without success.

"Father's clinic remained open after the invasion; he cared for his patients and soon treated many Polish soldiers wounded in the fighting.

"I mentioned that my father, Ephraim Borovski, was very highly respected. He treated everyone—rich and poor, Jews and Catholics alike. If someone couldn't pay, he accepted food for services, especially from the farmers near the village during the late harvest. He worked twenty hours a day treating the sick and wounded during those last days before the Germans overran our town."

Jacob's hand cupped the snifter, swirling the cognac, lost in thought.

His piercing eyes softened. "Let me tell you about my mother, Natasha. She was the family optimist, the mover and shaker, the antithesis of my father, who was a naturally reserved, serious person. Generous to a fault, she was educated as a teacher. She was also a talented classical pianist and singer who performed throughout the area.

"I vividly remember waking one night to the booms of heavy artillery fire in the distance. Two days later our town was shelled as the German army approached. Father gathered us together and formally apologized for having ignored Uncle Joseph's warning. He was so ashamed. That was the only time I ever saw my father cry."

Jacob's voice cracked. Hands clenched, he struggled for control.

"Organized resistance disintegrated very quickly," he resumed. "As the tanks and troops moved across the countryside toward Piotance, some people retreated to the cellars of their homes, others gathered a few belongings and headed east, in a futile effort to outrun the German army. Many died on the roads. The German pilots took particular pleasure in strafing roads crowded with women and children.

"We didn't flee. My father continued to treat people in his clinic located a few blocks from our home. The morning the Germans entered the town, he directed my mother, Anton and me to hide in the fruit cellar beneath the house. I remember he herded us into the cellar and closed the wooden trap door above us, leaving us in total darkness. We heard him shove a heavy storage cabinet over the door. He ordered us to stay there until he returned.

"A few hours later we heard gunfire, shouting and screaming, and then the tramp of boots through our house. The storage cabinet was shoved aside and a couple of soldiers came down the steps into the upper cellar and looked around. In the darkness of the cellar, they didn't find us. A short time later, they left the house.

"I'll never forget the unrelenting terror of that day. We had no conception of time passing. It was absolutely black, and the earthen floor smelled musty and damp. We sat on the ground, absolutely still, certain that the slightest noise would betray our hiding place."

Jacob paused and sipped his cognac.

"After what seemed an eternity, someone tramped down the steps, shoved the storage cabinet aside and lifted the trap door.

"It was Father. During the day the Germans had searched his clinic. They allowed him to continue treating the few civilians who were in his waiting room. The next day he was ordered to treat only German soldiers.

"To this day, I'm amazed that they didn't take him out and shoot him. He never made any attempt to conceal his identity. And his features were more Semitic than mine," he laughed.

"One of his patients was Maria Dosecki, a widow whose husband had died several years earlier from heart disease. Maria lived on a farm outside Piotance. She raised vegetables with the help of her two children. Her son, Paul, was ten and Theresa was my age. My father delivered both children, and our family sometimes visited their farm in the summer to buy fresh vegetables. We were acquaintances, not friends. Maria's family was Catholic and we were Jews.

"Maria came to the clinic just before the occupation, when it was clear that the Germans would soon overrun the area. Fearing for our safety, she

11

begged us to hide out at her farm. My parents didn't immediately accept her offer. However, the day after the Germans entered town, my father closed the clinic, telling a few patients that we were heading east toward Russia.

"Our plan was to stay with Maria until the Germans moved through, then head south through Czechoslovakia and Hungary to Yugoslavia and eventually to Palestine. Father had earlier closed his bank account, which had a substantial balance, and spread the word that we were leaving town.

"He couldn't get all his money from the banker, but he was able to convert some cash into gold coins, and (wisely as it turned out) he removed Mother's jewelry collection from their safe box. My mother packed essential clothing and a few precious heirlooms, including a family photo, which I have to this day.

"The roads east of Piotance were chaotic and it was relatively easy to blend in with the hoards of people. Three kilometers outside town, we turned north, following a trail that Maria used to come to town. It took only a few hours to make the journey.

"We expected to hide for a short time until things settled down, then head south. Staying with Maria was a huge risk, especially since the Germans had overrun the entire area. We didn't want to jeopardize her family with our presence. We had money, gold and jewelry; and Father was confident he could get us safely to Palestine."

Nancy and Dick watched as their old friend rose and threw a fresh log on the fire. The bark exploded in a shower of sparks, brightly illuminating the room.

Standing, his tall frame obscuring the fire, he turned to his friends.

"Do you really want to hear the rest? This is taking longer than I expected."

"Yes, of course. That is, unless it's too painful for you," said Nancy, wide-awake.

"Not at all. Actually, this is a catharsis of sorts. Strange how I've avoided telling you about those years. The events are so clear in my mind," he mused.

He returned to his chair, stretching his long legs in front of him and folding his arms, relaxed as he sipped his cognac.

"Despite our original plan," he resumed, "we didn't leave Maria's farm for five long years. It was simply too risky to try to move south without papers and with Germans guarding the railroads. Reaching Palestine was a dream that was never fulfilled.

"Life on the farm was dangerous, but in retrospect, it was relatively tolerable. Compared to the alternative, we were very fortunate indeed. We four children got along surprisingly well, despite our age and religious differences.

"After the fighting moved into Russia, life resumed some semblance of normality. A group of Polish collaborators ran the political affairs in Piotance. The schools reopened and Paul and Theresa went back to the parochial school in town, which was run by the nuns.

"Of course, whatever they studied, Anton and I also studied at night. After a time, they managed to borrow advanced textbooks on math and science, which they brought home. The nuns must have suspected something, but no one questioned their interest in such demanding subjects. My parents took turns teaching us. It was one way to pass the time because we couldn't be seen in town or even around the farm. Anton and I would study during the day and then all of us would be tutored in the evenings. We studied by candlelight, since the farm had no electricity. Anton's dream of becoming a physician like my father began to slip away. Those years were especially hard for him.

"The German patrols that occasionally made forays through the countryside were the most serious danger. The farm was isolated and we didn't worry much about neighbors visiting unexpectedly. But the patrols would simply appear down the dirt path beyond the house and barn. During the summer, we took turns keeping watch from the woods about a kilometer away. If we saw anything suspicious, we would run back and warn everyone.

"The patrols invariably were noisy and careless, giving us ample warning. The four of us initially hid in the hayloft of the barn beneath loose straw. One time we were almost discovered when one of the soldiers actually climbed the ladder to the loft with a pitchfork and poked around in the hay practically on top of us. Little Theresa Dosecki suddenly began to scream, creating a diversion. That gave Maria an excuse to spank her which the soldiers thought was very amusing. They left shortly afterward.

"We needed a safer hiding place or we surely would be caught. That evening we sat around the kitchen table, trying to figure out where to hide. Maria finally came up with a plan to build a shelter in one of the potato fields. Actually, it was a brilliant idea that saved our lives. In summer and early fall the fields were masses of low green foliage, which provided good cover. In the winter the fields were covered with dead weeds and rotting potato plants. The German patrols spent their time searching the barn, outbuildings and the house. They never tramped around the fields.

"We immediately set about executing Maria's plan. We found some scraps of lumber, cut limbs from a good-sized tree, shaped them into crude posts and fashioned an underground room. The lumber provided basic support and we lined the sides and floor with rocks. In the end we constructed quite a substantial hiding place.

"In some ways it resembled a grave." Jacob paused and sipped his cognac.

"Earth and plantings covered the trap door and nicely concealed access to our little shelter. The spot that Father selected was smack in the middle of Maria's largest field about thirty yards from the dirt trail and a hundred yards from the woods.

"Whenever the lookout spotted human activity coming our way, we would dash for the shelter. Once we were safely down the hole, Paul or Maria would cover it with dirt, and then continue working the fields around us. There was plenty of room for the four of us to sit, or even lie in the shelter. The difficulty was that we had to remain completely silent in total darkness. We soon learned to store a jug of water, some bread and a few potatoes in case we had to spend the night in the shelter. We even kept a bucket for human waste.

"We stayed in that hole for five days near the end of the war when the Germans were retreating through the area. Although it may seem like horrendous conditions to you," he regarded Dick and Nancy thoughtfully, "compared to the suffering of Jews in the death camps, we were relatively comfortable."

He rose and stretched before adding another log to the fire.

"Good grief, Jacob," Nancy shuddered. "You were essentially buried alive in that field."

"It was no place for someone with claustrophobia," he smiled. "Don't forget that Jews hid in attics, closets, cellars and other nooks and crannies in cities all over Europe. Our shelter was simply a country version of the city shelters.

"Of course, most of the Jews were eventually captured and herded off to the crematoriums. We survived. Seven million others were not so lucky.

"Looking back, I'm amazed that we were not discovered. After all, Paul and little Theresa attended school throughout most of the occupation, never revealing our secret. Although the nuns may have wondered about their insatiable appetite for books in math and science, they never questioned them. It's ironic that they both really hated those subjects," Jacob chuckled.

"Those nuns surely knew something was afoot at the Dosecki farm. And the neighbors never questioned Maria about how she was able to manage the farm with only the two children to help tend the crops.

"During the fall and winter months, our parents took turns teaching all of us together. Although Maria was illiterate, she consistently encouraged her children to get an education. My brother Anton was older than the rest of us. He got special attention in an effort to keep alive his dream of attending medical school."

"Until you mentioned him earlier, I didn't know you had a brother," Dick said. "Did he become a physician after the war?"

"Anton was the only one who didn't survive," Jacob whispered. "He died in January 1945, five months before the war ended. The war had turned against the Nazis—that became obvious when troops began to flow through Piotance in increasing numbers. Paul and Theresa brought us reports of the troop movements. The soldiers were well west of Piotance and retreating back toward Berlin, pursued by the Russians when Anton died.

"That was the most extreme winter of my life. I will never forget the cold, the snow and the brutal winds. I've never been so cold in my life. Food was practically nonexistent. We lived on potatoes and occasional wild game—rabbits, squirrels, anything we could trap or shoot.

"Anton came down with what seemed a bad cold. We were spending a lot of time in the shelter because of troop movements in the area. And the few medicines my father had taken from his clinic were long since gone. We couldn't risk having Anton stay in the farmhouse because he had a terrible hacking cough and would have been discovered. So we stayed underground. He coughed and coughed, night and day. There was nothing Father could do for him.

"He grew weaker. One bitterly cold night, he finally slipped away."

Jacob turned away, struggling to regain his composure.

"He was buried in an unmarked grave in the woods," he resumed. "The most difficult task of my entire life was to help my father dig my brother's grave. The ground was snow covered and frozen solid, but we had no place to hide the body. So we dug. We wrapped his body in a simple blanket—one we could scarcely part with.

"That evening, Father and I said the Khaddish by candlelight in Maria's parlor. Everyone—Maria, Paul, Theresa, my parents and I—witnessed the ceremony. We were able to dig up his remains and bury him in Piotance in the Jewish cemetery after the war."

Jacob buried his face in his hands. Dick reached across and gripped his arm.

"Now I know why your older son is named Anton," said Nancy softly.

"Yes," Jacob nodded. "And Paul, of course, is named after Paul Dosecki. He died in 1955 in an industrial accident at the shipyard in Gdansk. We didn't learn of his death until more than a year later."

Jacob shifted in his chair, detached, his face deeply shadowed. He rose and stretched once more, then went to the sideboard and poured more cognac.

"But to finish the story," he said.

"Shortly before Anton died—in September of 1944, I think—we were discovered by a German patrol. Next to losing Anton, that was the most traumatic experience of my life.

"It was late afternoon. Maria had gone to town scavenging for supplies and gathering news about the German retreat. Theresa was on lookout and my mother was in the house. A German patrol of three young soldiers— probably none of them were more than twenty years old—suddenly tramped into the barn without warning. They completely surprised my father, Anton, Paul and me. It was later that we learned why our warning system had failed.

"They must have heard us talking. They just appeared, rifles pointed directly at us, ready to fire. They started shouting orders in German, obviously suspicious and a little scared too. Although we understood they wanted directions to Piotance, we pretended not to understand.

"One brutally aggressive soldier poked and prodded us with his gun butt while the others watched and laughed. I was absolutely terrified. Still, we played dumb, hoping they would give up and leave.

"He knocked Anton and Paul to the floor and pointed the gun to their heads. Then he set to work on my father and beat him methodically and with apparent delight. This time, the other two soldiers joined in, taking turns beating him nearly unconscious. Father would sink to his knees, his hands protecting his head. They would force him to his feet with their bayonet. The image of those soldiers beating my father is one I will take to my grave.

"At one point," he resumed, "he was beaten unconscious from blows to the kidneys. I was certain they would kill him. There was nothing any of us could do to stop them. Finally, they herded us toward the front door of the barn. I assumed they were taking us outside to execute us."

"Your mother was in the house. What was she doing while all this was going on?" asked Nancy.

"Maria had just joined Theresa at the lookout when they spotted the three soldiers moving across the fields heading directly toward the house and barn. The soldiers were between the woods and the house and they cut off any avenue to warn us. Maria and Theresa watched the soldiers enter the barn. They dashed through the woods to the house, but it took longer than running down the dirt road. They got into the house without being seen. Our lookout system failed for the first and only time.

"Meanwhile, my mother had been working in the attic. She heard the noise and watched the soldiers enter the barn. She was completely helpless to do anything. She later said it was the most frustrating moment of her life.

"We were incredibly lucky, however. The soldiers failed to post a guard outside when they entered the barn. They were just kids, obviously not well trained and very careless. That proved to be a fatal mistake.

"When Maria and Theresa dashed into the house, Maria hid Theresa in the attic. She and my mother grabbed butcher knives and sneaked outside. They made their way to the small door at the rear of the barn. They could hear the soldiers making a lot of noise, laughing as they beat my father.

"Anton, Paul and I saw the door slowly open and realized they were coming into the barn. We immediately set up a diversion, yelling and screaming, pretending to help Father."

Jacob regarded his two friends in the dim light of the dying embers.

"I am so proud of those two women. I'll never forget the look on my mother's face when she saw my father bloody and limp on the floor, his body in the fetal position taking blow after blow. She was ready to kill them. And Maria was a tough Polish farmwoman who had endured nearly five years of war. She was equally prepared to repay the Germans for some of her losses.

"They never hesitated," Jacob continued, shaking his head. "Using some bales of hay as cover, they worked their way toward the front of the barn. At precisely the right moment, they leaped across the floor like a couple of tigers closing in for the kill, knives held high, poised to attack. The two who were working over my father never knew what hit them.

"Maria and Mother stabbed the soldiers in the back, right through the heart, almost as though they had practiced the maneuver. Those two soldiers were dead before they hit the floor.

"In the melee, Anton, Paul and I pounced on the third soldier, wrestled away his gun and threw him to the floor. Then we all set to work on him.

"It was a bloody mess. But I can guarantee, those soldiers never hurt another human being," Jacob said remorselessly.

"Of course, cleaning up the mess and disposing of the bodies was a major problem. Father took charge. He was battered and bruised but no bones were broken. I'm sure some of his later medical problems resulted from his beating.

"Maria remembered an abandoned well behind the barn that had gone dry years ago. Until that afternoon, the rest of us didn't know it even existed. We dragged the bodies from the barn and tossed them into the well. There was blood in the snow. We very carefully covered all traces of the slaughter, and threw some brush and other junk over the well.

"We did a good job. A few days later, another much larger patrol came to the house looking for the missing soldiers. They never found the bodies, despite spending hours searching the barn. After the war ended the following May and the ground thawed, we buried the bodies in a common grave deep in the woods. We didn't notify the Russian occupation authorities that controlled the area. We decided to literally let sleeping dogs lie," he said ruefully. "The remains are probably still there, in Maria's woods.

"You know," he confessed, "I never felt any remorse about those killings. Obviously, it was a simple case of survival. We did what we had to do to save ourselves. Even now, I feel no guilt.

"Those young men had families, I suppose, who must have mourned their loss. When it comes to self-preservation or to defending a parent or loved one, some very basic instincts take over.

"I've never told this story to anyone except Ruth. Our sons know nothing about those years. It was an unspeakably difficult time, one that I've tried to eliminate from my consciousness. We survived, thanks to our wits and to the courage of Maria, Paul and Theresa Dosecki.

"Here I sit with my closest friends on the night after reaching the summit of the Matterhorn, discussing the darkest years of my life," he said. "Perhaps it all came back precisely because of my exhilaration from the climb. It was terrifically satisfying to reach the summit."

Jacob rose and stretched. He sank back in his chair and regarded his two friends. He glanced at his watch. "It's nearly four o'clock. Have you heard enough for one night or would you like to hear the rest?"

"If you're prepared to continue, we're ready to listen," said Dick, glancing at Nancy. "We had no idea how you spent the war years. We knew that you were born in Poland. It was obvious you never wanted to dwell on that part of your life. We also knew, of course, that you had attended university in France where you met and married Ruth."

"This won't take much longer," Jacob assured them.

"When the Allies defeated the Germans, we celebrated the end of the war with Maria, Theresa and Paul. After those interminable years in hiding, we finally returned to our home in Piotance. As you might have guessed, the house had been destroyed. During their final retreat, the Germans resorted to a scorched earth policy. And what they didn't destroy, the Russians either confiscated or burned.

"Conditions were chaotic. The countryside was full of Russian soldiers who were almost as bad as the Nazis. They plundered what was left of people's property and raped women and girls—it was total anarchy.

"Clearly, we couldn't stay in town. Our house and my father's clinic were piles of rubble. Maria insisted that we all return to her farm, this time living openly with her and the children. Father decided the farm offered better protection than Piotance.

"Several weeks later, we gathered in the kitchen for an extended family conference. Let's see. My parents were in their fifties, although they looked much older. Maria was nearly sixty years old. Anton was gone, and Paul was a teenager. Theresa and I were children. Aside from being

18

malnourished, a common problem across Europe, we had come through the ordeal surprisingly well. We were extremely fortunate in that my parents still had a supply of gold coins and Mother's jewelry from before the war. We insisted that Maria take some of the coins—I don't know how much Father gave her, but she was able to live relatively well after the war. Certainly, compared to seven million other Jews, we were in great shape," he said bitterly. "We were all alive."

"There we were," he resumed, "six people, living on a rundown farm surrounded by utter chaos, preyed upon by roving bands of Russian soldiers who had deserted from the army.

"Sitting around the kitchen table, we mapped out a plan for the future. Father didn't want to rebuild his medical practice in Poland. By that time, we had some idea of the extent of the Holocaust. We knew that our relatives in Warsaw had been taken away, presumably to the ovens. Our only ties to Piotance were Maria and her children. Father wanted to leave Poland, and to get as far away from Germany as possible. He was reluctant to head east, since the brutality of the Russians nearly equaled the atrocities of the Nazis.

"He went around the table, asking each of us to speak, even us children. After a long discussion, he took charge. I'll never forget his enthusiasm as he proposed that all of us, including Maria, Paul and Theresa, try to make our way to France. The ultimate goal was to settle in America, the Promised Land.

"My father was utterly convinced that life for Jewish survivors would be infinitely safer in an area controlled by the Western allies, rather than the Russians. He proved to be correct in that assessment," said Jacob.

"Unfortunately, the only way to get to France was to walk. And hundreds of thousands of refugees were wandering all over Europe with little or no food, water, or clothing. To reach our destination, we would have to join the dispossessed, taking what we could carry, hoping to pass through the barriers already being erected to keep those in the east from reaching the western zones.

"Maria refused to leave the farm, convinced that as long as she could work the land, her family could survive. Theresa decided to stay with her mother. Paul, after some discussion, opted to join us, even though it meant leaving his mother and sister temporarily behind. His plan was to head west, away from the Russians, find shelter and work and then send for Maria and Theresa.

"Less than a week after our summit conference," Jacob smiled at the image, "we gathered our few belongings and packed them into a cart that we took turns pushing. We set off to the west and what we hoped would be a better life. It was tough to leave Maria and Theresa. Although civilian authorities had begun to restore order, life was still dangerous, especially in the country. Maria was perhaps the strongest, most self-reliant woman I have ever known. If anyone could survive alone, it would be Maria.

"Our journey west took us through Warsaw," he said. "The old city was virtually leveled. Of course, the Jewish section had been obliterated after the Warsaw ghetto uprising. There was no way to determine specifically what happened to our extended family, especially to the uncles, aunts and cousins on my mother's side of the family. It took ten years to establish with certainty that they all died in the Holocaust.

"We stayed in Warsaw only a few days because it was already clear that the Russians were settling in for a long stay. We wanted no part of the communists, whom my father considered no better than the fascists. We took advantage of the turmoil to cross the border to Germany on foot, pushing the cart. It was bizarre to enter the country that had caused so much human suffering.

"Three months after we left Maria and Theresa, we reached the American controlled sector of Germany.

"Paul had left us by that time, deciding to remain in Poland. He headed north toward the sea, and eventually made his way to Gdansk where he worked in the shipyards for about ten years. He never returned to Piotance. We never saw Paul, Maria or Theresa again."

Jacob locked his hands behind his head, his eyes focused on the distant past.

"During the war years, Anton, Paul and I were very close. After Anton died and Paul decided not join us in the west, my parents became my only companions. They suffered more on our trek west than during the years of the Nazi occupation. It's hard to describe the conditions in Europe during the summer of 1945. Just surviving from one day to the next was a major victory."

He looked around the spacious room. "Who would have dreamed that one day I would live in this comfort? I never take it for granted.

"After spending some months in a displaced persons camp in western Germany," he resumed, "we were allowed to leave. Father's medical training was an important factor in obtaining permission to go to France. We made our way to Paris and he began the bureaucratic process of proving his medical credentials to the French authorities. Then, just as life began to improve, a truck hit him as he crossed a boulevard and he was killed. He was on his way home from a meeting with the medical authorities.

"We learned later that he had been granted a provisional license to practice as a physician in France. I suspect he was focusing on that good news when he was killed. He died in the spring of 1946."

Jacob combed his hands through his thick white hair.

"Mother was devastated by his death. She was a very optimistic woman, full of life even in the most desperate circumstances. His death nearly destroyed her. And I was so preoccupied with my own grief that we both drew protective shields around ourselves and suffered alone.

"She finally pulled herself together, probably because of me. It had been my father's dream that I should receive a university education, and she began to focus on that goal. To support us while I finished the French equivalent of high school, she took odd jobs as a cleaning woman. She also occasionally offered piano and voice lessons. Of course we couldn't afford a piano, so she would travel to her students' homes.

"I studied and worked at odd jobs after school. I was a couple of years older than my classmates, but I soon caught up. I discovered a real passion for science and mathematics and achieved high test scores when I finished high school. By that time, I wanted a career in science. I took the competitive examinations for admission to the Ecole Polytechnique in Paris. My mother was so proud when I was admitted.

"I went straight through the university, completing my doctorate in chemistry in 1955. Sadly, Mother died in 1953. She had been in failing health for several years, probably brought on by the hardships we endured during the war.

"Dick," he regarded his friend, "as a physician, you probably know that Holocaust survivors suffered a variety of war-related illnesses."

"Yes. There's a large body of medical evidence detailing the post-war health effects of the Holocaust on the survivors," Dick said.

"Anyway," Jacob resumed, "two years after she died, I earned my doctorate. Aside from my mother, I had no strong ties in Paris. When an opportunity to join a research team at the University of Grenoble came along, I accepted. The laboratory at Grenoble was doing some interesting work and I became caught up in my research and teaching. My work consumed all my waking hours. That's when I realized that I had some modest talent for basic research and developed a real love for teaching."

"Modest talent?" Nancy laughed. "As a member of the National Academy of Sciences and a master teacher, you can hardly be categorized as a 'modest talent.' Students line up for hours to take your Principles of Chemistry course. Your research is recognized around the world. Face it, Jacob. You're a major reason why Cabot University is consistently ranked as a top tier public university."

He shook his head. "Be serious," he chuckled. "Let me finish this before we all fall asleep.

"Going to Grenoble was the right move for me," he continued.

Linda Kistler

"That's where Ruth and I met. She was a graduate student enrolled in one of my courses. From the first day of class, she sat in the back of the lecture hall and appeared to hang onto every word. I had my eye on her.

"She was always prepared. I knew she had a good mind. Her accent was quite heavy in those days, and it didn't take long to learn that she was also a Polish refugee. By the end of the first month of classes I asked her to dinner, and we quickly developed a serious relationship."

"Did you help her with her studies?" asked Dick, curious.

"Not at all. She was a brilliant student. In fact, her theoretical grasp of chemistry is much better than mine. I'm rather intuitive in my research, working out ideas in the laboratory, filling in the technical details later. Ruth is just the opposite. She meticulously develops the theory before she engages in laboratory experimentation. That's probably why we have been a successful research team. Our talents complement each other.

"Her experience during the war was very different from mine. She refuses to discuss the details of that period in her life, even with me. I'm not revealing many personal details when I tell you that Ruth's parents were wealthy. She was born in Krakow, the only child of a prominent, even aristocratic, family of merchant Jews. Shortly before the Germans overran the area, the family fled to the east. They managed to reach Russian-occupied eastern Poland where they lived in relative comfort until the Germans turned on Russia. They moved farther east into the Soviet Union where they were forced into a Russian labor camp. They spent most of the war in miserable conditions, but they survived. France was relatively welcoming to Jews after the war. Like my family, Ruth and her parents made their way to France. I never met her parents. They died just a few years after arriving in France.

"Ruth was only three years old when the Nazis attacked. She retains some vivid memories of that period which must have been incredibly traumatic. She rarely discusses those years, not even with me. Like many Holocaust survivors, she keeps the details locked within her psyche. You understand her need for privacy?"

They nodded.

Jacob looked at his watch and yawned. "I really didn't intend to spend the night reliving those years." He glanced out the picture window into the garden and beyond to the Matterhorn.

"It's already dawn. The sun will be up in less than an hour."

He looked across at Dick. "Yesterday at this time we were close to the summit of the mountain. Was it worth the effort?"

Dick laughed. "Twenty years from now, when the only climbing we'll be doing is struggling out of our rocking chairs, we can relive the entire experience."

22

Nancy pulled herself slowly from the chair, making no effort to conceal a deep yawn.

"I've had it for one night. Don't forget to turn out the lights when you come up," she reminded them. She kissed both men, climbed the wide stairway and quietly let herself into the corner room overlooking the garden.

The two men gathered their empty glasses and carried them into Hannah's immaculate kitchen. Opening the French doors, they walked onto the stone terrace. In the crisp morning dawn they gazed up at the brooding Matterhorn as the first rays of pink struck the peak. The colors of dawn slid rapidly down the face of the great mountain, invading the ridges and granite promontories, illuminating the snowfields they had traversed during their ascent of the peak.

Dick leaned against the stone wall, arms folded, and gazed up at the granite face.

"Now you know the whole story," Jacob said. "Without question, the war years shaped my life in ways I still don't understand. You know, I've never been very introspective, perhaps because I want to avoid thinking about those years," he mused.

"One fact is certain. The personal challenges in the last decades don't begin to compare to the hardship and loss we endured during that unspeakably brutal time. Life has been comparatively easy. My school years in France were relatively comfortable. Even the loss of my parents didn't have the impact of my brother's death. The daily struggle for survival in Poland is hard to explain. You had to be there.

"I vowed that if I survived, my life's work would honor Anton. At that point, I still dreamed of becoming a doctor. I gave up trying to become a physician shortly after we got to France. My work in science has proved to be intellectually stimulating and I don't regret my decision.

Dick stood in the early morning chill, hands in his pockets. He turned to his friend.

"As a physician, I occasionally thought it curious that neither you nor Ruth ever spoke of your early years. Now I understand. I also understand the source of your political convictions, your commitment to certain causes— your opposition to the Vietnam war, and your support for affirmative action, for example—must have been shaped during those early formative years."

With a final glance at the mountain looming above, they entered the chalet and went to bed.

Part II

Summer

Chapter 4

Graduation week in early June evoked the usual mixture of joy and sadness in the Cabot University community. Seniors indulged in a final orgy of parties and gatherings celebrating a major milestone in their lives.

Faculty typically approached graduation with ambivalence. Many were acutely aware that the unique bonds between faculty and students would forever be severed as graduates moved on to careers or graduate school. This June, their customary relief at the end of the grueling academic year was tinged with sadness at the loss of an important colleague. Jacob Borovski's death was close to the surface as faculty and students alike marked the end of the academic year. Commencement ceremonies, normally staged on the Commons among the massive oaks, were moved indoors when a three-day downpour turned the lush, green Commons into a shallow pond. Despite the soggy weather, more than 6,000 people gathered in the Johnson Fieldhouse to observe the ceremony.

Cabot University followed academic traditions handed down from European universities since the Middle Ages. The ceremonies began promptly at ten o'clock as the procession of soon-to-be-graduates entered the Fieldhouse to the strains of the brass choir's opening anthem and rousing cheers from the audience. Standing at their seats in academic robes, they watched the long procession of faculty and other dignitaries enter the cavernous Fieldhouse, led by the faculty marshal bearing the university mace. The platform party entered last and marched up the center aisle to the applause of onlookers and graduates alike.

Ruth and Nancy, clad in the colorful academic regalia of their respective alma maters, joined fellow faculty behind the colorful banners of their colleges—white designating the School of Arts and Sciences and drab brown for the School of Management. The procession slowly made its way through the black-robed throngs of graduates, smiling here and there at faces recognized in the crowd. They climbed the steps, took their places along the rows of seats on the stage and stood overlooking a sea of faces—2,000 graduates seated on the floor and 4,000 family and friends occupying seats overlooking the ceremonies.

The next hour was taken up with speeches of distinguished guests and University administrators, all seeking the spotlight for brief moments before the conferring of degrees.

The recognition of doctoral candidates was a highlight of the graduation ceremony. All successful doctoral candidates, many of whom were completing upwards of a decade of education and research, received individual public recognition. Called to the front of the stage to receive their degree, President Northrop announced their name and the title of their research dissertation. Then their Faculty Dissertation Chair placed the traditional academic hood, symbolic of the doctorate, on each graduate's shoulders amid robust cheers from the audience.

Three students of Ruth and Jacob Borovski received their doctor of philosophy degrees. As co-chairs of their dissertation committees, Ruth and Jacob would have participated jointly in the academic hooding ceremony for their graduates. In Jacob's absence, Ruth joined the Dean of the School of Arts and Sciences and slipped the doctoral hood over each candidate's head. One newly minted doctor of science bent over awkwardly as Ruth, who barely reached his shoulders, arranged the hood and then shook his hand. The young man accepted the congratulations of the Dean and the President, then turned back to Ruth and embraced her in a spontaneous gesture of respect and affection.

Tears welling, Nancy joined the graduates and guests who rose as one. Her natural reserve clearly shaken, Ruth returned to her seat as thunderous applause rolled through the vast Fieldhouse.

At the end of the ceremonies, the newly minted graduates marched from the hall as proud family and friends looked on. The faculty and administrative officers smiled at the sight. Once again, this special moment in the life of the university was over.

The pomp and ritual of the graduation ceremony reinforced the long tradition and ongoing mission of the university as a center for scholarship and research. It also indelibly stamped on the minds of the graduates their new status as alumni of one of the leading academic institutions in the country. A solicitation from the Office of Alumni Affairs seeking financial support was already in the mail.

Chapter 5

"We'll miss you, Ruth." Nancy glanced at her friend as she wheeled into a parking space in the short-term lot adjacent to the passenger terminal at the Hillsdale Regional Airport. She switched off the ignition and regarded her friend. "This is the first time that you and Jacob won't be flying with us to Coral Cay."

"I know. I'm trying not to think about it." Ruth gazed across the parking lot toward the terminal. "There's no sense in dwelling on the past. I understand that intellectually, but I can't always act on the knowledge. Right now, the best therapy for me is work. Spending the summer doing research with Paul and having Anton nearby in San Francisco is what I need."

Nancy lifted the trunk lid and signaled a skycap for assistance. Both watched closely as he piled Ruth's bags and boxes onto a cart and wheeled it to curbside check-in. Nancy stood aside while Ruth checked her bags and produced her driver's license for identification. They took the escalator to the upper floor.

After a farewell hug, Nancy watched as Ruth passed through the security check points without incident. The twenty-passenger propjet that would take Ruth to Pittsburgh for her connecting flight to San Francisco sat on the tarmac while the ground crew loaded the luggage and fueled the small plane. Despite the seven a.m. departure time, Ruth would spend most of the day flying across the country. With luck, she would arrive in San Francisco on schedule in mid-afternoon.

*   *   *   *

"How was your flight?" Paul retrieved his mother's baggage from the claims area and guided her past the baggage security attendant.

"The usual. A small plane to Pittsburgh, then one not much larger for the rest of the flight out here," she said.

"Are we going to see Anton today?" She searched the crowded claims area for her older son.

"We'll meet him for dinner. He was sorry he couldn't meet your plane." Paul glanced at his watch. "He's in the middle of a scheduled doctoral defense by one of his students," he continued. "No way to reschedule it. He'll meet us around seven o'clock for dinner.

"We can drop off your bags at my apartment," he said. They entered a broad corridor leading to the parking garage. "Then if you feel like checking out my lab, we can review my research and I can take a look at the materials

29

you brought along. Do you feel up to that?" Paul anxiously regarded his mother.

"Of course," she laughed. "I dozed a bit on the plane. Traveling alone on a six-hour flight is really a bore. A little work may help me adjust to the time change."

An hour later they drove through the broad gates of the Stanford University campus and parked near Paul's lab. Within minutes they were engrossed in the major research project begun by Jacob and Ruth that would now be completed by Paul and Ruth.

Chapter 6

Dick Atherton pushed the throttles forward, banked the twin-engine Beechcraft Baron and descended to five hundred feet in preparation for landing at the Coral Cay Resort in the British Virgin Islands. The flight from Hillsdale had been uneventful, interrupted by two refueling stops and an overnight stay in Miami. Nancy was subdued during the flight, gazing occasionally at the terrain 8,000 feet below, reading much of the time as they flew south toward their favorite early summer vacation resort.

The brilliant tropical sun beat directly into the cockpit. Dick throttled back, nudged the wheel forward, extended the landing gear and began his final approach to the narrow blacktop runway. Slipping past the familiar ruins of an abandoned sugar mill, he set the plane down and taxied to the tin-roofed terminal.

Nancy handled customs and entry formalities while Dick secured the plane, greeting as old friends the two ground attendants who also served as maintenance personnel at the tiny airport. Not much had changed on the island since their first visit with Jacob and Ruth a decade ago. What began as a brief celebration at the end of a difficult academic year became an annual ritual marking the beginning of summer.

Together, Dick and Nancy strolled from the terminal and greeted the attendant who would drive them the two miles to the oceanside resort. Minutes later their van passed between the stone gates of Coral Cay Resort. Waiving the check-in formalities, the driver delivered them immediately to their beachside cottage. While he unloaded the van and deposited their luggage in the spacious dressing room, Nancy and Dick slid back the double screen door leading to the flagstone patio. Removing their shoes, they walked a few steps along a sandy path, pushed aside masses of sea grapes and stepped onto the sandy beach.

The half-mile crescent of white sand beach faced the brilliant emerald waters of Coral Cay and the reef beyond. Waves lapped gently at their feet. A few resort guests lounged beneath umbrellas or in strategically placed hammocks, reading, sunning and floating on inflated rafts. Beyond the reef, a few sailboats tacked languidly along the Sir Francis Drake Channel. Dick glanced toward the boathouse and spotted the Cay's thirty-foot catamaran, Sea Spray, anchored just off the dock. Apparently no one had booked a cruise today.

"Ready for a quick swim before lunch?" Dick regarded his wife.

"I'll race you," said Nancy. Within moments they changed into swimsuits, lathered on a generous dose of sun block and splashed into the calm lagoon. The rest of the day was occupied in winding down from the flight, lazing on the beach and reading. Although both were painfully aware that Ruth and Jacob Borovski no longer occupied the cottage next door, neither spoke directly of their friends' absence.

The two couples had vacationed together so frequently at Coral Cay that they had come to consider it their own private resort. No longer would they exchange books on the beach, or engage in heated political conversations late at night over nightcaps, or swim nude in the warm water under the stars.

Over the next week, Dick and Nancy visited their favorite secluded beaches and neighboring islands, swimming and snorkeling, silently acknowledging the absence of their best friends. Coral Cay's spectacular scenery, clear emerald waters and brilliant sandy beaches constantly reminded them to savor their own good health, to revitalize their strong marriage, to begin anew.

Dick indulged his passion for scuba diving, joining groups of four or six divers under the watchful eye of resort personnel, exploring sunken wrecks and dazzling offshore coral reefs. Nancy snorkeled or sunned on the beach, often alone, reading and savoring the seclusion and solitude, interrupted only by the unobtrusive attentiveness of the resort staff.

Chapter 7

The summer months proved to be a productive research period for Ruth despite intermittent, intense bouts of grief. The long hours in the laboratory offered solace, challenging her to focus on her research to the exclusion of other thoughts.

She often worked alone, sensitive to Paul's need to complete final details on his doctoral dissertation. They invariably met for lunch; and Paul frequently joined her in the laboratory, looking over her shoulder, talking through problems, offering suggestions, providing comfort with his steadfast presence. Paul's Stanford associates welcomed her warmly into their research environment, aware of her formidable reputation, delighted to meet her, to explore her intellect, exuding the enthusiasm and curiosity of young scientists at the beginning of their careers.

Several evenings each week they met Anton in Berkeley, crossing the Bay Bridge to San Francisco, attending concerts, visiting Chinatown, discovering the galleries, museums and shops for which the city is famous. One of Ruth's favorite places was Golden Gate Park. There among the green spaces and winding paths, she and the boys whiled away many weekend hours walking and tramping along the beach, admiring the Golden Gate Bridge in the distance.

Ruth was pleased that Anton had settled into life on the Berkeley campus of the University of California and begun to build an impressive research and academic record. Despite her unspoken misgivings about his living arrangement with a young male colleague, she accepted his sexual orientation and loved him without reservations. Occasionally, Anton's uncanny physical resemblance to Jacob unnerved her, triggering painful flashbacks to her younger days in Europe.

Chapter 8

Two miles south of the Coral Cay Resort lay Devil's Cay, a tiny secluded bay rimmed by a broad crescent of white sand beach. Near the massive rocks marking the entrance to the Cay, Nancy lay face down and motionless on the emerald water, swim fins barely moving, examining the rich sea life below, snorkel tube clamped firmly in her mouth. Absorbed and unafraid, she watched as a large barracuda slowly meandered into view, gliding lazily among the reindeer coral formations fifteen feet below. A cluster of brilliant parrot fish and yellow sergeant majors ignored the intruder, pecking energetically at the coral as golden sunlight filtering through the water illuminated the scene.

Devil's Cay had been the favorite beach of the two couples from Hillsdale. They enjoyed countless hours swimming and snorkeling in the tiny bay at the secluded southern end of the island. While Jacob and Dick went scuba diving on distant reefs, Ruth and Nancy swam and snorkeled. Tired and refreshed, the women would settle on beach towels beneath a huge umbrella shielded from the sun's intense rays and read. Occasionally, they would glance seaward toward the tiny sailboats that dotted the horizon or feast their eyes on the changing cloud formations in the western sky.

Now, placidly floating face down in the water, Nancy felt an overwhelming sense of loss. The unique relationship with Jacob and Ruth over several decades had been irretrievably altered. Like Ruth, she understood that change was an inevitable fact of life. Emotionally, however, she could not surrender the past. The prospect of life at Cabot University without Jacob and the unique friendship they had forged over so many years was profoundly depressing. While close to Ruth, Nancy's stronger bonds of friendship had always been with Jacob. Ruth's natural reserve, perhaps an artifact of her early experiences during the Holocaust, presented a barrier Nancy never penetrated.

Swim fins barely moving, breathing easily and watching intently the teeming sea life on the sandy ocean floor, Nancy finally confronted the loss that Jacob's death created in her professional life. Who would lead the faculty in its inevitable battles with the administration? She felt inadequate to assume a leadership role on behalf of the faculty despite her consulting background and expertise in Human Resource Management. On a faculty dominated by males, she would never achieve the respect and confidence accorded Jacob. And she could not identify any other faculty member qualified to fill the void created by his death.

She worried that the absence of a strong faculty leader would encourage certain administrators, perhaps led by Tyler Hutchins, to radically reshape the university to fit their own vision. Over the years, Jacob stood as a formidable bulwark against several administrations that had sought to impose a conservative, even reactionary vision of the university's mission upon the faculty and students.

Nancy considered President Larry Northrop a notable exception to Cabot's generally mediocre administrative staff. However, Larry's barely suppressed anger following Dick's questioning remarks at the memorial service for Jacob last month surprised and angered her. Although Northrop subsequently authorized a search of the laboratories and storage areas in Starrett Science Center in the month following graduation, he had openly expressed derision and contempt when Ruth and Nancy initially approached him seeking an investigation. It was only after an influential member of the Board of Trustees independently insisted upon a quiet investigation that Northrop reluctantly agreed to review the university's procedures surrounding safeguarding and disposal of chemicals and toxins on campus.

Northrop's defensive reaction to the search puzzled her. Dick's publicly expressed concerns at Jacob's memorial service were not the first time questions about campus safety had arisen. Indeed, she and other faculty felt that an ongoing program to examine university health and safety procedures should be put in place. Each time the proposal was raised at faculty senate meetings, Tyler Hutchins led the administration in assuring the faculty that the university's health and safety procedures met and exceeded all state and federal requirements. Invariably, the matter was dropped.

Larry Northrop was furious with Dick, whose remarks had publicly embarrassed the university. The subsequent search of the science labs and storage areas had turned up nothing of consequence. The investigation was carried out quickly and discreetly. Only a handful of people were aware of the activity.

Nancy felt that the incident should not have precipitated the obvious coolness Larry had exhibited toward her since the memorial service in May. She rejected the possibility that a professional relationship begun in 1965 could be severed over an investigation and review of safety issues.

Larry Northrop had joined the faculty the same year as Nancy and Jacob. Rising through the faculty ranks to chairman of the Electrical Engineering Department, then Dean of the School of Engineering and finally Vice-President for Academic Affairs, he was a bona fide member of the Class of '65, one of the group of faculty whose friendship and professional association extended over three decades. Overwhelming support by the faculty figured heavily in his appointment as President more than twenty years ago when former President Jackson Starrett was forced to retire.

Linda Kistler

Nancy trusted and admired Martin Billings, Vice-President for Academic Affairs, far more than Larry Northrop. Billings, a professor of English for more than twenty years, reluctantly accepted the appointment as chief academic officer at Northrop's request in 1980. Although not members of the Class of '65, he and Ruth Borovski were part of the elite faculty group who exercised the academic leadership on campus.

A man dedicated to the intellectual growth and welfare of students, Billings was accorded extraordinary trust and respect by the faculty. As the chief academic officer of the university, he concentrated on academic matters, including curriculum and faculty tenure decisions. He enjoyed the confidence of the faculty, and focused his primary loyalties on the faculty and students of the university. Their support and approval of his actions were the principal reasons he continued in the position, despite his dislike for the administrative minutiae he dealt with daily. Recently, his personal goal was to serve the university for a few more years, then retire quietly to his winter cottage in the Florida Keys.

Nancy had little respect for most of Cabot University's other administrators. Tyler Hutchins, Vice President of Finance and Administration, was a particularly inept bureaucrat, one of several who had lost sight of the raison d'être for a world-class university. The faculty believed that Hutchins delighted in obstructing rather than facilitating the services sought by faculty and students.

Administrators all too frequently ignored the university's primary mission, that of educating and training the university's students. Intent on building minor fiefdoms, they engaged in petty internecine wars and obstructed faculty who dared to question their edicts. Unless a strong faculty leader emerged quickly to challenge the administration, Tyler Hutchins and his cronies would step into the void and impose even more heavy-handed bureaucratic regulations on the faculty.

Jacob's leadership was irreplaceable. Yet someone had to step up and lead the faculty, which was united in its commitment to protect and enhance the academic quality of the university's programs. A year ago, when the administration proposed major changes in teaching loads and imposed financial cutbacks in research support, Jacob led the faculty in successfully fighting the cutbacks. Who would fill that leadership role in the future?

Nancy had no illusions about the loss of Jacob's leadership. She fully expected Tyler Hutchins and his cronies to try to implement major changes in the months ahead, changes that would not necessarily be in the faculty and students' best interest. Cabot University had a long history of issuing onerous administrative edicts during the summer months when faculty members typically were off campus conducting research, on vacation or otherwise unavailable to challenge arbitrary decisions. Somehow, Nancy

36

and others would have to find a way to continue to influence the university's decisions. The gains under Jacob's leadership could not be frittered away.

*   *   *   *

Nancy peered through her snorkel mask as thousands of tiny silver fish swarmed across the coral field, then dashed upward to the surface. The sun's intense rays on her back and shoulders brought her back to reality. She lifted her head, spit out the snorkel tube and gazed out to sea, searching for Dick along the reef a quarter mile away. Seeing nothing, she treaded water and slowly searched the shoreline. In the distance the solitary beach umbrella stood guard over their picnic cooler and towels.

She watched as Dick emerged from the water, removed his fins and facemask and dragged his air tank up the beach to their umbrella. Perhaps sensing her gaze, he turned and scanned the sea, searching for her orange tipped snorkel tube. She raised her arm and waved. Depositing his gear, he grabbed his swim fins and returned to the water. Nancy slowly swam toward the beach to meet him.

Dick reached her and kissed her hard, evoking the familiar response his touch always produced. Silently demanding, his kisses became more insistent as he held her firmly in his arms. She wrapped her legs around his waist, returning his kiss with a passion that surprised and pleased both of them.

"When is the boat coming to pick us up? Do we have time...?" Nancy smiled.

"We've got plenty of time," he said.

Swimming in unison, they let the fins do the work as they raced for the beach. Reaching shore, they slogged through the deep sand to the umbrella and their towels. Their lovemaking was short and intense, each understanding the needs of the other. It was as though they felt an urgency to reaffirm their passion, to celebrate the joy of living. Later, they enjoyed a leisurely swim together, exploring among the huge rocks and into the channel, delighting in the coral gardens and brilliant tropical fish, occasionally retrieving a conch shell from the sand fifteen feet below.

An hour later a Boston Whaler, piloted by one of Coral Cay's water sports attendants appeared on the horizon. Jason, whose expertise with boats was legendary among resort guests, slowed the Whaler abruptly and deftly maneuvered the boat through the narrow sand bar guarding the beach. Near the shore, he shifted into neutral, steadying the boat in the shallow water. Nancy hopped onto the bow and crawled back to the bench seat while Dick handed over the folded beach umbrella, stowed the rest of their gear and climbed into the boat.

37

During the speedy ten-minute ride back to the resort, they soaked up the spectacular island scenery. Dense foliage covered the mountains that bisected the island. Masses of impenetrable greenery formed steep canyons descending to the secluded beaches that gave this exclusive and expensive resort its world-class reputation. Behind the boat, the tropical sun had already begun its slow descent into the western sea.

*   *   *   *

Meals at Coral Cay were served in an eighteenth century stone Sugar Mill, restored and transformed into an open-air dining pavilion. During daylight hours, guests feasted their eyes on the magnificent views beyond the sandy beach shaded by towering palms. In the distance the island of Tortola lay five miles across the channel.

Each evening the Sugar Mill was transformed into an intimate candlelit dining room, cooled by fresh ocean breezes. Formally dressed table captains strolled among the tables, catering to their guests' every whim as an island combo provided soft background music.

Hand in hand, Nancy and Dick strolled along the softly lighted path from their cottage to the dining pavilion, past masses of flowering bougainvillea and sheltered beneath a canopy of giant tulip trees. The natural beauty and serenity of the resort had already begun to work their magic even in the midst of their unspoken grief.

*   *   *   *

Nancy sipped her after dinner liqueur and gazed at the lighted palms marking the edge of the beach. She leaned back in her chair and turned to her husband. "Do you remember when Joe Scali died in 1981?" she asked quietly.

"What made you think of him after all this time?" Dick asked quizzically, an eyebrow raised.

"Come on, answer my question, please."

"Well, yes, now that you mention him, I vaguely remember something about it. He died young, as I recall. And wasn't he a member of the Chemistry Department along with Ruth and Jacob?"

"Right." Nancy's finger traced a pattern on the heavy tablecloth, seemingly absorbed, swirling the cognac in its heavy goblet.

"Well, some of us questioned whether chemical poisoning was a contributing factor in his death. Jacob, Ruth—a group of us—were so concerned that we drove to Philadelphia to discuss Joe's death with the university's Chairman of the Board of Trustees."

"I do remember," Dick nodded. "I also recall that the chairman was President of Capital Chemicals, one of the biggest chemical companies in the country. Didn't he ask Jacob to conduct a thorough investigation?"

"Yes. And Jacob asked me to join the ad hoc committee even though I'm not a chemist," Nancy said. "It was handled very quietly. Most of the faculty knew nothing about it."

"I also remember," Dick said, "that no evidence ever came to light implicating the misuse of chemicals in Joe's death. Why are you bringing that up on an evening like this?" Dick glanced around the pavilion.

"Because I can't help wondering if Jacob's illness was somehow linked to the chemicals he used in his research," Nancy said pensively. "I know it seems unlikely, but there is that small doubt in my mind, and it just won't go away. In fact, I haven't been able to get it out of my mind since he died."

"Nancy," Dick took her hand in both of his. "I'll admit Larry Northrop had to be prodded a bit, but he did finally authorize a search of the lab areas where Jacob worked. Ruth led the team that conducted the search and it was finished before she went to California and we left to fly down here. Ruth told both of us that nothing was found."

Gently, he continued, "The fact is that Jacob died of a particularly virulent form of pancreatic cancer that metastasized to his liver. It happens, and there's nothing medical science can do except make the patient comfortable and minimize the pain. Jacob was an extraordinarily strong person, physically and mentally. The fact that he lived only six months following the diagnosis is evidence of the virulent nature of his cancer and the collapse of his immune system."

Nancy refused to meet his gaze.

"Look at me," he touched her cheek.

"Jacob's gone, Nancy. We all have to adjust to his loss and get on with our lives."

Eyes glistening, she gazed across the romantic setting filled with guests savoring the evening. The soft candlelight emphasized the glow of her newly acquired tan and her black cocktail dress highlighted the gray flecks in her hair. Moments later, she returned his gaze. She smiled sadly and nodded her head. He leaned over and gently kissed her lips.

She sighed.

"The four of us have always considered Coral Cay our private hideaway, Dick. I'm having trouble accepting the changes that Jacob's death will bring. It's not just that we've both lost our best friend. The university has lost its most prominent professor and the faculty has lost its leader. There's no one to take his place. I also think about the students who will never be challenged and inspired by his intellect, his dedication to science, not to mention his sense of humor. His death is such a waste. I know I shouldn't dwell on it, but it's just terribly unfair."

She smiled ruefully, "You approach life so rationally, so deliberately. That's one aspect of your character that appealed to me when we first met. Somewhere in your medical training, you apparently learned to deal with crises—even death—dispassionately. I envy your control and calm, especially now. After all, we both lost our best friend. I just need more time to adjust."

Together they sat quietly listening to the trio of musicians and the soft sounds of the island.

"Sorry," she concealed her tears, absorbed in the amber liquid in her goblet. "You should know by now that emotional control isn't my strong suit."

Dick reached for her hand, smiling with infinite tenderness. "I love you precisely because you express your emotions so openly. Don't ever change."

"Now," he said rising from the table, "let's dance for awhile and then walk back to the cottage along the beach. With luck we can spot Orion and the Pleiedes tonight."

An hour later, they slipped away, descending the broad stone steps to the darkened beach. Removing their shoes, they wandered arm in arm along the beach, the gentle surf at their side, taking turns identifying the constellations of stars spread like an enormous umbrella above them. Standing in the quiet surf, they paused to view the twinkling lights of Tortola and the silhouette of a yacht silently motoring past the resort, heading for a sheltered anchorage at the north end of the island. As they reached their cottage, a brilliant shooting star bisected the heavens and plummeted into the ocean beyond the reef.

Lulled by the intense silence of the starry night and the sounds of gentle surf, Nancy slept soundly for the first time in weeks.

*   *   *   *

Shortly after 3 a.m. Dick slipped silently out of bed. He paused to regard the naked form of his wife revealed in the dim light of a patio lamp. She stirred but did not awaken. Opening the sliding screen door carefully, he stepped across the patio to the sandy path leading to the beach. Brushing aside the sea grapes in the dim light of a waning quarter moon, he found a beach chaise and sat down. There, in the darkness and solitude of Coral Cay, he surrendered to the grief he had so carefully controlled. Thirty minutes later, he returned to the cottage. He lay silent and motionless beside Nancy until dawn when he rose, donned his trunks and swam slow laps in the quiet lagoon. The exercise failed to lift his spirits.

He would continue to display the exterior strength and calm that was essential to Nancy's well being. However, despite his intention to turn aside her concerns, their conversation the previous evening lingered in the back of his mind throughout the rest of the week.

Chapter 9

Heavy rain poured through the open window, soaking the flimsy gauze curtain and darkening the wooden sill next to the bed. Clad in shorts and T-shirt and sprawled across the bed in his shabby room, Kevin Parks was awakened by the distant rumble of Saturday morning traffic on Main Street.

As the minute hand on his bedside clock crawled past eleven o'clock, he reluctantly roused, sweaty and restless from ten hours of fitful slumber. For the past two months his craving for sleep was insatiable. Twelve, even fifteen hours a day were not enough. He was overcome by a deep fatigue, a fog of exhaustion. Productive research, usually an energizing source of exhilaration, had become impossible. Never much interested in food or drink beyond burgers, fries and cokes, his eating habits became even more erratic. Even his passion for science fiction paperbacks held no appeal. He failed to recognize in his behavior the symptoms of clinical depression or to realize that Jacob Borovski's death was the trigger that led to his paralysis.

Strangely, for the first time in weeks he awoke refreshed. It took only a moment to realize the source of his well being. At last he had a plan of action. And last night he thought of someone he trusted, someone who would listen, perhaps offer encouragement and most important, share his secret.

He rolled over and closed the window. One arm flung across his forehead, he reconsidered his decision to bring Tony Amonte into his plans. In the damp gloom of morning, he began to doubt the wisdom of confiding in his old friend. Tony probably knew more about the campus than anyone else alive. But could he trust him? Although Tony knew nothing about chemistry, he wasn't stupid and he might ask questions Kevin couldn't answer, at least not yet. Whether he talked to Tony now or later, eventually he would need his help. Perhaps a visit to Tony should wait a while longer.

Kevin's friend, Tony Amonte, had been head custodian at Cabot University until his retirement a few years ago. Kevin worked part-time for Tony for four long years, and he knew from experience that janitors eventually saw and heard just about everything important on campus. If they didn't hear or see the action directly, they learned about it from the secretaries and clerks working in offices all over campus.

As a needy undergraduate student, he qualified for a work-study program that helped pay his tuition and gave him some cash to live on. Although the program paid barely subsistence wages and limited students to fifteen hours of work each week, the money paid for his meals.

Kevin looked back on those years with a mixture of anger and shame. Some lucky work-study students actually got to grade papers, answer phones in a Dean's office or assist the secretaries with administrative chores. He noticed that the choice work-study jobs usually went to attractive female students. By the time he heard about the program, the only jobs available were for student janitors. The janitorial work wasn't difficult, merely demeaning. It actually was a lot easier than the manual labor he had endured on his father's farm during high school. The smirks of passing students as he lugged bucket and mop, scrubbing and waxing floors in buildings all over campus were impossible to ignore. Kevin's undergraduate years were consumed by his studies and work.

Student janitors coordinated their hours with the head custodian, Tony Amonte. For reasons unknown to him, Kevin's scheduled fifteen hours each week were restricted to Friday afternoons, all day Saturday and Sunday morning. To make matters worse, he was assigned to work directly under Tony.

Initially, he resented being under the watchful eye of the head custodian. However, as the weeks and months flew by, Kevin slowly warmed to his new boss. Tony was a good teacher. He showed him how to efficiently mop and wax the floors and clean the lavatory toilets. Gradually, the two developed an easygoing relationship, a give and take he never experienced with his peers. Amonte treated Kevin as an equal, and the janitorial crew was less condescending than the students who sat in classes with him and competed for grades.

During his freshman and sophomore years, Tony and Kevin developed a standard work routine. Late each Friday afternoon they would meet in Connors Hall. There, in a windowless basement storage closet, the janitors stored their buckets, mops, rags and the large buffers used to polish the endless halls in the four-story building that housed the business school. As the work week drew to a close, the two would sometimes spend an hour slowly storing their equipment, cleaning up and shooting the breeze before punching the time clock and checking out. During those times, they would gossip about the latest campus scandal, complain about the students, faculty, administrators and life in general.

Kevin was amazed at Tony's storehouse of knowledge about Cabot University. He knew everyone on campus from the President down to the newest custodian and secretary. He delighted in recounting tales of the faculty's idiosyncrasies, and their occasional sexual liaisons that invariably took place late at night in offices and laboratories where faculty and students presumably were engaged in important research.

Tony's service to Cabot University dated from the late 1950s when he arrived in Hillsdale, a recent Italian immigrant. He became a fixture around the university, having participated in its transformation from a sleepy liberal arts college into a world-class research university. The campus building boom of the late '60s and '70s presented opportunities for advancement from lowly janitor to head custodian. In the process he absorbed an encyclopedic knowledge of the university. He knew every nook and cranny on the campus, observed the successes and failures of several Presidents and other top administrators and was on a first name basis with most faculty members.

For four years Tony Amonte was one of Kevin's few human connections outside the classrooms, labs and the library where he spent most of his waking hours. An easygoing Italian with strong religious and family values, Tony Amonte was pleasantly surprised at the relationship that developed between the strange but brilliant young student and himself. Kevin was mature for his age, had a good work ethic and took directions well, unlike many other students in the work-study program.

Tony sensed that his young charge endured a fair amount of subtle ridicule from his classmates. He concluded that Kevin's sullen exterior masked a decent kid from a poverty-stricken background that alienated him from the typical middle and upper class students that comprised the student body.

He admired Kevin's obvious intellectual abilities and pitied his utter lack of social skills and inability to relate to his peers. He never knew that Kevin had grown up on a farm less than ten miles outside Hillsdale, a rundown property where his father still lived.

Gradually, Tony drew the young student into his family, inviting him to Saturday night supper with his wife and their two teenaged children. Embarrassed and shy, Kevin initially found excuses to decline the casual invitations. Finally, he joined them one Saturday night for Rosa's spaghetti and meatballs. Like her husband, Rosa was a warm, unpretentious first-generation Italian. Their children were in awe of the young student their father invited to supper. Gradually, Kevin relaxed in the warmth of the Amonte home. In time, Tony's family replaced the family Kevin had abandoned years earlier.

Life changed when Kevin entered graduate school. He received a research assistantship, primarily because Jacob Borovski championed his application, having identified him as an excellent prospect for doctoral work. His days as a student janitor finally ended. Although no longer working for Tony, he continued his relationship with the family, joining them about once a month for dinner in their modest home a mile from campus.

Three years ago, Tony retired from Cabot University at the age of seventy. He soon discovered that he didn't enjoy the retired lifestyle, and Rosa quickly tired of his presence underfoot during the day. Three months after his retirement party, he began working twenty hours a week handling the cash register at a popular pizza parlor on Main Street near the campus. Kevin made a point of buying pizza at least once a week, mainly in order to talk to his friend.

Tony's intimate knowledge of the campus would be invaluable in Kevin's search for the toxins he was convinced had contributed to Jacob's illness and death. But consulting Tony at this point might be premature. Kevin needed to know more about the specific classes of chemicals that were known toxins and carcinogens. Tony could help him later, after Kevin had a better idea what he was looking for.

Chapter 10

Kevin stretched, pulled back the flimsy curtain and checked out the street activity below. It was nearly noon. Time to hit the road. He grabbed the towel from the hook on the back of his bedroom door and walked down the dark hall to the shabby bathroom. He showered hurriedly, pulled on a fresh T-shirt, a pair of dirty cutoffs and his sneaks.

Heading downstairs to the front door, he mentally laid out his plan of attack. Confiding in Tony Amonte could wait. First, he would begin the library search. It was the logical preliminary step in his quest to find the cause of Jacob's illness. He reviewed again the crude plan he had worked out last night, checking for flaws in his approach. He would search, identify and catalog a comprehensive range of toxic chemicals, then cross-reference each chemical to studies of known or suspected carcinogens. Finally, he needed an inventory of all chemicals in use at Cabot University, whether in student laboratories or in funded research projects. He would lay out the database, download the data, analyze and manipulate the information to isolate all toxic chemicals that were known or suspected carcinogens and match that list against the inventory of chemicals present on the campus.

Somewhere in the administrative computer system the university maintained inventory records of all purchases. It was simply a matter of hacking into the system and downloading the detailed inventory records to his private database.

Kevin was confident he could break into the administrative computer system. He knew from experience that computer hacks were not nearly as difficult as non-techies believed. After all, he'd hacked into the academic computer system more than a year ago, and those records were more closely guarded than financial records like purchasing data.

The firewalls designed as system safeguards were not impregnable. Once he broke into the system, finding and downloading the data he sought was a trivial exercise. He knew that several local networks linked all computer systems on campus. That meant that he could probably hack into the administrative computer network through the library network. His search would begin in the library.

A new computerized catalog and search system had been installed recently in the main library. The internal system was linked to major libraries around the country to facilitate research. The library system was a state of the art design that had gained national attention when it went online six months ago. The new system streamlined the older, more cumbersome research methodology Kevin had used when he prepared the bibliography for his dissertation two years ago.

Before Kevin could build his database, he needed to learn how to navigate the new system. Then he would search every source for chemicals that were known or suspected carcinogens. He mentally cataloged the few carcinogens he already knew: benzene, a commonly used laboratory chemical, was one. He began to visualize the database he would build. He would not simply catalog the chemicals; he would note their chemical properties, perhaps their chemical composition, common uses and other characteristics.

He recalled from casual reading that dioxin, the chemical found in Agent Orange, a defoliant widely used in the Vietnam War, was thought to have contributed to premature cancer deaths of Vietnam veterans. He was supremely confident that understanding the chemical composition and other properties of the active chemicals in Agent Orange would not be a problem.

He made a mental note to include medical databases in his search. The medical literature could be a useful source of data reporting possible links between cancer and chemicals. He would start by identifying the known chemical carcinogens, reviewing their medical symptoms and follow wherever his research led him. His spirits lifted. He felt energized and alive for the first time since Dr. Jacob's memorial service.

Leaving the rooming house on Baxter Street, Kevin walked half a block to Main Street and headed for the local restaurant that featured all day breakfasts. Minutes later a pimply-faced kid punched his order into the computer and he paid his bill. He grabbed a wad of napkins from the metal dispenser, tossed a handful of ketchup packets on the tray and made his way through the noontime crowd to a booth at the rear of the restaurant.

He ate his breakfast quickly, watching a high school student damp-mop the floor nearby. Taking a ballpoint pen from his shirt pocket, he sketched a rough outline of a tentative research plan on a paper napkin. Ten minutes later he folded and put it in his pocket. He left the restaurant and ignoring a light drizzle, walked along Main Street, turned right at Monument Square and headed up the hill toward campus and the main library.

Kevin despised the tedium of library research. He viewed it as a necessary but deadly boring chore. During his undergraduate days, he had avoided the library as much as possible, enrolling in science and mathematics courses, disdaining the liberal arts courses that required extensive library research and writing. Walking across the quiet campus in the afternoon humidity, he recalled the bibliographical research he had completed for his dissertation thesis two years ago. The literature search had consumed more than two months, time he would have preferred to spend on the laboratory experimentation he loved.

Today, however, he strode purposefully through the wrought iron gates and up the driveway in front of Old Main, then cut across the Commons and entered Memorial Library. Cabot University's main library was an ultra-modern structure housing more than three million books and periodicals. The second floor of the red brick and glass structure housed one of the most comprehensive collections of scientific journals and books in the country. He swiped his student ID card through the card reader at the library entrance and crossed the massive marble lobby to the broad stairway leading to the second floor.

The university's recently installed state of the art computerized library search system offered fast, efficient access to huge databases located on the campus, around the country and the world. Although he had not explored the new system in depth, he was certain that his computer expertise would facilitate mastering the search techniques quickly. He would build his database in short order.

At the top of the stairs he turned left, opened the glass doors to the reference area and took a seat at the bank of computer terminals. He picked up an instruction sheet for accessing computerized databases and began to read.

The search software proved to be surprisingly user friendly. Kevin sought out a reference librarian who recognized him as a graduate student and one of the more proficient computer users on campus. She pointed out a few helpful shortcuts within the search program to assist him.

Within minutes, he logged onto a huge database housed at the National Institutes of Health in Maryland. He began to enjoy the process of moving through the search menus, drilling ever more deeply into the subject of chemical toxins. Using keywords as references, he quickly focused his search, fingers flying across the keyboard, staring intently at the monitor in front of him. Thanks to the helpful librarian who provided the restricted access codes, he logged in and began to search several databases.

Unlike his earlier library research, he would not waste time copying journal articles and other references; he could simply log on and read information directly from the original source materials. Library research would never be a favorite activity; now, however, computer technology would save extraordinary amounts of time, allowing him to focus his energies on identifying and then analyzing the specialized data he sought. Using the Internet for access, he could query databases that otherwise would have taken weeks to search.

It was a simple task to search the library's own vast in-house collections of scientific, medical and business journals and citations that were accessible on line. The system greatly facilitated drilling down on a specific topic in ever increasing detail. Kevin's search for links between chemical toxins and cancer would be easier and more detailed than he imagined. In any event, this exercise would help him develop techniques in accessing many computerized library databases, a skill that would prove useful when he resumed research on his dissertation.

Kevin smiled to himself, realizing that the research design he sketched out earlier that day could be completed in an afternoon. He decided to extend his study, to conduct a far more comprehensive review than originally planned. By the end of the afternoon he identified more than twenty potentially useful information sources. For the first time in two months, he felt alive, focused and energized.

As the afternoon slipped away, Kevin grew increasingly confident in his ability to search through masses of current and past research on chemical toxins. He was elated, convinced that his work would yield the data he needed. If Jacob's cancer were linked to chemical toxins, he would identify and prove the connections.

He worked quickly and efficiently, oblivious to the buzz of activity around him. The reference librarian glanced his way from time to time. She smiled to herself. She had hooked still another student on the new system.

Kevin left the library as the sun disappeared behind Connors Hall. He retraced his steps across the Commons, enjoying the fragrance of freshly mowed grass and the soft breeze that stirred the branches of the giant oaks guarding the broad sidewalks. Here and there, couples lounged on the wooden benches bordering the walks or sprawled on the grass, basking in the warmth of the sun's fading rays. He left the campus and walked down University Avenue toward the rooming house he called home.

Turning onto Main Street, he realized that his search was just beginning. Today he had only established the feasibility of the study and identified several databases that merited further examination. But proving a link between specific chemicals and the type of cancer that killed Jacob was merely the first step. He would also need to identify sites on the campus where those chemicals were used or stored, then somehow prove that Jacob (and perhaps others) had routinely been exposed to them and had suffered harm as a result of their exposure.

He wondered about possible sources of toxic chemicals. The only large chemical manufacturer in the area was the Capital Chemicals plant in Oakton, ten miles south of Hillsdale. He vaguely recalled that both Jacob and Ruth had worked at Capital's Oakton Division before joining the faculty at Cabot University. They might have continued with a consulting arrangement in recent years. A major employer, Capital Chemicals enjoyed an excellent reputation as a place to work. Kevin planned to apply for a research position in the company's laboratories after he finished his doctorate.

Capital was a huge company engaged in the manufacture and sale of basic chemicals for industrial consumption. The Oakton plant concentrated on the manufacture of chemicals used in polymers. He needed to investigate the company further. Obviously, any major chemical manufacturing facility would have procedures in place to dispose of its waste. Could he somehow get into the facility and explore their processes for storage and disposal of the waste byproducts of the manufacturing process?

The comprehensive nature of the library's computerized databases opened new avenues to search. He need not restrict his examination to science and medical sources. He might also review some local history, especially the development of industry and the history of Capital Chemicals Company and its activities in the area.

Also, were there other chemical companies in the area that he didn't know about? He remembered his father telling him about working at a chemical plant during World War II. Although the company had paid excellent wages, working conditions were dreadful. Kevin wondered whether that had influenced his parents to oppose his decision to major in chemistry nearly ten years ago.

He turned his thoughts to Cabot University. Was it directly involved in the mystery? Both Ruth and Jacob Borovski had taught and conducted research at the university for many years. In fact, their professional lives were linked more closely with the university than with Capital Chemicals. It seemed more likely that Jacob's cancer was connected to his work on campus than to his consulting activities.

Crossing Main Street at the traffic light, he casually wondered whether other faculty or staff at the university had died of cancer during the past decade. Given the size and ages of faculty members, it was likely that a few had died of cancer. Then he remembered Dr. Atherton's cryptic comments during his eulogy for Jacob. He had mentioned that a number of faculty had died of cancer and seemed concerned about the issue. Although the parameters of the problem were becoming clearer, a huge amount of work lay ahead. In the meantime, he would keep his ideas to himself. He needed more data. Before he talked to Tony Amonte, he would flesh out his theory with facts, not speculation.

*   *   *   *

The computer search begun that summer afternoon would become an all-consuming obsession. Although he would eventually gain an encyclopedic knowledge of chemical toxins and their possible relationships to cancer, Kevin would not appreciate the irony that his analytical talent, identified and nurtured by Jacob Borovski, would produce his first and final brilliant contribution to scientific knowledge. His work would validate Jacob's initial judgment that he had a brilliant mind for science. Jacob did not live to witness the fruits of his pedagogy nor the meticulous application of the research techniques he had nurtured in his student. Jacob had trained Kevin well. Ruth would later acknowledge that his assessment of Kevin's potential as a research chemist had been on the mark.

Chapter 11

Late in August Paul Borovski wrapped up the final details of his dissertation and was awarded his doctoral degree at Stanford University's small summer graduation ceremony. Nancy and Dick Atherton flew west for the occasion, surprising and pleasing Ruth and her sons. The low-key nature of the occasion suited Ruth for whom holidays and ceremonies like graduation were proving especially painful.

Following a final round of parties, Paul and Ruth packed a few belongings and set out on a 3,000-mile cross-country trek to Hillsdale. A watery sun pierced the early morning fog as mother and son headed east across the Bay bridge, moving easily against commuter traffic approaching San Francisco.

"Sorry to be leaving the Bay Area and all your friends?" Ruth glanced at her son from the bucket seat of Paul's Mazda Miata.

He smiled. "Sure," he admitted, glancing at the rear view mirror, then expertly switching lanes and picking up speed. "After all, I've spent a third of my life out here. The weather's terrific in the summer, there's good hiking in the Sierras, and Stanford was a great place to study. The only downside is the winter rains and the possibility of a major quake.

"Oh, well, I'll be back here probably about as often as I'll get to Hillsdale. It won't be the same, I know." He tuned the car radio to KQED, adjusted the sound to a comfortable level and grinned across at his mother.

"Ready for some new adventures?"

"Always," Ruth replied. "As long as you forgive me if I sleep across the desert east of Reno."

"What do you know about that stretch of highway?"

"Several years ago Jacob and I drove back from the West Coast after one of his climbing expeditions in Yosemite. I learned firsthand that the countryside from Reno to the Wasatch Mountains near Salt Lake City is best viewed from the air." Paul laughed as the car left the foothills east of San Francisco and entered the Sierra high country leading to the Continental Divide and Reno beyond.

*   *   *   *

The lush, verdant farms of central Pennsylvania were laden with fruit and produce ripe for harvest when they traveled across the state a week later. The afternoon sun was sinking toward the distant hills west of Hillsdale when Paul finally braked to a stop in his mother's driveway. Nancy, Dick and Hillary greeted them with hugs and cold drinks. His mother's friends had opened, aired and cleaned the house that had stood empty since June.

Cocktails and dinner at the Atherton home awaited their arrival. Standing an hour later on Nancy's deck, Ruth gazed across the river toward the town and the university buildings visible on the far ridge. Silhouetted against the western sky, the campus gleamed serenely in the reflected sun.

"Glad to be home, Ruth?" Nancy asked.

"Yes, although it still seems strange without Jacob."

"No doubt it will be difficult for a while."

"Spending time with Paul and Anton was just what I needed. Do you realize that Paul left home almost ten years ago, and Anton twelve years ago? It was a pleasure to get to know both of them again. They were a real comfort. I worked in the lab during the day; and we spent a lot of evenings and weekends together. Jacob would be so proud of both boys. They're mature, kind human beings who've begun to develop very successful careers in science and academe. I hope I can maintain this new relationship with them."

"That should be relatively easy with Paul in Cambridge," said Nancy. "Perhaps we can plan a couple of trips to Boston. We can see Paul and visit my parents at the same time."

"Yes, and Paul and Anton have promised to come here for holidays. Although it really depends on how involved they become with their research."

*   *   *   *

Paul stayed in Hillsdale long enough to help Ruth unpack and settle back into her home, leaving the week before Labor Day and driving to Cambridge where a position as Assistant Professor in the Chemistry Department at MIT awaited. Boston was only an hour by plane from Hillsdale, six hours by car. Before he left California, Paul had promised Anton that he would spend as much time with their mother as possible, working with her on their joint research and helping her through the first year of loss. He intended to keep his promise. Assisting with the research begun by his father and carried on by his mother would not be a chore. Perhaps in time he would make significant contributions in his parents' field.

Immersion in the research she loved and working with her sons proved to be the therapy Ruth Borovski needed. Although she still experienced periods of unremitting grief, the healing process had begun. She felt increasingly confident she could carry on her research and teaching schedule at Cabot without Jacob.

Two weeks before fall classes were scheduled to begin, Ruth felt relaxed and rested. Still, returning home and the first few days in her office and laboratory were painful ordeals, bringing back a flood of memories. She recognized the need to continue the grief therapy she had sought in Palo Alto during the worst bouts of depression. She made a mental note to ask Dick Atherton to recommend a staff psychiatrist at Essex Medical Center.

Chapter 12

As August drew to a close, Kevin Parks abandoned any pretense of work on his dissertation. He spent countless hours in Memorial Library, deserting his research in the chemistry labs. He became ever more secretive and belligerent when Ruth prodded him to get back to his research. Occasionally, he stretched out on a bench in the laboratory rather than return to his rooming house a half mile away.

His physical appearance and personal hygiene regressed to his past slovenly habits. He became more unkempt and grew a full beard, neglecting to keep his brown shoulder length hair in a ponytail. His fall wardrobe consisted of filthy jeans and T-shirts. With the coming of cooler weather, he donned a shabby red ski jacket picked up at the Salvation Army used clothing store. In habits and appearance he would have been mistaken for one of Hillsdale's homeless persons had he not been so well known by the university staff. Instead, the campus security forces ignored him, tagging him as just another weird student, allowing him to wander the campus unmolested.

Concerned by his apparent lack of research progress, Ruth questioned Kevin about his mysterious, apparently all-consuming preoccupation. Sullen and disrespectful, he refused to offer the slightest hint of his current work. She encountered him frequently in the science library, but rarely saw him in the laboratory space he had been assigned.

Ruth hesitated to confront Kevin. She had not supervised him directly while Jacob was alive, nor had she taken an active interest in his research project. She decided to adopt an attitude of helpful waiting. Perhaps in a month or two he would get back on track with his research and finish his dissertation.

*　*　*　*

Shortly before Labor Day and the formal beginning of the fall semester, Kevin disappeared from his usual campus haunts. Disclosing his plans to no one, he hitchhiked northwest to Buffalo, obtained directions from a helpful gas station attendant and visited the Love Canal area, an infamous community in suburban Buffalo. Nearly fifty years ago, a residential area of the blue-collar town had been contaminated with dioxin, a hazardous chemical that was virtually unknown to residents. Decades later, following an investigation by the Federal government in the 1970s, hundreds of residents of the community were relocated from their contaminated homes to a safer environment. Although the incident had received wide coverage twenty years earlier, the matter had been largely forgotten. He wanted to view the site of the Superfund project for himself.

His off-campus odyssey next led him to Fernald, Ohio, site of an important nuclear weapons plant. With the help of an angry and disillusioned worker he met in a bar near the plant, he evaded plant security, gaining entry into one of the nation's top-secret weapons plants. For several days he roamed at will inside the huge complex, observing the methods used to store highly radioactive wastes generated in the manufacturing process. He watched intently as eighteen-wheelers loaded with hazardous waste materials lumbered out of the complex, heading for the huge nuclear storage facility at Savannah River in South Carolina.

Thanks to his new buddy, he met several other Fernald workers at the same local bar. After a few beers, they revealed the depth of their fears. Disgruntled and angry, the workers convinced Kevin that their future health was in jeopardy. Captives of generous salaries and fringe benefits, they continued to work in an unsafe environment despite their fears. Kevin returned to Hillsdale having seen with his own eyes the results of chemical contamination. The trip had been more revealing than he had imagined.

*   *   *   *

The day after Labor Day Ruth unexpectedly encountered Kevin leaving the science wing of the library. Dismayed by his disheveled appearance, obvious lack of personal hygiene and by his disappearance from his usual haunts during the past three weeks, she asked him to stop by her office that afternoon.

An invitation to meet in Ruth Borovski's office was a command that Kevin could not ignore. His advisor would doubtless insist on a report on his research, but he had no progress to report. Within a few hours he would have to decide whether to confide in her, to reveal the information he had gathered during his disappearance from campus. And to justify his recent activities, he would be forced to disclose his growing suspicions about the nature of Jacob's death.

Part III

Fall

Chapter 13

Labor Day weekend found hoards of new and returning students descending on Cabot University in a chaotic scene that was duplicated at campuses across the country. Rousing from its summer doldrums, the spruced-up campus braced for another year. Shepherded by parents, envious siblings and assorted hangers-on, the freshmen descended on Saturday. Despite obvious efforts to appear cool, they exuded an aura of anxiety during the required campus tours and orientation lectures, familiarizing themselves with the place they would call home for the coming year.

Oppressive heat and humidity produced late afternoon thunderstorms that marred the traditional outdoor reception and cookout for entering freshmen and guests, and cut short host Larry Northrop's usual welcoming speech.

For freshmen, the holiday weekend passed in a blur of manic activity. Mountains of clothing, hi-fi and television equipment and laptop computers were hauled from vans and cars to tiny rooms in the rabbit warrens of the freshmen residence halls. Glum expressions and occasional tears were observed as freshmen lingered over emotional farewells.

On Sunday and Labor Day, the shrill cries of returning students punctuated the air as they settled into the more spacious upper class residence suites. Cocky sophomores, veterans of the academic pressures and social life of the university, savored the precious few hours before Tuesday classes, heading for their favorite downtown haunts in the Main Street bars and restaurants.

The juniors and seniors were more serious, bracing for the academic rigors ahead and perhaps recalling the tragic events of the past spring. The graduate students, especially those in chemistry, gathered in small groups, sober, glum, a few openly grieving for Jacob Borovski, whose legendary chemistry lectures would no longer motivate them to labor on.

Perhaps reflecting her own unacknowledged depression, Nancy thought the beginning of fall classes was less exuberant than usual. The freshmen looked younger than ever, a reminder of the widening age gap between those bright, eager but immature intellects and her own maturity. Senior faculty, many of whom returned from a summer absorbed in research and writing elsewhere, exchanged greetings with colleagues, plowed through mountains of accumulated mail and prepared for the fall teaching and research challenges. Many were subdued as the unspoken loss of the university's most distinguished professor weighed heavily.

*   *   *   *

At a meeting early in June with the Dean of the Arts and Sciences School, Ruth Borovski had accepted supervisory and mentoring responsibility for Jacob's three doctoral students, including Kevin Parks. Although her workload doubled instantly, she welcomed the additional assignment as both challenging and therapeutic. Guiding six students through the research and writing labyrinth that comprised the doctoral program in chemistry would be her private gift to Jacob.

Kevin Parks quickly emerged as a major problem. Late in August, at the request of the chair of the Chemistry Department, Ruth convened Kevin's five-person dissertation committee. Their task was to evaluate Kevin's progress toward the doctoral degree. During the three-hour meeting, the committee concluded that Parks had not demonstrated satisfactory research progress. The committee unanimously voted to issue an ultimatum. Failure to complete and defend his dissertation by next May would lead to permanent dismissal from the doctoral program at Cabot University. As his dissertation committee chair, Ruth signed the warning letter and personally delivered the official notice to the student.

"Kevin, you know that I'm now the chair of your dissertation committee. The committee met last week and reviewed the materials you gave me in early August. After evaluating your progress to date, the committee unanimously agreed to take the action outlined in this letter." She handed him a sealed envelope.

"This is not a pleasant task for me, Kevin. I hope you understand."

"What's in the letter?" he asked, feigning ignorance.

"An official notification that unless you complete your dissertation, defend it and finish your degree by next May, you will be permanently dismissed from the doctoral program. There will be no more extensions beyond May.

"I managed to convince the committee and department to extend your research assistantship through next May. Your tuition, fees and other university costs will be paid, plus you'll receive a stipend of $15,000 to live on for the next nine months," she continued.

"Did you vote to issue this ultimatum?" he asked, ripping open the envelope.

"Yes, I did."

Kevin glared at her, his dark eyes glinting in the afternoon light.

"For reasons that make good sense," Ruth said. "You've been a student in the doctoral program for the past five years. The university has supported your work and provided you with living expenses. Most graduate stipends end after four years. You've gotten more support than any other student in the program since I've been on the faculty here at Cabot."

"The university's resources are limited," she continued. "I convinced the committee to give you more time because of Jacob. He was your dissertation chair, and you need time to adjust to me as your chair. I realize that you're having a difficult time, along with the rest of us. That's why we approved the extra year."

Kevin looked away.

"Do you understand what this is all about?" she asked.

"Yeah, I get it. Finish the dissertation or else. And I have until May to get everything done."

"This is not impossible, Kevin. Just focus your energy on your research and come to me when you need help. That's what I'm here for. I don't know what you've accomplished over the summer since I wasn't on campus. However, others on your committee spent the summer working on campus and they say you simply disappeared."

"Oh, so you've got spies checking up on me?"

"No more than on any other graduate student," she said mildly.

"Exactly what did you accomplish in the last three months?"

"A lot. But nothing I want to discuss right now. I'll get back to you when I have some research results."

"I'll expect you to give me some results soon—in a couple of weeks, not months, Kevin."

"Right."

"You know where to find me. I'm either here in my office or in the lab about fourteen hours a day. And you can always call me at home or send me some results by e-mail. I'll review your work and get back to you quickly," Ruth said.

"Yeah, right." He headed for the door. "Got any more good news for me?" he asked over his shoulder.

"No. Just get to work and show me some research results. If Jacob were here, he would insist on seeing results now, not later." Kevin closed Ruth's office door none too gently.

Chapter 14

The semester got underway in earnest and Ruth became completely absorbed in her multiple roles of researcher, graduate student mentor and teacher. She spent most afternoons and many evenings working on her own research. She found solace in the long hours in the laboratory and in her office where she advised her graduate students. Students appreciated her accessibility, knowing she was available to review their plans, check their research data and probe for flaws in their methodology.

Twice weekly she meticulously planned and delivered the introductory undergraduate chemistry lectures that had made Jacob a campus legend. More than three hundred freshmen typically enrolled in Chemistry I each fall semester. Chemistry I, a foundation course required of all engineering and science students, was critical to success in advanced courses in various majors.

Although her teaching style was less flamboyant than Jacob's, the students responded with admiration and respect. Like Jacob, her academic standards and expectations were high. Students soon realized that Cabot University's world-class science reputation required intense dedication.

In contrast to some tenured full professors, Ruth took her teaching responsibilities as seriously as her research. The summer months with Paul in California were not devoted exclusively to research. She also designed the Chemistry I course syllabus, selected the text and prepared the detailed lecture notes, multimedia presentations and laboratory experiments she would deliver in the fall.

Ruth's lectures were delivered in the steeply tiered lecture hall in Starrett Science Center. Students attended the lectures, and then met twice a week in small recitation sections. A cadre of chemistry graduate students supported and supplemented her lectures, conducted the small recitation sections and monitored the required weekly laboratory sessions. Nothing was left to chance.

The course served as a filter for the undergraduate and graduate programs in chemistry. Its primary objective was to identify promising students who were encouraged to major in chemistry. Along with physics and calculus, the course was the foundation for virtually all the university's programs in science and engineering. The assignment of a senior faculty member to teach Chemistry I (first Jacob and now Ruth) emphasized its importance in the curriculum.

*　*　*　*

The Columbus Day holiday in mid-October marked the first major break in campus routine during the fall semester. The three-day weekend allowed many students to return home for the first time since Labor Day. Some students blew off the weekend at keg parties, athletic events and other activities. A few students used the time to catch up with class assignments and projects that had already begun to pile up.

Paul Borovski flew to Hillsdale from Boston to visit his mother and review their research progress since the summer in California. Utilizing e-mail and computer links to transfer data, their research grant was proceeding on schedule and had begun to produce interesting findings. Ruth observed over the previous summer that her younger son was rapidly maturing into a superb research chemist. Landing a faculty position at MIT confirmed her assessment of his research potential. She was comforted by the knowledge that Jacob would have been pleased with Paul's intellectual curiosity and disciplined approach to research.

On Saturday, the first day of the three-day break, Ruth and Paul spent a long day in Ruth's laboratory, absorbed in research. Starrett Science Center was virtually deserted, faculty and students taking advantage of the long weekend. Late in the afternoon they were interrupted.

"Who's this guy, Mother?" Paul glanced up from the workbench startled by the bearded and disheveled figure heading their way through the otherwise deserted lab.

"It's Kevin Parks," Ruth whispered, rising from the bench to greet her student. For a few awkward seconds Paul failed to recognize Kevin as the graduate student who had spoken so eloquently at his father's memorial service the previous spring. Belatedly he reached across the lab table and shook his hand.

"Kevin, it's good to see you," said Ruth. "You haven't spent much time in the lab recently. At least I haven't seen you."

She glanced at Paul. "I'm ready for a break. How about you? And Kevin, can you join us?"

"Sure," said Kevin. "I could use some coffee."

Gathering the pile of computer printouts, Ruth locked the laboratory door and walked down the hall to her office. Settling down on the leather sofa and chairs grouped around a low coffee table, they exchanged pleasantries while Ruth served mugs of steaming coffee.

"What research are you working on, Dr. Borovski?" Kevin asked politely. Ruth sketched briefly the joint NSF grant they were working on.

"Kevin, how about giving us an update on your work?"

"I haven't spent much time recently on my dissertation research," he admitted defensively, "but I haven't been loafing, either."

"Kevin has a deadline to finish his doctorate by next May," Ruth told Paul. "And the administration won't extend the deadline or Kevin's financial support."

"There's plenty of time to finish my research and graduate next May," said Kevin confidently. "My research plan is all set. The data collection and basic research will take only about a month. Then I figure I'll need another couple of months to analyze the data and write up the results. No big deal."

Ruth frowned. Kevin's occasional flashes of arrogance annoyed her.

"Every graduate student in the world minimizes the time and effort required to finish a dissertation." She smiled. "Even Paul, who earned his doctorate only three years after his undergraduate degree, needed an extra six months to finish those so-called last minute details. Dissertation committees are demanding."

She continued to probe. "I've seen you working on the library reference computers and browsing in the stacks at all hours of the day and night. Obviously, you've been busy. If you're not working on your dissertation, what exactly are you doing?"

Perhaps wanting to impress Paul, a contemporary he had admired from afar, Kevin disclosed some details of his work. "I've been working on a personal research project, Dr. Borovski. After Dr. Jacob got sick—before he died—I got interested in figuring out how someone could suddenly get cancer and die within six months." He sat back in his chair, arms folded.

"Of course, everybody thinks cancer is just an unlucky roll of the dice. They're wrong. I intend to prove that Dr. Jacob's death could have been prevented. That's what I've been working on," he confessed matter-of-factly.

Kevin settled his thin frame lower into the elegant leather chair, propping his filthy sneakers on the polished mahogany coffee table. Animated, his dark eyes gleaming with alarming intensity, he fleshed out his theory. "I think Dr. Jacob was the victim of some unidentified chemical contamination that destroyed his immune system and triggered the cancer that caused his death."

In stunned silence, Ruth and Paul listened to Kevin sketch a disjointed and rambling theory of death by chemical poisoning. Oblivious to his surroundings and ignoring his audience, he spun a scenario that rationalized the seemingly senseless death of his mentor. Ruth regarded Paul across the coffee table, disbelief and dismay etched on her face. It didn't take a trained psychiatrist to recognize that Kevin Parks had lost touch with reality.

Obsessed, Kevin launched into a detailed description of his research methods and disclosed his visits to contaminated sites in Love Canal and the nuclear facility in Fernald, Ohio. He described the computer searches that occupied his late evening hours at the library. Speaking so fast that his listeners could barely follow his thoughts, he offered a rudimentary outline of his search of medical and chemical databases.

"I've made tremendous progress. Before long I'll be able to prove a direct link between Dr. Jacob's cancer and some of the toxic chemicals we work with every day in our labs right here in this building." He stopped and took a deep breath. "I'm getting close to pinpointing the exact cause of his cancer."

Kevin sat back at last. He smiled at Ruth and Paul, awaiting their congratulations.

After an awkward silence, Ruth finally spoke. "Kevin," she said gently, "your first priority is your doctoral research. Nothing is more important than completing your degree."

Kevin often avoided eye contact during conversations with faculty. His habit of gazing into the middle distance focusing on a point known only to him annoyed Ruth intensely because she was never sure he was paying attention. Now he gazed directly into Ruth's deep brown eyes, as if trying to read her innermost thoughts.

"You don't get it, do you?" he shouted aggressively, sensing pity and withdrawal in their faces.

"You'll see. I just need a little more time to prove I'm right." Without another word, he grabbed his lab notebook and left the office.

Ruth gathered up the coffee cups, and rinsed them in the tiny sink. Shaking her head in disbelief, she said, "I knew Kevin was troubled by Jacob's death, but I'm stunned at his behavior. This looks like a full-blown obsession. He's always been a bit strange, even in the best of times. I'm no psychiatrist, but I've always thought his mental state was fragile at best. He may have slipped over the edge. I should have kept track of his activities more closely," she worried.

"Don't blame yourself. You and Dad both knew Kevin has a weird personality," Paul reassured her.

"It looks like he's simply freaked out," he continued. "He can't cope with the reality of Dad's death. He also may be rationalizing the likelihood that he won't finish his doctorate and will be forced to leave the university. And if he doesn't finish his degree, he won't have much chance for a good job in research. Employers are willing to overlook some idiosyncrasies in talented people with doctorates, but Kevin won't have the credentials."

"What do you suggest?" Ruth asked, locking the office door behind them and walking down the hall to the lab.

"I don't think there's much you can do at this point," said Paul, "except to somehow distract him from this crazy obsession and pull him back to his dissertation research. And I haven't a clue how you might go about it.

Apparently the possibility he'll be kicked out of the doctoral program hasn't sunk in yet."

He and Ruth entered the empty lab. "Mother, this is not your problem. He's responsible for his own actions. If he wants to throw away his future, that's his decision."

The hours flew by as mother and son mapped out their next series of tests. They set timelines and divided responsibilities for reaching research goals over the next two months. At seven o'clock, Ruth and Paul left the laboratory in Starrett Science Center, determined to take a break on Sunday and enjoy a brief respite from their work.

Chapter 15

Seated around a roaring fire in the stone fireplace in Nancy and Dick Atherton's living room, Ruth and Paul related the earlier encounter with Kevin Parks.

"Ruth, you can't be responsible for the actions or obsessions of your graduate students," Dick said. "Sure, you're concerned. But Kevin has to make his own way. He's an adult—I assume he is at least twenty-eight years old. I agree with Paul, the best you can do is try to convince him to get back to his doctoral research."

"We all know a little about this young man's background." Hillary Gardner stretched her feet closer to the warmth of the fire. "Even though his father lives on a farm not ten miles from here, he apparently never visits home. If I didn't know better, I'd say he looks like one of Hillsdale's homeless people. You say he's brilliant, and I believe you, Ruth. But he has some obvious personality and behavior problems. Jacob tended to overlook those problems," she observed. "Maybe the time has come for him to either produce some decent research or just leave the university."

"But I feel I'm letting Jacob down if Kevin doesn't complete the program successfully," Ruth protested.

"You have a lot on your plate right now, Ruth," said Hillary. "You've doubled your research and advising chores by accepting Jacob's students. You and Paul have your own research to complete. You don't have time to deal with this student's problems on top of everything else." Hillary sipped her espresso and reached for a second piece of biscotti.

"That young man has always been a misfit," noted Dick. "I recall Jacob said he had few friends, no money and a dysfunctional family situation. With the notable exception of Jacob, apparently he was unable or unwilling to relate to his peers or to the faculty.

"You're all probably correct," said Paul. "In the months since Dad died, he may have lost touch with reality. But that's not your problem, Mother. You have obligations for his research and doctoral program, not his personal problems. Besides, we've got our own research deadlines."

"I'm well aware of that. Still, I think someone has to intervene." She wouldn't let the matter rest.

"If you need to do something, why not simply confront him, insist that he drop this crazy hunt for toxic contaminants and use the dismissal threat to get him back on track? Force him to meet with you weekly. Get in his face. Monitor his progress daily, if necessary," Paul suggested.

"Better yet," he continued, "threaten to call his committee together and dismiss him at the end of this semester. Don't wait until next May. If that doesn't get him moving, nothing will."

Chapter 16

Monday before the four-day Thanksgiving holiday, Kevin made what he thought was a significant breakthrough in his work. In response to Ruth's repeated warnings, he had finally resumed his research in the lab next to hers. Each day he worked under her direct supervision, and met twice weekly in Ruth's office to review his progress. To her relief, Kevin began to produce some significant research output.

However, Kevin continued to spend long evenings in the science library refining and enlarging his computer search for toxic contaminants. Early in his search, he identified and analyzed the chemical composition of a group of chemicals, many of them found in the university's laboratories, that were widely recognized as carcinogens. It had taken a week to link two medical databases and design a complex program to match selected chemicals and specific types of soft tissue cancers.

Well after midnight one November evening he felt a rush of excitement as his complex design for linking databases bore fruit. For the first time, he tested the program for specific matches. His program indicated that long-term exposure to asbestos, a known carcinogen, was a strong contributing factor in the development of lung cancer and asbestosis, a fatal lung disease. No surprise there, he thought. But at least the program seemed to be working.

Digging deeper into the data, he found a series of citations for studies of shipyard workers dating from the 1930s and 1940s. Workers exposed to asbestos during the construction of World War II naval vessels had been found to suffer abnormally high rates of lung cancer and asbestosis many years later. The medical correlations were suppressed or ignored until the 1970s when class action lawsuits were filed against major producers of asbestos products. The courts ultimately found the companies liable, requiring them to compensate survivors or their families.

Kevin had been vaguely aware of the correlation between lung cancer and asbestos fibers. These results confirmed his confidence in his program design. Now he could search the databases for similar associations between chemical substances and cancers.

Hunched over the keyboard, he tapped a few keys, sat back and awaited results. In a matter of moments, his program spewed out a list of chemicals and related cancers. As the lines of data appeared on his monitor, he was shocked to find an unexpectedly long list. He doubted the validity of his findings. Perhaps his program had some hidden design flaw.

A complete analysis would have to wait; it was past midnight and the library would close at 1 a.m. The room was deserted except for one other student, and he brusquely acknowledged the librarian's reminder that the library was closing shortly.

Kevin hurriedly transferred his software and data files to several floppy disks, taking care to erase all traces of the program and his analytical results from the university computer network. He logged off, slipped the disks and printouts into his backpack and knotted the flap. With a nod to the librarian guarding the exit, he left the building.

He smiled as he jogged across the deserted campus toward University Avenue. The evening's work validated his original design, and his program worked. Perhaps it needed some fine tuning to be sure there were no bugs, but that was not a problem.

Soon he would link the cancer that killed Dr. Jacob to specific substances, chemicals that likely were found right here on campus, probably in Starrett Science Center. Ruth Borovski would recognize his accomplishments. Perhaps someday he would be honored around the world for having made the first definitive connection between specific toxic chemicals and certain cancers. The value of this research far outweighed the trivial doctoral project everyone thought he was focused on.

He slowed to a walk as he rounded the corner onto Main Street, completely deserted now except for an occasional car cruising through the blinking yellow traffic lights. Walking rapidly along the quiet street, he sketched out his next step. He needed to access, copy and analyze the medical files describing Jacob Borovski's final illness. Those records were stored at Essex Medical Center in Oakton. Access would be difficult, probably more difficult than the library work he had already done.

He would hack into the hospital's computers, he decided. Failing that, he would somehow steal Jacob's hardcopy medical records. He wondered idly whether the unauthorized accessing of private medical records was more illegal than hacking into the restricted medical databases he had already accessed.

What the hell, he mused, if his hacks were detected, he already was in trouble. One more hack wouldn't make much difference. His search was too important to let a few privacy laws get in his way. His confidence soared. With tonight's breakthrough he had just proved he could access databases across the campus, across the country and virtually anywhere in the world.

The more serious problem was to cover his electronic tracks so his unauthorized review of records could not be traced. It would not be easy, but he had fellow hackers he could call upon. He would quietly consult a few students in the Computer Science Department, graduate students like himself, who shared his opinion that tapping into restricted databases was a challenging way to demonstrate electronic and intellectual prowess.

At one-fifteen, he quietly let himself into Mrs. Ledbetter's rooming house and climbed the stairs to his room. He tossed his ski jacket in a corner and propped his backpack on the floor against his battered dresser. Reaching down, he wearily pulled off his sneakers and sprawled fully clothed across his unmade bed.

As sleep overtook him, he remembered Ruth Borovski's invitation to Thanksgiving dinner at her home. For sure, Paul and Anton Borovski would be in Hillsdale. Maybe he could run some of his ideas by them privately. He would have to go. An invitation to his advisor's home was a command performance. At least the food would be good, he thought as he drifted off to sleep.

Although the university was officially closed for the four-day holiday, the library and laboratories would be open except on Thanksgiving Day. Ruth Borovski doubtless would be busy with her sons and not expect him in the lab. He could use the extra time to continue his search. With luck, he could make some real progress.

Chapter 17

Thanksgiving dawned clear and cold. Kevin slept late that morning, aware that the library and the other campus academic buildings were closed. When he finally awoke shortly after noon, he grabbed a cup of coffee and donut at the outlet down the street and returned to his room. Taking his printouts from his backpack, he spread them across his unmade bed. For the next few hours he reviewed the data he had generated over the past few days.

The Borovski Thanksgiving gathering began in late afternoon and typically lasted well into the evening. Kevin left the house shortly after four o'clock and began the two-mile trek to the Schmidt Farm area and Ruth's home.

Walking down deserted Main Street, he turned onto Market Avenue and headed for the river bridge a mile away. Crossing the river, he hiked up Shawnee Hill and turned into the area. He arrived as dusk settled over the town. As he strolled up the driveway he hesitated for a moment, enjoying the spectacular view of the town and Cabot University, which dominated the ridge west of town. He watched, the streetlights blink to life all over Hillsdale and heard the distant clock atop Old Main toll the hour. Beyond the garage, he glimpsed the large sloping lawn leading to a dense hardwood and pine forest and the darkened river far below.

The Borovski home, a spacious traditional colonial, was brightly lighted. Through a front window he saw a group of people gathered in the living room near the fireplace. When Jacob Borovski was alive, Kevin was a regular visitor to this home. After he entered the doctoral program and began working under Jacob's direct tutelage, he had been invited to every Thanksgiving celebration. Out of respect for his mentor, he always attended, despite acute discomfort at large social gatherings.

He rang the doorbell.

"Hello, Kevin. Happy Thanksgiving."

Paul Borovski extended his hand and directed him to an upstairs bedroom where his ski jacket and ever-present backpack were added to the mound of coats on the bed. Retrieving a bottle of inexpensive white wine from his pack, he headed downstairs in search of Ruth, and made his way through the throng of guests to the kitchen.

The festivities were well under way. Judging by the number of cars parked in the driveway and on the street, Kevin estimated that Ruth had invited at least thirty people. Apparently, he was the last to arrive. Drinks in hand, the guests were clustered around plates of hot and cold hors d'oeuvres near the living room fireplace, in the kitchen and in the large family room, talking and laughing with the easy familiarity of old friends.

He found Ruth putting the finishing touches to the turkey gravy at the stove while simultaneously directing the final preparation of the feast being assembled on the center island that dominated the kitchen. Kevin awkwardly thrust the bottle of wine in its plain brown bag into Ruth's hands.

"Thanks so much, Kevin," Ruth smiled, touched by his gift, especially since she knew that even an inexpensive bottle of wine would put a dent in his meager budget.

"Here," she said, thrusting the large slotted spoon into his hand, "would you mind stirring this please—just keep it from sticking on the bottom. Let me get you a glass of wine or some mulled cider if you prefer."

"Some cider, thanks," said Kevin, accepting a steaming mug of the spicy brew. He took a generous sip and began stirring.

Relieved to have an assignment in the midst of the laughter and conversation around him, he methodically stirred the gravy while Ruth assisted several others who were busily arranging platters of turkey, vegetables and salads in a colorful array on the island, which would serve as a buffet table for the feast.

Nearby, Anton Borovski carved the second of two large turkeys that had been roasted to juicy brown perfection. He raised his carving knife in friendly greeting. Kevin glowed with pleasure at the simple gesture.

The Thanksgiving guests were mostly faculty members and their families, several foreign students and Ruth's graduate students and spouses. Nancy Atherton's husband, the physician whom Kevin had last seen at Jacob's memorial service, wore jeans and a dark red chamois shirt, blending in with the casually dressed faculty and students. Even Nancy, who like Ruth, always dressed rather formally while on campus, wore dark woolen slacks and a bright sweater. Ruth, however, wore a simple dark woolen dress, reflecting the formality of her European background.

Always a gracious hostess, Ruth entertained with simple elegance. She circulated among the guests, making the foreign students feel welcome, pouring wine and cider, replenishing the hot and cold hors d'oeuvres trays. Despite himself, Kevin began to relax, enjoying the bustle and camaraderie around him.

When the dinner was assembled, Ruth invited everyone to gather together. She nodded silently to Anton, who offered a brief prayer of thanksgiving. In the silence of the moment, a wave of pain engulfed Kevin, reminding him again that Jacob Borovski would no longer host the Thanksgiving celebration. That role had passed to Anton, the elder son. In the pause following the prayer, Ruth momentarily seemed to lose her composure. Recovering quickly, she invited the guests to help themselves to the food and to take seats in the dining room or the playroom, in which round tables had been set with crystal and silver flatware to accommodate the crowd.

Kevin was among the last to serve himself, hanging back to see where Ruth, Paul and Anton Borovski would sit. As usual, they selected the dining room, joining Dick and Nancy Atherton and Hillary Gardner and her son Neil, who was home from college.

Kevin loaded his plate and quickly took the last seat in the formal dining room. Aglow under the soft light of a crystal chandelier, an arrangement of winter mums was nestled between white candles. The heavy mahogany table was covered with an antique damask tablecloth that Kevin knew was one of the few Borovski treasures that somehow had survived the Holocaust. Silver flatware, English china and leaded crystal wineglasses acquired by the Borovskis during their long marriage glowed in the candlelight.

The conversation ranged from casual to serious, with Ruth bringing up the recent election of a Democrat to the White House. The national health care proposal was a major factor in the election. Its potential impact on the medical profession drew strongly negative comments from Dick and Hillary.

*   *   *   *

"Kevin, perhaps it isn't fair to ask you about your research at the dinner table," said Ruth, trying to draw him into the conversation. "You might find it helpful to get together with Anton and Paul and me during the weekend, perhaps tomorrow afternoon at the lab," she suggested.

"From what Mother has told me about your work, I might have some ideas that will help you along," said Anton. "We're both working in the same general area of polymer analysis, and my lab at Berkeley has come up with some interesting findings during the past couple of months. I'd look forward to seeing your work and comparing results."

"You were doing some really interesting research when we talked in October," Paul joined the discussion. "I guess you can't keep scientists out of the lab, even during a holiday break," he laughed. "Let's all meet tomorrow afternoon in your lab."

Kevin shrugged, caught off guard. "I guess I can meet you tomorrow," he said vaguely.

Though he was frustrated at the hitch in his plan to spend most of the next three days and nights in the library, there was no convincing way to avoid a meeting. More seriously, if Anton and Paul asked probing questions, they would quickly realize how little progress he had made. His hours in the lab were designed to convince Ruth that he was working seriously on his dissertation. He had successfully avoided giving her specific data on his research. In reality, he'd accomplished nothing substantive during the past two months, despite the impression given to Ruth.

"So, what time do you want to meet, Kevin?" Paul pressed him.

"How about two o'clock tomorrow afternoon?" Kevin suggested after an uncomfortable pause. He resumed eating.

"Fine. That's settled then." Paul looked across the table at his mother and nodded.

Kevin was relieved as the conversation turned to other issues, and he was able to quietly eat and listen to the others.

Shortly after nine o'clock Kevin sought out Ruth.

"Thanks for inviting me to dinner," he said awkwardly.

"You'll always be welcome here, Kevin," said Ruth, continuing to measure fresh coffee into the top of the large coffee machine. She opened the sideboard and set out an assortment of brandies and liqueurs.

"I'll be going now."

"Do you need a ride back to your room?"

"No. I'll walk, thanks."

Ruth paused. "When did we agree to meet tomorrow in the lab?" she inquired, opening the side door near the garage.

"Is two o'clock okay with you?"

"Fine. We'll see you then."

A blast of cold air hit him as he made his way among the cars parked in the driveway. He glanced at the brilliant starlit sky, turned up the collar of his ski jacket, slung his backpack over one shoulder and thrust his hands deep into his pockets. There was practically no traffic as he headed down the hill and across the bridge toward the distant lights of Hillsdale.

Less than an hour later he entered the rooming house off Main Street. Mrs. Ledbetter's three other student lodgers were away for the holiday weekend, and the ramshackle house was deserted except for its owner. Feet up, Mrs. Ledbetter was stretched on her recliner in the dingy living room, a half empty bowl of popcorn on the stand beside her, engrossed in a television program. She didn't bother to greet him as he walked past the door headed for the stairs.

Upstairs in his room, he unknotted the top flap of his backpack. He rummaged inside the pack and pulled out a sheaf of computer printouts. He propped two pillows against the headboard and settled back to continue the tedious line-by-line examination of his latest computer hack, searching for coding errors that would indicate flaws in the program he had designed.

For more than three hours he studied the numbers and symbols on the papers spread across the bed. Oblivious to the indistinct murmurs of the television downstairs and the street noises outside, his concentration was complete. He noted small changes here and there, scratched notes in the margins, reminders to modify several codes and equations. It was 2 a.m. before he finally was satisfied. He threw the papers onto the faded rug beside the bed and without bothering to undress, fell asleep.

*   *   *   *

"I think Kevin's finally adjusting to Jacob's death and working with me as his advisor," Ruth remarked to Nancy as they began the task of cleaning up after the last guest's departure. "He seems to be making progress on his research since I read the riot act to him last month. At least we're meeting regularly now to discuss his work, and he's spending time in the lab where I can keep an eye on him."

"You'll know soon enough whether he's back on track," said Nancy. "Your meeting tomorrow should give you and the boys a chance to review his work. You may even be able to assess whether he can finish his dissertation by the May deadline. I really hope he can pull it all together and finally graduate. Seems like he's been hanging around the university forever," she laughed.

*   *   *   *

Ruth, Paul and Anton parked the car behind Starrett Science Center and walked to the rear entrance of the complex. Although the university was officially closed for the Thanksgiving break, the building was unlocked. Ruth's photo ID badge gave them access, and the campus security guard stationed in the lobby nodded in recognition. Ruth, following security procedures, signed the register and noted their arrival time.

They entered the bank of elevators at the rear of the deserted lobby and rode to Ruth's fourth floor office and the chemistry lab area. She unlocked her door and brewed a pot of coffee as they waited for Kevin Parks to appear.

Half an hour later, they headed for Kevin's lab space located next to Ruth's larger, private laboratory.

"I should have known he wouldn't be here on time." Ruth was disgusted.

"Not surprising, based on what you've told us," said Paul. "We can take a look at your own work. The afternoon won't be wasted."

"Right. Let's get to it," said Ruth. She stuck a post-it message on Kevin's door directing him to come to her laboratory.

She unlocked the door to her lab and switched on the overhead lights. "Anton, let me show you some of the results Paul and I generated over the past couple of months. Even though it's not exactly your specialty, you may find it interesting."

An hour later, satisfied that they had brought Anton up to speed on their current research, they traded passwords and access codes for later use when they would communicate by computer.

The internal university networks at Cabot University, MIT and Berkeley would provide the necessary electronic links between their office and lab computers. Using the Internet would greatly facilitate data transfer and speed up messages among the three scientists. Because each had personal computers with modems for data transmission in their offices, they could transmit research results and other information easily and securely among their laboratories. They made plans to share weekly updates by computer, thus avoiding lengthy delays in moving their research forward.

An hour later, it became clear that Kevin would not honor the appointment set the evening before. "I give up," said Ruth. "There's no point in waiting any longer. I'll follow up next week and get a complete accounting of his progress. I don't intend to let that young man off the hook," she said grimly.

"You promised us you would relax a bit this weekend, Mother. Forget this little episode," Anton advised. "Don't let it spoil the rest of our time together. I have a ten o'clock flight back to San Francisco Sunday morning, and Paul's got to drive back to MIT tomorrow."

They signed out of the building and trekked across the deserted Commons beneath giant oaks whose barren limbs stretched into the fading light of a pewter sky. They did not see Kevin Parks emerge from the library. Head down, the omnipresent backpack slung over his left shoulder, he hurried toward the building they had just left.

Chapter 18

Ruth walked down the hall on Monday morning and stuck another note on Kevin's laboratory door ordering him to meet in her office on Wednesday at three o'clock. As Wednesday afternoon drew to a close, she was not surprised that he again had failed to keep the appointment. Angry, she resolved to track him down and confront him. Today, she would accept no more excuses.

She headed for the library reference section with its computers offering free Internet access. Hurrying across the Commons through a cold rain, she swiped her ID card releasing the security gate and she climbed the wide steps to the second floor science stacks and computer reference area. Her hunch was correct. Kevin Parks sat at a computer terminal, oblivious to the muted activity around him, staring intently at the color monitor.

Ruth tapped him none too gently on the shoulder and openly scanned the data displayed on the computer screen and the computer printouts spread around his work area. Her customary civility completely deserted her.

"Kevin, did you forget you had an appointment with Paul, Anton and me last Friday afternoon?"

Startled, he looked up. "Ah, Dr. Borovski, I didn't forget our meeting, I just got involved with work here. I was late getting to the lab. You had already left."

"You were at least two hours late, Kevin. We waited for you. Your behavior these last few months and especially missing still another appointment is inexcusable. And why didn't you have the courtesy to telephone and set up another meeting? Didn't you see the note I left on your door? I suspect you haven't been near your lab all weekend," she refused to let him off easily.

"You don't understand, Dr. Borovski. I think I'm really onto something that might explain why Dr. Jacob contracted cancer and died," Kevin exclaimed, his face flushed. "I can't get back to my dissertation research— this work is much more important. Besides, if my theory proves out, any research I do in polymer chemistry will be trivial in comparison."

"Kevin," Ruth said, quietly, "are you still obsessed with the absurd notion that Dr. Jacob's death is somehow linked to a toxic chemical problem? I thought we laid that idea to rest months ago. You promised me you would get back on track with your dissertation research."

She pointed to the monitor and reached for his printouts. "Are your working on your dissertation now or wasting time on this utterly futile search?" Although her voice was deadly calm, her demeanor exposed her anger.

"Forget the dissertation research, Dr. Borovski. Let me explain." Kevin took the printouts from her and pushed back his chair. He rose, his lanky frame towering above her. Animated and intense, he was anxious to convince her. "I think there really is a link between Dr. Jacob's cancer and his exposure to chemical contamination right here on campus. I'm sure of it! I just need a little more time to prove it and then together we can eliminate the problem so others won't get sick and die."

Ruth glanced around the area, reached for a nearby chair and motioned for Kevin to sit down. She pulled her chair closer to the computer monitor. She regarded Kevin with a mixture of pity, sympathy and sadness. His mental state was far more serious than she had imagined. He needed psychiatric help. How could she possibly convince him that his frantic search for toxic contamination was an irrational reaction to the grief and depression that had naturally followed Jacob's death?

"Kevin, I do understand your struggle with Dr. Jacob's death. You're trying to convince yourself that his death was not simply an ugly trick of fate," she said quietly.

She glanced around. Although the area was not crowded, other students had begun to look their way, annoyed by the disturbance but interested in this confrontation between a senior faculty member and a student.

"Look, this is neither the time nor place to discuss these issues. Just log off the computer, gather up your work and walk with me back to my office," she ordered firmly. "What I'm going to tell you should be discussed privately in my office, not in the middle of the library."

Kevin didn't argue. He shoved his papers into his backpack, logged off the computer network and followed her from the library. Silently, they walked the short distance across the Commons to Ruth's office. She poured two cups of coffee and motioned Kevin to the sofa as she took the chair opposite him.

"Kevin," she began softly, "What I'm about to tell you is known to very few people on this campus. I'm taking you into my confidence because I'm fond of you personally and I respect you as a scientist. I know how impressed Jacob was with your intellectual capacity and potential to become a superb research chemist. However, you absolutely must keep this conversation confidential," she warned.

He nodded assent.

She paused for a moment and sipped her coffee. "Your obsession with my husband's death is, in my view, unhealthy and counterproductive." Kevin refused to meet her gaze. He shifted on the sofa, his knee jiggling nervously.

"Surely you realize that the last six months have been very difficult for me and my sons. Our close friends and colleagues who knew Jacob loved him as much as you."

"Let me tell you something. Your theory that some undiscovered source of chemical contamination contributed to his death, in fact, was discussed and evaluated by Jacob himself shortly before his death."

Kevin's eyes lit up. He wasn't wrong! Even Dr. Jacob had his suspicions.

"A few weeks after Jacob's memorial service, the university took unprecedented steps to investigate the matter. I am telling you in confidence that the possibility that chemical poisoning contributed to Jacob's death has been examined by some of the best occupational health experts in the country."

Kevin interrupted, his eyes brilliant with excitement. "I know about this, Dr. Borovski. A few weeks before he died, I visited Dr. Jacob in the hospital. I overheard him talking about this with his friend, Dr. Atherton. I think Dr. Gardner was in the room, too," he confessed.

"Let me continue, Kevin. Please don't interrupt," said Ruth. "During the two weeks between final examinations and graduation, you may remember that Starrett Science Center was temporarily closed for interior repainting. No one was allowed in the building.

"In fact," she said, "immediately after the memorial service, the administration authorized an interdisciplinary team of experts— occupational health authorities from Harrisburg and Philadelphia, along with several experts from OSHA in Washington—to make an exhaustive search of every laboratory, lecture hall, maintenance and storage facility in this building. I was in charge of the team."

Kevin was stunned.

"We turned this building upside down, examined every possible nook and cranny, checked every conceivable possibility that might help us identify and locate any chemical contaminants that could have contributed to Jacob's illness.

"What did you find?" Kevin interrupted her again.

"Nothing, absolutely nothing," Ruth said, pain in her voice. "The laboratories in Starrett Science Center are absolutely clean. They are being operated in compliance with all federal and state safety requirements. The chemicals used in our classes and laboratory research projects are similar to those used throughout the country. There is no reason to believe that Jacob's death was linked directly or indirectly to toxic chemicals. All of our toxic chemicals are being properly managed, stored and accounted for.

"Kevin, we couldn't conduct a public search of Starrett Science Center," she explained. "That would have created unnecessary anxiety—possibly a panic—among the students and faculty. That's why the building was closed for two weeks. And you must honor my need to maintain confidentiality on this. Believe me, if there were a contamination problem on this campus, we would have found it. Do you honestly think that I would leave any possible source unexamined?"

"No," he admitted.

"Now, it's time for you to stop fantasizing that Jacob's death is linked to some undiscovered contamination," she said firmly. "It's time to move on.

"No one, not even you, Kevin, misses Jacob more than I. One painful conclusion I reached during the last six months is that we all must move on. Jacob would have wanted that. We must fill our lives with work, family, the things we love to do. He wouldn't want us to waste precious time grieving when so much needs to be done."

Kevin sat mute, confused and dismayed. He was stunned to learn that a high level investigative team had secretly examined the science building without his knowledge. Aware that others had seriously considered the possibility of toxic contamination now convinced him that his theory had merit. Maybe they just hadn't looked in the right places.

Could he confide in Ruth, trust her as she had confided in him? He decided to take the chance.

"The analysis I've been doing on my own is coming at the problem from a different direction," he revealed. "I'm using the library reference computers to access several medical databases. The idea is to correlate specific types of cancers with known chemical carcinogens. Then I can narrow my search to specific chemicals. It's sort of a magic bullet approach as opposed to your shotgun approach. You know that my math skills and computer expertise are probably the best in the entire Chemistry Department. You can bring in a bunch of environmental experts to search all you want. They don't know what they're looking for. When I get done with this study, I'll know precisely what to look for. If anyone can link chemical contamination and cancer on this campus, I can."

His eyes glowed like brilliant black coals. "With my analysis, I'll be able to link specific chemicals—chemicals we use in the university's laboratories all the time—and known cancers. Then it's just a matter of correlating the type of cancer that killed Dr. Jacob with the specific substances that triggered it," he said.

"The fact that you and the administration thought a chemical might have triggered Dr. Jacob's cancer shows that my idea is not irrational. It may take a little more time, but I'll eventually find the answer."

"Kevin, listen to me," Ruth interrupted angrily. "There's nothing more to be done. Some of the best minds in the country have examined this problem, searched the building, evaluated our procedures for storing and using our chemicals, reviewed the university's safety standards. We all reached the same conclusion—there is absolutely no link between the environment on the campus and Jacob's death. You're wasting time. Worse, you're jeopardizing completion of your doctorate," she said, her normally serene voice becoming strident. "We've done everything humanly possible to identify an external source of chemical contamination at Cabot. It simply doesn't exist."

She rose and walked to the window and gazed down at the Commons, struggling to regain her composure. She turned to face him.

"Kevin, give it up. Move on. Finish your research and get your degree," she said harshly. More than anyone else on this campus, Jacob wanted you to complete your degree.

"Let me tell you something else. Very few faculty in the department or throughout the university for that matter, care whether or not you finish your degree. You're just one more student in the pipeline. The Dean considers you a hanger-on—a perpetual student, unwilling to leave the university and get a job. And most of the faculty feel the same way.

"I'm sure Jacob wouldn't support this futile obsession—and that's what it is, Kevin. He would want you to complete your degree. Instead, you dishonor his memory by acting this way."

Kevin's eyes glistened with tears. Her words stung deeply. She took both their coffee mugs, went to the sink, rinsed them and poured fresh coffee, allowing him to regain his composure.

Returning to her chair, she handed him a fresh cup. Sipping silently from her own, she regarded him sympathetically over her half-glasses. Perhaps one more personal revelation would convince Kevin of the futility of his work and help him begin to recover. She set her coffee cup on the table.

"Kevin, do you remember that I left Hillsdale right after graduation last June to spend the summer with Paul and Anton in California?"

He nodded.

"The boys and I worked together on some of the joint research that Jacob and I had already begun. During July, despite my best efforts to focus on research, I became badly depressed. I realized it was a delayed reaction to Jacob's death in April. The finality of his passing caught up with me, and I had a really difficult time coping.

"We recognized what was happening. I was unable to function in the lab, which has always been a refuge for me. Paul and Anton persuaded me to see a psychiatrist who specialized in grief therapy.

"I've never needed a psychiatrist before," she confessed, "perhaps because Jacob and I were very close. Together, we dealt with life's blows without outside help. Besides, Jacob was so strong mentally that whenever I needed advice or encouragement, I knew exactly where to look," she whispered, her face a mask of unspoken sadness and loss. "Jacob was not only my husband, he was also my mentor and best friend," she looked away, fighting for control. "Perhaps that's why I felt his loss so deeply.

"Despite my best efforts, I simply could not cope with my loss. I visited a young female psychiatrist whose specialty is helping people deal with the death of a loved one. As often as two or three times a week, we met during the rest of the summer. Gradually, I began to feel better. In early September when I came back to Hillsdale, I was ready to return to teaching and research, confident that I could carry on.

Although I'm now dealing with Jacob's loss, I still need therapy from time to time. Every two or three weeks, I visit Dr. Jerry Siegel, a very fine psychiatrist at Essex Medical Center. With his help I'm learning to live without Jacob and carry on my work, despite the strong presence I feel every time I walk into this building."

She had Kevin's full attention.

"Kevin, except for my sons, the only person who knows this is Dick Atherton. He arranged for me to meet Dr. Siegel. Don't misunderstand; I'm not ashamed that I need therapy to deal with my loss. I'm just reluctant to discuss my private life with anyone.

"I'm telling you this now because I believe you need help in dealing with your grief, just as I did."

Kevin refused to meet her gaze.

She pressed on. "I have an appointment with Dr. Siegel tomorrow afternoon. I want you to come with me," she said firmly. "You'll feel much better about yourself. If you don't want to see my doctor, I can arrange for you to talk to another psychiatrist. You need to take this first step by coming with me tomorrow and talking to a professional."

He began to refuse.

She interrupted him. "We can go together. I'll wait for you and drive you back to campus. And don't worry about the cost. Your student health insurance covers visits of this sort.

"You need this, Kevin," she continued gently. "You'll feel so much better about the loss of Dr. Jacob. You'll feel better about yourself, but you've got to take the first step. You can do this."

Kevin leaned forward on the sofa, hands covering his face. The floodgates opened and he sobbed uncontrollably. The grief he had denied for months came pouring out. Ruth rose and sat quietly on the sofa beside him, her arm around his shoulders.

Finally regaining a measure of composure, he tried to apologize. Wordlessly, Ruth went to her desk and returned with a supply of tissues and a glass of water. The loud buzz of the telephone startled them. Ruth answered the phone, spoke briefly with a student, replaced the receiver and turned back to Kevin to find that he had risen to leave.

"Well," she smiled, "how about a visit with my favorite doctor?"

"If you really think I should talk to him, I guess I can go with you," he said resignedly. "Where should I meet you and when?"

"Be here in my office by 2:30," said Ruth. It takes about twenty minutes to get to the hospital and another ten minutes to the office. And Kevin, no more excuses. Be here," she said firmly.

She followed him the few steps to her office door, touched his arm and opened the door.

"I know you'll feel better after you talk to Dr. Siegel."

"I doubt it," he said sadly.

"Be here tomorrow, Kevin," she ordered.

Returning to her desk, she telephoned Dr. Siegel's secretary at Essex Medical Center.

Chapter 19

"Ruth, I have a note that you called," said Jerry Siegel an hour later.

"I know this is short notice, but I wonder if you can squeeze in a visit with one of my students. I'm no psychiatrist, but I believe this young man desperately needs help." She summarized Kevin's background and her concerns regarding his emotional state.

"I'll talk to your student first, if you don't mind waiting. Then I can give you a preliminary assessment during your session."

Ruth need not have worried that Kevin would fail to appear the next afternoon. He knocked on her office door at 2:25 looking tired and drawn. During the twenty-minute drive to Essex Medical Center in Oakton, he was subdued but outwardly calm. Ruth was relieved. Perhaps Kevin finally realized that he needed help in dealing with the trauma of the past six months.

They emerged from the elevator and entered the fifth floor offices of Dr. Jerry Siegel in the hospital's psychiatric wing. A young forty-year-old physician, Siegel sported a full dark beard and spoke with a strong Bronx accent. Considered by some on the medical staff as a sixties-style hippie, he was surprised to find that he enjoyed the pace of life at Essex Medical Center in rural Pennsylvania. The three-hour drive to New York City allowed him to combine the best of both worlds—a stimulating professional environment in a rural setting and the opportunity to stay close to family and friends in the city.

Siegel was young, energetic, talented and thoroughly professional. He related well to young college students. In his few short years at Essex Medical Center he had built a thriving practice treating troubled young people.

Jerry Siegel looked forward to meeting Ruth Borovski's student, curious about the problems the young graduate student would present. Ruth and Kevin were ten minutes early for the three o'clock appointment and took seats in the reception area. Kevin began to display signs of anxiety, tapping his foot and shifting uncomfortably in the soft chair. Ruth's efforts at quiet conversation failed, and she was relieved when Jerry Siegel emerged from his office, greeting her with a warm smile and introducing himself to Kevin.

He ushered Kevin past the receptionist into his inner office and closed the door. An hour later, they returned to the reception area where Ruth was waiting. She was surprised and dismayed to see that Kevin eyes were red-rimmed and puffy. He was clearly distraught. Siegel spoke quietly to his secretary as Kevin stood aside, avoiding Ruth's gaze.

He turned to Ruth. "Dr. Borovski, I'm recommending, and Kevin has agreed, to admit himself to our psychiatric unit for evaluation. The minimum time he will be hospitalized is thirty days."

Shocked, Ruth turned to Kevin. "I didn't expect Dr. Siegel to suggest that you stay," she said, "but he is a better judge of the help you need than you or I. Your well being is his first priority. If Dr. Siegel believes you need hospital care to deal with your problems, you've got to listen to him. Now is the time to resolve the issues that are making your life so difficult. Your job now is to follow the doctor's orders.

"If you wish, I'll contact your parents and tell them where you are. I'll also notify the university of your absence."

"I'm willing to sign the admission papers," said Kevin, avoiding her gaze, "but I don't want my family to know about this. I haven't talked to them in a long time and this is none of their business.

"What about my research? If I have to stay here for at least a month, I'll only get further behind in my work. And I haven't got any money to pay for this." He ran his fingers through his long hair, agitated and close to losing control.

"Don't worry about your research," said Ruth. "I'll do my best to convince the university to give you an extension of time to finish your degree. And definitely don't worry about the funds to pay for your medical care. Your university health insurance will cover practically all the costs. I'll personally take care of the rest. As for notifying your family, of course I'll respect your privacy. No one will know you are here.

"I'm proud of you for making this decision, Kevin. As soon as Dr. Siegel allows you to have visitors, I'll be back to see you. Also, you know Dr. Atherton and Dr. Gardner are both on staff here. I'm sure they'll look in on you as well."

"One more thing." Kevin lowered his voice. "Would you go to my room and collect that data I've been working on—you know—the disks and printouts related to the studies we talked about?

"I didn't tell you about another little analysis I began last week" he whispered. "There are some papers in my room that I don't want anyone but you to see. I broke into the university's administrative computer to get the data. Some of those papers and disks are in my backpack. The rest are on the dresser in my room at Mrs. Ledbetter's."

"Not to worry," Ruth assured him. "I know where you live. I'll get the disks and papers—anything related to our discussions. I'll store them at my home, if you wish." She frowned, thinking.

A moment later she smiled. "I can tell your landlady that you're working on a special project for me and will be out of town for a month or so. That way, your privacy will be protected, and I'll have a reason for collecting the papers from your room."

"Thanks, Dr. Borovski. I'm sorry to ask you to do this for me."

"No problem, Kevin. Just concentrate on getting well."

"If you will excuse us, Ruth," Jerry Siegel interrupted them. "I need to take Kevin to our facility and get the admission process started. I'll be back shortly." Siegel smiled reassuringly over his shoulder as he led Kevin from the office.

*   *   *   *

"What's going on, Jerry?" Ruth asked fifteen minutes later, seated in Siegel's office. "I had no idea you would want to admit Kevin. I'm amazed that he would agree to it. Is his condition that serious?"

"Based on my initial evaluation, I believe Kevin is suffering from clinical depression, probably triggered by the death of your husband, but also complicated by his failure to complete his dissertation and possibly influenced by his apparent estrangement from his family. I haven't had time to more than touch on any particular issue. I need to safeguard his privacy, but since you seem to be the one person he trusts, I can tell you a bit more.

"He's displaying obsessive-compulsive behavior with some underlying psychosis. In my opinion, a period of hospitalization with intensive therapy for thirty to sixty days is clearly warranted. We'll treat him with a combination of chemical therapy and counseling to try to get at the underlying causes of his problems.

"I've already begun the chemical therapy. When I left him a few minutes ago, he was beginning to calm down. I think he's relieved that someone is going to help him deal with some difficult problems that probably developed over a long period of time. Your husband's death was simply the precipitating factor in a situation that may date back to his childhood.

"You did this young man a real service in bringing him here. The early prognosis is actually quite favorable. His willingness to accept professional help will put him on a path to recovery. Ruth, he understands that you have his interests at heart. He was surprisingly receptive to my recommendation that he spend some time in the hospital.

"As for not notifying his family of his hospitalization, I think we can honor that request. After all, he's almost thirty years old. He's an adult and perfectly capable of making that decision. Apparently he has been estranged from his family for years, although they live just outside Hillsdale.

"By the way, he offered a somewhat incomprehensible account of his recent activities in trying to identify some sort of toxic contamination as the precipitating factor in the cancer that ultimately led to your husband's death. What do you know about that?"

Ruth explained the university's actions over the past few months. She related the final conclusion by health officials that nothing on the campus could be linked to Jacob's death and outlined her sketchy understanding of the work Kevin had begun independently, unaware of the university's secret investigation.

"Jerry, I think Kevin's work during the past six months is simply his response to Jacob's death and his irrational fear that he can't finish his doctoral research without Jacob's guidance. Frankly, he may also be reluctant to deal with me as chair of his doctoral committee" she said.

"I took over that responsibility after Jacob died. He may have problems dealing with female authority figures. You should know that Kevin has asked me to collect some computer disks and printouts from his room. I'll do that, of course; and I'll look over his work, but I seriously doubt that it will yield anything of value."

*   *   *   *

Before Ruth left the hospital, Jerry Siegel promised to phone her when Kevin was ready for visitors. She would honor Kevin's request not to notify his parents. She would inform Cabot University officials and Kevin's dissertation committee that he was involved in an off-campus assignment for her. His absence would scarcely be noticed.

On her way home, she stopped at Kevin's rooming house, paid the next month's rent and asked for permission to collect some papers from Kevin's room. The landlady was so absorbed in a television game show that she barely glanced at the check and waved her upstairs toward Kevin's room. Ruth entered the room and quickly gathered the papers on his dresser. She put them into his backpack, which was crammed with computer disks and printouts. Lifting the heavy pack onto her shoulder she left the house without disturbing Mrs. Ledbetter.

The following day Ruth stopped by the Chemistry Department office and told Nathan Golding, the Chemistry Department chairman, that Kevin Parks was doing some important off-campus research related to her federal grant and would probably need an extension on the deadline for completing his dissertation. He agreed to the extension provided Ruth convinced the rest of Kevin's dissertation committee of the validity of the project and the need for the extension. He didn't probe deeply into the nature of Kevin's assignment.

With luck, Kevin would be released from the hospital before Christmas, only a month away. During the long semester break she could spend some uninterrupted time helping him make progress toward completing his dissertation research.

*   *   *   *

The month between Thanksgiving and the Christmas recess was a period of intense activity on the campus of Cabot University. Classes for the semester ended on December 10. Following a three-day reading period, the entire student body endured a frenzy of final examinations, completion of research papers and other projects they had neglected during the semester. The deadline for all academic work was December 21, the official end of the semester. Faculty would issue final grades or assign grades of Incomplete for work not completed by the deadline. As Kevin's dissertation chair, Ruth simply issued a grade of Incomplete for his dissertation. No one questioned his absence.

Part IV

Winter

Chapter 20

Early in December, long before classes and final examinations officially ended on the twentieth, the campus took on a festive air in anticipation of the coming holiday season. An enormous spruce wreath, dressed with hundreds of tiny white lights and a huge red bow, hung from the Old Main clock tower, carrying on a tradition begun decades earlier and symbolizing the school's early Protestant origins.

The public areas of the academic buildings and residence halls displayed Christmas wreaths and miniature trees. Secretaries in the administrative and academic offices across the campus tried to outdo each other in designing elaborate holiday decorations. Even the lamps along campus walks sported green boughs and red bows, and the face of Old Main's huge clock took on a red glow for the holidays. When the season's first snow arrived on December 11, the campus was transformed into a winter postcard.

Academic departments traditionally hosted elaborate parties for faculty, students and staff. Restrictions against alcohol were temporarily ignored and the entire campus celebrated the season with food and drink. Between parties, faculty members frantically graded final examinations and forwarded students' semester grades to the registrar, who was charged with processing and mailing grade reports to the university's 8,000 students in early January.

In downtown Hillsdale, the light poles along Main Street and University Avenue became enormous candy canes. Every store blazed with lights and Christmas decorations as throngs of shoppers invaded the boutiques and specialty stores. Not to be outdone, the regional mall outside town was crowded with shoppers in a buying frenzy that began the day after Thanksgiving. Even the local churches were packed with parishioners enjoying programs of Christmas music. Touched by the holiday spirit, everyone celebrated the season.

By December 20, students had packed their belongings, vacated the residence halls and headed home, delighted to celebrate the end of another semester with a four-week break from classes. Finally, the campus quieted, virtually deserted except for a sizable contingent of foreign graduate students. Unable to afford visits to their home country, they remained in Hillsdale, using the vacation period to work on research and catch up on sleep.

Many Cabot University faculty typically used the month-long semester break to continue their research at a more leisurely pace and to attend numerous professional meetings scheduled in January. Some combined professional meetings with a week or two of vacation, typically in a warmer climate.

This first holiday season since Jacob's death was painful for Ruth, despite maintaining a full schedule of activities designed to keep her busy and involved with friends and colleagues. She celebrated Chanukah with members of her synagogue, finding solace in the rituals of her faith. Paul and Anton Borovski made daily phone calls to their mother and left short e-mail messages on her computer at the lab. Aided by weekly visits to her psychiatrist, Dr. Jerry Siegel, Ruth dealt with the holiday season, fighting occasional bouts of overwhelming grief.

Nancy and Dick Atherton would spend the holidays as usual in Massachusetts with Nancy's elderly parents. They invited Ruth to join them, suggesting a visit with Paul at MIT, or perhaps enjoying a concert at Symphony Hall or simply relaxing. She declined, citing a need to concentrate on her research undistracted by classes and student demands. Nancy didn't press the issue, sensing her friend needed time alone.

Two days before Christmas Nancy and Dick, accompanied by Hillary Gardner, who would join her parents and son in Concord, flew to an airport outside Boston. Both physicians looked forward to a break from their work at Essex Medical Center. Weather permitting, they would make the short return flight to Hillsdale on New Year's Eve.

Ruth planned a quiet Christmas day, hoping it would pass uneventfully. The Borovski family had never celebrated the holiday, not even when their sons were children.

During the late afternoon hours of Christmas Eve, following her therapy with Dr. Jerry Siegel, she visited Kevin Parks in the psychiatric wing. His hospital stay had been extended another thirty days. Jerry assured her that the additional time was essential to Kevin's long-term recovery.

Ruth looked forward to her visits with Kevin, who seemed genuinely pleased to see her. They met in the comfortable lounge reserved for patients and guests and spent an hour in casual, relaxed conversation. They discussed in general terms the progress of his treatment and Kevin's plans to return to campus late in January. He didn't inquire about activities at Cabot, nor ask about her research, nor mention the toxic contamination theory that had obsessed him during the previous six months.

On Christmas morning, following brief phone calls from her sons, Ruth sat down in her study to review the documents she had retrieved from Kevin's room a month earlier. In her rush to complete final examinations, issue grades and prepare a research paper for an early January professional meeting, she had temporarily put aside the task of examining the papers that led to Kevin's breakdown and hospitalization.

With a pang of guilt, she wondered whether Kevin's current problems might have been avoided if Jacob had survived and continued as his mentor. Although Jerry Siegel didn't deny that Jacob's death had been a factor in Kevin's breakdown, he had assured her on several occasions that his illness involved a series of traumas dating from his childhood and teenage years. Adhering to ethical standards and patient privacy issues, Siegel didn't elaborate further.

Taking a steaming cup of coffee from the kitchen, she dumped the papers from Kevin's backpack onto the desk in her study and sorted them into piles. She put the computer printouts in chronological order and stacked them neatly on the floor for later review. Next she tackled the pile of scientific and medical journal abstracts and studies that Kevin had copied. She set aside the random scraps of paper densely covered with Kevin's cramped handwritten notes. An hour later she began to read.

Much of the information was a straightforward scientific search and evaluation of toxic chemical contaminants. He had followed his usual disciplined bibliographic search, printing out abstracts of scientific articles on various categories of chemicals. She separated the abstracts from the scientific studies that Kevin had printed in full and put them aside into a second pile. She smiled. Whatever his unhealthy mental state, Kevin Parks knew how to efficiently conduct a literature search. Jacob had taught him well. He also had used his well-developed computer skills to accumulate a wealth of information from computerized databases in a very short period of time. If only her other graduate students were equally proficient researchers.

She reviewed the abstracts and the scientific papers. Kevin had focused on studies describing some of the most lethal chemical carcinogens— benzene and dioxin, among others. Ploughing through the pile of documents littering her desk, the floor and a nearby table, she sorted through a second set of abstracts and articles. These papers from medical journals detailed the medical effects of toxic chemicals. They were compiled from external medical databases, not from the scientific databases that comprised Cabot's primary reference resources.

Kevin somehow had accessed external databases stored on computer servers in medical schools around the country, at the National Institutes of Health in Maryland and the Centers for Disease Control in Atlanta. Scanning the medical studies, she noted that they invariably described various types of cancers, mostly soft tissue cancers. Several explored in general terms the possible links between toxic chemicals and cancer.

Several studies examined possible links between various types of cancers and nuclear waste contamination. A few papers described activities at government-run sites in Fernald, Ohio and the Savannah River works in South Carolina, the country's only manufacturing facility for producing tritium, a highly radioactive substance used in the production of hydrogen bombs. Kevin had collected scientific and medical studies dating back to the 1970s, many concentrating on dioxin, a controversial toxic chemical that had contaminated an area called Love Canal outside Buffalo, New York. The controversy over dioxin extended back to the Vietnam defoliation project, when the chemical was an ingredient in the defoliant known as Agent Orange.

Much of the data appeared to be completely unrelated to Jacob's illness.

Sadly, Ruth realized that Kevin's obsession had led him far from his doctoral research in polymer chemistry. She blamed herself for failing to supervise his research more closely. Because he had been a fixture in the university's chemistry laboratories for so long, her department colleagues tended to ignore him. She was now guilty of the same neglect. Jacob's death and her own grief did not excuse her. She had ignored the symptoms of his mental illness, symptoms that he probably exhibited months before his hospitalization.

Ruth was grateful that Jacob would not know the impact of his death upon his favorite graduate student. Hopefully, intensive therapy and the passage of time would enable Kevin to return to a healthy and productive life. Time would tell. In the meantime, she would monitor his progress in therapy more closely, visit him frequently and help him deal with Jacob's death. Perhaps encouraging him to complete his thesis as a lasting tribute to her husband would be an effective incentive.

Ruth left the study and walked through the living room to the kitchen. She replenished her cup of coffee and she leaned on the counter, gazing out the large kitchen window at the peaceful scene before her. The ice-clogged river that bordered her property lay far below. It meandered past the town of Hillsdale, bathed in the late morning sunshine of a perfect winter day. On the distant ridge to the west she spotted the white clock tower atop Old Main silhouetted against the azure sky. This panorama was her favorite view in the world. It never failed to give her a sense of belonging, and solace.

Thanks to Jerry Siegel's counseling, the frequent bouts of overwhelming grief were diminishing. On this first major holiday without Jacob, she was increasingly confident that she had come to terms with his death. She had begun to cope.

She returned to the study where the last chaotic pile of random notes written in Kevin's cramped spidery script awaited. She scanned each scrap, sorting them by subject matter into notes related to toxic chemicals, cancer and related medical data, nuclear data and finally, she put a few scraps in a miscellaneous pile.

Unfolding a ruled page in Kevin's nearly indecipherable writing, she barely glanced at the list of names. Without further thought, she wadded it into a ball and tossed the sheet into the wastebasket. She paused. Later she would be unable to explain why she hesitated, then retrieved the sheet, smoothed it and examined it more closely.

She had assumed the paper contained the list of authors that Kevin had used in his search. Irritated, she tried to decipher a few names. She realized with a shock that some of the names were familiar. She pulled her chair closer to the desk and began a line-by-line deciphering of the scrawled names. She put a check mark beside each name she recognized. Puzzled and increasingly anxious, she found that nearly thirty names on the list were those of present and former faculty members at Cabot University. Several other names seemed vaguely familiar. Perhaps they were university staff members employed in the past.

Clearly, her original assumption was off the mark. This was not part of Kevin's review of technical studies. She ran her finger down the list slowly and wrote the department and academic area of each name she recognized in the margin of the paper. The faculty names were associated with academic disciplines across the university—from liberal arts, business, music, engineering and science.

Kevin had penciled in a date in the left margin beside each name. Following some names, a second date had been written. With mounting excitement, Ruth realized that the first set of dates was clustered during the five-year period from 1965 to 1970. Could this be a list of faculty who came to Cabot University between 1965 and 1970, a period of great growth in the number of faculty and students at the university? Jacob Borovski and Nancy Atherton joined the faculty in 1965. Ruth came in 1970 after resigning from Capital Chemicals Company's Oakton Division. Sure enough, her name appeared near the bottom of the list, while Nancy and Jacob's names headed the list.

There also were names of faculty who had left the university. Gabby Fotanzi's name leaped off the page. She had left the university after losing a bitter battle to earn tenure in the mid-1970s. Smoothing the wrinkled sheet more carefully, she checked the second date that had been inserted beside Jacob's name. With a sinking feeling, she realized that April 14 was the date of his death.

She quickly scanned the remaining names with dual dates. She recognized the names of Jackson Starrett and Kenneth Compton, both former Presidents of Cabot University, who had died some years earlier. Sure enough, if memory did not fail her, their date of death was inserted beside each name. At the bottom of the list she also recognized the name of Steve Cox, a young faculty member who had died in the crash of his private plane more than ten years ago.

Why would Kevin Parks catalog the names and dates of death of selected faculty from the past? Noting Jacob's death was not surprising, but why would he compile such a list, how did he select these names and perhaps most puzzling, how did he learn what appeared to be the exact dates of death of these people?

She could not answer her own questions. Reluctantly, she placed the single sheet of paper in a manila folder. She would show this item to Nancy and Dick later.

She gathered each pile of materials and inserted them in large manila envelopes. She labeled each one and filed them in the bottom drawer of her file cabinet. She would return the data to Kevin after he was released from the hospital. On second thought, if Jerry Siegel gave permission, she might discuss the materials with Kevin. Restored to good health, Kevin probably would have no use for them.

Chapter 21

Kevin Parks spent Christmas Day with Valerie Chapman, a Cabot University undergraduate and fellow patient in the nearly deserted psychiatric unit of Essex Medical Center. Both young people would remember the day as the most depressing holiday of their lives.

They had no visitors. Jerry Siegel, both students' psychiatrist, strongly advised Valerie's parents against a Christmas visit, despite their expressed desire to see their daughter and a willingness to make the two and a half hour drive from Philadelphia to Oakton. Kevin had been estranged from his parents for nearly a decade. In his eyes, they no longer existed. His family knew nothing of his hospitalization, and he had no intention of contacting them.

Following a failed suicide attempt in early December, Valerie Chapman had formed a tenuous bond with Kevin. The two were the only patients in the psychiatric unit under the age of thirty. Had they not been patients at Essex, their paths would never have crossed on the campus. Thrown together by circumstance, they shared common links with their doctor and an intense isolation in the sterile surroundings of the psychiatric lockup.

Jerry Siegel made morning rounds as usual, spending more than an hour each with Kevin and Valerie, trying to brighten the dismal holiday for his young patients. "I've given you permission to leave the hospital grounds for a few hours if you want," he told Kevin at the end of his visit. "It's cold, but actually rather nice today. I'm going down the hall to visit Valerie Chapman and I'll write a permission slip for her, too. Maybe you both would enjoy a walk downtown later today." He jotted a few notes in Kevin's medical file. "See you tomorrow at the regular time in my office," he said casually.

An hour later Kevin met Valerie in the hall outside their rooms. Together they wandered into the nearly empty commons area where the hospital staff served them a quiet Christmas dinner. Despite their well-intentioned efforts, no amount of forced holiday gaiety could alter the depressing atmosphere within the unit, and the staff failed utterly to lift their spirits.

"Want to take a walk downtown?" Kevin asked as they finished off their dessert. "Jerry promised to leave passes at the front desk. We can get out of here for a couple of hours. There won't be a problem as long as we only take a walk. I guess they trust us not to do anything stupid."

They signed out under the watchful eye of the head psychiatric nurse on duty, indicating Memorial Park as their destination, and promising to check back into the hospital by five o'clock. Wearing jeans, heavy sweaters and ski jackets, they put on dark glasses as they emerged from the hospital into a sunny but cold early afternoon. Gloved hands in pockets, they trudged across a huge expanse of frozen grass and blacktop parking lot, and passed through the main gate.

Leaving the hospital grounds behind, they walked briskly toward Oakton center, passing through the quiet residential area near the hospital, not speaking, absorbed in their private thoughts, painfully aware of past Christmases spent in far different surroundings. Valerie gazed with unconcealed longing at the brightly lighted Christmas trees visible through the windows of spacious homes whose driveways were littered with parked cars, evidence of the family gatherings going on inside.

Kevin ignored the scene around him.

The village center was an easy twenty-minute walk from the hospital. Strolling down one side of the wide main street, they stopped occasionally to view the shop windows laden with Christmas offerings. They passed the village diner, a local landmark, now closed and dark. A few minutes later they walked through the open gate to Memorial Park, a gathering place and recreation area bordering the river. They sat down on a bench near the water's edge and stared across the slowly flowing river, laden with huge chunks of ice.

Kevin and Valerie made an unlikely pair. Valerie carried herself with the grace of a ballerina, her shoulder length flowing blond hair pulled back in a pony tail, stylish muffs protecting her ears from the biting cold. Her designer ski jacket and jeans contrasted sharply with the unkempt appearance of her companion. She was compulsively fastidious about her personal grooming and painfully thin. In addition to her failed suicide attempt, she was being treated for bulimia, a serious but relatively common, eating disorder.

Kevin Parks cared nothing for appearances. Except for the brief interlude following Jacob's death when he had shaved his beard and trimmed his long hair, he ignored both his appearance and personal hygiene. Once again, he sported a full beard that effectively concealed his face. His dark hair had grown to shoulder length, which he rarely drew into a ponytail. Never particularly aware of personal hygiene, he showered only at the hospital staff's insistence, and his clothing came directly from the Salvation Army's used clothing store.

Despite their disparate appearances, they shared several things in common. Both were students at Cabot University, Valerie a senior and Kevin in graduate school. Both had suffered traumatic experiences that landed them in Essex Medical Center's psychiatric unit. Both were patients under the care of Jerry Siegel, whose specialty was the treatment of depression in young people.

Both were undeniably brilliant. Valerie, a perfectionist, had always excelled in school, loved to read, enjoyed classical music and jazz and was fond of modern art. European History was her major, and her grades placed her in the top three percent of students at Cabot University. She was admitted to membership in Phi Beta Kappa, an honor accorded a select few of the top liberal arts students.

Kevin, equally brilliant student in science and mathematics, generally scorned the arts. His musical tastes, such as they were, ran to country and western. He had never explored the worlds of art or classical music beyond the required introductory courses he took as a freshman. Except for an expertise in computers developed during his lonely undergraduate years, and a passion for science fiction paperbacks, he had no hobbies or outside interests.

*   *   *   *

Valerie gazed silently across the placid river and began to talk, opening up to Kevin for the first time, revealing a life of unimaginable wealth and privilege.

"Sure you want to tell me about yourself?" he asked.

"Why not? What better time than Christmas? And why not with someone I'll probably never see again after we both get out of the hospital."

"Be my guest, let it all hang out." Kevin said. "I'm actually a very good listener."

"You don't know anything about me, Kevin, except you probably know why I'm in the loony bin."

"Yeah, well, it's kind of hard to conceal a suicide attempt. I heard you OD'd on some drugs and then tried to finish it off with booze," he said softly.

"I guess nothing is a secret in a psychiatric wing.

"Actually, I still think it was a rational thing to do," she said defensively. "Some days—today, for instance—I'm sorry I botched the job so badly. Now Jerry Siegel's working to convince me that suicide is no way to deal with my issues. In fact, he says it's a pretty dumb thing to do, especially since I'm supposed to be so intelligent."

"So why did you try it?" Kevin glanced at her face, and then looked away.

"If you really want to know, this will take some time. I probably should fill you in on my background a bit," she said. "Let me tell you what it was like growing up rich. From what I can tell, your parents weren't too well off."

"No."

"Anyway, you know I'm from Philadelphia—well, not Philadelphia, but one of the 'burbs, Bryn Mawr to be exact. That's one of the Main Line towns, lots of big estates. It's where the old money lives. I grew up there, sort of."

"Not bad," said Kevin.

"My father is Executive Vice-President of a big drug company in the city—you would know the name if I told you since your field is chemistry. I adored my dad. Notice the past tense on that, Kevin?"

"Yes."

"When I was a kid he was away from home a lot, traveling on business, getting ahead in the company. When he came home from a trip, he'd bring me a neat gift from whatever faraway place he visited. I used to be sad when he left, but really glad when he got home. He's in marketing. Typical outgoing marketing type, always laughing, loves people, they like him, you know the type.

"Mother, on the other hand is beautiful, really cool."

"You must have your mother's looks," Kevin said quietly.

"I suppose my looks come from my mother and my personality from my dad," Valerie continued.

"My grandparents are both dead now, but they were wicked wealthy. Since Mother was an only child, she inherited all the money. My grandparents set up a big trust fund for me when I was born. I don't know how much money is in it, but I get it all when I turn thirty—that is, if I live that long."

Kevin frowned.

"I grew up with lots of pets," she changed gears, smiling now. "We had two golden retrievers, plus I got a pony when I was five and later a horse for my thirteenth birthday. I also had lots of cats, a couple of gerbils and some birds. I really love animals. At one point I thought about becoming a veterinarian, but then I learned you needed to know a lot of science and that cooled me on that career," she said.

"When I was only six, my parents sent me to a private primary school run by the Quakers near my home. This was the same school Mother attended when she was a child. For the first couple of years, I was allowed to live at home and commute to school. Later, I boarded at the school, which wasn't too bad, except that I could only go home on weekends so I didn't get to play with the animals or ride my horse. After I finished eighth grade, I went to a prep school outside Boston, just like my mother.

"It got to the point that I hardly ever went home. That's the disadvantage of boarding school. I really didn't see what was happening to my parents because I wasn't with them except on short vacations."

"What about your summers?" asked Kevin.

"During the summers I spent two months at a coed summer camp on Cape Cod. First, I went as a camper. Later, I got to be a counselor. I really loved that camp. I played all sorts of sports, plus we had a big show that we put on every year during parents' weekend and I acted in four or five plays. I also acted in plays during my years at boarding school. I was pretty good.

"One thing about private schools, Kevin. The classes are small, and you can really learn. There's a lot of pressure to get into the Ivy League schools or some place that's academically outstanding. I learned to write, spent a lot of time reading, studying history, literature, classical music and art. Of course, I also spent a lot of time listening to Phish and the Grateful Dead.

"Am I boring you?" she asked sharply.

"Nope. Keep talking."

"I was accepted at a couple of Ivy League schools, but I decided to come to Cabot because it was closer to home. I thought I'd see my parents more often. It only takes a couple of hours to get home from here. During freshman orientation week, I soon realized that most of the kids didn't come from my sort of background. So I haven't told many guys about myself. My friends just know that I live near Philadelphia and went to high school in New England. It's easier to fit in if I don't talk about my background.

"As far as choosing a major, I don't have a clue about what I want to do after graduation. I ended up majoring in European History by accident. It's a good major for me—it's easy, I enjoy writing the term papers and doing the reading for history and literature. I figured out a long time ago that I could cram like mad before a test and pull mostly A's without much effort. It gave me a chance to party and hang out when I wanted to. If I majored in math or science, I'd have spent most of my time in the library studying.

"Instead, it's been an easy four years here. Easier than boarding school. I get along with people, study pretty efficiently during the week so I can drink and party every weekend. I realize now that I've been drinking and doing way too many drugs. At least that's one thing I learned from Dr. Siegel."

Kevin said nothing.

"Don't get excited." She caught his scowl. "I don't do much besides grass. But I do love vodka tonics. I've got to cut back on drinking, too."

"So, what made you decide to wipe yourself out?" Kevin asked. "Sounds like a pretty good life to me."

"It's hard to believe that everything happened only five weeks ago. It seems like a long time since Thanksgiving. In fact, Jerry Siegel showed me that my problems were building for at least a year. I just didn't realize it. I began to really look forward to the weekends, to the parties, to drinking and fooling around.

"Jerry says I was depressed and began to drink and party too much. A couple of times I passed out and don't even remember how I got back to my suite in the residence hall. Then I started to gain weight, a total calamity as far as I'm concerned. A friend on the women's cross country team told me that you can eat and drink all you want, then go to the bathroom and throw up, then go back for more. It works, too. I got into the habit of binge drinking and purging every weekend. I'd probably still be doing it except that Thanksgiving break came up and I went home to celebrate with my parents.

"I drove to Bryn Mawr after classes on Wednesday afternoon expecting the usual big celebration to have already begun. Instead, the house was quiet. Mother and Dad told me that we were having Thanksgiving dinner by ourselves, just the three of us.

"You've got to understand that this is very unusual in my home. My parents always had a big Thanksgiving party. They often invited twenty or twenty-five friends for a huge feast. Not this year, though."

Kevin sat beside her, watching the flowing river, listening intently to Valerie's recounting of a life completely alien to his own. Occasionally, he walked to the water's edge and skipped flat stones across the ice-jammed surface. For the most part, Valerie seemed to be unaware of his presence, absorbed in her own world.

"Thanksgiving was really weird—it was just too quiet. Dinner was served in the late afternoon. The maid had just cleared the appetizer course. I remember that a Mozart CD was playing in the background. I'll never be able to listen to that music without remembering what happened that day." She began to cry.

Kevin reached into his jeans, pulled out a wad of paper tissues and handed them to her. Moments later she resumed her narrative.

"We were seated at the dining room table, just the three of us, waiting for the arrival of the roast turkey. My dad always made a big deal of carving the turkey.

"I still can't believe he was so casual. It was like he was talking about the weather, not about ending my parents' marriage, a marriage that had lasted more than thirty years. He just said, 'Valerie, your mother and I have something to tell you.' I started to smile, thinking he was going to announce some awesome vacation plans we would take together during semester break—something like that.

"Then he said, 'we've decided to file for divorce, and we wanted to tell you this news together, to assure you that this is an amicable divorce. We both love you and will remain close to you.'

"He was speaking so quietly that I thought I'd misunderstood him. Then he repeated that this was an 'amicable' divorce, as though any divorce is amicable."

Turning to Kevin, she asked, "Has anyone in your family ever gotten divorced?"

"No such luck," he said bitterly. "My dad had too much fun beating up my mom to let her get a divorce. Besides, I think she was afraid of leaving him—afraid she would have to go on welfare to survive.

"Forget I told you that," Kevin said sharply, directing the conversation back to Valerie.

"What happened after your dad dropped the bombshell?"

"Strange, I remember the whole scene perfectly clearly, but everything was in slow motion. I turned to Mother to see how she was reacting. I know now that she was devastated, although she never shows her emotions and she wasn't about to lose control at the dinner table. That would be too uncivilized," she laughed weakly.

"My mother is always super cool. I never know what she's thinking. Dr. Siegel explained to me that some people have problems showing their emotions. That's Mother. I remember growing up loving my father so much because he was always laughing, a big hugger. Of course, it helped that he constantly brought me gifts. In fact, it was incredibly easy to manipulate him. If Mother wouldn't give me something I wanted, I just went to Dad. I'm not too proud of the way I managed him." Her voice was tinged with regret.

"Anyway," she continued, "there we were at the dinner table, waiting for the damned turkey. And everybody was being terribly civilized, ignoring the bomb they'd just dropped on me.

"In retrospect, I'm actually proud of the way I kept the whole charade going. I wasn't an amateur actress in prep school for nothing," she choked.

Kevin impulsively reached out and took her gloved hand in his.

She tossed her hair. "I was in total control. We might have been discussing my grades from last semester. Dad gave a totally lame explanation about wanting to take a different path in the years ahead. He kept emphasizing that I wouldn't have to worry about money. The trust fund would take care of that. Of course, that wasn't his money anyway. It came from Mother's side. Besides, I've never had to worry about money in my whole life."

Valerie fell silent, seemingly absorbed in the scene before her, watching the river flowing by, studying the spacious homes lining the distant bank.

"Anyway," she said, "I figured if they could be calm and rational about the divorce, so could I. I've got to admit, though, the turkey tasted like cardboard and the mashed potatoes were paste. I downed two glasses of

Linda Kistler

dad's expensive chardonnay so fast I had to excuse myself before dessert to visit the bathroom and throw up the whole mess."

"The conversation during the rest of the meal was absolutely normal, my parents discussing the presidential election as though everything was fine. Mother went on for a time about some charity ball that was coming up during the Christmas season. In other words, Kevin, my Thanksgiving dinner was like most other holidays in the Chapman family—very proper, very civilized," she concluded.

She looked at him. "Since this seems to be true confessions time, now it's your turn to tell me how you landed in the loony bin. You haven't been exactly forthcoming, you know. I don't even know where you grew up."

"But you haven't told me why you tried to do yourself in," he said.

"Later. That's enough for now. Tell me about yourself," she demanded.

Kevin opened up to Valerie as he had not done with anyone since childhood.

"For sure, it's not a pretty story, Valerie. Actually I grew up on a farm only a few miles outside Hillsdale," he began. "I graduated from Hillsdale High School ten years ago, and probably would have ended up working in a mill or the local canning factory if I hadn't gotten a scholarship to Cabot. There was a chemistry teacher at the high school who thought I showed some talent in science. Science and math always came easy for me. She talked to the admissions people at the university about me. After an interview, I filled out some forms and the university offered me a combination of scholarship and a work-study program. It was actually pretty easy.

"My mom wanted me to go to college, but Pop never liked the idea of a kid of his getting a college degree. He figured the whole damn family should spend our lives working like dogs on the farm. God, I hated that farm—up at dawn to milk the damn cows, feed the rest of the animals, then hop on the school bus and ride for half an hour to school. Reverse the process in late afternoon. The work never ended. I couldn't participate in school activities because I had to work. Actually, I never had much interest in school activities, anyway. I wasn't any good at sports, never tried out for any school plays. I might have been interested in the chess club but they always met after school and I had to catch the bus home.

"I've got three younger brothers and a sister, and we all worked our butts off on the farm. Going to college was a way off the farm, and I jumped at the chance."

"So why haven't your parents come to visit you?" Valerie asked.

"My mom is dead and I haven't seen Pop or my brothers and sister for years. They don't know I'm here, and they'll never know, if I have anything to say about it."

106

"Why? Are you ashamed of being sick?"

He glanced sideways at her profile.

"Well, if you really want to hear the ugly details, I guess there's no reason you can't know."

Valerie was interested. This strange young man's problems were a welcome diversion from her own.

He began offhandedly, as though the events he recounted had long since lost their ability to wound.

"The bottom line is that Pop is a brutal son of a bitch. He beat my mom regularly—that is, after he finished beating us kids. He really got his jollies from beating us, and he used any trivial excuse to take us on. We never could do anything right, especially me. Maybe he was especially hard on me because I'm the oldest. It didn't matter that I earned top grades in high school, or that my sister was valedictorian of her class a few years after I graduated. Nothing we did was good enough for him. All he cared about was the farm.

"What really used to bother me was how he treated Mom—the bruises, black eyes, the endless criticizing of everything she did. I realize now the bastard is a 24-carat sadist. Growing up, I didn't even know the meaning of the word. I just knew none of us could satisfy him, could never earn his approval.

"What I remember most about my high school years is the work. The fucking chores never ended. We worked morning, afternoon and night, usually until dark. During our so-called summer vacations, everybody worked eighty hours a week—except Pop, of course. He fancied himself some kind of manager who was real good at delegating tasks. He made sure there was a lot of work for everyone, including Mom, then he would take off and join his buddies for drinks about four o'clock every afternoon.

When Pop came home after dark, everybody tried to stay out of his way. He was usually drunk as a skunk and mean as a cornered rat. That's when the beatings usually took place. He would inspect our work, and then decide that what we had done wasn't good enough, or that we hadn't done enough. Then he would start in on us, usually beginning with me, then working his way down the line.

"That's how it was until I was about thirteen years old. Then one night, right after he'd finished beating my mom, Pop took me out to the barn and he came on to me." Kevin revealed the awful truth quietly, his face impassive, eyes focused intently at some distant point across the river.

Valerie thought she had misunderstood. "You don't mean…" she began, stunned. She glanced at his profile in the late afternoon sunlight.

"Yeah, I mean exactly what you're thinking."

"What did you do?"

"The first time it happened, I got into a wrestling match with him that turned into a fist fight. Trouble is, I lost. He gave me the worst beating of my life—he was a lot stronger than me, and I never won a fight with him. He's over six feet and weighs about two twenty-five. When he finally pinned me to the floor in the barn, he got exactly what he wanted."

Kevin momentarily lost control. He sat silently on the bench for a time, hunched over, his fists clenched. Finally, he gazed across the icy river to the far shore as though the winter scene demanded his full attention.

Valerie was silent. Then she reached out and took his hand. He didn't resist.

Moments later he resumed. "I've never told anyone before what happened to me—not Dr. Borovski, not even Dr. Siegel. For about three years, until I enrolled at Cabot University, Pop forced me to give him sex—sometimes oral, sometimes butt fucking—it didn't much matter." Turning away again, he shielded his face.

"The worst part is that after awhile, I just let him do it. I didn't even fight back. Sometimes, when I think about it, I can almost convince myself that nothing could have stopped it. I guess the sex was easier than putting up with his beatings.

"It became a pattern, almost routine—once, sometimes twice a week, usually after he'd been drinking. At least he laid off beating my mom and the others. Later I developed a technique for mentally turning off. I would just blank everything out of my mind. It was like I could go outside myself. What was happening to my body—the abuse—wasn't happening to me. I sometimes do that even now—when I don't like what's going on around me. I can turn everything off.

"I think Mom realized what was happening because she worked like crazy to help me get into college," he resumed. "She used to secretly phone my chemistry teacher to ask her to help me get into Cabot. Mom took a few beatings because she encouraged me to go to college. I'm not proud of leaving my mom and brothers and sister in that situation. At the time, all I could think about was getting away myself.

"Anyway, the scholarship to Cabot changed my life. Once I left home, I never went back. For the first couple of years, I would call Mom occasionally when I figured Pop would be out in the fields or in some bar.

"You never see your mother and brothers and sister?" Valerie asked gently.

"Mom died four years ago. The old lady who owns the rooming house where I live stopped me one day and told me to check out an obituary in the paper. Said she was real sorry about my mother. She gave me a strange look when she realized I didn't know until she told me.

"I don't know what happened to my brothers and sister. Once, about three years ago, I think I spotted my sister downtown, walking out of McDonald's. Her back was toward me so I wasn't sure. I just turned around and walked the other way."

The two sat lost in thought.

"Kevin, I don't know what to say," said Valerie. "My parents' divorce is trivial compared to what you put up with for years."

He finally faced her directly. "Whatever you think, don't pity me," he said grimly. "I left home a long time ago. The only one who mattered to me was Mom, and she's dead. I figure my sister and brothers could leave the farm any time they want, just like I did. As for Pop, for me he doesn't exist. The day I left for college I vowed never to speak to the bastard again.

"Besides, that part of my life has nothing to do with being here at Essex," he said. "I'm here because Dr. Siegel says I'm depressed. He says it was brought on by Dr. Jacob's death. Jerry also says I've developed an obsession about how he died."

Valerie was puzzled. "I remember last spring when the memorial service was held for Dr. Borovski. I never had a class with Dr. Borovski although I remember seeing him around campus. The science majors in my residence hall say he was an awesome teacher. Classes were canceled and a lot of students went to the service. Did you go?"

"I not only went, I spoke on behalf of Dr. Jacob's students," a touch of pride crept into his voice. "I never gave a eulogy before. I was really nervous about speaking in front of so many people, afraid I'd mess up, maybe break down, but I got through it without making a total ass of myself."

"You know the woman who visits me about once a week?" he abruptly changed the subject.

"I think so. She's short, always well dressed, has a nice smile?"

"Right. That's Dr. Ruth Borovski, Dr. Jacob's wife—his widow," Kevin corrected himself. "She's my dissertation chairman. She had a lot to do with getting me admitted to Essex. I made the mistake of telling her about my research on toxic poisons. She doesn't believe me either—nobody does," he said gloomily.

"She thinks I'm depressed about losing Dr. Jacob. She's probably right about that," he admitted. "She practically forced me to talk with Dr. Siegel. Then I made the mistake of telling him that I think Dr. Jacob died from toxic chemical poisoning, and that I'm convinced the university is at fault. I guess that's when he decided I need to stay here and work this out."

"Next to Dr. Jacob, Ruth Borovski is the one person in the world who encouraged me to work toward my doctorate," he continued. "They both treated me like a member of their family, although they have two sons of their own. I often got invited to their home for holidays and sometimes for parties with other students." He seemed quietly pleased.

"Since I've been in the hospital, she usually visits me once a week. I guess she feels a little responsible since she's the one who brought me to see the doctor in the first place. She arranged for an extension on my dissertation. I don't know how she managed it, but she's pretty good at pulling strings with the administration. They were going to kick me out of the doctoral program if I didn't finish my dissertation by next May. When I get out of here, I'll go back to Cabot and finish my work."

The pale sun had already slid below the horizon. Dusk signaled the rapidly approaching winter darkness, and the temperature began to drop.

"We'd better start back." Valerie shivered. Kevin glanced at his watch. "Right. If they send a team out looking for us, we'll lose our privileges."

He walked the few yards to the shore, searched for a flat stone and threw it violently across the water into a slag of ice floating down the river. Together, they turned away from the river and walked quickly along Oak Street through the village center and up the hill to the hospital. Banks of sodium vapor lights cast a garish orange glow over acres of empty parking lots as they made their way to the main entrance. Entering the gaily-decorated lobby, they headed for the psychiatric wing, signed in and noted the time of their return.

Kevin hesitated, standing uncomfortably in the brightly lighted corridor, searching for words to end the day. Finally, he turned and headed toward the far corridor and the safety of his room. He regretted having revealed the sordid details of his life to this strange, but beautiful girl he hardly knew. Valerie Chapman had somehow overcome barriers he had erected years ago. He would not lower his guard again, not to Jerry Siegel or Ruth Borovski or anyone else.

Chapter 22

Sprawled across her bed in the darkened room, the sounds of Phish blasting through her headphones, Valerie Chapman tried to ward off the panic attack that threatened to overwhelm her. In the past month, the music and the prescribed anti-depressants helped control her anxiety. Sometimes, though, they didn't do the job. As she waited for the new dose to take effect, she relived each of the many Phish concerts she had attended over the past five years. They were her mantra of memories that lifted her far from her sterile surroundings.

With help from her therapist, she was beginning to deal with her parents' pending divorce. Although she had made progress during the past month, she was not ready to leave the hospital. The psychiatric unit had become her safe harbor, a place where she could deal with the internal chaos that sometimes overwhelmed her.

She changed CDs and in the stillness heard a quiet tap on her door.

"Mind if I come in?" Kevin asked, looking sheepish.

"How long have you been standing there?" she asked.

"Only a couple of minutes," he said.

"You can come in as long as you don't mind listening to Phish," she said. She left the door ajar as he walked past her into the room. A strictly enforced hospital rule required open doors whenever patients received visitors in their rooms. She unplugged her headphones and adjusted the volume low enough to avoid complaints from the staff. Motioning him toward the room's only upholstered chair, she flopped on her stomach across the bed. She regarded Kevin quizzically, a tiny smile on her face.

"So, what brings you here?"

He slouched deeper into the chair and looked away.

Valerie had never met such a strange young man before. Aware of her undeniable beauty and accustomed to frequent propositions from males since her early teens, she wondered whether he was permanently damaged from the sexual abuse administered by his father. She now understood why he had never displayed a sexual interest in her. Could she turn him on sexually? It might be an interesting challenge.

"Want some candy?" she motioned toward a gift-wrapped box open on the desk.

He reached for a chocolate.

"You must think I'm a real creep," he began, "telling you that shit about my past. Don't know why I spilled my guts to you. I haven't even told that stuff to Dr. Siegel. I shouldn't have laid all that on you."

"I let my guard down, maybe because it's Christmas and we're the only patients left in this joint. Whatever you do, please don't tell anyone else—especially not Dr. Siegel—what I told you. If you do, they'll never let me out of here."

"No one will learn anything from me," she assured him. "Actually, your story made me realize how lucky I've been—at least I think both my parents still love me, even though they can't stand each other. Their divorce is nothing compared to what you've had to deal with.

"And I don't have to worry about money like you. I've always had lots of money. My parents saw to it that I got into the best schools. All I had to do was study, and that wasn't too hard. You had to scrounge up money to go to school and still make great grades to keep your scholarship."

She was silent, debating whether she could trust him.

"I haven't really told you why I'm stuck here at Essex," she said, finally. "Maybe you'll trust me more if you know why my parents threw me in the loony bin."

"I never talk to anybody around here except Dr. Siegel. Your secrets are safe," said Kevin.

She plunged ahead, reliving those awful days a month earlier when her world had unraveled like a ball of yarn.

"Remember I told you my parents were really cool when they told me about the divorce during Thanksgiving dinner?"

"Yeah."

"Anyway," she continued, "after dinner and in the early evening we all sat around the fire and made nice—like nothing was happening. Since both of them seemed really in control, I went right along with the pretense. It was as though we all thought the divorce was not a big deal. It was all really weird.

"Mother came to my room later that night, wanting to talk. That's when she told me my dad was moving out—in fact he'd already moved out two months ago. He spent the weekend at home to keep up appearances because of me. She wanted to talk about the financial situation. She gets to keep the house—after all, she inherited it from her parents. It really belongs to her. I told her that was no big deal. She kept talking about the money, went over the details about the trust fund I'll get when I'm thirty. I didn't pay much attention.

"What really upset me was that she told me that my father had already moved in with someone who works in his company. The killer blow is that this bitch is only 27 years old. So, he's screwing around with a woman half my mother's age and only a few years older than me. God, the whole scene makes me sick. I hate him."

Kevin listened intently, his dark eyes avoiding her gaze.

"I don't know what to say," he shifted in his chair. "I can't imagine living in a big house like you describe, having a lot of money."

"Let me tell you the rest. I left on Saturday night—no reason to hang around, and drove back to school. I thought I could deal with the divorce as well as anybody. If it didn't bother my parents, why should it bother me.

"I managed to stay cool for three days. Then one night about ten o'clock while I was studying in my room, I got a huge panic attack. In the midst of it all, I decided I didn't want to live anymore—a perfectly rational conclusion under the circumstances.

"I've gotten panic attacks since I was around thirteen, and I have a prescription to help control them. I just grabbed the bottle and took about twenty pills all at once. Then I washed the pills down with half a bottle of vodka. Nice combination, huh? It almost did the trick. I don't remember much over the next couple of days.

"One of my roommates came back from a movie at about eleven-thirty and found me unconscious on my bed with the empty bottle of vodka. She got really scared. She knew instantly what I had done.

"She ran down the hall to the residence life counselor who called an ambulance. They admitted me to Hillsdale Hospital where they pumped out my stomach. The combination of drugs and alcohol kept me in intensive care for several days until I was stabilized. It was relatively easy to bring me back from the overdose. Dealing with my depression has been a lot harder.

"My parents came up from Philadelphia—they actually drove up together—isn't that a laugh? On the doctor's recommendation, they had me committed to Essex Medical Center for psychiatric care. Although I don't remember much about it, I lost control when I saw Mother and Dad together. I started screaming and yelling. I totally flipped. The doctors gave me a shot and I was transferred here.

"Right now, Dr. Siegel won't allow my parents visitation rights until I sort out a lot of stuff that's messing up my head." She paused, listening to the music. "So here we are. Nothing like spending Christmas in the loony bin to make you realize there's no place like home."

Chapter 23

The 90-minute flight from Massachusetts to Hillsdale was swift and uneventful. With his wife in the seat beside him and Hillary Gardner occupying a rear seat, Dick Atherton eased back the throttles, extended the flaps and banked onto final approach to Hillsdale Regional Airport. A weak mid-winter sun hung low on the western horizon as the plane touched down and Dick taxied toward the civil aviation hanger and his tiedown spot. He made a final inspection of the plane, and then headed for Essex Medical Center.

Fifteen minutes later, Hillary dropped Nancy Atherton and her baggage at home, three doors down the street from her own home. The blinking red light on the message machine greeted Nancy when she entered the study next to the bedroom. Ruth's slightly accented voice came through when she pressed the replay button.

"Nancy and Dick, welcome home. I hope your visit with your parents was fine and that they are well. Please call me after you get settled. There's no rush, nothing urgent. Perhaps you, Dick and Hillary can join me for a simple New Year's Eve supper if you haven't anything else planned. Talk to you soon."

Nancy hit the delete button.

She unpacked, emptied the boxes of gifts and put them under the tree, turned on the lights and touched a match to the dry kindling in the fireplace. The house warmed and the fresh scent of the Christmas tree filled the air. A check of the empty refrigerator convinced her that dinner with Ruth was a great idea.

Later, the four friends relaxed around the fireplace in the Borovski living room, each privately determined to ignore their unspoken grief on this first New Year's Eve without Jacob. Quietly at ease, they sipped after dinner liqueurs, savoring the Beethoven piano concerto on the audio system and the warm glow of the fire.

"Your phone message implied you wanted to talk, Ruth. Anything happen at school while we were away?" Nancy asked idly.

"Nothing much. The lab was very quiet. The campus was essentially deserted. I finished the final draft of the paper I'm presenting at the ACS meetings next week in Chicago. Paul is co-author on the paper, and both he and Anton will be at the meeting with me. I'm looking forward to it."

She changed the subject. "I've been monitoring Kevin Parks' progress as a patient in the psychiatric unit at Essex—by the way, he's coming along well, according to Jerry Siegel. You might be interested to know that when Kevin was admitted, he asked me to collect some papers from his room at

Mrs. Ledbetter's. I brought them back here for safekeeping but didn't get a chance to look at them until Christmas Day. I assumed it was data related to his doctoral thesis.

"When I visited him on Christmas Eve, he asked me to take a look at his work. The data he was so concerned about was research he'd been doing on toxic chemical contamination. That topic is completely unrelated to his dissertation research.

"From what I can gather, he responded to Jacob's death by somehow convincing himself that toxic chemicals were an important factor in his illness. This notion is the source of the full-blown obsession that Jerry Siegel is helping him deal with.

"Anyway, I spent Christmas afternoon reviewing the papers I collected from Kevin's room."

She summarized Kevin's research.

"I have no idea whether what he's collected makes sense or not," she concluded. "This topic really requires the expertise of an environmental health expert, not a graduate student or a polymer chemist like myself.

"So why not simply turn the papers over to someone who can evaluate them?" Dick asked.

"I can do that, of course. However, I promised Kevin I'd safeguard his papers. He wants to keep this confidential and I don't want to violate his trust, especially since it's related to his psychiatric problems," Ruth said.

"What intrigued me about his research was that in the middle of this stack of papers, I came across a list of names—including Jacob's and some other current and former faculty members. Many of the people on the list have died. Others have left Cabot and taken jobs elsewhere. Let me get the list."

She went to the study, returning with a folded sheet of lined paper, and she handed it to Dick. He glanced at the paper, shrugged and passed it on to Nancy, who checked the names carefully. "I recognize just about every name," she said finally. "You're right, these are faculty who came to Cabot around 1965 with Jacob and me. I would guess they probably came between 1965 and 1969. I think there are a few administrative staff mixed in with the faculty."

Leaning over the back of Nancy's chair, Ruth pointed to the list. "Notice there's a second date inserted after some of the names.

"Beside Nancy's name is only one date—1965. But there are two dates beside Jacob's name—1965 in the first column and April 14, over on the far right. That's the date he died—a date I won't forget. That's why I looked at the list more closely. Joe Santi and Beth Ferguson are on the list. It looks like they also joined the faculty in 1965," she pointed out the dates in the first column. "Didn't Beth die about ten years ago from cancer? And we all know that Joe died back in 1981 from cancer."

Ruth handed the paper across the coffee table to Hillary. Intrigued, she set down her drink and examined the list closely. "This could be a list of faculty who came to Cabot between 1965 and 1969 and who have either died or moved away," she speculated, handing the paper back to Nancy.

"Look," Nancy pointed out, "some fairly recent dates are inserted after faculty who haven't worked at the university for years. See, here's Gabby Fotanzi. She left here more than twenty years ago, after she was denied tenure. Kevin Parks can't possibly know her. He would have been just a child when she was here."

"Look here," said Nancy, excited now. "There's a fairly recent date beside her name. The last I heard, she was working at a small college outside Chicago," she recalled. "I got Christmas cards and notes from her for a few years after she left Hillsdale. Then we lost touch with each other. We probably haven't been in contact for at least ten years. I'm not ready to speculate about what this second date means," she said.

"But why would Kevin develop this list? What possible interest or connection can he have with these people, except for Jacob, of course?" Hillary interjected.

"I was going to ask Kevin directly when I visited him the day after Christmas," said Ruth, "but when I mentioned the list to Jerry Siegel, he asked me not to discuss anything even remotely connected with Jacob's death. He said it might set back his recovery. Kevin hasn't brought up anything about his papers or research since I told him three weeks ago that the university agreed to extend the due date for his dissertation."

"I'll phone Gabby tomorrow and find out if anyone from the university has contacted her recently," Nancy volunteered.

"Good idea. A phone call will probably clear it up," agreed Dick.

The next afternoon a digitized voice informed her that Gabriela Fotanzi's phone was no longer in service. She made a mental note to try to track down Gabby on the Internet.

Chapter 24

A heavy downpour shrouded the campus in a gloomy mid-afternoon twilight. February had been a cold and miserable month, typical of late winter in Hillsdale.

Nancy Atherton's mood matched the weather. She hurried along the broad sidewalk between Connors Hall and Old Main, head bent against the wind and rain, an umbrella and her raincoat providing scant protection against the elements. She pulled open the side door to the administration building and climbed the narrow rear stairs to President Larry Northrop's private offices, stowed her rain gear in the visitors' closet, and greeted the President's administrative assistant, Jane Foley.

"He's running only five minutes behind schedule," said Jane. "You're next on today's agenda." Ten minutes later Jane ushered her into the office, closing the door softly behind her.

Larry Northrop stepped from behind his desk, a warm smile welcoming his old friend and colleague. Nancy and he had been close professional colleagues and friends for several decades, their relationship becoming more formal after Larry became President in 1980.

A technocrat and professor of both physics and electrical engineering, Larry rose through the faculty ranks before turning to administration. An international authority on high-speed semiconductor devices, he pioneered research essential to the computer revolution. For ten years Northrop pursued a typical academic career of teaching, research and consulting. In 1975 when he was appointed Vice-President for Academic Affairs, he abandoned his academic lifestyle and took on the role of senior administrator.

He came to enjoy his administrative duties and developed a strong leadership style. In 1980, when the former President retired, Larry Northrop became the unanimous choice as Cabot University's sixth President. Northrop honed his skills as a superb administrator, fundraiser and advocate for the university. His organizational strengths, keen intellect and bold academic strategies brought prestige and recognition to Cabot University. Under his leadership, the school entered a period of dynamic growth and became recognized as one of the country's elite universities.

Larry led Nancy to the leather sofas in front of the handsome fieldstone fireplace whose light and warmth helped cut the gloom. Nancy moved quickly to the purpose of the meeting.

"Larry, I want to alert you to a matter that has troubled several of us recently. We think it's serious enough to bring to your attention."

Larry regarded her quizzically. "I'll admit the staff was a bit curious about your visit, especially when you declined to tell Jane the purpose of the meeting. She is getting quite a reputation as my gatekeeper. Obviously, Nancy, my door is always open to you. What's the problem?"

"Unfortunately, the problem may relate indirectly to Jacob Borovski's illness and death." Northrop settled back on the sofa, arms folded. "Larry, recall that after Jacob died you authorized and a team conducted a thorough search of his laboratory and office area to see whether some kind of chemical contamination might have contributed to his illness?"

"Yes, of course. Didn't Ruth and the Borovski sons participate?"

"Right."

He leaned forward. "The search turned up nothing. Everyone was satisfied that lab chemicals were not a factor in his death. Why do you bring that up now, almost a year later?" Larry's smile and obvious puzzlement took the edge off his words.

She sighed, and then plunged ahead. "It's hard to discuss this without seeming melodramatic—even a bit paranoid. However, several of us—my husband, Ruth Borovski and some others—believe there may be a problem traceable to this campus that contributed to not only Jacob's death, but also to the deaths of an unusually large number of other faculty and staff."

Northrop raised an eyebrow.

"Recently, we analyzed some data, using rather sophisticated statistical models. Our results tentatively indicate that the number of cancer deaths among faculty and staff here at Cabot is much higher than national and regional norms published by the Centers for Disease Control in Atlanta. The studies also suggest that the number of cancer deaths is too large to be a random happening—bad luck, if you will."

Northrop absorbed the information without comment. Finally he said quietly, "Nancy, if I understand your implication, this is a very serious matter. What objective data can you possibly have uncovered to substantiate it?"

There was no turning back. Nancy took a deep breath, surprised at the tension she felt and at the sudden change in the tone of the discussion. "This is a preliminary study. Admittedly, more work needs to be done. That's why I came to you. Obviously, we need to maintain complete confidentiality about this until we evaluate the dimensions of the problem and perhaps work out a plan to deal with it. We've traced some data back more than thirty years."

"You're not authorized to access the university's personnel records." Northrop interrupted her coldly. "Those records are confidential under federal and state privacy laws. Faculty members have no legal right to the kind of information you apparently obtained for your study. I need to know who violated university regulations and exactly how you got your hands on confidential data."

"Larry, let me assure you that our information was obtained outside the university," she lied. "We haven't violated any laws, but we do need your authorization to develop more detailed data from university files. That's why I asked for this meeting," she said evenly.

"Let me summarize where we are at this point." She redirected the discussion. "We have evidence suggesting that an unusually large number of faculty and staff who came to Cabot in the 1960s have died of various types of cancer. We don't want to be alarmists, but our initial studies show that cancer deaths at Cabot University are more than five times the expected number based on age, sex and other factors. Further, we've informally traced a number of faculty and staff who came to Cabot in the 1960s and who left the campus for one reason or another—resignations, failure to earn tenure, the usual reasons. Several of those faculty have either died from cancer or been treated for cancer. In our opinion, the clustering of cancers here at Cabot may—and I emphasize the word may—represent a cancer hot spot. And that leads us to question whether these cancers may be due to some source of contamination."

Northrop tried to interrupt, but Nancy overrode him, determined to lay the whole story on the table.

"Let me finish, Larry. After we identified the high rate of cancers on campus, we tried to pinpoint the locations on campus where these people worked. The objective, of course, was to see whether the cancers were clustered in a confined area. To try to pinpoint a source of contamination. Either because we don't have enough information or because there is no clustering, we haven't made much progress on that," she admitted.

Northrop tried to interrupt her again. He failed. Nancy was on a roll.

"We also briefly studied the number of deaths from heart disease," she continued. "Most of us have been on the faculty for a long time. We know everyone. It wasn't hard to identify people who died of heart attacks and strokes. The incidence of heart disease at the university contrasts quite dramatically with deaths from cancer. Deaths from heart disease appear to be normal for the age groups examined (people on campus now in their fifties and sixties). We concluded that the number of cardiac deaths is normal for the population studied."

She paused and took a deep breath.

"Well, Nancy, you and your friends certainly have been busy," said Northrop dryly. "Your assumption that some sort of serious health hazard exists on campus takes some getting used to. In fact, before I give any credence to your studies, I'll have to review the data myself and have the staff evaluate your analytical models. I assume you're prepared to turn over the information for the university to examine."

Nancy anticipated the request and stalled. "I can't promise to share our information until I consult with the others. I don't have to remind you," she continued, "that Ruth Borovski is a superb scientist and also knowledgeable in statistics. And she has professional colleagues across the country who can supplement and validate her work. My husband and Hillary Gardner are physicians with in-depth medical knowledge of cancer, heart disease and other serious diseases. All of us are utterly convinced that a serious problem may exist. We want your cooperation in gathering more data for analysis.

"We'd like a cooperative effort to begin right away," she continued. "Surely the university wants to get to the bottom of this as much as we do. In our view, the evidence gathered so far is compelling enough to warrant further work. That's why I requested this meeting and why I didn't discuss the subject with your staff."

Larry Northrop gazed into the fire, calmly reviewing his options, considering alternative strategies. He could not appear unresponsive to the group's concerns, although his initial reaction was to dismiss out of hand the notion that a serious, ongoing, health problem existed on his campus. The issue had been investigated in the past with negative results. These people just couldn't seem to drop the matter.

On the other hand, given the stature and reputations of those apparently involved, he couldn't treat the matter lightly. If Nancy's assertions were shown to have substance, the students, faculty and staff of the university may be in jeopardy. He had a legal and ethical obligation to deal with the issue.

He returned to his earlier question. "Where did you find your data, Nancy? Surely you don't expect me to have any confidence in data from an unknown source. Exactly how did you track down people who left Cabot University years ago? I can't accept your findings, even if they are preliminary, without knowing your sources."

"Our sources are confidential," she understood exactly what Larry was trying to do. "We believe the data are accurate. Surely you know I wouldn't bring unreliable information to your attention. You know me better than that," she responded angrily.

"We need access to the administrative computer system to verify whatever data are on file relating to deceased faculty. Obviously, we understand the need for others to verify our work before we go public with it. We welcome your support and collaboration to get to the bottom of this." She ignored the frown on Northrop's face.

"That's why we've come to you directly. We want an internal investigation and analysis. We could assist your staff, save some time," she volunteered. "Searching the university's personnel records for the last three decades is not a trivial task, I know. If you authorize the analysis, Ruth and I will set aside some time and work on it very quietly. If you want staff personnel to conduct the work, that's your decision, although there's a risk the study will leak to the public."

He nodded, a small smile forming. As usual, Nancy had her options covered before she came to him. A professor of management, she was clearly capable of reviewing and analyzing the data. Ruth Borovski or her friends could manage scientific aspects of the analysis. The real issue was whether to bring his own administrative people into the loop or allow Ruth and Nancy direct access to the personnel records they sought and let them conduct their own analysis.

"Let me think about how I want to proceed, Nancy," he rose from the sofa, signaling the end of the meeting.

"I intend to get to the bottom of this issue once and for all," he assured her. "That's the least I can do to honor Jacob's memory, although I doubt that anything of substance will be found. After all, we've looked for contamination in the past and found nothing. Let me deal with the data acquisition and privacy issues and I'll get back to you shortly."

"Thank you, Larry. We appreciate your willingness to listen." They shook hands somewhat formally as she left the office.

Nancy gathered her raincoat and umbrella and headed across the Commons to Ruth's office in Starrett Science Center. She found her colleague in her lab and quickly summarized her meeting with the President.

"Let's give Larry a week to get back to me," said Nancy. "If we don't get a response, I'll phone his office and apply some pressure."

"I think Larry will accept our offer to conduct the computer analysis. That's preferable to bringing other administrative people into the loop," said Ruth.

They were wrong.

Ten minutes after Nancy left the President's office, Tyler Hutchins, Vice-President of Administration and Finance, entered Northrop's office. After a brief private conversation with Northrop, he left through the outer office, sweat beaded on his shiny forehead and his normally fleshy face was flushed. Porky Hutchins clearly was agitated.

Five days later, Nancy received a voice mail message from the President directing her to call for an appointment as soon as possible. His prompt response was encouraging.

Chapter 25

Nancy's eleven o'clock appointment with Larry Northrop was delayed twenty minutes because the President was running behind schedule. Seated in the outer office, she watched with amusement as Tyler Hutchins rushed past Jane Foley and barged unannounced into the President's office. He was carrying a sheaf of papers that looked like computer printouts. Shortly thereafter, the Director of Human Resources joined the group in the President's office.

As she waited, Nancy reviewed her long relationship with Tyler Hutchins, Cabot University's current Vice-President of Finance and Administration, and one of the most powerful administrators on campus. Universally detested by faculty and students alike, Hutchins had been an administrator for nearly thirty years. She recalled vividly the day in 1970 when Hutchins earned his brutally descriptive nickname. An anonymous student had angrily shouted him down during the antiwar rally following the Kent State killings, calling him Porky. Hundreds of students took up the nickname. From then on, Tyler Hutchins was called Porky behind his back by students and faculty alike.

Nancy suspected he was well aware that the entire campus community called him Porky. The nickname matched his demeanor and basic nature. Short and heavy set, he had the pink, delicate skin of one who had not spent much time at the beach. Hutchins bore an uncanny resemblance to that most maligned of farm animals. With advancing age, the deep-set eyes, nearly lost in folds of fat, were magnified by thick glasses. A bushy mustache failed to soften the flat nose and prominent nostrils above a leering mouth. A crudely concealed bald spot completed the image.

Never known for his charisma or sense of humor, Tyler Hutchins had been a pompous, pretentious and overweight junior faculty member in the Psychology Department. Despite having joined the faculty along with Nancy and Jacob in 1965, he was never part of the faculty group that had risen through the academic ranks, developing national and international reputations in the process. His academic career was singularly mediocre, his teaching the butt of crude jokes by students, his professional research a blank page.

Rumored to be a favorite of several influential local politicians, Tyler Hutchins received tenure in 1970, not because of his academic and research achievements, but based upon his political connections. His political cronies convinced then-President Jackson Starrett to grant Porky a lifetime tenure appointment and the rank of Associate Professor. His research record was a glaring shortcoming that might have been overlooked had he not posted an equally dismal record in the classroom. From his first semester on campus, he had not related well with students. They despised him and went to great lengths to avoid his classes. His assessment of most students' academic potential was equally low.

Having secured tenure, Hutchins set about climbing the administrative ladder, using his political connections to grease an appointment as Assistant Comptroller. Totally ignorant of the financial workings of a university, he spent the next fifteen years learning the language of finance, ingratiating himself with a series of equally incompetent administrators including Jackson Starrett, the university's President during the turbulent years between 1965 and 1980. While other administrators managed the day-to-day complex internal functions, Hutchins curried political favor, succeeding first at the local level and subsequently with the state politicians in Harrisburg.

His tireless cultivation of politicians brought increasing power and influence within the university. When financial support for higher education became increasingly important, Hutchins became the university's point man with the state legislature. He was a familiar figure lurking in the halls of the capitol, hanging out in the local watering holes frequented by politicians.

He accompanied the President to Harrisburg where lobbying the legislature for additional funds was an important priority, especially when Cabot University became part of Pennsylvania's public university system during the 1980s. Members of the education and appropriations committees frequently dined with Hutchins, allowing him to pick up the tab. His success in extracting generous public support for the university assured him an increasingly powerful role in university affairs.

Two years ago the university trustees promoted Hutchins to Vice-President of Administration and Finance in a general reorganization of administrative functions. The faculty viewed his promotion as evidence that people do indeed rise to their level of incompetence. Nancy, among others, wondered aloud what managerial lapse led the President to appoint Hutchins to the second most powerful post at the university. Porky had wandered far from his academic position in the Psychology Department. Nancy smiled to herself. The skills of a psychologist might be essential for survival in a top administrative post in academe.

The meeting in the President's office finally ended and the principals filed out. Hutchins, whose battles with Nancy Atherton over the years were legendary among the faculty, barely nodded as he left.

Five minutes later, Nancy was ushered into the President's office.

"Thanks for coming by on such short notice," the President greeted her. Nancy was not surprised that Larry Northrop seemed more businesslike today.

"I appreciate your getting back to me so quickly, Larry," she responded cordially. "How do you want to proceed with the analysis and investigation?"

"First, let me explain what I've done since you brought this matter to my attention." He returned to his desk, motioning her to a seat across from him. Nancy sensed that this would not be a repeat of the friendly fireside chat they had enjoyed the week before.

"I asked Tyler Hutchins to have Mary McGraw in Human Resources prepare an analysis and summary of employee deaths from all causes at the university over the last thirty years. I didn't discuss your concerns in detail with either Tyler or Mary. They spent several days reviewing old records and produced a summary report this afternoon—just a few minutes ago, in fact. He, Mary and I went over the information together. Here is what they found. I have no reason to doubt their findings," he reached for a printout.

"To summarize the results, there doesn't appear to be an unusual number of deaths of faculty and staff from any cause during the last five years," he said, flipping the pages. "Tyler says the oldest records—those before 1975—are in long-term storage or have been destroyed. In any event, they're not in the computer system. Therefore, we can't analyze any data prior to 1975. Still, there's no evidence of an unusual number of deaths from cancer over the period analyzed. If you're relying on memory and anecdotal evidence to build your theory and analysis, it can't be verified," he concluded.

"In order to completely respond to your concerns, I also asked Tyler to check the university's records on industrial accidents, specifically looking for instances of chemical contamination in the labs by students or faculty. His review turned up nothing over the past fifteen years. Sure, we've had accidents on campus, but Cabot University has one of the best overall safety records in the country when it comes to work related accidents and campus safety.

"In summary, there's nothing to worry about either from chemical contamination or plain vanilla industrial accidents in our laboratories. We have a superb safety record. I'm proud of it." He set aside the stack of printouts. Fingers forming a tent under his chin, he awaited her reaction.

Nancy was silent, disappointed but not surprised.

"Perhaps you and Ruth are having a delayed reaction over Jacob's death," he suggested, finally breaking the silence. "His loss was a serious blow to the university and to many of us personally. It's not surprising that you and others would have difficulty adjusting to his death. He was a powerful force on this campus. His absence continues to be felt."

Nancy remained silent, waiting for him to continue.

"My advice to you and your associates is to put this matter behind you and get on with the business of teaching your students and conducting the research that is so important to the university." Larry Northrop smiled thinly.

The President's conclusions were not unexpected. Nancy had prepared for this meeting, privately convinced that the official university response would be to deny that a problem existed. She was certain, however, that the last thing Larry wanted was regulatory agencies or the media to get wind of the group's concerns.

Her response was direct and to the point.

"Perhaps I didn't make myself clear last week," she said quietly. "We have enough evidence to warrant a more thorough examination of university records. We believe our data are reliable enough to take to OSHA and we're prepared to begin the process right now. We would prefer to keep this confidential until we can independently examine the university's records. We could narrow our search to specific records that we want to verify. However, if you won't allow us to review those records, we will go forward without that review.

"Frankly, I don't care if university records are in long-term storage and not on your computers. We've offered to conduct a targeted study at no expense to the university. This isn't a trivial matter, and we believe you have an obligation to facilitate an internal investigation of the records. We're confident it will confirm what our external analysis already shows."

"Nancy, I've just told you that we've completed an internal review that supports my conclusion that nothing is amiss," Larry Northrop angrily interrupted her, slapping his hand on the pile of computer printouts.

"I'm not convinced, Larry," Nancy said coldly. "We want to review the data independently. However, we will go public based solely on our own data, if necessary.

"Let me renew our offer to conduct an objective internal analysis and evaluation on a pro bono basis," she concluded on a more conciliatory note.

She had gone too far.

Larry Northrop understood precisely the implications of her thinly veiled threat. The issue had just escalated to a higher level. Nancy recognized the warning signs that Larry Northrop was rapidly losing control of his legendary temper.

She tried conciliation one last time.

"Larry, we're trying to protect the university from publicity that might be very damaging. Frankly, I don't understand why you want to disregard the information we've gathered."

"Because whatever data you've gathered is inaccurate and unreliable, Nancy. And you refuse to reveal its sources and your methodology. I've reviewed all the available data with Tyler and Mary," he said heatedly. "Their work was thorough and their conclusions were straightforward. Your concerns have no validity. Speaking for the university, I consider the matter closed." His grim demeanor spoke volumes. Further argument was futile.

The President's condescending tone infuriated Nancy, and fueled her resolve.

"If that's the university's decision, I promise you that federal and Pennsylvania OSHA agencies and other available sources will be notified. We intend to get to the bottom of this. The issue won't be ignored," she warned.

"Whatever," he said with a dismissive wave of his hand.

The interview concluded, President Northrop sat at his desk as Nancy left his office.

Nancy was badly shaken. She had hoped to convince Larry to provide the necessary records, if only to protect his own reputation and keep the issue confidential. Ruth, Dick and Hillary had doubted that Larry would cooperate, while agreeing that the offer had to be made. They were right. Nancy clearly had misjudged Northrop. She would not make that mistake again.

She ignored the sunny skies and the warm breeze hinting of spring as she hurried across campus to Starrett Science Center. The sidewalks were crowded with students and faculty, some heading toward classes, others toward the Student Center for lunch. Entering the building, she crossed the lobby, skirting the enormous two-story bronze rendition of the DNA double helix molecule that dominated the area. Pushing her way into an already crowded elevator, she punched the fourth floor button.

She found Ruth and Kevin Parks in Ruth's office, totally absorbed in a computer printout on the desk. Kevin Parks, disheveled and unkempt as ever, his face once again concealed behind a full dark beard, was speaking excitedly, his black felt pen slashing across columns of data. Their concentration was so complete that both were startled as Nancy entered the room.

"Sorry to interrupt, but I have a one o'clock class and we need to talk," said Nancy, pointedly ignoring Kevin.

"Is this about your meeting with Larry?" Ruth asked softly.

"Right. It wasn't a great success."

Kevin watched the exchange between the two professors, openly curious. Nancy intercepted his gaze and wondered whether he realized that his own cryptic notes had been the focus of the meeting.

"Please excuse us for few minutes." Ruth handed the printout to Kevin. "Take this back to the lab and review the items we've marked," she directed.

"Then make the revisions and run the program again with your new data. I'll meet you in the lab shortly."

Kevin gathered his data, stuffed it into his backpack and left. Ruth shut the door behind him.

"What happened? Judging from your expression, I suspect Larry Northrop wants no part of any investigation."

"You and Dick and Hillary were right. He won't cooperate. He also brought in two more administrators, Tyler Hutchins and Mary McGraw from Human Resources. Larry apparently asked them to review the university's data and report back to him. They've convinced him there's no problem. By the way, records before 1975 aren't stored on the administrative computer. They're in long-term storage, and Larry has no intention of digging for more data.

"Our esteemed leader," she continued, "added insult to injury by implying that you and I may be experiencing a delayed reaction to Jacob's death. Wouldn't you know he'd resort to sexist condescension," she seethed.

"The bottom line, however, is that we won't be getting any corroborating data from the administration. Either we continue this on our own, and that's probably a dead end, or we follow through on my threat to contact the federal and state OSHA and try to get an external investigation going.

"The fact is, I really don't want to go public with this just yet," said Nancy. "I'm really angry, Ruth—first because I lost my temper when I realized that Larry wouldn't help us, and also because he was so damned condescending."

"Don't blame yourself," Ruth interrupted. "I'm sure you handled the situation as best you could under the circumstances. If the administration won't cooperate, we do have alternatives.

"Let's get together at my house this weekend. We can sit down with Dick and Hillary and figure out how to proceed. I'm depressed, too. But I guess I didn't really expect the administration to cooperate."

* * * *

Students and faculty moving down the hall near Ruth Borovski's office ignored the bearded student slouched casually against the wall, head back, seemingly dozing. Kevin Parks heard every word of the exchange inside the office. He was elated. Ruth Borovski and Dr. Atherton were trying to persuade the administration to launch another investigation into Jacob's death. More important, they apparently had examined and were treating seriously the data he collected prior to his enforced hospital stay.

He headed down the hall to the lab, a smile lurking behind the beard. As a condition of discharge from the psychiatric unit at the medical center, he had convinced Dr. Jerry Siegel that his obsession about Dr. Jacob's death was under control. How easily fooled the psychiatrist had been! Kevin admitted he had been depressed, but he was not suffering from an obsession. He would not rest until he proved that some substance on the campus of Cabot University had killed Jacob Borovski and many others. Granted, he hadn't yet identified the deadly substance. Now, after nearly a year, others believed him. The administration's refusal to cooperate would not deter him from his search or from feeding information to the two professors who had taken up his cause.

Chapter 26

Kevin Parks first successfully hacked into the university's computer systems during his undergraduate days. Initially, administrators were lax in implementing computer security across the campus. He hung out with computer science students whose personalities and work habits matched his own. Late at night and on quiet weekends, he and a small gang of students invested hundreds of hours perusing some of the school's most confidential and sensitive data—data that was strictly off limits to students.

One summer night several years ago, his random hacking produced some priceless information. He stumbled onto the single most sensitive file in the university's network. That key file listed the computer usernames and passwords for all faculty and staff. Scanning the list of names and passwords, he jotted down President Larry Northrop's username and personal password. The password was priceless because the President could directly access all of the university's vast administrative and academic computer networks.

Most faculty and staff enjoyed limited access to specific computer systems based upon demonstrated need. As a doctoral student, Kevin was authorized to access specific internal research networks to facilitate his research. He also frequently tapped into external networks and bulletin boards relating to chemistry and physics located around the world.

During one of his first hacks, Kevin used the President's password to enter the administrative computer system, the repository for sensitive financial, administrative and personnel records. Later, he gained unauthorized access to student grades, transcripts, admission and financial aid data and other confidential student records maintained in the academic computer network. He examined student files, including the transcripts of every student enrolled at the university over the past ten years. It would have been child's play to alter grades, including his own. He didn't take advantage of the opportunity.

Cabot University, like other educational institutions, constantly upgraded its computer security measures to safeguard its confidential systems. As a standard security precaution, computer access codes were altered every three or six months. Late the previous fall, following several well-publicized electronic break-ins by student hackers at other universities, the university engaged computer consultants to evaluate its security systems. As a result, computer security was significantly upgraded. Despite the expensive precautions to prevent unauthorized access, technology specialists believed the complex computer systems and networks continued to be vulnerable to clever and determined hackers.

Engineering and computer science hackers typically consider security systems an intellectual challenge, a game of cat and mouse whose objective is to defeat the power and authority of administrators. Tiring of computer games, they spend countless hours exploring the arcane security systems in usually futile attempts to break the codes and access forbidden data. Most efforts are designed to prove the hacker's technical wizardry, not to corrupt the data or damage the systems.

Despite the fact that unauthorized access to university computer systems is illegal and subject to possible federal felony charges, a few undeterred students continue to successfully invade university, military and corporate computer systems around the country. Some, but not all, are eventually apprehended.

Many hackers believe that the severe penalties only make the game more exciting. Incidents of damaging hacking continue to surface. Among computer science students, undetected system violations continue unabated and unpunished.

After he entered graduate school, Kevin spent less time hacking computers. However, occasionally late at night and on weekends, he continued to access the university's most secure systems. He made a point of checking the President's access codes frequently, memorizing the changes as they occurred. He had no intention of allowing his hard won skills to become obsolete. For perverse reasons which Kevin himself probably could not articulate, he also periodically accessed administrative and financial data. He never altered or deleted data. Access alone was a private ego trip, a reaffirmation of his computer prowess.

Kevin did not share his secret knowledge until he met Valerie Chapman at Essex Medical Center. There, in a fit of late evening bravado, he revealed his hacking prowess, boasting of his success in breaking into administrative computer systems. After both students were discharged and returned to the university, he invited Valerie to the chemistry lab on a snowy Saturday night in February. He demonstrated how to hack the system through Ruth Borovski's personal computer. To his disappointment, Valerie displayed little interest in his hack or even perusing her own academic records or the data of friends.

*   *   *   *

Kevin sat at the computer in Ruth's lab tediously keying in arcane chemical data to test a new set of algorithms. With luck, the revisions would generate some research results his advisor would approve. Tonight he would access the administrative computer and search the personnel records even more carefully. This time, he would examine the report that administrators had produced for President Northrop. He would put his computer expertise, knowledge gained from many hours of lonely hacking, to work in a productive way.

Ruth entered the lab moments later and found him engrossed in the computer task she had assigned. He seemed energized and focused, committed to completing his research and earning his doctoral degree. Relieved that his attitude and work habits had greatly improved since his hospitalization, she felt less guilty about her role in his hospital admission and psychiatric treatment. Although Kevin would always be something of a social misfit, never completely adjusted to the world around him, she found his recent dedication to his research a hopeful sign.

Kevin glanced up as she entered, then resumed working. For the first time in weeks, he was engaged in his own chemistry research, settling down to an afternoon in the laboratory, inserting the changes his advisor had laid out for him. He would hack the administrative computer later tonight, long after Ruth had left for the day.

*   *   *   *

Fingers flying across the keyboard, he accessed the administrative computer system. Based on the conversation he had overheard outside Ruth's office the previous afternoon, the two professors wanted to corroborate the handwritten data Ruth had found in his backpack several months ago. They were unaware that the data had, in fact, been taken from one of his earlier hacks of the administrative computer. Nancy Atherton's request to examine university data was redundant. They already had the information.

Should he reveal his source? If he did, they would know he had hacked the administrative computer, a security breach they might feel obligated to report. Better to wait a few days and see what developed. Meantime, he could hack the system again and look for more complete data on the deaths of the faculty and staff he had jotted down on his handwritten list. Kevin smiled. Finally, his work was yielding results. Others were beginning to believe that Jacob Borovski's death was not simply random bad luck.

Chapter 27

Shortly before ten o'clock Kevin successfully accessed the administrative computer system using President Northrop's password. Clicking through the menu-driven command structure, he located the Human Resources Information Module. The Module's on-line Help assistance detailed the program's features and provided a key to deciphering the system's command structure. He spent fifteen minutes scanning the help section, learning how to navigate the database, identifying the files and contents of each data field and matching the codes to data fields.

Moments later he accessed the master file of deceased, former and inactive employees. He knew that Dr. Jacob joined the faculty in 1965. He identified the employment records dating from 1960. They appeared to have been scanned into the computer. But Northrop had told Nancy Atherton that records prior to 1975 were either in long-term storage or had been destroyed. Why would Northrop lie about it? Was he trying to hide something important? A careful analysis of the data in front of him might be adequate to support his theory that an unusual pattern of deaths had occurred on the campus.

He scanned the names in the master file of deceased, inactive and former employees. It took only a moment to find the column reporting the status of each name. A "D" in the column identified the person as deceased, an "L" as someone currently on paid leave, a "U" as someone on unpaid leave, and an "R" as someone who had resigned. Scrolling down through the file, he was surprised to find many names coded with a D. Some names corresponded to those he had identified during his earlier brief search, but many more names needed to be added.

He would prepare a new, more complete list. Using the system's SQL programming language, he set up a temporary file into which he copied all deceased employees' names and the vital statistics he would need. With a few keystrokes, he gathered the name, sex, social security number, last permanent address, academic department and office location by building name, floor and room number and length of employment at the university. He named the file LN1 and hid it deep inside the Human Resources Information module.

He created a second file into which he copied each dead employee's name, social security number, date of birth, date of death, cause of death and the name and address of the deceased's next of kin. He saved the file as LN2, again hiding it in the HR Information module. He would use the two files to develop a spreadsheet and manipulate and analyze the data as he saw fit.

It was too dangerous to download the two new files onto a floppy disk or print the data directly from the administrative computer to Ruth's lab computer where he was working. His hack might somehow be traceable. Ideally, he thought wryly, he should be sitting at the computer in the President's office, impossible under any circumstances.

The safest approach would be to download his new files from a computer terminal in the library's computer lab that was open to students and faculty. At this time of year the library was usually crowded with students working late into the evening. The library computer lab was open until midnight.

One more student occupying a terminal wouldn't attract much attention. He would copy the files to a floppy disk there, then return to Ruth's lab, analyze the data and print out his results on a small printer that was independent of the campus computer network.

With one final review of the data in his two files, Kevin logged off the system. He flipped off the lights in Ruth's lab, locked the door and walked across the Commons to the library. Its lights blazed a warm welcome through the spectacular two-story atrium lobby, even at eleven o'clock. He trotted up the broad steps to the building, pushed open the oversized glass doors, swiped his student ID card through the automatic entry and crossed the main lobby.

Turning left, he took the carpeted stairway to the lower level that housed the library's fifty personal computer terminals and associated printers. Although the room was designated for student use, faculty and staff frequented it as well. Anyone having access to the main library could log onto the university computer network and also gain entry to external databases and the Internet.

Perhaps fifteen students were scattered throughout the large room at this late hour. Staring intently at their monitors, they were oblivious to the activity around them. The soft hum of the equipment was interrupted by the clicking of keys as students tapped their keyboards. Occasionally, one of the printers mounted along a far wall spewed out a report into the impatient hands of a waiting student.

Kevin surveyed the room, recognized none of the students and selected a terminal several seats away from the nearest neighbor. He sat down in front of the computer. Using the President's access name and password, he quickly called up the Human Resources Information Module. In a few seconds he found the two files he had just created, checked their contents, then saved them to a floppy disk. Then he reviewed the floppy disk to assure that the information was intact. He deleted the two files LN1 and LN2 from the administrative computer network. Although the files had been automatically archived when he saved them at the lab, he knew that after a period of one week, the archived copies would be deleted from the system. If his activity remained undetected during that period, no one would know the data had been copied to an external computer.

The likelihood of detection was low. Even if the copying were discovered and found not to have been initiated by President Northrop, the computer trail would stop at this terminal in the library. By the time that unlikely event occurred, perhaps hundreds of students would have logged onto the campus computer networks via the terminal. His trail would be safely obliterated.

At eleven forty-five Kevin logged off the administrative computer, tossed the floppy disk with his purloined data into his backpack, shut down his terminal and sauntered upstairs to the library checkout area. As he moved toward the exit, he noticed a janitor beginning his evening cleanup. He waved casually to the solitary librarian staffing the checkout desk, passed through the electronic gate and left the building.

Back at the front entrance to Starrett Science Center he punched his unique six-digit access code into the black box with blinking red lights. Hearing the familiar click as the lock electronically released, he opened the heavy glass door and entered the lobby. He hesitated for a moment at the bank of elevators, then walked to the left stairwell and trotted up the four floors to Ruth's laboratory.

Entry to individual labs and offices in Starrett Science Center was restricted after seven o'clock in the evening. Authorized graduate students gained access to a lab or office by swiping their coded plastic ID card through a card reader mounted on the wall by each door. Like other doctoral students who often worked late, he had access to the building and to his own and Dr. Borovski's laboratory. He could not gain entry to her office down the hall nor to any other labs and offices in the building. He swiped his card through the card reader and heard the familiar click as the lab door unlocked.

Entering Ruth's darkened lab, he flipped the switches for one bank of lights and made his way among the mass of equipment and lab benches to Ruth's personal computer. He turned on the computer and the small inkjet printer attached to it. After a moment's delay, the familiar Windows screen appeared. He inserted the disk into the drive and selected the spreadsheet program icon from the desktop screen. He copied his two files containing the personnel data into the spreadsheet. He waited a few seconds while the data from LN1 was read into the spreadsheet and watched as the data file appeared on the screen.

The spreadsheet was a jumble of data. It would have to be reformatted to be useful. He was satisfied, however, that the data transfer was successful. With some formatting changes, Kevin could manipulate the information and prepare a useful analysis. He saved the new spreadsheet file back to his floppy disk, then followed the same procedure with the LN2 file. He merged the two files into one large file for analytical purposes.

Two hours later, his work complete, he printed the results along with copies of each data file. He saved five new spreadsheets back to his floppy disk, and made a second complete backup of his data. When he was certain that all traces of his work on Ruth's computer could not be detected or reconstructed, he turned off the computer and printer.

It was after one o'clock when he trekked across the deserted campus toward University Avenue. In the distance, the library lights had been extinguished. The campus settled down for the night. Walking along the side of Old Main, he glanced toward the familiar corner office of President Larry Northrop. Lights blazed from that office and the outer office. His heart skipped a beat. Well, he thought, I'm not the only person working late. Let's hope the President wasn't trying to access the computer system while I was using his password. It was too late to worry about that now.

Backpack slung over his shoulder, he headed downtown. Ten minutes later he was back in his room at Mrs. Ledbetter's. He dropped his pack into the corner, removed his running shoes and down jacket and collapsed across the bed. Pulling a soiled blanket over his body, too exhausted to strip to shorts and T-shirt, he fell asleep.

*   *   *   *

Awakening at dawn, Kevin dragged himself out of bed and groped for the printouts in his backpack. He turned on his bedside lamp, spread the papers across the bed and reviewed last night's work. For the next hour he pored over his analysis, comparing the data hacked from the Human Resources database with the scientific data on the incidence of cancer he'd gathered over the past several months off the Internet.

Shortly after seven o'clock, he phoned Valerie Chapman. "Sorry to wake you up, Val, but I've got something important to talk about. How about meeting me in the campus cafeteria in half an hour?"

"Are you treating me to breakfast?" she asked sleepily.

"Yeah, sure. Just be there."

Thirty minutes later he entered the noisy cafeteria, crowded with students cramming breakfast before heading for classes. Valerie had saved a seat for him at an empty table overlooking the terrace. Waving a greeting, he pushed through the food line, grabbed two bagels and two cups of coffee, paid the cashier and headed for her table. Dropping his backpack on the floor, he greeted this strange, beautiful girl who was now his friend and confidant.

"Thanks for coming," he began.

"You're welcome," she bit into her bagel.

"I got the data Dr. Atherton asked the President for, and I've spent most of the night analyzing it."

"I thought she wanted personnel data, the kind that's confidential. How did you get your hands on it?"

"You weren't interested when I tried to show you how to hack the administrative computer. Don't ask me to explain now, you don't want to know. What's important is that the data confirm what I've been saying all along. A lot of people at Cabot University have died of cancer—I found a bunch of other names last night, far more than I had on my original list.

"The cancer deaths on campus since 1975 are about eight times the expected number based on the national and regional statistics I compiled months ago. I'm sure that Dr. Jacob and the others were killed by something on this campus, and I'll bet you that it's some kind of chemical or environmental contamination."

"Aren't you jumping to conclusions awfully fast, Kevin?" Her skepticism surprised him.

He frowned. "Look, Val, you're no scientist and you hate math. You can't judge the data. Trust me, I know the evidence is strong. Now I need some ideas on how to deal with this."

She looked across the table. "My advice is simple, Kevin. If you think this information is really important, you've got to show it to Dr. Borovski and Dr. Atherton. And if you do that, there's no way you can hide the fact that you've stolen data from the university's computers. And if the administration ever finds out, you'll be in really deep trouble," she said seriously, watching his reaction.

"Come on, Val, cut the lecture. Help me figure out how to tell them what I've got without letting them know I hacked the admin computer."

"You're the genius, you figure it out," she retorted. "Get real. Maybe it's time you told them the whole story—what you've been up to for the past few months." She rose and left the cafeteria without a backward glance.

Chapter 28

"Where did you get this data, Kevin?" Ruth Borovski asked angrily.

"I thought you wanted it. Why worry about where I got it?" Kevin didn't expect applause from his advisor, but he wasn't prepared for her violent reaction.

"This must have come from the administrative computer system," her voice rose. "Don't you understand that unauthorized access to confidential computer files can lead to felony charges? Do you want to completely destroy your career at Cabot University and possibly end up in prison?"

She leaned back in her desk chair. "I shouldn't even be looking at this data because I'd be considered an accessory to the theft. Kevin, you've put both of us in a terrible position." She took a deep breath, her lips a thin line.

"Why don't you just check out the data," he grumbled sullenly. "When you see these results, maybe you'll decide a computer hack isn't such a big deal. Just look at the data and my analysis," he pleaded. "I haven't had time to analyze it completely, but I've reached a few obvious conclusions."

Glaring at him over her half glasses, she reluctantly leaned forward over the sheaf of printouts and began to read. Silently, she flipped through the printouts, casually reviewing Kevin's work. Despite her anger, she began to examine the data more closely. Moments later, now fully absorbed, she jotted occasional notes in the margins of the spreadsheets littering her desk. For ten minutes only the rustle of papers broke the silence in the office as she sorted through his analysis. Absently, she reached for her coffee mug, sipping the dark brew.

Finally, she settled back in her chair and regarded Kevin. "This is some piece of work," she said quietly. "I wish you were as thorough in your dissertation research as you apparently have been with this data."

"What do you think?"

She sighed. "If these data and your analysis are as reliable as I believe they are, we may be sitting on a real time bomb."

"I had to show it to you, Dr. Borovski," Kevin's dark eyes gleamed. "It proves I was right all along—something on this campus is causing cancer—there are simply too many deaths for them to be random events. I can prove that Dr. Jacob and a lot of others didn't have to die."

"Wait, Kevin," Ruth interrupted. "If your analysis is correct, you may have identified a serious problem, perhaps linked to the campus, possibly even to this building. But this doesn't prove that Jacob and the others you've identified were victims of toxic contamination. This may be the first step in an investigation. On its face, it proves nothing."

"But we're onto something big. I'd bet my life on it! Don't you want to get to the bottom of this?"

"Of course I do. Granted, you may have identified a problem here on campus. But Dr. Jacob and the others are gone; you can't alter that reality. You must accept Jacob's death and deal with it, however difficult that is. You can't dwell on the past," she said more gently.

"I know." His dark eyes teared and he glanced away, struggling to regain control. "During my stay in the hospital Dr. Siegel helped me begin to deal with it. I've accepted it—at least intellectually—in my head, I mean. Sometimes, though, I get really down. It's hard. I just want to talk to him, get his advice, hang out with him in the lab.

"Don't misunderstand. You've helped a lot—you probably saved my life when you got me admitted to the hospital. And I will finish my dissertation. I'll prove to you and everybody else that I can do it.

"But you can't just ignore what I've found," he pleaded with her, pointing to his data. "Everybody on campus—students, faculty and staff— may be at risk. If you ignore what I've found, you and Dr. Atherton are as guilty as the fools in the administration who've hidden the problem all this time. You'll be part of this cover-up!"

"Once again, Kevin, you're jumping to unwarranted conclusions," Ruth said calmly. "It's premature to attribute any motives to the administration— good or bad—at this point. All we have is some statistical data that seems to suggest an unusual number of cancer deaths among people who worked here. You're not being logical; you're ignoring your scientific objectivity because Jacob was involved. We've got a long way to go before we can attribute these deaths to a cancer hot spot. And we can't presume that the deaths were caused by an environmental problem, nor can we assume the administration has deliberately hidden the problem."

He stared at her in disbelief.

"Don't misunderstand, Kevin," she tried to soften her criticism. "I've known Larry Northrop for many years. He's an ethical man who cares deeply about this campus and everyone here. Although he resisted our requests for information, I don't think there's anything evil in his actions. He wouldn't knowingly put anyone in jeopardy. He thinks this issue is irrelevant."

"But he wouldn't give Dr. Atherton access to the data she asked for," Kevin retorted stubbornly.

"How do you know about that?"

"I was here the other day when she told you," he mumbled.

She seemed satisfied with his lame explanation.

"I prefer to think President Northrop believes this is not important enough to pursue any further," she said firmly, "and until we have evidence to the contrary, don't assume any evil intent by the administration. Let's not waste time trying to sort through motives. However, I won't be satisfied until we have a complete explanation of these findings. I can promise you that."

Ruth reached into a desk drawer for a manila folder. She put Kevin's data into the folder and opened her briefcase.

"Kevin, thank you for bringing this information to me. I don't know—I don't want to know—how you managed to get your hands on the data," she touched the folder. "You realize, of course, that the personnel records of faculty and staff are confidential right along with all student records, including academic grades. You can be subject to criminal prosecution if you broke into the administrative computer."

She smiled grimly as she put the folder into her briefcase. "If you got these records illegally, I'm probably an accessory to your wrongdoing because I've just reviewed them. However, I guess it's too late to worry about that now. We need to consider what to do next. I'll discuss this with Dr. Atherton and perhaps a few other people."

She opened her office door. "If you'll trust me to safeguard this material, I'll take it home and study it more carefully to verify your methodology and analysis, perhaps run it by some other experts. I assume you have a backup disk for this data?"

He rummaged through his backpack, found a disk and handed it to her. "I've got another copy back in my room. Nothing is stored on a hard drive anywhere—it's all on floppies. You and I have the only two. What do you want me to do now?"

"Nothing, Kevin. Wait until I get back to you. I need a couple of days to consult with others. I'll be off campus at a conference in New York until Sunday. I won't have time to deal with this until next week.

"By the way, does anyone else know about this?" she asked.

"I told Valerie Chapman earlier today. She persuaded me to show you the data, but she wants no part of this. Unfortunately, she's doubtless figured out that I hacked the administrative computer," he said.

Ruth frowned. "Who is this girl?"

"She's an undergraduate I met at Essex Medical Center. Don't worry," he said confidently, "she won't discuss this with anybody but me. I won't involve you and the others in my hack. That's my secret. Believe me," he bragged, "if you need more data, I can get it for you."

"You've done quite enough for the moment," she responded dryly. "Kevin, I'm now involved in your wrongdoing, and if I show this data to others and take the disk and spreadsheets for safekeeping, we may both be in legal hot water."

She sighed. "What's done is done. Right now we need a strategy for proceeding. I'll try to get back to you sometime next week."

"Meantime, get back to work on your dissertation research," she directed, pointing a finger at him. "If you just concentrate your efforts, you can finish the research in a couple of months, then spend the summer writing your results. You could earn your degree by the end of August."

She ushered Kevin from her office, dialed Nancy Atherton's extension, and waited impatiently for the recorded greeting to end. "I need to talk to you." She spoke into the silence at the other end. "How about this evening at my house? If Dick and Hillary are available, would you ask them to join us? I'll make dessert and coffee. Consider it a bribe to get you all to come over," she said. "If I don't hear from you, I'll see you around eight o'clock."

Chapter 29

"Please take a look at the material Kevin Parks handed over to me this afternoon. It won't take long to review the data and spreadsheets."

"What's all the mystery about, Ruth? Can't you just tell us about it?" Hillary asked.

"No. Just read it," said Ruth. "You'll figure it out."

Half an hour later, having examined the documents and working on their second cups of coffee, the group gathered in front of a blazing fire.

"Dick, what's your opinion of this data?" Ruth greatly respected the analytical mind of Nancy's husband.

"Actually, I'm not terribly impressed," he shrugged. "It's interesting, but certainly not strong enough to accuse anyone of negligence or wrongdoing. I doubt there's anything sinister behind it. It looks rather insubstantial to me."

"I agree." Hillary Gardner closed the file and tossed it on the coffee table. "If the inference is that the university has experienced an unusual number of cancer deaths over the past few decades, these spreadsheets don't make the case, at least not to me. What's Kevin Parks trying to prove?

"One thing is certain," Hillary continued, "he apparently still hasn't gotten under control the crazy obsession that landed him in the psychiatric unit. I guess two months' hospitalization wasn't enough. Probably one of us should tell Jerry Siegel that his patient needs more help. That's one concrete step we can take.

"As for the data itself," she said, "I'd disregard it. Sure, it looks like a lot of people apparently have died from a variety of cancers while employed at the university. Granted, Kevin's preliminary statistics seem to indicate a higher incidence than normal, but I'd want more evidence than the work of a graduate student. I don't know if six or eight or ten times the normal incidence of cancer at the university implies a possible cancer hot spot or not.

"Besides, the notion of something amiss on the campus has been around for a long time." She looked over at Ruth. "The investigation right after Jacob's death wasn't the first time this issue has surfaced. I remember an incident about twenty years ago when Joe Santi died. Wasn't he a chemistry professor?"

"Yes. And his name is on Kevin's list," Ruth gestured toward the file on the coffee table. "Joe was actually the first to die from the group who came to Cabot in 1965. He died in 1978, a couple of years before Larry Northrop became President. Joe was barely forty years old. He was a brilliant teacher, an organic chemist and researcher." She gazed into the fire, recalling the tragedy two decades earlier.

"Some of the details are beginning to come back to me," said Ruth. "Jacob was worried that Joe might have died from exposure to toxic chemicals. A small group of us got together and drove to Philadelphia to discuss our concerns with the Chairman of the Board of Trustees.

"The Chairman of the Board of Trustees at the time was the President of Capital Chemicals, and Jacob knew him rather well. He used his connections with the company to arrange a meeting." She turned to Nancy. "You went with us didn't you?"

"Yes, I vaguely remember something about it," Nancy admitted. "I think only four of us went to that meeting and Jacob spoke for all of us. Your memory is a lot clearer on this than mine."

Ruth glanced at her friend. "Maybe I have more at stake than you. I think the meeting was in January and we ran into a nasty snowstorm in the Poconos. It must have been on a weekend because we visited the Chairman at his home in Bryn Mawr, I believe. We were late because of the storm, and the meeting only lasted about an hour. Then we turned around and drove home the same day."

"It's beginning to come back to me," said Nancy.

"I recall the Chairman was cordial, but cool," said Ruth. "In retrospect, it took a fair amount of arrogance, not to mention chutzpah, for us to contact the Chairman of the Board of Trustees directly. Give him credit, though," she continued, "he listened, probably because of Jacob's reputation as a scientist who was consulting with Capital at the time. Anyway, Jacob laid out our concerns in his usual forceful style," she smiled. "The rest of us just offered moral support.

"The Chairman didn't commit to anything that day, but he promised to take the matter under advisement. I do remember he chided us for failing to follow the normal administrative lines of authority. We bypassed the President and the rest of the Cabot administration at the time, a ploy that didn't endear us to any of them," Ruth chuckled.

"Our trip ultimately produced the desired result. Within a month, the university's Board of Trustees approved an investigation into the circumstances surrounding Joe Santi's death. The discussion and approval took place in executive session, so faculty and students knew nothing about it. Naturally, we didn't discuss it with the rest of the faculty.

"Jacob was in charge of the investigation. I know that he was extremely thorough. After all, if something were really amiss, all of us—faculty, staff and students—might be at risk. I was part of the team that searched every lab, every storage area. We also reviewed in detail every procedure regarding the handling, storage, even the purchase of chemicals for use on campus. That was the first time such an investigation was conducted, at least that I'm aware of," Ruth said.

Nancy broke the silence, unwilling to let the matter rest. "Maybe my memory is flawed on this, but I seem to recall that a major rumor around campus at the time was that Joe's wife, Martha, received some sort of payoff from the university. If nothing was found, why did the administration apparently give her compensation?"

"There never was any acknowledgment of a payoff to Martha," said Ruth. "That was just an unsubstantiated rumor. Still, it wouldn't surprise me if she received compensation. After all, she and Joe had three young children. Joe probably hadn't built up much in the way of savings. The Board of Trustees could authorize such payments. Perhaps they just wanted to recognize Joe's contribution to Cabot University."

"That was probably the only investigation of laboratory procedures until last summer when you led the investigation after Jacob died." Nancy said sadly. Ruth rose and stood in front of the fire, hands outstretched toward the warmth, lost in thought. With a sigh, she began gathering the empty cups and dessert plates.

"About six months after Joe died, Martha and the children moved back to the Midwest, their home before coming to Hillsdale. I think we exchanged Christmas notes for a couple of years, but that stopped a long time ago. I have no idea where she is now," she said over her shoulder, heading toward the kitchen.

Dick Atherton glanced at his watch. "It's almost midnight. Hillary and I have a seven a.m. staff meeting. He turned to his wife and Ruth. "What do you propose to do next?"

"We've got a few alternatives," said Nancy. She ticked them off. "We can do nothing. That would be easy, especially since you and Hillary aren't too impressed with the data. Or we can ask someone with expertise in this sort of thing to take a look at the data and give us an opinion. Finally, I probably could confront Larry Northrop with the data," she said, "but I hardly think that's a rational alternative, given the reaction I got last week. Furthermore, if I go to Larry, he'll know the administrative computer has been hacked.

"Ruth and I can verify that the people on Kevin's list have died. Kevin's data are reliable," Nancy reminded him.

"Whether the statistical analysis is reasonable is another question. I think the best alternative is to ask someone with expertise in statistics to evaluate the data independently. An expert wouldn't need to know the source of the data, or even the location. We can camouflage the details," Nancy said.

"It's obvious Kevin got those names from university personnel files," said Dick. "If you pass along the data for someone else to review, how are you going to protect Kevin? And what about the apparent breach of the campus computer system?" Dick asked. "Larry Northrop can't ignore that. And are you just going to ignore it?"

"For the time being, yes," Nancy retorted.

"Just a minute," said Ruth, excited for the first time all evening. "We have an expert right here on campus. John Campbell has both a Ph.D. in biology and a medical degree. I should have thought of him earlier. He's an expert on blood diseases and the interaction of the environment, pollution and disease. Why don't I talk to him, show him the analysis and ask his opinion? At least he might give us some ideas on how to proceed."

"I don't know, Ruth," Nancy said doubtfully. "John would probably realize the data relate to the campus, even if we disguise it. I know his research is highly regarded, but he would be one more faculty member with knowledge of what we're doing. It might be hard to keep it confidential. I think we should look for an expert outside the campus.

"Perhaps Paul would know someone at MIT who could do the analysis, or Anton at Berkeley," Nancy suggested.

"You two need to work it out." Dick stood up, closing out the discussion. "Hillary and I have contacts at the Centers for Disease Control in Atlanta, but I'd hesitate to submit a report compiled by a student whose data sources and research methodology are suspect. I don't recommend going that route, at least not yet."

"We obviously need to confirm Kevin's analysis," Ruth agreed. "He said he took the raw data and manipulated it using statistics he gathered from an on-line medical database and from the National Cancer Registry. While I think it's reasonably good work, I'd feel more comfortable if someone else reviewed it before we start sounding alarms with the federal or state OSHA groups.

"At times like these I really miss Jacob," Ruth said. "Although he often worked intuitively, he was a much stronger mathematician and statistical analyst than I. He could have assessed this information very quickly and judged its validity and Kevin's reliability as a statistician. He'd know exactly how to proceed."

Nancy looked up and met Dick's gaze. This was one of the few times since Jacob's death that Ruth had spoken his name directly and admitted her loss.

"Ruth, you know John Campbell better than the rest of us," said Dick. "If you think he can be trusted to keep this confidential, then show him Kevin's data and ask for his opinion. We all agree that a level of cancer deaths eight or ten times the national or regional average may be significant, if in fact, that can be verified. Another question is whether environmental factors are involved. Maybe John will have some ideas on how to proceed.

"Or call Paul and Anton. Maybe they can recommend someone qualified to offer an expert opinion on the data we have."

* * * *

"Hi, Mom," Paul Borovski recognized the caller ID number as he picked up the phone the following evening. "What's up? You never call me in the middle of the week."

"Paul, I need a favor. And please don't ask me to explain what's going on."

"Go ahead."

"Can you recommend a statistician at MIT who can review some data for me and give me an expert opinion very quickly?"

"Sure. This place is loaded with those types. But why would you need someone from here? Can't you find someone at Cabot to check your data? And what sort of data needs to be analyzed? Is it connected to your research?"

"Slow down, Paul. I don't want someone here to evaluate the data. The issue may be fairly serious. I don't intend to discuss it with you now, and it isn't connected with my research. I'll explain everything later.

"The analysis will probably require only a day. And I'll pay the going rate for a one day consulting assignment. And yes, I need the work done quickly."

"Let me ask around. I can't think of anyone offhand, so it might take a few days. How fast do you need this? It might help me line someone up if I could describe the type of statistical analysis you want."

"I can't go into detail with you, Paul. Please just find someone competent with statistical models who can spend a day analyzing some data." Ruth sounded frustrated. Paul knew better than to press her for more information.

"When you find someone, give me a call," she directed. "I'll overnight air express a package to you and you can pass it on. And please don't open the package," she warned.

"Really, Mom, you're making this seem very mysterious. Anyway, I'll do what I can and get back to you by the weekend."

"Thanks. I'll explain everything later." She hung up.

145

Chapter 30

Increasingly frustrated, Kevin awaited a response from Ruth Borovski. A week should have been ample time for her to consult with others and get back to him. He regretted confiding in her in the first place. Ruth and her friend Nancy Atherton were prominent faculty members, part of the campus establishment. Faculty, even those as responsive as his advisor, usually supported the administration on campus issues. He doubted they would oppose the President and administration on a controversial issue, particularly one that, if proven, could damage the administration's reputation.

If cancer deaths could be traced to environmental contaminants on the campus, students and faculty continued to be at risk. Nothing would be gained by waiting for his advisor's help. He would continue to search the campus on his own. Eventually, people would be forced to recognize the problem and deal with it.

*   *   *   *

Kevin hurried across campus in the cold March rain, mulling over his next move. Perhaps now was the time to visit Tony Amonte, the head custodian he worked for during his undergraduate days, the man who befriended him, who welcomed him into his home. During Amonte's decades at Cabot, he had seen the campus grow from a cluster of four buildings into a vast educational complex sprawling across more than 200 acres. He might be able to help.

Intending to visit Tony after he left the hospital, Kevin had stopped by the pizza parlor where Amonte had a part-time job working the lunch trade. The cashier told him that Tony had quit two weeks before Christmas to care for his wife, who was ill.

Now, two months later, it was time to visit Tony. Besides, he wanted to see how Rosa was coming along.

*   *   *   *

Kevin walked along the quiet street, glancing occasionally at the numbers nailed above the doorways of the modest homes. The area hadn't changed much since his undergraduate days when he visited the custodian's home weekly, often staying for supper and an evening of TV with Tony's wife and kids.

He felt guilty about not having visited the neighborhood since Tony retired. It was convenient to occasionally stop by the pizza parlor for lunch and catch up with Tony's news. He had completely lost touch with Rosa and the kids.

Located in an older, working class section of Hillsdale, the neighborhood was home to carpenters, mechanics, factory workers and semi-skilled laborers. The houses were neatly maintained, set back from the sidewalk with small plots of grass fronting tiny porches. Detached one-car garages distinguished a few homes, but most people parked their cars along the curb of the narrow street.

The street was quiet this late afternoon. Few homes showed signs of life behind the thin lace curtains. Here and there, television sets glowed through rain spattered windows as the afternoon talk shows droned on. The rain was finally easing and the sky was brightening in the west, promising better weather tomorrow.

He unlatched the gate in the low wooden fence enclosing the front yard of the cottage at number thirty-three, walked along the narrow sidewalk and up the concrete steps to the tiny stoop. Before he could knock, his old friend opened the glass storm door, stepped outside and engulfed him in a bear hug.

"Long time between visits, Kevin. How's the dissertation coming along?" Tony looked up at the slender student he had known for nearly a decade.

"Good, Tony. Sorry I haven't come to see you and Rosa in awhile. I've had a few problems. Things kind of fell apart for me."

"I know, I know—word gets around," said Tony, pulling him inside.

Kevin had forgotten how much he cared about this old man, walking painfully now, slowed by arthritic knees, the penalty for a life of manual labor. When Kevin was hired as a student janitor in a part-time campus work-study program, Tony Amonte became his first boss and, in time, his first adult friend. As head of janitorial services, he worked his student staff as hard as his full-time employees. Cabot University's buildings and grounds were meticulously maintained, enhancing the spectacular setting and adding luster to the university's academic environment.

Kevin worked on the janitorial staff in return for a waiver of his undergraduate tuition. The program was part of the university's financial assistance for needy students. Tony Amonte, an Italian immigrant, empathized with the brilliant but strange and lonely student and he took Kevin under his wing. They spent long hours together during the school year and in the summers when Kevin worked full time in the maintenance department. The three undergraduate years working for Tony taught Kevin some practical skills that would later prove invaluable. He not only learned how to repair everything from stopped up toilets to electrical light switches, he also explored every nook and cranny on the campus.

Janitorial work during the academic year presented opportunities to clean (and inspect) faculty offices, laboratories, even the computer facilities. It was during this period that Kevin obtained master keys to every building on campus, a theft that Tony may have suspected, but never confronted him with. Those keys gave Kevin and a few other student hackers access to computers that were off-limits to students. In return for access late at night and on quiet weekends when the probability of discovery was negligible, two computer science students taught Kevin the basics of hacking, a skill that would later prove invaluable.

*   *   *   *

"Come in, come in," Tony whispered, "but be quiet. I just gave Rosa her medication and she's almost asleep. Sleep is a blessing because her pain is relieved. The doctors say they can't do much for her except try to keep her comfortable. It's only a matter of days or a few weeks at most," he confided sadly.

"I'm sorry, Tony. Rosa is more of a mother to me than my own mother and I didn't even know she was sick until a few weeks ago." Kevin's dark eyes glistened in the dim light of the hallway that ran the length of the tiny home.

"I've spent the last year dealing with my own problems. I let everything else go."

The old man and the young student entered the small living room where the television set displayed a picture with the sound muted. Tony clicked the set off, motioned Kevin to a soft chair and sat down on the sofa.

"Can I get you some coffee, my boy? I remember you used to consume more coffee than anyone I ever knew."

"No, thanks," he said, looking around the familiar room. "Oh well, what the hell, I'll share a pot with you if it's no trouble."

The old man shuffled down the hall, leading the way past the bedroom where Rosa slept. The kitchen was situated at the rear of the house overlooking a small back yard and a paved alley beyond. Tony measured generous portions of coffee into the pot and as the water dripped through the grounds, the two sat down at the ancient round oak kitchen table.

Kevin glanced around the homey room that had been the scene of some of his happiest times as an undergraduate. Tony and Rosa practically adopted him during his sophomore year after he entered the student work-study program. The Amonte children were typical boisterous teenagers during those years. It was hard to realize that they were now young adults and that once plump and buxom Rosa Amonte was wasting away from cancer. A lot had changed in the past year.

"How are Tony, Jr. and Maria these days?" he began.

"Fine. Tony's got a job in Texas as an auto mechanic and Maria is finishing her freshman year at Penn State. Maybe this family will finally get its first college graduate," he said proudly. "She has the brains to do the work, and I think she'll stick with it. Tony was always crazy about cars and he seems to like Houston. His job pays pretty good. He's got a girl friend, now. He says he's happy," he shrugged. "I guess the boy just wasn't cut out for college."

He pulled two mugs from the shelf and poured the steaming coffee. He took a bag of cookies from the cupboard and brought it to the table.

"Still take your coffee black?"

"You remembered," said Kevin.

"These cookies aren't bad, but not as good as Rosa's homemade biscotti." Kevin helped himself to a second one.

"Remember when you visited years ago? We always ended up here at the kitchen table." The old man seated himself opposite Kevin. "By the way, I went to the memorial service for Dr. Borovski last spring and heard you talk. You did good."

"Thanks."

"I also heard you had some problems after Dr. Jacob died. Did you really spend some time in the loony bin?"

"Yeah." Kevin shrugged his shoulders and glanced away. "Got a little depressed. Didn't see how I could get along without Dr. Jacob. I'm okay now, though. Dr. Ruth Borovski took over as my dissertation advisor. She's been a big help. She's almost as tough as Dr. Jacob," he said ruefully. "I'll probably finish my research in the next couple of months, maybe finally get my degree the end of the summer. I may actually have to go out and work next fall," he laughed.

"Good, Kevin. Time you moved on. You been a student too long." Tony glanced out the window above the sink at the darkening sky. "You ain't here to shoot the breeze or talk about your studies, boy. What's on your mind? Tell me what's going on."

"It's a long story. Maybe I shouldn't involve you. You got a lot to deal with right now."

"Now I'm interested. Out with it," he demanded. "Rosa won't need more medication until after the eleven o'clock news. I got four hours to listen."

Thirty minutes later, Tony got up from the table and poured more coffee for Kevin and himself. He had listened closely, interrupting occasionally to clarify a point.

149

"Let me get this straight. You think some sort of toxic chemicals or other contaminants are killing people at Cabot University. Is that what you're telling me?"

"You got it."

"Well, now, that's a real stretch. You better be careful who you tell your story to or you'll land right back in the loony bin."

Tony's reaction was not what Kevin wanted to hear.

"Hear me out, dammit. I've got some statistical evidence to support my conclusions."

"I don't know anything about statistics. I just know your idea is crazy," retorted Tony.

"I'm not finished. Will you listen to me?"

"Go on."

"I showed my data to Dr. Borovski. She's taking it seriously. She and Dr. Atherton are trying to get the administration to listen. I think President Northrop is stalling, hoping the problem will go away."

"Do Professor Borovski and Dr. Atherton actually believe you?" Tony was skeptical. "This sounds like a cockamamie story if I ever heard one. And I'm surprised those two faculty are involved."

"Well, they went to the President about it. And the President refused to listen to Dr. Atherton and basically kicked her out of his office. Tony, believe me, the problem is real. We've got to identify the source of the contamination and force the university to clean it up. I figured you might have some ideas about where shit like toxic chemicals might be stored. You worked at Cabot for forty years. You know everything there is to know about the facilities. Where could it be stored?"

Kevin leaned forward, elbows on the kitchen table.

"Son, you're barking up the wrong tree. I know the procedures for getting rid of chemical waste from the labs. We've got a manual that spells it all out. The university complies with all the federal and state regulations— at least they did before I retired. I can't speak for the situation right now. I'm positive that while I worked at Cabot, there was nothing wrong with the way chemicals or other waste materials were handled."

Tony sighed. "If it'll put your mind at rest, I can go over what I know about the procedures the school used for a lot of years. And those procedures probably haven't changed in the last two years."

"Tell me," Kevin demanded.

Tony settled back in his chair. "Basically, all the used chemicals from lab experiments and other waste materials are stored in a small room on the fourth floor of Starrett Science Center—the room's about the size of a walk-in closet. It's actually close to Dr. Jacob's old office. One weekend around the end of each quarter, an environmental waste disposal company from

Philadelphia sends a panel truck to the campus and hauls the stuff away. The disposal people wear protective clothing and masks—the usual gear for removing hazardous materials. They minimize publicity by doing the removal on a weekend when not many people are around.

"I don't know where they haul it to. It's probably disposed of somewhere around Philly. I assume it's done legally since it's a big company that specializes in that type of work. When I was still working at Cabot, it was a routine job, although I always made sure at least two extra people worked in Starrett the weekend they came.

"I think the school bid the work out and the same company had the contract for at least the past ten years. The operation was first rate, Kevin. If there was any storage or disposal problems, they happened a long time ago," he said.

"That's the point," said Kevin excitedly. "Most of the people who died came here in the sixties when the university grew a lot—built more buildings, students started coming from around the country, not just from Pennsylvania. The people who died of cancer worked here maybe fifteen to twenty years, and the deaths began to mount up during the late seventies and eighties. So whatever caused their cancers took a long time to develop.

"How did the university dispose of toxic wastes back in the fifties and sixties?" Kevin asked.

"How the hell do you expect me to remember that far back? I have trouble remembering what I ate for breakfast." Tony slapped his hands on the table. He cocked his head toward the bedroom.

"Wait a minute." He shoved back his chair and went into Rosa's room. Through the open door, Kevin watched him lean down, whisper a few words, rearrange the covers, then gently close the door and return to the kitchen.

"You're asking about procedures from a long time ago," Tony resumed. "People didn't care much about toxic waste then. The tree huggers and environmentalists didn't get a lot of attention until the last twenty years or so."

"All the more reason to figure that toxic chemicals could have caused the cancers," said Kevin, his voice rising. "Don't you see the possibility? I think toxic wastes are still stored somewhere on campus that nobody knows about."

"No way, Kevin. That's impossible. It's just not rational. Besides, most toxic waste dumps are near old factories, places like that, not on a high-class university campus. Besides, I know every nook and cranny on that campus and I can't imagine where such a dump might be located."

Tony regarded his young friend closely. "You been smoking something, Kevin?" he asked quizzically. Maybe the kid still was a bit crazy, maybe the mental problems that landed him in the hospital weren't cured after all. Kevin's flushed face and glittering black eyes were not reassuring.

"It wouldn't have to be a very big dump, especially if the waste was really toxic," Kevin rambled on, lost in speculation, ignoring the old man. "The pieces of this puzzle are finally starting to fit together," he said.

"Let me tell you what I found last summer when I began working on this. I went digging through some old historical records stored in the library archives," he related. "Back in the early 1970s, somebody wrote a fairly comprehensive history of the school from its early days as Cabot Academy up until it was renamed Cabot University.

There was a section on how the early donors to the university's endowment fund helped the school to expand and attract great faculty and students. Two companies, Capital Chemicals and Saxton Controls, made large donations to the school in the late 1940s or early 1950s—somewhere in that time period. Apparently those multimillion-dollar donations were an important part of the school's early endowment.

"I never heard of Saxton Controls, so I looked it up in a listing of U. S. corporations but I couldn't find any record of it. I did learn that Capital Chemicals bought out a local company, Oakton Industries, in the early sixties. And Capital is one of the biggest chemical companies in the world."

"Now it's coming back to me," mused Tony. "I remember Saxton Controls. It was a small division of a New Jersey company that operated some kind of secret plant right outside Hillsdale during World War II—long before your time, son," he chuckled.

"The plant was built along the river, maybe three miles north of town. Whatever they manufactured required a lot of water because the plant had huge pipes that pumped water from the river into the plant and then back out.

"The workers at the plant earned high wages and put in a lot of overtime. They made big bucks, especially for those days. I was lucky to make $50 a week at the same time some of the Saxton workers bragged about taking home $200 to $300 a week. They also hinted that they were helping win the war, but I never put much stock in that. Lots of companies around here helped win the war. There was even a big plant ten miles up the river that built heavy tanks during the war. Whatever they made at Saxton was top secret. The workers could have lost their jobs, or worse, if anyone leaked what was going on at the factory.

"Right after the war," Tony became more animated, his voice rising, "rumors floated around town that the plant had something to do with making the atom bomb. Nobody took that talk seriously because the government said the bombs were developed out in New Mexico and built in Tennessee and somewhere in Washington State. If Saxton Controls had anything to do with those weapons, it was probably some sort of internal mechanisms or assembly operations," he said.

"The plant operated for a few years, then closed down. The place was boarded up and a big fence kept out the curious. Finally, maybe twenty-five or thirty years ago, the buildings were torn down and a housing development was built on the site. It became prime real estate and some nice homes were built overlooking the river.

"Most people who worked at Saxton have either died by now or they left Hillsdale long ago. Some of the employees had moved up here from New Jersey and they pretty much kept to themselves. When the plant closed, I guess those folks went back to Jersey.

"Kevin, even if the plant generated toxic waste of some kind, it was at least three miles away from the university. There's no connection to toxic waste and the school that I can see."

"Wrong, Tony," said Kevin, flushed with excitement. "What if there was a reason for that large donation to Cabot back about fifty years ago? What if the school stored some of their toxic waste on the campus? What if those materials were nuclear waste?"

"Whoa, fella. You're getting way ahead of reality now," Tony shook his head. "We don't even know what the company manufactured. You got no reason to suspect that Saxton produced nuclear or toxic waste. Hell, thousands of plants all over the country produced secret stuff for the war effort. The nuclear stuff was concentrated in only a few locations. We know that now. For sure, none of that stuff was around here.

"As for toxic waste, I suppose there's a remote possibility that the company used chemicals in whatever they manufactured. Even so, you can't assume that toxic waste somehow ended up on the campus. That's just crazy."

In the harsh glare of the overhead florescent light, Tony's skepticism was tinged with pity.

"Your theory is off the wall, kiddo. It's like something out of a bad television movie. You're a scientist, and I'm just a dumb custodian. But your idea is stupid. Even if it was true, any toxic waste would have been carted away years ago.

"Still," he mused, "I wonder why Saxton Controls gave the university so much money. Maybe Cabot did some research for Saxton during the war," he speculated.

"But so what?" He leaned back in his chair and regarded Kevin across the kitchen table. It was time to change the subject.

"Son, you're making a bunch of wild assumptions here. You better keep those ideas to yourself," he warned. "Nobody's going to take you seriously. They'll think you're a nut case.

153

"So, what did you find out about Capital Chemicals in your search?" Tony moved to a safer topic.

"Not much. Of course, everybody knows they're a huge multinational company. I know that Ruth and Jacob both worked at the Oakton Division before they came to the university," Kevin said. "Maybe that's why a bunch of officials from Capital came to Dr. Jacob's memorial service."

"Kevin, Capital Chemicals is more likely to have stored chemicals on campus than Saxton. I remember back when Jackson Starrett was President of the school—Starrett Science Center was named after him, you know. Anyway, Starrett was a scientist and he was supposed to be a good friend of the President of Capital Chemicals. A lot of chemistry and physics graduates went to work in their laboratories."

"Since the Borovskis had some connection with Capital, Ruth might know what the company manufactured in Oakton during the forties and fifties," said Tony.

"Have you asked her?"

"No."

"The university always had a cozy relationship with Capital," he continued. "If any chemicals were stored on the campus from a company, it's a lot more likely they came from Capital than from Saxton. Still, anything stored on campus that long ago couldn't possibly be around the school now. There's just no way," he shook his head.

"Anyway, where could they be hidden? Kevin, just forget this. Don't waste your time hunting for something that doesn't exist—at least not now. For a couple of minutes, you had me almost believing there might be something to your idea."

"There **is** something to it," Kevin retorted. "You're like everybody else, Tony. You can't believe the university could screw up on something this important. My theory's not only possible, I'll prove it to you and everybody else." He shoved back his chair and headed for the kitchen door.

"Wait a minute, Kevin. Don't go off mad. Sit down and have another cup of coffee. Let's talk about something else for a change."

He glanced at his watch.

"I thought you wanted to see Rosa. She'll be waking up any time now. She'd be really disappointed not to see you, even if it's only for a few minutes. She's in bad shape," he said sadly, "but at least her mind is as sharp as ever when she's not doped up with painkillers. The fact is, Kevin, you may not get another chance to talk to her."

"It's that bad, huh?"

"Yeah, that bad," said Tony bleakly.

"All right, I'll stay till she wakes up." He settled back in his chair. "But let me talk through my theory some more," said Kevin stubbornly.

"Kevin, you're really obsessed with this. Can't we talk about something else?"

"No," he retorted. "Tony, let's assume there are some old toxic chemicals on campus. Where could they be hidden?"

"That's just the point," Tony shouted, slamming his fist on the table. "The only place on campus where chemicals are stored is Starrett Science Center. And I know those wastes have been regularly hauled away for years," he said.

"But Starrett Science Center is relatively new," Kevin interrupted. "The original science building was Connors Hall, and it's positively ancient. There's a plaque in the entrance hall dating that building around 1890. What happened to the chemicals when that building had a lot of science labs? Could chemicals still be stored there?"

"No way," Tony retorted. "After Starrett was built about twenty-five years ago, Connors Hall—it was called Science Hall then—was closed. The building was completely gutted except for the outside walls and load bearing beams. They even took out the floors. Then the building was redesigned for the Business School. The whole project took about three years. What you see is really a new building disguised behind the brick and ivy of the old structure. For sure, all the chemicals from the old labs were removed when Connors was renovated—probably long before then. There's just no chance that chemicals could be stored anywhere but in Starrett. Face it, Kevin. There's no toxic waste dump at Cabot University. Forget it."

Kevin slumped deeper into his chair.

"Maybe you're right," he sighed. "Still, I'll take a look around Connors Hall just to be sure. Any chance you have a master key for that building, Tony?"

"No. I turned in all my keys when I retired. Why do you need a key? The building's open until eleven o'clock at night. Just go in and look around if you want. You won't find anything."

"It won't hurt to check it out anyway. What about the basement of the building? Can I poke around there without arousing suspicion?"

"Sure. There's some heating and electrical equipment down there. Also some storage and maintenance closets."

"I wouldn't mind checking out those closets," Kevin said. "For sure, I'll need a master key to get into them."

Tony regretted mentioning the closets. It only fueled the kid's obsession. Still, it wouldn't hurt to check them out if it would finally convince Kevin his search was futile.

"I can probably get you a key," he said reluctantly. "I visit the guys in the maintenance shops about once a month, just to shoot the breeze, find out what's happening. I know where the master keys are kept. I'll get you one next week. Just promise to give it back to me and don't make a duplicate," he warned.

"Great. Maybe there's nothing in those closets, but at least I should make sure."

Rosa's voice, weak from drugs and sleep, interrupted their conversation. Tony rose and went into her room. He came to the door and motioned Kevin into the tiny room off the kitchen that had been converted to a sick room.

Kevin left the Amonte home a short while later, saddened to see the wasted body of Rosa, the kind Italian woman who had treated him like a son. He was glad that he had waited and spent time with her. Rosa had been a surrogate mother to him. She had showered him with love, fed him, scolded him about his unkempt beard and offered unsolicited advice along with unconditional affection.

Hers was a love he would not find elsewhere, not even in the Borovski home. Ruth Borovski would never be a surrogate mother. Her innate European reserve raised a barrier he could not penetrate. Dr. Jacob, on the other hand, had been a father figure, albeit a demanding one, since their first encounter in freshman chemistry.

He trusted Tony and Rosa Amonte more than anyone with the possible exception of Valerie Chapman. He could be himself with them, confident that his welcome was secure. Despite his long absence during the past year, he knew the Amonte door was open to him day or night. On the other hand, he would never consider dropping in uninvited at the Borovski home, not even when Dr. Jacob was alive.

He checked his watch under a street lamp and headed back to campus, hurrying along dimly lighted streets, past mostly darkened homes. Folks in this neighborhood were usually in bed by eleven o'clock because the work shifts in the local mills began at seven.

*   *   *   *

Entering the campus, he cut across the Commons to the library. Taking the granite steps two at a time, he opened the glass doors, swiped his plastic sensor card through the security box and reached the main floor. The library closed at midnight on weekdays. There was still time to search more old records in the university archives before the building closed. He needed detailed information about Connors Hall and knew exactly where to look.

The university archives were housed in a separate, locked room on the basement level. He would need a librarian to give him access. The reference librarian reluctantly led him to the basement. "You know the building closes in only forty-five minutes," the librarian pursed her lips and glared.

"Right. Thanks for letting me in." No need to make the old lady angry. He closed the door and went to work. During his preliminary search last summer Kevin found the oldest campus records, some dating back to the 1800s. Several large folios lay on top of the stacks along the rear wall. Standing on a small stool, he tilted the top folio and read the faded label. The unwieldy folio contained architectural blueprints and detailed drawings for the school's oldest buildings, Old Main and Science Hall.

Bingo! Possible pay dirt on the first try. He pulled the folio from the shelf and carried it to a nearby table. Untying the dark brown ribbon, he lifted out the yellowed and faded drawings and blueprints. The drawings were nearly impossible to decipher. He pulled one print and laid it under the reading lamp. He could barely make out the architect's name and address in the bottom right corner. The blueprints looked like they hadn't been touched in many years. Working carefully, he examined the hand printed headings on each document, placing them face down on the table, searching for Science Hall's architectural drawings. He found four large blueprints labeled Science Hall, which appeared to be the drawings for the original four-story building that had been renamed Connors Hall after the building was renovated. Why, he wondered idly, was the original science building renamed Connors Hall after it was renovated? Some day when he had more time, he would find out.

Beneath the rendering of the building exterior, he found the three-by-two foot blueprints detailing the plans for each floor. Although the prints had darkened and were badly frayed along the edges, he could easily trace the exterior shape of the building and the dimensions of the interior spaces.

The original basement level was the last blueprint in the package. Leaning over the table, arms spread wide, his hands anchoring the edges of the print, he studied the faded print. Taking a deep breath to calm his racing heart, he examined the bottom right corner of the blueprint. A small separate rectangular sketch was set neatly apart from the exterior dimensions. Offset from the front of the building, the drawing detailed what looked like a small room extending beneath the granite steps at the building's main entrance.

According to the drawing, the room extended beyond the brick plaza facing the building into the grassy and treed Commons area. Before the transformation of Science Hall into the business school, a large room— perhaps a storage area—apparently existed in the basement. Either Tony Amonte never knew about the space or he had forgotten to mention it to Kevin.

Surprise, surprise, he laughed aloud. If the drawings were accurate, the dimensions of Science Hall's basement differed in one important respect from the renovated basement of Connors Hall. Moving the print directly under the table lamp for better viewing, he pulled up a chair and studied the diagram inch by inch. Obviously, the basement area did not exactly correspond to the exterior dimensions of the upper floors. More important, the extension under the plaza and part of the Commons area was not reflected in the architectural drawings for the renovated business school.

He pulled out the first floor blueprint from the stack of papers. The first floor of renovated Connors Hall featured a large interior lobby with a bank of elevators along one side and the original handsome central staircase leading to the upper floors.

Students leaving the building by the main entrance walked down the wide, shallow granite steps to a spacious brick plaza, a popular gathering place for students and faculty. Clusters of benches were scattered around the edge of the plaza. Broad sidewalks beyond the plaza branched off to the library and other academic buildings and cut diagonally to Old Main on the far side of the Commons.

Kevin glanced at his watch. Fifteen minutes until the library would close. He placed the blueprint for the first floor of old Science Hall on top of the basement blueprint leaving an overlap at the bottom.

Yes! The difference in the two prints was unmistakable. The small storage area in the original basement of Science Hall did not extend to the floor above. Mentally, he visualized the room tucked away beneath the granite steps and extending under the plaza at the entrance to what was now Connors Hall.

The public address system quietly sounded a gong and a voice announced that the library would close in ten minutes. Damn! Kevin rummaged through his backpack, and tore two sheets from his lab notebook. Placing the lined notebook paper over the basement blueprint, he traced a rough outline of the storage room, noting the location of the exterior wall on the east side and its relationship to the entrance, granite steps and plaza. He copied the blueprint label, including the architectural firm's name, address and date of the drawings.

Gathering the blueprints, he replaced them in their original order, inserted them in the large folio and laid it on top of the stacks. He would photocopy the entire set of prints later. Given the faded condition of the paper, he wasn't confident of success. However, if that failed, he could make more accurate copies with good tracing paper. The lights flashed twice, signaling that the building would close in five minutes.

Stuffing his crude sketches into his backpack, he closed the flap and slung it over his shoulder. He left the archives room, walked upstairs past the checkout desk and through the electronic gate to the glass doors.

The late day rain had moved on, leaving the clean damp fragrance of wet grass and crisp cool air. Stars glowed brilliantly in the dark sky as he jogged across the Commons. Back at Mrs. Ledbetter's, he sat on the edge of the bed and pulled out his rough sketches, too excited to think about anything but the newly discovered room in the basement level of Connors Hall.

He would phone Valerie Chapman tomorrow and ask her to meet him in the library. Together, they would study the blueprints and figure out what to do next. Stripping off his jeans and sweatshirt, he wondered why Tony Amonte apparently had forgotten about the old storage room. Had he deliberately avoided mentioning the room? Maybe he'd just forgotten it. He had a lot on his mind with Rosa.

Crawling under the covers, he decided not to tell Tony about his discovery until after he picked up the promised master key to Connors Hall. Nor would he confide in Dr. Borovski or Dr. Atherton. They were too wired to the administration to be trusted. Except for Valerie Chapman, he would work alone as always.

Chapter 31

Nancy's repeated requests to meet with Larry Northrop failed. Each time she phoned the President's office, she met with a thinly disguised runaround. On one occasion she was informed that Larry was out of town. Second and third requests were denied because the President was said to be unavailable for the next several weeks.

The message was clear. President Northrop was avoiding her. So be it. If he wanted to ignore her, she and Ruth would continue without the administration's cooperation.

She phoned Ruth's office just before her mid-morning lecture.

"This will only take a minute, Ruth. I've been trying to see Larry for the past two weeks. Clearly, he's decided to ignore us. When I tried this morning, the secretary said he is unavailable for the next two weeks. That translates into no meeting for at least a month.

"Did Paul ever recommend someone from MIT to examine the data? I still think that's better than showing the materials to someone here on campus."

"Paul called me about an hour ago," said Ruth. "He's got someone lined up to look at the data. I'll Fed Ex the package this afternoon. Paul thinks the work will take a week or two because the professor doing the analysis is fitting it in around his regular research. According to Paul, he is an expert in both statistics and environmental science. If anyone can make something of this data, he should be able to ferret it out."

"That's good news. Even if it takes a bit longer, I feel better about using someone off campus. Then if there's nothing significant in Kevin's analysis, we won't look completely stupid," Nancy laughed.

"Right. I've written a brief explanation of the data and outlined what I want in the way of statistical analysis that I'm enclosing in the package. I've been vague about the source of the data, implying it's related to a chemical plant, not to the campus."

"Good. Be sure to keep a copy of everything in a safe place, preferably at home, Ruth."

"Already done."

An hour later the package was on its way to Cambridge. It was time to be patient and await the results of an independent analysis.

*   *   *   *

Kevin could scarcely suppress his glee as he and Valerie Chapman followed a student librarian to the basement archives. They waited

160

impatiently while the student unlocked the door, turned on the lights and left.

"We're onto something big—I know it, Val. Look what I found last night."

Valerie shook her head. "I've never seen you this hyper, Kevin. Chill out. It can't be that important," she groused.

"Wrong, Val. It's incredibly important. I've found the smoking gun— what I've been looking for since Dr. Jacob died." They sat down at the long table in the middle of the room and Kevin turned on the table lamp.

"Don't keep me in suspense," Valerie demanded.

"There's a secret storage area beneath the plaza in front of Connors Hall. I'll bet you a burger and fries that's where the toxic waste is stored that nobody on campus admits to knowing about," he exclaimed. "Let me show you."

"Yeah right, Kevin," she said. "Show me."

He lifted the folio of architectural drawings from the top shelf and removed the blueprints. From the bottom of the pile, he pulled out the original blueprint of the basement level of Science Hall. Speaking quickly, he pointed out the space extending beneath the steps and plaza from the old Science Hall, and then compared it to the detailed drawing of the basement of the renovated Connors Hall.

Unconvinced, Valerie spread the two faded blueprints side-by-side and examined them in detail. She looked up. Perhaps Kevin wasn't totally crazy.

"Believe me now, Val?" asked Kevin.

"Well, I suppose that might be a storage area," Valerie admitted. "You probably should check it out. Whether toxic waste is stored there is something else again. And it's a long way from a smoking gun. Even if there is a storage space down there, how do you propose to get into it?" she frowned.

"Tony Amonte is getting me a master key," Kevin confided. "With that key, I can open any door on the campus. We can sneak into faculty offices, go through files, find exams, anything we want," he bragged.

"Whoa, Kevin. Don't include me. I won't be part of this if you decide to start checking out faculty offices."

"Ok, ok, just kidding," Kevin grinned. "I won't do anything stupid."

"Let's go over to Connors Hall right now," he suggested. "We can take a quick look around, then check things out more carefully when I get the key."

"I thought you wanted me to copy the drawings or at least made a decent diagram of this," she gestured toward the blueprints. "After all, European history majors are used to examining diagrams of old cathedrals. Why not a building at Cabot University? I have a pretty good eye for detail."

161

"Yeah, right. Take a few minutes to do that. I brought along some tissue paper for tracing." He reached into his backpack and retrieved a package of white tissue paper.

Valerie went to work carefully tracing the complete blueprint of the old Science Hall basement level, and then repeating the process for the newer blueprint of renovated Connors Hall. Shortly after noon they left the library, emerging into late winter sunlight and mild temperatures, joining the mobs of students heading to lunch and mid-day classes. They walked along the broad sidewalk to Connors Hall, and entered the building through the main entrance. On their left, a narrow stairway led to the basement level.

Minutes later they completed their search of the basement area beneath the front entrance. Unlike the early blueprints they had just examined, the east wall of the basement was solid plaster, broken only by a solitary wooden door near the stairwell. Disappointed, they turned the door handle. The door was unlocked. They stepped inside, flipped the light switch and closed the door. Several concrete steps led down to a small room, a space not much bigger than a large closet. Mops, a floor waxer and cleaning supplies were stacked neatly in the dimly lighted space along with some wax dispensers and partially depleted jugs of cleaning fluids. The room was a janitorial closet used to store cleaning equipment and supplies.

"Big deal, Kevin. You've found your storage closet," Valerie taunted him. "There's nothing down here that matches those old blueprints."

"Yeah, right. Maybe this isn't the storage area we're looking for. If those plans were accurate, that room should be behind this wall, extending out under the steps and plaza." He pointed to the east wall along which were stacked three file cabinets. "Maybe when they renovated this building, they just walled that room off," he speculated. "And what if they sealed off the room without emptying it out? Maybe twenty-five years ago, nobody cared what was in that storage room."

"Get a life, Kevin. Admit it, the whole idea of toxic waste is a fantasy." She regarded him with a mixture of pity and exasperation.

"Maybe those old blueprints for Science Hall were simply inaccurate," she said more gently. "There's obviously nothing here."

"But if the old prints were accurate, that area under the steps and the plaza was probably just walled off," he countered.

"No, Kev," said Valerie, depressed. Her friend was unwilling to face the reality before him. "Tony told you the whole building was gutted. Even the floors were removed. If there was a storage room, they probably cleaned it out along with all the other debris and sealed it off. That would explain why this wall is covered over."

Kevin didn't argue further. Disappointed, he switched off the light and closed the door.

"We might as well check out the rest of the basement," said Kevin. They walked slowly along the hall, peering into rooms in which broken desks, beat up and discarded file cabinets and an assortment of classroom tables and chairs were stacked to the ceiling.

"This is a dead end," said Valerie. "If there was a storage area down here a long time ago, it sure isn't here now. Forget it, Kevin." They retraced their steps back along the corridor and upstairs to the lobby.

"I just can't believe this. I'll get that master key and check out every single room in this building," said Kevin stubbornly. "I'll do it on my own."

"Suit yourself," Valerie shook her head.

"How about a burger for lunch? My treat," Val offered as they left the building and headed across campus. During their stay at Essex Medical Center, she had learned that junk food sometimes diverted his attention from what was clearly an unresolved obsession.

He shrugged. "As long as it's your treat."

Chapter 32

Tony Amonte phoned Kevin later in the week, agreeing to meet him at Sal's Pizza Shop. Seated in the crowded restaurant on Main Street, Kevin and the old man shared a large pepperoni pizza, two bags of chips and cokes.

"Here's the master key. It'll open every door on the whole campus," Tony nervously looked around as he slid the key beneath his hand across the table. "If you make a copy of this key, I swear I'll come after you with a hammer. I mean it, Kevin. Don't duplicate this key."

"Don't worry. I'll check the building out and get the key back to you in a few days."

Kevin didn't mention the blueprints of the old Science Hall or the newer set of prints for the renovated Connors Hall. There was no point in discussing an apparently nonexistent storage room. Tony was preoccupied with caring for Rosa. He was sure the end was near.

*   *   *   *

Long after midnight, Kevin returned to Connors Hall, locked for the night, the offices and classrooms darkened. The campus was deserted as he approached the building's side door. He inserted the master key, half expecting it not to work. Unlike Starrett Science Center, this building apparently was not alarmed. He had noted earlier that day the absence of the telltale television cameras like those mounted in the lobby and stairwells of Starrett and Old Main. He slipped quietly into the darkened building, illuminated only by dim red exit signs.

He paused inside the door while his eyes adjusted to the darkness before heading toward the front of the building and the main entrance. Using the exit signs for guidance he entered the lobby, which was dimly lit by the reflected outside floodlights that illuminated the plaza. Staying close to the wall, he headed for the stairway to the basement level.

Reaching into his backpack, he pulled out a small flashlight and focused the beam on the steps. He slowly made his way down the narrow steps to the basement area that he and Valerie explored a week ago. Only the single door of the janitor's storage closet broke the east wall near the stairwell. He shined the light toward several rooms that fed off the main corridor on the right. Walking down the hall, he twisted the knobs on several doors. Locked. Each time, the master key slid quietly into the locks.

He unlocked two rooms at the end of the hall and found them empty, layers of dust coating the floors, the air musty with neglect. He sneezed. He did not step inside or otherwise disturb the rooms.

Except for the elevator near the middle of the floor, the basement level apparently served as a storage area for the rest of the building. His inspection complete, he headed back down the hall and the stairs leading to the lobby.

Discouraged, he checked his watch and began to climb the stairs, then retraced his steps and faced the closet tucked beneath the stairwell. As he expected, the door was locked. He inserted the master key and slowly turned it. After initial resistance, the bolt action released. He pushed open the door and cautiously entered the room, leaving the door ajar behind him.

He turned on his flashlight and quickly swept the beam around the room. The janitorial supplies were in place, and except for a neatly stacked pile of coveralls in the corner, the room was undisturbed from his and Valerie's earlier visit.

Pointing his flashlight upwards, he realized for the first time that part of the ceiling was actually formed by the underside of the steel staircase leading from the basement to the lobby. He cast his light around the room one final time. A metal glint caught his eye.

A dual light switch was mounted on the far wall, partially hidden by a file cabinet. Stupid place for a light switch, he thought. Awkwardly, he reached behind the file cabinet and flicked one switch. Nothing happened. He tried the other switch and a dim fluorescent light mounted in the ceiling flickered briefly, and then lit, brightly illuminating the room. He quickly closed and bolted the door, tossing his flashlight back into his pack.

The storage room appeared larger than he remembered when he and Valerie had checked it out earlier. Slowly, he inspected the room in minute detail, drawn to the dual switch he had just discovered. Suddenly he realized that the wall on which the switch was mounted was different than the others. This wall wasn't plastered. It was covered with wallboard crudely held together with long strips of tape.

He hadn't noticed it earlier because the file cabinets reached nearly to the low ceiling. The wall was painted the same shade of bile green as the rest of the room. In their hurried inspection, neither Valerie nor he had noticed the difference in construction. He reached above the file cabinets along the wall and rapped his knuckles against the wallboard. A dead hollow sound came back.

The wall was directly opposite the entry door and flush with the exterior wall of the building. Heart pounding from a quick surge of adrenalin, he realized that if his orientation and sense of direction were correct, the wall covered an area directly under the exterior granite steps and brick plaza in front of the building.

He suppressed a laugh. Those old blueprints were accurate after all! The old room shown on the early architectural drawings for Science Hall might lay just behind the janitors' room he was standing in. He walked toward the cabinets, preparing to push them aside and get at the exterior wall.

Footsteps sounded directly above his head. Someone was approaching the stairs. He switched off the florescent light, and waited, his heart pounding.

The footsteps paused at the bottom of the stairs. A powerful flashlight beam swept along the crack beneath the door. He didn't breath. The footsteps finally retreated down the hall, only to return a few minutes later and pause outside the door. Someone rattled the doorknob, testing the deadbolt lock he had secured minutes earlier.

After an interminable period that he decided later was probably only thirty seconds, the guard slowly made his way upstairs to the lobby. Kevin didn't move for another ten minutes. Then, gathering up his backpack, he took his flashlight and cautiously opened the door.

With a final look around the room, he hoisted the backpack over his shoulder and locked the door, testing that it was securely bolted. There would be no more exploring tonight. He would wait until he had the proper tools to search behind the wallboard. Holding onto the railing, he crept up the dark stairs to the lobby.

He moved silently down the corridor to the side door he had entered an hour earlier. Safely outside the building, he walked casually along the sidewalk to the plaza and front entrance. Keeping to the shadows, he sat down on a bench and scanned the front of the building. It didn't take long to orient himself and pinpoint the area he had just explored.

Elated, he stood and raised a clenched fist toward the darkened building and starlit sky.

"Yes!" he shouted.

He turned and trekked back to his room.

Part V

Spring

Chapter 33

Spring arrived, seemingly overnight. The huge lawns that spread across the Commons shed their winter skin of dusty brown and like a wily chameleon, took on the chartreuse brilliance of early spring. Giant oaks and maples, barren silhouettes over the past six months, brought forth their canopy of leaves, casting abundant shade across the campus. Masses of colorful rhododendron and azalea presented a showy extravaganza.

The warm spring breezes lured hundreds of students from classrooms and laboratories. Clad in the uniform of the day—cutoffs, tank tops and sandals, they thronged to the Commons. A few students pretended to study. Most simply hung out in groups of twos and fours, staking out grassy patches, sprawling on colorful blankets sporting the Cabot Cougar logo, plugged into headsets listening to music, reading, sleeping. Everyone— students and faculty alike—savored the brief respite before facing final examinations scheduled for later in April.

Oblivious to the scene around him, Kevin Parks jogged along the broad sidewalk toward Starrett Science Center. Head down, hands anchored in the pockets of his dirty jeans, his backpack loaded with books and computer disks, he was completely self-absorbed.

Visualizing the likely outcome of the upcoming meeting, he fought to control his rising panic. He searched desperately for convincing reasons to persuade Ruth Borovski that he deserved more time to complete his dissertation. There was no way his name would be on the June graduation list. He hadn't even begun to put his experimental results into a rough draft. He braced for the inevitable.

In reality, he no longer felt compelled to finish his degree. The doctorate that had consumed his waking hours over the past few years was a trivial pursuit. His search for toxic contamination on the campus was a far more important priority, one that engaged all of his intellectual and scientific skills.

Now he had to decide whether to take Ruth more fully into his confidence. Should he tell her about his analysis of the old Science Hall blueprints in the library archives? Could he convince her that the secret space in the basement of Connors Hall might contain the toxic waste he had spent the past year searching for?

Certainly, his disclosures would explain the lack of progress on his doctoral research. However, given her furious reaction to his hacking into the university's administrative computer, he could hardly expect her to endorse a break-in of Connors Hall. She probably wasn't interested in his discovery. Besides, she apparently was unimpressed with his preliminary statistical analysis of cancer deaths on campus. He had given her the data more than a month ago and she hadn't bothered to get back to him about it.

He sprinted up the granite steps and entered Starrett Science Center. Crossing the nearly empty lobby, he punched the up arrow at the bank of elevators and waited. He got off at the fourth floor and walked along the hall, glancing into the polymer laboratories where he and Dr. Jacob had spent so many wondrous hours.

He knocked softly on his advisor's office door. Telephone in hand, Ruth Borovski opened the door and motioned him to a seat on the leather sofa. She turned back to her desk and quickly ended the conversation.

"Thank you for being prompt, Kevin."

She eyed him silently, trying to gauge his mood. "I think you've been avoiding me in the lab, or haven't you been spending much time in the lab?" she began mildly, a faint smile removing some of the sting in her words.

"Well, I've been busy with other things. I've worked a little on my research, but I won't be ready to defend my dissertation until late in the summer at the earliest." There was no point in beating around the bush.

"But your extension runs out the end of June," she reminded him. She waited for him to respond.

Silence.

She sighed and turned to the computer printouts spread over her desk, seemingly engrossed in the data. Finally, she sat back in her chair and faced him directly. "I've consulted with the rest of your dissertation committee, the chair of the Chemistry Department and the Dean of Arts and Sciences," she said. "They absolutely refuse to grant you another extension. If your dissertation isn't finished by June 30, there won't be another extension."

"Oh."

"You've known that June was the final date for months, Kevin. However, if you totally focus your efforts—work fifteen-hour days for the next couple of months—I think you can meet that deadline," she tried to sound upbeat.

Silence.

"What were the results of the experiments we discussed last month?" She tried another tactic.

"There are no results. I didn't finish inserting the algorithms." He gazed out the window, staring intently at the puffy cumulus clouds perched above the distant hills.

"Why not, Kevin? Didn't you understand my suggestions?"

She waited, the ticking of her desk clock the only sound above the soft hum of the air conditioning.

"I just didn't feel like working on it," he mumbled, avoiding her gaze.

"What exactly have you been doing since mid-March when we last talked?" she asked.

He leaned forward on the sofa, elbows resting on his torn jeans, his fists propping up his chin.

"Well," he began, "I've looked at a few things in the lab. Most of the time I've been searching for toxic wastes—the stuff that killed Dr. Jacob— the shit that's hidden somewhere on this campus," he stared at the carpet, seemingly absorbed in the intricate oriental weave.

"Remember that statistical analysis I gave you on the number of cancer deaths on campus?" He finally looked at her.

She nodded.

"Whatever happened to it?"

"Nothing, Kevin. I reviewed it again and concluded that your analysis was flawed. I put it aside. Do you want it back?" she turned to a horizontal stack of papers on her desk.

"No. You might as well trash it."

He retreated more deeply into his shell, avoiding eye contact, his lips set in a stubborn line.

For reasons she could not articulate, Ruth refused to concede failure with Jacob's most brilliant student. She removed her half glasses and placed them carefully in the middle of her desk pad. Perhaps shock therapy would work.

Gripping the arms of her chair, she displayed a side of her personality she rarely revealed to students. "Kevin, you've got to move beyond this obsession of yours. When you were released from the hospital, Dr. Siegel was convinced that you could deal with Jacob's death. I thought so, too. Apparently we were wrong. I spoke to Jerry just last week. He said you haven't met your therapy appointments for the past month. That's not a good idea."

Receiving no response, she pulled her chair closer to him, leaned forward, forcing him to meet her gaze.

"I want you to promise you'll see Dr. Siegel now—this week. Therapy sessions will help you concentrate on your research, get back on track. Am I making myself clear?"

He sat silently; the only sound the nervous tapping of his sneaker against the carpet.

"I can't promise anything," he said finally, "I'm really busy right now."

She pounded her fist on the desk. "Perhaps I'm not making myself clear, Kevin. If you don't finish your dissertation by the end of June, there will be no more extensions. Your financial aid will end. You won't be a doctoral student at Cabot University any longer," she shouted, hoping to force a response.

171

Silence.

She took a deep breath and sighed. "I wasn't going to tell you this today, but you leave me no choice. I've already discussed your research with the directors of two major laboratories. If you finish your dissertation, I can set up job interviews for you. With your degree, you can join one of the best research labs in the country, be part of a team that is carrying on Dr. Jacob's work.

"But not without your degree!" she shouted. "Wasting precious time on this crazy effort of yours is completely counterproductive," she threw up her hands, disgusted that she had lost control.

"You just don't get it," he protested, finally engaged. "It's here, on this campus and I've **got** to find it. I'm telling you, it's not a futile effort! I know what I'm doing." He slumped deeper into the sofa. "I'm right and I'll prove it. You and everybody else are blind to what's been happening on this campus for years." He glared at her.

"Let me repeat, Kevin," said Ruth grimly. "Get on with your research. You've run out of time and excuses." She retrieved her half-glasses, twirled them absently, searching for a way to reach her brilliant but troubled student.

The silence grew. Kevin refused to meet her gaze. His left knee jiggled uncontrollably, his filthy sneaker tapped a rhythm both ignored.

She gave him one last chance. "Do you want to discuss in detail exactly what you've been up to this past month?"

"I guess not. You wouldn't believe me anyway, so why bother? When I've found the evidence, you and your friend Dr. Atherton will be the first to know," he said defiantly.

"Give it up, Kevin," she said sadly. "If I thought that something on this campus contributed to Jacob's death, I wouldn't rest until I uncovered it. Surely you know that. Face reality. There's no evidence to support your theory, and this obsession is destroying your future. Drop it and get on with your life.

"Jacob would give you exactly the same advice that I'm giving you now," she said grimly. "Finish your dissertation. You have a brilliant analytical mind, enormous talent in the laboratory and your training equals the best in the country. But you've got to complete your research—I can't do it for you.

"You've lost a lot of time since you left the hospital. If you don't earn your degree, you'll spend the rest of your life cleaning test tubes," she said disgustedly.

"Do you think you're the only person who was traumatized by Jacob's death?" she lashed out. "Every day since he died I've fought my own battles with grief and depression, battles you can't possibly imagine." She turned away.

She faced him again. "Your behavior dishonors his memory. Do you understand that? He was convinced that you had the intellect and talent to make a real contribution to scientific knowledge. All you lack is the will."

Kevin recoiled from her attack.

She walked to the coffee maker that was always on. Moving to the small sink, she rinsed the pot and prepared fresh coffee. The diversion helped calm her.

Ruth made one final effort. "Don't you realize how much Jacob cared about you? Precisely because he respected your talent, I chose you from literally hundreds of his former students to speak at his memorial service. He would be appalled that you haven't finished your degree." She made no attempt to conceal her dismay.

"Your failure is also mine," she admitted sadly. "I share a major responsibility for your lack of progress. Apparently, I'm not able to motivate you to carry on. Do you really think this obsession is worth destroying your opportunity for a productive, challenging career and a decent life?"

She slumped back in her chair, exhausted, defeated.

"This really is your last chance, Kevin," she said softly. "Your dissertation committee took a formal vote this morning. As your advisor, I've been directed to warn you that if your research is not completed by June 30, you will be removed from the doctoral program. Terminated. The Dean's Office will notify you in writing. The letter is being mailed today."

Kevin dropped his head. When he finally gazed out the window, Ruth noted the moisture in his eyes. He knew this ultimatum was coming and thought he was prepared for it. Still, the finality of her words was a blow he could not conceal.

"I guess that's it, then," he whispered. He stood up, grabbed his backpack and opened the door.

"Kevin, Jacob often told me you were his most brilliant student. If you value his memory, you'll get yourself into the lab and do whatever is necessary to finish your research."

Kevin regarded this petite woman, brilliant and successful in her own right, the wife of his surrogate father. His dark eyes glinted dangerously, his lips a thin line nearly invisible in the tangle of his unkempt beard. "Anything more you want to tell me?" he asked.

"No."

It was over and both knew it. He slowly shook his head. He closed the door and walked down the hall past the research labs. Not waiting for the elevator, he entered the stairwell and ran down four flights to the lobby. He passed the huge double helix sculpture without a glance, pushed open a glass door and left the building. Turning right onto the broad sidewalk, he headed for Connors Hall.

Chapter 34

"I delivered the doctoral committee's ultimatum to Kevin," Ruth related to Nancy that evening. "It made absolutely no impression on him, but at least I tried."

"What's he been up to over the past month?"

"Apparently, he's still looking for toxic waste. I doubt that he's found anything substantive. He's clearly close to the edge psychologically— probably even more obsessed than before his breakdown last year. And he didn't take kindly to my suggestion that he resume his therapy with Dr. Siegel. Oh, yes, his appearance is even more slovenly, if that's possible."

"Did you tell him you sent his data to MIT for an independent analysis and that the result was inconclusive?"

"No," said Ruth, a note of finality in her voice. "Maybe his theory has some validity, but if one of the best environmental scientists in the country tells me the analysis is inconclusive, I don't see any point in pursuing it. I give up. Maybe it's time to put the entire issue behind us and move on with our lives. Let Jacob rest in peace."

"It's your decision, Ruth," Nancy said, depressed. "Certainly, Dick and Hillary think we've obsessed a bit over this ourselves."

"They're probably right."

*   *   *   *

Shortly after midnight on Saturday morning, Kevin mentally thanked Tony Amonte as he slid the master key into the well-oiled lock and slipped unobserved into Connors Hall through the side door. His backpack bulged with tools. Two hammers, a crowbar, a small saw, pliers, Phillips and flat screwdrivers, a sharp knife for cutting wallboard, several rolls of duct tape, a towel and two heavy flashlights comprised his arsenal. Making his way along the dark corridor, he felt energized and alert. The waiting was finally over. He would soon have the answers he sought since Dr. Jacob's death a year ago.

Since his meeting with Ruth more than two weeks ago, he had been lethargic, unable to shake a deep fatigue and depression. The reality that his academic years at Cabot University were ending had begun to sink into his psyche. He didn't fight the fatigue, nor take the medication for depression prescribed by Dr. Siegel.

He holed up in his cluttered room at Mrs. Ledbetter's, slept sixteen hours a day, read and reread his favorite science fiction paperbacks, rousing himself occasionally to review the drawings Valerie had sketched of the basement level in Science Hall. He avoided the research laboratories in Starrett Science Center, the building that held so many memories.

He made no attempt to analyze his lethargy. Occasionally venturing out to a local convenience store, he stocked up on chips and nachos and the six-packs of colas that sustained him. Even his usual diet of pizza, burgers and fries was tasteless. He slept and waited for the end of semester exams when Connors Hall would be deserted and the possibility of discovery minimized.

On two separate evenings, when the air was warm and filled with the scent of blooming flowers, he visited the campus library, seeking solitude in the archives room, studying once again the architectural drawings for Science Hall, renamed Connors Hall decades earlier to honor some long forgotten benefactor.

* * * *

For the first time since his disastrous meeting with Ruth Borovski, it was finally safe to revisit the janitor's closet beneath the stairs in Connors Hall. The building's three large lecture halls had been taken over for Cabot University's final examination period. For six days a week, hundreds of students trekked to the business school's classrooms and lecture halls where they endured the four-hour final examinations required in every course. During the exam period the building remained open until 1 a.m. to accommodate students completing projects in the large computer lab on the first floor. Lights blazed in classrooms and offices until dawn.

Now, final examinations had been written and computer projects completed. The campus was virtually abandoned. Only the seniors remained, and they would spend the next seven days during Senior Week drinking, partying and celebrating until graduation. Summer school would not begin for another two weeks.

* * * *

During the past year the campus buzzed with rumors that the academic computer system had been hacked, and that certain faculty and administrative offices had been violated. Campus security officials never acknowledged the break-ins. Privately, however, the chief of security vowed to apprehend and punish the intruders.

The administration, responding to the perceived security problems, launched a massive program to secure all academic and administrative buildings. Connors Hall was the last to be secured because the building was considered a low risk site compared to the expensive science laboratories and Old Main with its administrative offices and sensitive student and administrative records. Soon, the campus would be secure, impenetrable to unauthorized entry.

In early April workers began installing an elaborate security system throughout Connors Hall. Like those already in place in Starrett Science Center and Old Main, the system would be card activated. When it became operational, evening access to the building would be restricted to authorized cardholders with photo IDs. Unobtrusive television cameras mounted at each entrance would record anyone entering the building. The date and time of each access would automatically be logged into a remote computer that would compare magnetic cards with photos of authorized users. The entire system was scheduled to become operational on May 1.

Kevin's access to Connors Hall would be restricted in less than a week. Tony Amonte, who twice had demanded return of the master key, added to the urgency. Time was running out. The chance to investigate the storage room behind the wallboard and whatever contents might be hidden there would slip away. It was now or never. Kevin was prepared to work through the weekend, if necessary.

A surge of manic energy replaced the lassitude that had dogged him over the past two weeks. He smiled. The fools in the administration would never believe that a single student could wreak such havoc on their precious computer systems, not to mention breaking into Connors Hall. After his search was over, he would show the administration the flaws in the university's computer system.

*   *   *   *

Kevin made his way along the dark corridor to the basement stairway off the main lobby. He extended his left arm, occasionally touching the wall for guidance, his eyes focused on the glowing red exit sign and the dimly lit lobby ahead. Beyond the lobby, through the row of glass doors, massive floodlights illuminated the granite steps and front entrance to the building.

He squinted, lowering the visor of his baseball cap to shade his eyes and preserve his night vision as he neared the lobby. Cautiously, he peered outside the glassed front doors. The plaza appeared deserted. Rather than walk directly across the open lobby to the stairs, he kept to the shadows around the edge and hurried down the basement stairwell. He fumbled for Tony's master key in his jeans pocket. Protected now from the lighted lobby, he groped for the recessed door beneath the steps. Grabbing the doorknob, he found the lock and inserted the key. He felt the dead bolt release.

Success!

He entered the musty room, closing the door behind him. In the pitch-black darkness of the closet, he lowered his backpack to the floor, unzipped the pack and searched the contents, finally feeling the large flashlight on the bottom. Switching on the low beam, he scanned the room. It appeared undisturbed from his last visit. Reaching into his pack, he pulled out a towel and carefully stuffed it along the crack beneath the door. Security people were not likely to check the building tonight. But if someone did enter the building and check out the basement, they might spot the light seeping under the storage room door.

He propped the flashlight on a bench and set to work. He wrestled three empty file cabinets away from the wall, careful not to disturb the thick layer of dust on their tops. Fully exposing the back wall beneath the stairwell, he aimed the flashlight beam directly onto the faded green wallboard. He dug out his crowbar, the hammer, pliers and the wallboard-cutting knife and laid them neatly on the floor.

Using his hammer, Kevin systematically tapped softly, first vertically, then horizontally. With a magic marker pen he carefully marked small black X's at six-inch intervals wherever the wall sounded hollow. In ten minutes he had finished tapping and marking the entire wall. He stepped back and examined his work. No question about it, the shape outlined by his X's formed the outline of a door. Beyond the marked area, his tapping produced the dull thud of solid concrete or stone.

If the area he had just outlined were, in fact, a door, he would cut through just enough wallboard to find the doorknob and lock, push open the door and shine the flashlight into the room he was certain lay beyond. He would enlarge the open area until he could inspect the room. If necessary, he would get a larger saw and cut through the door to reach his goal. The file cabinets were five feet high. A small opening could be concealed when the cabinets were replaced against the wall. If he had to cut away a lot of wallboard, it might be impossible to hide the hole.

He set to work.

With his cutting tool, he pierced the wallboard halfway between the marks outlining the vertical space. A doorknob, if there was one, could be on either the left or right side. Working quickly, he was surprised at how easily the tool sliced through the wallboard. In a few moments he had cut a twelve-inch square. He inserted the tool along the cut. Using his fist, he punched the area sharply. The wallboard fell away with a soft pop and thudded to the floor inside the hole. Grabbing a flashlight, he directed the beam into the hole and looked around. Six inches behind the hole his beam illuminated what appeared to be a heavy oak door, stained dark brown, covered with dust and grime.

His heart leaped. The old plans were accurate! A room lay behind the wall.

He angled the light upward. On his knees, he craned his neck and spotted the top of the door and part of the frame. Directing the beam to the right, he found a dull brass plate surrounding a round hole where a doorknob was missing. Shining the beam to the left, he found the edge of the doorframe and two rusty hinges. Twisting his body, he stuck his right arm into the opening and, using the flat of his palm, explored as far as he could reach. Almost immediately, he encountered something metal below the small opening he had cut.

"Shit!" he hissed aloud. Not only was the doorknob missing, leaving an empty hole, two heavy steel bars were attached across the door for good measure.

Carefully, he pulled his arm from the opening and slumped back against the wall. Surrounded by his tools, sweating and breathing heavily from the exertion, he rested and examined his options.

Despite the risk of discovery, perhaps the best alternative was to enlarge the hole enough to crawl through, force open the door and worry about the consequences later. Hiding his work could wait until he learned what was behind that door.

He set about tearing down the wallboard. Adrenaline pumping, he worked quickly and efficiently, cutting huge chunks of crumbling wallboard and piling them neatly on the floor. The air soon filled with fine particles. Minutes later the heavy metal bars and plates securing them to the wooden door were fully exposed. The hole was now a gaping gash four feet across by three feet high.

Perspiration dripped from his beard as he worked. He stopped for a moment, stripped off his shirt and wiped the sweat from his eyes. The steel bars and the empty brass plate where the knob had been removed were now fully exposed. Why, he wondered, had the door been barred and then sealed behind the wallboard? Someone must have wanted to keep the curious out of the room.

Despite the obstacles, Kevin was elated. At last, he had confirmed that the original building blueprints in the library archives were accurate. Behind that door he was convinced he would find the sub-basement extending under the front steps and plaza in the front of Connors Hall. But the steel bars were a serious and unexpected problem.

Actually getting into the sub-basement might prove far tougher than he anticipated. Exhausted by the unaccustomed heavy labor, his initial elation began to slip away. He took another break, groped around in his backpack and pulled out a can of warm cola. Resting his aching back against a file cabinet, he popped the tab and took a long swig, thankful that he had thought to bring along a drink. He munched on a pack of cheese crackers and relaxed, occasionally aiming the flashlight beam into the hole and contemplating his next move.

Removing the heavy bars without making an enormous amount of noise might be impossible. For sure, he didn't have the proper tools to cut through heavy steel. And if he enlarged the hole any further, he could forget about concealing his work. On Monday morning, the first janitor entering the storage room would know someone had broken in.

Worse, even if he somehow managed to remove the bars and break through the door tonight, there was no telling what he might find. Having waited a year for this moment, he would not be rushed. He would make public his findings when he was ready. Now, however, the safe hours of darkness were rapidly slipping away.

He reviewed his options, approaching the situation analytically, forcing himself to think calmly. First, evaluate the problem and develop reasonable alternatives. He could stop now, get more tools and possibly invite Tony or Valerie to help. Or he could continue working alone through the weekend.

But if he worked during the day, what was the likelihood he would be discovered? Probably fairly high, he decided. Should he gamble that no one would visit the janitor's closet until Monday morning? It's decision time, he told himself. But he needed more time to think, to evaluate the alternatives.

He checked his watch.

Almost four o'clock. Dawn would arrive in another couple of hours. Although the campus was quiet, surely someone from security would tour the building during the day. Why risk discovery and blow his chances when success was so close?

He suppressed a visceral need to continue working. He crawled slowly to his feet. With a final sweep of his light into the gaping hole, he tossed the remaining broken wallboard into the hole, cleaned up the loose debris as best he could and shoved the file cabinets back against the wall.

He smiled, satisfied with his efforts thus far. The file cabinets completely concealed the hole. The dust had been disturbed, but hopefully not enough to arouse the suspicion of a casual observer. Besides, who would expect a janitor's storage closet to be the object of a break-in? The young janitors now working at Cabot University were not as observant as old timers like Tony Amonte. He would finish before Monday. It was time to quit for the night.

He tossed the tools into his backpack, pulled on his sweatshirt, hoisted the backpack over his shoulder, turned off the light and opened the door. The building was quiet as a tomb. Standing in the dim light outside the closet, he locked the door, listened as the dead bolt slid into place and retraced his steps to the lobby.

Keeping to the shadows in the lobby, he peered into the darkness beyond the entrance doors. Beyond the floodlit plaza, the old-fashioned lamps illuminating the sidewalks across the Commons stood silent vigilance over the slumbering campus. The campus was utterly deserted. With a final glance toward the basement stairwell, he retraced his steps in the deep gloom along the corridor to the side door he had entered hours before.

He left the building and jogged silently across the damp grass toward the front gate. Concealed by the canopy of oaks and maples lining the avenue, he left the campus as the clock atop Old Main tolled four a.m.

As he turned onto Main Street, a police cruiser moved slowly toward him. Damn! What possible reason could he give for being on Main Street at this hour? He slowed to a walk, stuck his hands in his pockets and averted his face, seemingly deep in thought. The cruiser came alongside and stopped, its engine idling. He glanced toward the car and caught the lone patrolman's stare. He waved casually as adrenalin surged through his tired body. Walking slowly, he passed the closed shops and cafes. After an interminable delay, the cruiser slowly moved away from the curb and continued down the street.

By the time he reached the front steps of Mrs. Ledbetter's house, his heart had slowed to normal. He slipped into the darkened house and up the creaking stairs to his room at the end of the narrow hall. Without turning on a light, he laid his backpack on the floor beside the dresser, pulled off his sneakers and pants and was asleep almost before he hit the bed.

Chapter 35

He woke with a start. Bright sunlight streamed across the bed. The faded gauze curtains drifted back and forth in the warm breeze through the open window. Someone was laboriously cranking a sputtering lawn mower right next to his ear. The distant hum of heavy traffic on Main Street warned him that the hour was late. He rolled over on his belly, pulled back the curtain and looked outside.

The street below was empty except for the next-door neighbor and his lawnmower. Two kids on skateboards glided into view, racing along the sidewalk, rolling toward the Saturday mid-day action on Main Street. He heard Mrs. Ledbetter rattling her kitchen pots in the otherwise quiet house. The other students who rented the shabby rooms in the decrepit house had already left for the summer. He and an elderly drunk, Mark Miller, were the only paying guests.

He lay back, replaying the events of a few hours before, savoring his discovery, elated with his progress. He rolled out of bed, pulled on his pants and headed down the hall to the toilet. Ten minutes later he dialed Valerie Chapman from the phone on the stand near the front door. She agreed to meet him at Sal's in five minutes.

"Where have you been the last two weeks?" Valerie asked truculently.

"Well, hello to you, too," he drawled, following her to an empty booth in the rear of the busy hangout. "I could tell you I've been holed up in the lab working on my dissertation," he said.

"Not likely," she said sarcastically.

"You got that right," he admitted. He motioned for a waitress.

"You guys decide what you want?" the waitress slapped paper mats on the table and set some ice water in front of them.

"How about a large pizza—the works—and two colas?" Kevin asked.

"Don't tell me you're treating me," Valerie raised an eyebrow.

"We'll figure out who's paying later. I'm starved." The waitress wrote out the order and headed for the kitchen.

Kevin leaned over the table. "Actually, Val, I've been checking out that basement storage area in Connors Hall."

"Get a life, Kevin," she exclaimed. "You got me down here to tell me that? That was a dead end a couple of weeks ago, remember? I was with you when you checked it out."

"It's not a dead end now," he said.

"Your shrink was right, you really are obsessed," she interrupted him. "You're cruising for another stay in the loony bin. And wait till your advisor hears about what you've been up to."

181

"Wrong, Val. I'm not crazy and Ruth Borovski won't be hearing about what I've found. At least not yet."

She frowned. "Get to the point, Kevin. Don't jerk me around. I've got better things to do than hang around this joint."

He waited while the waitress delivered the pizza and drinks. Eyes on the beautiful girl sitting across the table, Kevin wolfed down a huge slice of pizza. With an uncharacteristic display of manners, he carefully wiped his mouth and beard with a paper napkin before continuing.

"I found it," he announced, lifting his paper cup and saluting her.

"Found what?"

"Remember those old architectural drawings for Science Hall—Connors Hall, I mean? The ones I showed you last month."

"Yeah, yeah. In the library," she said impatiently.

"Those old drawings were completely accurate. We just didn't look carefully enough. I went back last night and searched that storage closet again."

"Wait a minute!" she interrupted. "You actually spent last night inside Connors Hall? But all the classroom buildings are locked up tight. Everybody's taking a break before graduation next weekend.

"Oh, no," she rolled her eyes. "Don't tell me. You actually broke into a campus building?"

He nodded, a satisfied grin on his face.

"Whoa. So, how did you get in? Just opened the door and walked right in?" she asked skeptically.

He nodded again.

She glared, "You really are nuts, Kevin. Do you realize the trouble you'd be in if they caught you?"

"They didn't catch me and they're not going to catch me," he gloated. "I've got a master key for the whole damn campus. Hell, I could sneak into the President's office if I wanted to."

"And exactly how did you snatch a master key?" she eyed him suspiciously.

"Tony Amonte gave it to me."

"Wow. You mean the old guy who used to be a janitor?" Valerie was stunned.

"Yup, he's the one. Now are you ready to listen?"

She nodded.

"Here's the situation. What we thought was the outside wall under the basement stairwell was actually made of wallboard, not plaster like the other walls. I cut through the wallboard and guess what I found?"

"No," she whispered softly. "Don't tell me, let me guess. You found the room? The one in those old drawings? Oh, my God, you're telling me you were right?" she shrieked.

"Shut up for a minute and listen to me."

Kevin savored a rare moment in which he had the upper hand and her undivided attention. He glanced around the restaurant and lowered his voice. "There's a sealed door behind that wallboard. I'm positive it leads to the sub-basement. Probably when they renovated the building a long time ago, they just sealed off that area under the steps and the plaza."

"Great! So you've proved that the drawings were correct. Well, don't keep me in suspense. What did you find? Was the room empty? Or did you find that great big toxic waste dump you've been obsessing over for the past year," she teased him, eyes sparkling.

"You know, Val, you can be a royal pain in the butt." He finished off another wedge of pizza and took a long swallow of cola, dragging out the suspense.

"Actually, I ran into a small problem," he confessed.

"Oh, right. I should have guessed. Still another small problem," said Valerie. "It's always something."

He pounded the table. "Val, will you shut up and listen to me just once without interrupting?" he hissed.

"Okay, okay, I'll be a good girl," she leaned forward and gazed into his eyes, her fingers drumming a steady beat on the Formica tabletop.

His heel began a nervous staccato on the tile floor. She reached beneath the table and grabbed his knee. Her hand lingered longer than necessary on the inside of his leg. Startled, he moved away, burrowing deeper into the corner of the booth.

"Pay attention, Val. I worked until about four o'clock this morning. This is it," he said softly.

"I'm this close." He held his thumb and index finger half an inch apart.

"Remember, Connors Hall is ancient, built in the late 1800s. It's the oldest building on campus after Old Main. Connors was the science center until maybe twenty-five years ago. For almost a hundred years, the labs were located in Connors Hall along with all the science departments— physics, biology, you name it. Then they built Starrett Science Center and moved everything over there."

"Until you showed me those drawings in the library, I had no idea that Connors Hall had ever been anything but the business school," Valerie admitted. "Probably a lot of people, even faculty, don't know it was the old science building."

"Let's assume I'm right about what happened during the renovation," said Kevin. "The area was sealed off when they converted the building for the business school. It's conceivable that the stupid builders left some chemicals stored in the sub-basement area. Maybe the administration even knew about it," he speculated. "I'll bet you $100 I'm right," he concluded. "Whatever killed Dr. Jacob and a bunch of others on this campus was sitting right under our noses."

"Whoa, Kevin," she cautioned. "Slow down for a second. Listen to me for a change."

"First," she pointed her index finger at him, "you haven't got $100 so there's no bet." She giggled.

"Second, you found a blocked off door hidden behind some wallboard. So what? No big deal. Until you know what's behind the door, you haven't found anything."

"Shit, Val. You're really stupid when you want to be. I spent the whole damn night cutting through the wallboard!" He lowered his voice when the couple in the booth across the aisle glared at them.

"The door is secured by two heavy steel bars forming a big X across it." He crossed his arms to demonstrate. "I didn't have the time or the tools to cut through steel bars. So I just cleaned things up and moved the file cabinets back in place in case somebody checks the room today. I'm going back tonight to finish the job."

A trace of fear raced across Valerie's face.

Kevin leaned forward, determined to convince her. "Don't you see, Val," he said softly, "that area is a perfect place to store discarded chemicals. It's out of the way in the basement and nobody pays any attention to that part of the building. All kinds of junk could have been sealed in that room for twenty-five or thirty years—remember, the building housed the science departments for decades.

"Until fairly recently, nobody worried about disposing of toxic chemicals," he continued. "Why do you think there are toxic waste sites littering the whole country? Public awareness of the problem is finally beginning to sink in. Even now, very few people give a damn about toxic waste and environmental pollution," he concluded.

"You're probably right about that," Valerie admitted. "But it's still a stretch to jump from discovering an old door behind some wallboard to proving there's a toxic waste site right here on campus.

"Get real, Kevin, I won't believe you've found anything important till I see it myself."

She reached across the table and drained the rest of his cola, eyeing him, her blue eyes teasing and challenging.

"Some buddy you are," he said, disgusted. "I'll find out what's behind that door if it kills me." He grabbed the drink from her hand and slammed it down on the table.

"Dammit! I was gonna invite you to come along with me tonight. Bet you're afraid to spend the night with me," he leered.

Valerie nibbled at a cold slice of pizza. With thumb and forefinger, she daintily lifted a large round of pepperoni, wrapped it in a napkin and put it into her fanny pouch. Kevin raised an eyebrow.

"Mid-afternoon snack," she explained.

"Take the whole piece," he invited.

"Nah, just the pepperoni."

"Do you really want a partner tonight?" she asked, eyes dancing, rising to the challenge. "I've got nothing better to do. After all it's just another Saturday night in downtown Hillsdale. Why not? I can always brag that I spent the weekend before graduation hanging out in the basement of Connors Hall with a really weird geek."

Kevin put his elbows on the table. "You're chicken," he sneered.

"No I'm not," she retorted. "We're in this together. I accept your invitation!"

"You won't be sorry." Kevin grinned as they slapped high fives to seal the pact.

"And Dr. Borovski won't think I'm crazy when we find the stuff," he yawned and stretched his legs under the table, brushing her bare legs, actually relieved that she would be sharing the night's adventure.

"Trust me, Val," he said solemnly. "I'm onto something really big. I intend to blow this campus wide open and nail a few administrators in the process," he said.

"Yeah, right. The last time a guy told me to trust him, I ended up needing an abortion," she replied. He stared at her, speechless at her offhand revelation. He would never understand this beautiful girl, despite the countless hours they had spent together in the Essex psychiatric unit.

He dug into the pocket of his worn jeans, searching for cash. "You got any money?" he asked. "If you wanna be part of the action, it'll cost you. For starters, I need a heavy duty hack saw to cut through those bars, and I'm broke."

She unzipped her fanny pouch, pulled out two twenty-dollar bills and tossed them onto the table. "My contribution to our excellent adventure," she grinned.

"Thanks." He folded the bills and checked the food tab. "I'll meet you in front of your apartment about midnight. Wear dark clothes and be prepared to work. Oh, yeah, it's gonna be hot in that room. This won't be a picnic, Val," he warned. "Cutting through those bars and getting into the room may take all night. Better get your beauty rest this afternoon." It was his turn to tease.

"Don't worry about me, I'll be ready," she retorted. "Just make sure you bring the right tools and don't forget the master key."

Kevin made a gun with his thumb and index finger. He pointed at her. "Bang, bang," he laughed. "See you tonight—midnight, outside your apartment," he said. He slid from the booth and ambled along to the cashier by the door. He smiled. Tonight would be a lot more interesting with her along.

Valerie sipped the rest of Kevin's coke and casually watched him pay the cashier with one of the bills she had just provided.

Kevin walked outside into bright sunshine and headed down Main Street to Johnson's Hardware store. Ten minutes later he erupted angrily in a noisy argument with a store clerk, disputing the price of a cheap hacksaw. He couldn't know that his vitriolic outburst would be an important piece of evidence placing him in the Connors Hall basement that night.

Valerie strolled back to her apartment, clicked on the television and fell asleep watching a tennis match.

Chapter 36

He waited in the darkness near the entrance to her apartment building, sheltered by the low branches of a giant spruce tree.

Strange, he mused. He and Valerie were not exactly friends. He didn't have any friends, unless you considered Dr. Jacob a friend even though he was dead. After his last meeting with Ruth Borovski, he certainly couldn't consider her a friend. With the possible exception of Tony Amonte, his short list of friends came down to a single person, Valerie Chapman. Although they remained casually in touch following their treatment in Essex Medical Center, the shared intimacy of the psychiatric unit quickly faded when they returned to campus. Their psychiatric problems were not strong enough to forge lasting bonds.

Despite different backgrounds and interests, Kevin was glad Valerie had agreed to accompany him tonight. She would share his adventure and witness his success. She might even help with some of the work. Tonight he would prove his theory that toxic waste was stored on campus. He would link the deaths of Dr. Jacob and many others to toxic waste. That would be his final tribute to his mentor. For the first time since Dr. Jacob's death, he was at peace.

Finally, he would charge the stupid administrators who had ignored the problem, even when senior faculty members brought it to their attention. There would be plenty of blame to pass around, beginning with the President. He would show that the entire administration was guilty of criminal negligence. He would prove his theory to the skeptics, to Ruth Borovski and Nancy Atherton. And Valerie Chapman would regard him in a different light. He would no longer be the weird graduate student.

He got to his feet and brushed off the spruce needles that clung to his jeans. Sheltered by the tree, he watched Valerie open the glass entrance door of the building and step outside into the warm evening. She glanced around, suddenly appearing vulnerable and uncertain.

"I'm by the tree on your right," he said quietly. Startled, she peered into the darkness and walked slowly in his direction. He stepped from the shadows, his heavy backpack slung over his shoulder.

"Ready for your big adventure?" he asked.

"Ready," she said quietly.

They walked the three blocks to the intersection of Main Street and University Avenue. The streets were empty except for a few boisterous students weaving unsteadily down the street, headed for the residence halls on campus. Shops and restaurants close early in Hillsdale, even on a warm spring Saturday night. The late movie had emptied out more than an hour ago.

They turned up University Avenue toward Old Main, two anonymous students strolling quietly along the avenue. An occasional light glowed from the upstairs bedrooms of Hillsdale's most prominent families. The town was preparing for sleep.

Kevin broke the silence. "We'll jump over the stone wall near Old Main," he whispered. "We could go through the main gate, but I want to stay away from the lights around Old Main. Then we'll cut directly across the grass to Connors Hall. Even though the place is deserted, there's no point in advertising our presence."

"You're in charge," she said meekly. As they approached the main entrance in front of Old Main, she slowed. This little adventure might not be such a lark after all.

"What's the matter? Getting cold feet?" he glanced down at her.

"No. But we'll be in big trouble if we get caught," she said. "I don't want anything to mess up my graduation. My mother would have a stroke if I get into any more trouble, especially after my hospital stay. Dad's so wrapped up with his new girlfriend he doesn't care what happens to me."

"Nothing's going to happen except that we turn this whole campus upside down. You'll see," he displayed a show of bravado he didn't completely feel.

They scrambled over the low rock wall at the edge of the campus and made their way across the grass toward the plaza in front of Connors Hall. A casual observer seeing them in the dim light of the sidewalk lamps would assume they were students returning to their residence hall.

Arms around each other, they strolled casually to the side entrance of the building. Illuminated by a single bright floodlight above the door, they stood exposed for a few seconds while Kevin unlocked the door. They slipped quietly into the building and paused, waiting for their eyes to adjust to the dim interior. The building was silent, shrouded in darkness except for the red exit signs over the door and down the hall.

Kevin took her hand and guided her along the now-familiar corridor to the front lobby. Hugging the wall, they made their way to the stairway leading to the basement. For a few seconds they were exposed in the ambient light from the floodlit plaza beyond the main doors. He led her confidently down the familiar dark stairs to the basement.

Laying his backpack against the door to the janitor's closet, he unzipped the flap, fished out the heavy-duty flashlight and turned it on, shielding the beam. He pulled Tony's master key from his jeans pocket and unlocked the door.

Grabbing his heavy backpack, he pulled her inside the janitor's closet and closed the door. He twisted the dead bolt and, taking the dirty towel from his pack, stuffed it along the crack at the bottom of the door.

Then he flipped on the wall switch, flooding the room with light from the overhead fluorescent. He surveyed the room. Evidence of his work from the night before was obvious. In his haste to leave before dawn, he hadn't realized how much debris was in plain sight.

Valerie looked around. "This place is a mess. Even our do-nothing janitors would notice all this junk. You're lucky they didn't find this rubbish. Oh well, I'll help you clean it up before Monday. No one will know we've been here," she assured him.

"Let's get to work," Kevin checked his watch. "We've got about five hours to finish this." Taking the tools from his backpack, he arranged them neatly on the floor. Together, they wrestled the file cabinets aside, exposing the full extent of Kevin's work the previous night.

"Wow, you really have been busy," Valerie whispered, checking out the gaping hole and heavy steel bars crossing the exposed door to the sub-basement.

"Right. Are you here to help or just stand around and talk?" he asked, irritated and tense. "Even with these tools, breaking through that door won't be easy."

"Okay, okay. Just tell me what to do."

They labored without pause for the next three hours, first enlarging the hole to expose the entire door from the floor to the height of the file cabinets. Kevin hoped that the cabinets, when pushed back against the wall, would conceal their work. In addition to the steel bars blocking the door, they discovered that heavy nails had been pounded into the frame to further secure the door. Pulling the nails proved to be time-consuming but manageable. At last, they were ready to tackle the steel bars that were anchored diagonally across the door from top to bottom.

Kevin reached into his backpack and pulled out the large hacksaw. "See, this is what some of your money bought for our little adventure. The asshole clerk gave me such a hard time about the price that I almost slugged him. He finally knocked off a couple of bucks because the handle was chipped." He showed it to her.

"Yeah, and my bucks paid for your lunch too," she said dryly.

"A guy's gotta eat, and I'm broke," he retorted.

He positioned the hacksaw against one crossbar near the bottom of the door below the lock. Tentatively, he began to saw at a forty-five degree angle in the cramped space between the door and the bar. The grinding noise screeched through the room. He stopped, handed Valerie the saw and took the flashlight.

"I'd better check the noise level in the lobby upstairs before we do much more. Give me time to get upstairs, then start sawing," he directed. He unlocked the door, closing it softly behind him. Faintly, she heard him climb the stairs to the lobby. She waited a few moments, then carefully placed the hacksaw in the groove and slowly began to work the blade back and forth.

Standing in the middle of the lobby near the stairs to the second floor, Kevin listened, relieved. The screech of metal against metal was barely audible. A security guard walking through the lobby might not notice it.

He ran downstairs.

"I could hardly hear you," he said, taking the hacksaw from her and resuming work. "We gotta take the chance. Without the saw, we'll never cut through these bars."

Single cuts through each bar would not be enough. He estimated that the steel bars were perhaps one-half inch thick. It would be impossible to bend them out of the way. He would need to make four cuts—one at the end of each crossbar. Then he could lift them out.

Two hours later the heavy work was done. Sweating and exhausted, he slumped to the floor. Together, they inspected their handiwork. The two bars lay on the floor near the pile of steel shavings. Finally, the heavy wooden door was accessible, ready to be opened.

For reasons he could not explain, Kevin suddenly was in no hurry to pry open the door.

Valerie got to her feet and wiped off the back of her shorts. "Now what are you waiting for?" she demanded. "Let's see if anything is behind that damned door. You're acting as if you don't want to know. We haven't got all night, as you reminded me several hours ago." She checked her watch. "Why don't you just do it? You've waited long enough. This is your big moment and you certainly have my undivided attention."

He glared at her. He scrambled to his feet, placed his thin shoulder against the heavy wood door and pushed.

Nothing. The door was stuck.

He moved back a step, thrust his shoulder against the door and pushed. With a load screech, the door gave way. He lost his balance and nearly fell into the black opening. Grabbing the doorframe, he recovered as Valerie clutched at the back of his shirt and pulled him back.

A heavy musty smell gagged them momentarily. He reached for the flashlight and directed the beam into the dark hole. When the dust settled, the flashlight illuminated several rotted wooden steps leading to the earthen floor of the sub-basement. Then the unmistakable odor of chemicals assaulted them. They staggered back into the cleaner air of the storage room.

"Quick, Val, get something over your nose and mouth—a rag, a hankie, anything. The fumes could be toxic," Kevin gasped. He found a dirty T-shirt in his pack and tossed it to her. She tore the shirt in half, covered her nose and mouth with one piece and handed the rest back to him. Bent double, gasping and choking, they ignored the need for caution and opened the door to the corridor and fresh air.

For interminable minutes, they lay coughing and gasping in the corridor outside the storage room. Finally, Kevin ordered, "You stay here. I'll go back inside and check the air."

He cautiously opened the door, closing it quickly behind him. With his foot he kicked the towel along the bottom of the door to block the fumes. He went to the open door to the sub-basement and directed the flashlight beam down the rotted steps to the hard packed earthen floor some five feet below. Then he pointed the beam beyond the steps into the murky darkness.

He thought his heart would burst. There, like soldiers on parade, he spotted rows of 55-gallon drums receding into the murky darkness at the rear of the sub-basement. Kevin went back to the storage room door and let Valerie inside. Ignoring the fumes, he took her hand and led her to the open door to the sub-basement, shining his light on the rows of drums, neatly stacked, sealed for untold decades.

"There they are," he whispered.

"My God, Kevin," she gasped. "You were right all along. You really weren't crazy."

"Count them," Kevin ordered. He directed the flashlight beam along the rows as she began to count. Twenty-five large barrels were arranged in five neat rows. Nearly indecipherable markings, covered with years of grime, were stenciled on the side of each barrel. Aiming the flashlight beam onto the nearest barrel, they could make out faded markings on the steel tops.

"There's no doubt about it, those drums are full of chemicals. What kinds of chemicals is another question," he could hardly breath.

Stacked on each side of the wooden steps were perhaps twenty smaller steel containers. Kevin thought the drums were probably ten gallons each. Faded markings were barely visible on each container.

"Damn," he swore. "Val, check out the bottoms of those barrels." He directed the beam toward the earthen floor. "Some of them have completely rusted out. And look at the floor—it's just packed dirt," his voice rose.

"Some dickhead stored this shit down here, then sealed up the room and left the God damned stuff to rot. Look! Even some of the small drums are leaking. At least some of the chemicals have spilled out and soaked into the dirt floor.

"Look at the soil around the big barrels." He flashed the beam around the room. "See, it's discolored, darker than the rest of the dirt. Some of them have leaked, too. Probably most of this floor is contaminated with chemicals."

191

In the dim light, surrounded by tools and debris, breathing through the thin cotton T-shirt, Valerie turned to Kevin, stunned at the enormity of their discovery. "What if this stuff really is toxic? Let's get out of here before we inhale any more of these fumes." She panicked, terrified at the implications. Suddenly, she began to cry.

Kevin gathered her in his arms and held her close, patting her awkwardly, trying to comfort her. "Easy, take it easy. We can deal with this. Trust me, things are going to be okay, Val. You're my buddy, you can't let me down now, not when we've found the cache," he whispered calmly.

Slowly, she regained control. She stepped out of his embrace, wiped a few tears on her sleeve. "Sorry. I panicked a little. The fumes are making me nauseous," she smiled faintly, her face streaked with dirt and sweat. He reached for her again. Without thinking, he suddenly leaned down and kissed her gently on the lips. Surprised, she responded slowly, then more urgently, moving her arms up his back and pulling him toward her, seeking his tongue. Kevin found himself aroused for the first time in many months.

He drew back. "Wait," he whispered, "let's not begin something we don't want to finish in this dump."

"Right," she giggled, her confidence restored. "You might want to consider investigating this situation further when we get out of here," she regarded him in the harsh light of the storage room.

"That's a promise," he grinned. "Now let's figure out what to do next."

On hands and knees, they crawled to the dark sub-basement entry. Kevin reached for his backpack and retrieved a small instrument.

"What's that?" Valerie asked suspiciously.

"It's a portable Geiger counter. I scrounged it from the lab last summer in case I wanted to test something for radiation," he explained. "You never know when a device like this will come in handy. I need to check for radiation down there."

He stooped and gingerly put one foot on the rotted top step, cautiously shifting some of his weight. The step snapped with a dull crack and thudded to the earthen floor. Kevin regained his balance and stood up in the entrance to the sub-basement.

"Here, hold the light," he handed her the flashlight. "I'll jump down and get a closer look." She didn't argue. Hanging onto the doorframe, he dropped the five feet into the hole, sprawled forward and scrambled to his feet.

"Are you okay?"

"Yeah, fine."

Brushing the dirt from his hands, he reached up for the flashlight.

"There's a smaller flashlight in my pack. Get it and shine it on these small drums near the steps," he said. She found the flashlight and seated herself at the edge of the rotted stairs, her legs dangling into the sub-basement. She pointed the beam onto the ten-gallon drums.

"I gotta believe that whoever left this stuff here knew it was toxic," Kevin said, deeply angry. "Somebody in the administration sealed off this area. They're responsible for this mess."

"If the building was renovated a long time ago, maybe they just forgot about it. Or maybe they thought sealing it off was okay," Valerie speculated. "You've got to admit, they sealed it off very securely."

"I doubt they forgot it," Kevin retorted. "The size of this cache is amazing. We wouldn't use this volume of chemicals in the research labs in five years. And our labs are much bigger now than they were years ago.

"I can't imagine how the university could have accumulated so much waste. These barrels probably contain years of discarded chemicals that were never removed. It's a classic example of a toxic waste dump—and it's right here on campus."

He bent over and cautiously tipped one of the small drums. He leaped back. "Damn! This drum is leaking! See, the ground is damp beneath it," he exclaimed, taking care not to touch the contaminated soil. Valerie's beam focused on a trickle of fresh black liquid oozing from a rusty hole the size of a quarter near the bottom of the drum.

"I'll bet that some—maybe all—of these containers are leaking. They may be nearly empty. This crud just seeped into the soil over the years." He tilted two adjacent barrels and found wet, black soil beneath each one.

"Toss me a rag and shine your light toward the back," he directed. "There's something stenciled on the sides and tops of the barrels." He propped his large flashlight atop an adjacent drum. Gingerly, he rubbed the side of the barrel, revealing faded marks that Valerie, crouching above Kevin in the open doorway, couldn't read.

"Well, what do you know," Kevin whispered. "Here's a skull and crossbones. The classic symbol for poison. But it hasn't been used for years.

"Look here," he rubbed the side of the barrel. "This looks like a name and address." He directed his flashlight beam to the side of the barrel.

"Ever hear of Saxton Controls?" he asked.

"No, but I'm not a science major."

"Tony Amonte mentioned that name to me a month ago. Before that I didn't know much about them either," he said, "Saxton is the name stenciled on this barrel. The company may know what's in these barrels, but I think it's no longer in business," he speculated.

Valerie held the flashlight steady while Kevin wiped decades of filth from the rusty side of the leaking barrel. "The paint is badly faded, but it looks like the complete address is here. Saxton is located at Hillsdale RD#3. That's north of town along the river. The old road to Scranton goes through that area. Tony Amonte said there was a factory out that way a long time ago. Now, there's only a bunch of relatively new houses," he said.

Valerie tossed him a clean rag. He wiped his hands carefully. "I remember as a kid riding my bike along the river on the old road. If there was a chemical company in that area, it sure as hell isn't there now," he said. "We can check it out later," he said, wiping his sweaty forehead and beard on his shirtsleeve.

He wiped more filth from the top surface of the barrel. "Whoa," he exclaimed, "There's a date on this barrel! It says 6-29-48. Do you suppose this stuff has been sitting down here since 1948? That's more than fifty years ago! Incredible!"

"There's enough dirt and crud on these barrels to believe it could be fifty years," Valerie observed.

"If that date's accurate," he continued, "these barrels were stored here long before the building was renovated. According to the records, Science Hall was renovated into the business school and renamed Connors Hall about twenty-five years ago."

"No wonder you never heard of Saxton Controls," exclaimed Valerie. "These barrels may have been stored here since long before we were born."

"Right," said Kevin. "They may not even be university property. For sure, they've been stored here a hell of a long time. Maybe this stuff had nothing to do with our chemistry labs," he said. "There's just too much volume. It had to come from off campus, probably from this Saxton Controls outfit. There's no way we could use that many chemicals—or whatever is in these barrels. But why would a commercial company store materials here?"

Kevin stared up at Valerie from the cramped sub-basement, his filthy T-shirt soaked with sweat, his forehead and arms gleaming, dark beard glistening in the dim light. The dark shadows closed around him as he stood, hands on hips, surrounded by the cache of chemicals.

He set to work. "Before we do anything else, I'm going to check the room for radiation. It's remotely possible some sort of nuclear contamination is here along with the chemicals." He switched on the Geiger counter, checked some meters and set a few controls. He moved slowly around the room as Valerie's light illuminated his path. Occasionally, a faint click was heard.

"There's definitely some low level radiation here, but I won't be able to identify the source until we get some samples out of here and analyze them."

Valerie scrambled to her feet in the entrance. "Shouldn't we just leave? Maybe we're being contaminated right now." She started to panic again.

"Relax, Val. The counter is not registering much radiation. Whatever is here won't kill us, at least not if we don't stay too long," he said sarcastically.

"Oh, thanks, Kevin. That's very reassuring," she retorted.

"This really is amazing," he ignored her, finally coming to grips with the enormity of the discovery. "How long have I tried to convince people that something is wrong on this campus, that too many people are dying of cancer? Nobody listened. They said I was crazy. Well, I was right all along. We've got the evidence right in front of us," his voice cracked.

"Valerie, the chemicals leaking out of these containers are probably toxic; and they've been sitting here for half a century. Some of it has seeped into the ground and spread God knows where. Look at this floor. It's just hard packed dirt. And look at the stains," he said.

He stared up at her from the bottom of the rotted steps. "Do you understand what I'm saying?"

"Yes."

"Here's my theory. Over the years, as these barrels eventually rusted out, whatever they contained slowly seeped into the ground, maybe deep enough to reach the water table." He paused, thinking hard.

"Is that possible?"

"Yes, of course. Do you know that the campus water supply comes from two deep wells out behind the heating plant?" he asked.

"No. How would I know or care about where we get our water?"

"Val, the heating plant is less than a hundred yards from here! There's an outside chance that whatever's leaked out of these barrels has worked into the water supply. The whole campus may be drinking contaminated water!" he shouted.

"Oh, Kevin! Is that possible?" asked Valerie, panic rising again. "If you're right, then those people you talked about may have gotten sick and died needlessly. And others may be sick right now and not know it." She was close to tears again.

"Yeah, and I probably shouldn't be mucking around in this soil, and both of us shouldn't be breathing these fumes."

He tossed his flashlight up to her and tried to hoist himself from the hole. Valerie grabbed his arm and pulled as he struggled onto the floor. Panting, he crawled into the center of the room. They flopped on the floor, gasping for breath. He reached into the backpack for a clean towel and wiped the dirt and sweat from his hands and face. He checked the bottoms of his sneaks and cleaned them off.

She began to cry. "Hey, this is no time for tears," he gently wiped away her tears. "We should be celebrating—we just found what I've spent the last year searching for," he said softly. "Don't worry, you won't get sick from this. Our exposure has been too limited," he spoke with an assurance he didn't feel.

"But what a mess! What are we going to do?" she brushed her hair back and looked at him, tears streaking her tanned face.

He glanced toward the dark hole, pulled his knees close to his chest and laced his arms around them. He was silent for a few moments. Finally, he scrambled to his feet, pulled her up and away from the gaping hole.

"We can do nothing more right now," he said decisively.

He looked around the room. "There's no way we can put this back together like we found it. And there's no need to hide our work. Before this weekend is over, the whole world will know what's been going on at Cabot University," he vowed.

"I need a little time to figure out what to do next." He glanced at his watch. "It's almost five o'clock." He tossed the dirty rags into his backpack. "We gotta get out of here before daylight. The janitors typically don't work on Sunday, but I don't want to be seen around this building. I doubt that anybody will check this closet today anyway," he said.

"I really need your help," his voice softened as she avoided his gaze. "We have to come back here one more time—tonight. I can't do this without you."

"I don't know if I have the nerve to sneak in here again," Valerie shivered despite the heat and humidity in the room. Her voice trembled.

"We'll be together," he said gently. "Trust me. I haven't been wrong yet. Nothing's going to happen to us. You saw how easily we got in. We can do it again. This job will take another night to finish, that's all. Besides, Sunday night is the deadest night on campus," he reminded her.

"If anyone comes in here, they'll see this mess. Should we just leave those barrels exposed?" she asked doubtfully.

"Yes. And don't argue with me."

He gathered the tools and flashlights and stashed them in his backpack. "I'm beat. We both need some rest," he said. "We'll figure out what to do later. I need a little time to plan how to get the stuff out of the hole, and I need to check the library for information on Saxton Controls. If I know what the company manufactured, I'll have a better idea of what's in those barrels," he said, thinking aloud.

"Come on, we'll come back tonight."

Kevin hoisted the backpack over his shoulder without a backward glance toward the gaping hole and the sub-basement beyond. He opened the outer door and waited for Valerie. He flipped off the light switch and carefully locked the door as they left. Side by side, they climbed the stairs to the lobby and glanced through the glass doors to the plaza outside, barely visible in the gray light of dawn.

"Can I come back to your apartment?" he blurted out, surprised at his own boldness.

She hesitated for an instant. "OK. It's more private than Mrs. Ledbetter's. Nobody will bother us with questions."

Retracing their steps to the side entrance, they left the building. Hand and hand, the two students jogged across campus to University Avenue. They reached Main Street as dawn signaled the beginning of another day.

*   *   *   *

Ten minutes later, as the sun climbed above the eastern hills beyond the river, Valerie and Kevin reached her apartment building. Unobserved, Kevin waited patiently while Valerie unlocked the door to her apartment and led him inside.

"Where's your john?" he asked abruptly. She pointed to the closed door near the bedroom. Without waiting for an invitation, Kevin headed for the bathroom. Moments later Valerie heard the shower running. She went to her bedroom, rummaged through the closet and pulled out an old pair of baggy sweatpants and shirt. Crossing to the bathroom, she banged a warning on the door, tossed the clothes inside and retreated to the kitchen.

Kevin showered and pulled on the ill-fitting sweats, leaving his filthy clothes, sneaks and socks in a pile on the bathroom floor. He strolled barefoot into the living room as the early morning sun cast a shaft of light across the beige carpet. Without speaking, he sprawled face down on the sofa opposite the television set and within seconds, he was fast asleep.

Valerie popped the tab on a can of beer, tore open a fresh bag of chips and came into the living room. She set the beer and chips on the coffee table and stared at the strange young man with whom she had just spent the most extraordinary night of her life. His damp hair and beard darkened the light fabric of the sofa. Barefoot and in her sweats, he looked surprisingly vulnerable. Smiling, she put his heavy backpack in a corner near the front door and closed the drapes across the slider leading to the tiny deck overlooking the swimming pool. She turned out the lights.

Gathering Kevin's filthy clothing from the bathroom, she tossed them in a corner of her bedroom. Before she closed the bedroom drapes, she checked the lock on the slider to the narrow balcony overlooking the parking area below. She undressed quietly and threw her own sweat-stained and soiled garments into the corner. Naked, she entered the bathroom and stepped into the shower. As the first needles of hot water struck her face, waves of bone deep fatigue and emotional exhaustion overwhelmed her. Dripping, she wrapped herself in an oversized towel, returned to the bedroom and locked the door between the bedroom and living room. She found a clean extra-large Cabot Cougar T-shirt and collapsed across the bed. She would deal with her feelings toward Kevin Parks later.

*   *   *   *

Kevin awoke with a start, his heart pounding. Disoriented, it was a moment before he realized that he was lying on the floor of Valerie's living room. A door slammed and faint laughter drifted into the room. The voices receded as tenants from across the hall left the building. He checked his watch. It was nearly one o'clock. He had slept more than seven hours.

He felt refreshed and energized despite waking up on the plush carpet instead of the sofa. He yawned and stretched, basking in the quiet coolness of the dusky room. Rolling onto his stomach, he surveyed the apartment. Not bad. Amazing what a little money will buy. He glanced toward the closed bedroom door. She must still be asleep. He got to his feet and headed for the bathroom, making no effort to be quiet. A few minutes later, having brushed his teeth with Valerie's toothbrush, he explored the small kitchen. Opening the refrigerator, he helped himself to a generous portion of orange juice directly from the paper carton.

"That's an absolutely gross habit," Valerie observed, walking noiselessly into the kitchen behind him.

Kevin jumped. "Yeah, right. Sorry" he said sheepishly. "So how long have you been standing there?"

"Long enough," she retorted. "The glasses are in the cupboard. They're meant to be used," she lectured. "I hate people who drink from open cartons." Her smile took the edge off her words. She regarded him mischievously, her long blond hair tangled from sleep, huge blue eyes mocking him. They regarded each other awkwardly, suddenly strangers.

"I'm not much of a breakfast eater," she said, finally breaking the spell. "But I can make some coffee and there are some bagels in the freezer."

"Sounds terrific," he suddenly realized he hadn't eaten since noon yesterday at the pizza joint. She measured coffee, added water and turned on the coffee maker. She padded barefooted around the tiny kitchen, clad only in the oversized Cabot Cougar T-shirt and a pair of bikini panties, clearly outlined beneath the thin T-shirt.

Kevin stared, astonished at the casual way she flaunted her body. Valerie Chapman was doubtless the most beautiful girl he had ever laid eyes on. Without thinking, he impulsively reached across the counter and unplugged the coffee maker. Compelled by a latent and deeply repressed sexuality, he touched her shoulder and slowly drew her toward him. They faced each other, bodies lightly touching in the close confines of the brightly lighted kitchen.

"Remember what we started last night?" he whispered.

"My memory's pretty good, Kevin," she said softly.

Without warning, he bent his long thin frame and kissed her gently on the mouth, his hands cupping her face. She stepped back, bumping into the counter. Undeterred, he pressed slowly forward, gently pinning her against the counter, an arm reaching around her waist and drawing her closer.

Slowly, she began to respond. Her arms encircled his waist, melding his body to her own through the thin T-shirt. What began as a tentative kiss, a question and an invitation, surged with urgency neither could deny. Kevin reached behind her and flipped the light switch. Locked in a tight embrace, he put both arms around her tiny waist, as they slowly, soundlessly danced to unheard music through the living room to the bedroom.

Their lovemaking was swift and urgent. Kevin, the neophyte lover, eagerly yielded to Valerie's superior experience. She guided him with her hands and mouth, her movements revealing a level of sexual expertise he gratefully accepted but later wondered about. He couldn't wait. With a muffled shout, he lost himself in her body. She responded by pulling him closer, their voices rising together.

They made love through the long spring afternoon, first with the urgency of lovers exploring a new world together. Then more slowly, they began the journey toward the peace and security of experienced lovers. In the space of a quiet Sunday afternoon they came together, physically and emotionally bonding, discovering in each other pleasures neither dreamed existed.

That afternoon, in a fusion of exploration and lovemaking, they began the process of healing the crippling wounds of abuse and parental neglect that had shaped their lives. The physical and psychological traumas of the past that had nearly destroyed them would no longer control their lives.

They interrupted each other with revelations of young lives warped by abuse and fear. Kevin, the child of abuse, confessed his darkest secrets and exorcised the demons that even Dr. Jerry Siegel had never touched. He reveled in the strength of his resurgent manhood.

Valerie, the slender blond beauty, revealed a fragile self-image concealed behind a cocky, aloof exterior. The trauma of her parents' divorce seemed more manageable. The healing process each had begun during their psychiatric treatment took hold at last. As the barriers melted away, they grew confident that this commitment would not end with the betrayals that had nearly destroyed them in the past.

Their traumas—Valerie's bulimia and pain following her parent's divorce, Kevin's unrelenting episodes of sexual abuse during his teenage years, the panic and loss of Dr. Jacob, the months of darkness in the psychiatric unit and Kevin's seemingly futile search for answers over the past nine months—all yielded to new perspectives. For the first time in their young lives, Kevin and Valerie experienced a fulfillment they had never known before. Inextricably bound together by their past, they embraced a new beginning, confident of a future of limitless possibilities.

*   *   *   *

They finally opened the bedroom drapes as the sun, a massive red ball, slowly disappeared beyond the row of maples bordering the asphalt parking lot. Kevin, clad once again in Valerie's sweatpants and shirt, casually observed a lone figure dive into the pool. He turned from the window and regarded Valerie across the unkempt bed.

"There is still work to do on campus, Val," he sighed, reality finally intruding.

She ignored him. "I don't know about you, but I'm starved. Strange, sex never made me hungry before," she confessed.

"You're hungry because you haven't eaten anything for nearly a day. Well, no food anyway," he corrected himself, flopping onto the bed beside her.

Giggling, she reached for him. Feeling no positive response, she rolled out of bed, retrieved her T-shirt from the floor where she had tossed it hours earlier and pulled it over her tousled hair.

"We can eat while you figure out what to do next," she decided. She padded into the kitchen, turned on the oven and pulled a large pizza from the freezer. She twisted the tops from two cold beers, handed one to Kevin and raised her own.

"Cheers." They saluted each other.

Kevin found another bag of potato chips on top of the refrigerator, searched the cabinets for plates and napkins and set them on the small dining table nestled in a corner of the living room. Half an hour later they had devoured the large pizza, the chips and two more beers.

Relaxed and more contented than ever in his life, Kevin stretched his long legs beneath the table, nudging Valerie playfully.

Valerie's long blond hair had fallen over her face. She regarded him thoughtfully, her blue eyes serious, suddenly subdued. "I guess we can't avoid dealing with that cache of toxic chemicals or whatever is in those barrels stored smack in the middle of the campus.

"Have you figured out a game plan for tonight?"

"I haven't had time to give that problem much thought. Probably because I've been kind of busy," he smiled the contented smile of a bearded Cheshire cat. "Shouldn't take long to figure out something," he said.

"Well, we've only got tonight," she reminded him. "Tomorrow morning the first janitor into the storage room will find the mess and sound the alarm. Maybe we should let the administration figure out what to do. That's one alternative."

"No. I don't trust the administration, Val."

"I've been thinking about the stuff we found—whatever is in those drums is poison, otherwise they wouldn't have the skull and crossbones markings," she stated the obvious. "But maybe you're jumping to the wrong conclusions. I can't see how those chemicals—whatever they are—can be responsible for a lot of people dying of cancer at Cabot. That's a real stretch, Kevin. I'm no scientist, but it just doesn't seem possible."

Kevin tried to interrupt.

"Wait a minute," she raised her hand, determined to continue, "let me finish before you start punching holes in my nonscientific, perfectly rational, theory."

He settled back in his chair, arms folded across his chest, the superior smirk of a scientist on his face.

"Let's assume," she continued, "that those barrels *are* full of toxic waste. If the dates on the barrels are right, they've sat there for about fifty years. Thousands of students and faculty have used that building and most of them *didn't* get cancer—at least not that we know about. From what you've been able to find out, a few people on campus have died of cancer during the last twenty years. I'll grant you that much. But most of those people probably didn't work in Connors Hall—Science Hall—whatever it used to be called. Also, thousands of students attended Cabot during those years and we haven't heard about a cancer epidemic among the graduates.

"I don't understand how waste materials that were sealed off in a sub-basement storage area, apparently undisturbed, for so many years could cause cancer," she concluded.

She gathered the plates and bottles and went into the kitchen. "It's a real stretch to go from finding those waste materials last night—that's plenty serious enough—to jumping to the conclusion that toxic waste has caused a bunch of cancer deaths among the faculty at Cabot University," she said over her shoulder, loading the dishwasher. Throwing the pizza scraps and empty beer bottles into the trash basket, she returned to her seat.

"Are you finished now, Val?" He looked at her quizzically.

"Yeah, I guess so."

"Good. Now listen up." Kevin leaned toward her, his dark eyes brilliant, totally focused. "I'm well aware we haven't proved that whatever is in those barrels is responsible for deaths on campus or even that people are being contaminated by toxic waste." He shifted in his seat. "We have a lot of work to do before we can reach any conclusions. For example, I need to analyze the substances in those barrels to figure out exactly what's there, how long it's been stored there, who Saxton Controls is and what they manufactured."

He raised his finger. "We do know that some of the barrels have leaked into the soil in the sub-basement. That's a fact. The soil must be tested to see how deep the leakage extends into the ground.

"The worst-case scenario is that toxic waste has seeped into the water supply for the entire campus. I suspect that's exactly what's happened. If I'm right, everyone who drank the water from those deep wells over the past twenty or more years may be at risk. I'm sure that the water is tested periodically, but those tests may only be looking for certain bacteria. If they haven't been tested for the specific chemicals in those barrels, they won't find them.

"My worst fear is that those barrels contain not one or two isolated chemicals, but a whole group of toxic chemicals. A witch's brew."

"Whoa, aren't you getting ahead of things, Kevin? Admit it, we don't have any idea what's in those barrels. I haven't taken a chemistry course since prep school," she confessed. "I wouldn't know how to test whether a solution is toxic or volatile. How can you tell?" she asked curiously.

"I already have a pretty good idea based on the odor and viscosity of the liquid. The materials that soaked into the soil were very thick and possibly even volatile. I've got to analyze the solution to identify its chemical composition."

"You're right," Valerie agreed.

"It'll take a thorough investigation to get to the bottom of this," Kevin continued. "Based on what I saw last night, I would expect both state and federal Environmental Protection Agencies to be involved. And it's likely that the federal EPA will eventually have jurisdiction over the cleanup. I'll bet you $100 right now that this dump is so lethal that it will be designated for Superfund Cleanup.

"Make no mistake, Valerie, what we found last night is very serious. I'll stake my life on that prediction. What bothers me most about this whole situation is that the university administration may have deliberately hidden those barrels right here on campus among thousands of students," he exclaimed. "If we could prove negligence by the administration, more than a few heads would roll," he smiled, pleased at the prospect.

"Well, we can't prove anything until somebody tests the stuff," Valerie reminded him. "That's probably the role of some government agency. How do you propose to notify the university administration that we've found this stuff?

"Why don't we just sit back and watch what happens when the janitors find the mess tomorrow?" she suggested. "Chances are, they'll never know who found it unless we come forward and admit it."

"Wrong, Val. Our fingerprints are all over the place right now."

He sat silent, thinking.

"Let's go," he said abruptly, reaching for his sneaks and socks.

"You going to clue me in on your plan?" she asked over her shoulder, heading toward the bedroom closet. She slipped into a pair of tight jeans and sweatshirt.

"First stop is the library. I want to know more about Saxton Controls." He picked up his backpack and headed for the door. He turned back to the living room. "Have you got a camera?" he asked.

She rummaged through a desk drawer, and handed Kevin a small digital camera. He slipped it into the front pouch of the backpack. They left the apartment, Valerie locking the door and sliding her key chain into her jeans pocket.

"Shouldn't you tell Dr. Borovski what we've found?" she asked as they hurried toward the campus in the warm evening dusk. "After all, she's your advisor and she has a lot of influence on campus. She could make sure the chemicals are removed properly. Maybe you should call her tonight before we go back into the building."

"She's the last person I can talk to now," he said grimly. "We had our last meeting about my research two weeks ago. She told me I'm being thrown out of the Ph.D. program. If I don't finish my dissertation by the end of June, I'm history. And there's no way I can finish it by then. For sure, the administration will be glad to see me go," he said bitterly.

"I gave her my analysis of cancer deaths on campus more than a month ago. She supposedly reviewed it and decided that it's insignificant—said it doesn't prove anything. She wouldn't even talk about it, just kept bitching about my dissertation. Now you know why I won't trust any faculty."

"I'm sorry, Kevin." They reached the campus and walked along the broad sidewalk toward the library. "Maybe if you work like crazy, you'll be able to finish. Besides, when they see what you've found in Connors Hall, the administration might let you stay on," she suggested.

"Not a chance," he said. "My college days are over. At least you'll graduate next weekend. I'm glad for you, whatever happens."

Chapter 37

Sunday was the slowest day of the week on campus. With classes ended, the library was nearly deserted. They entered through the broad glass doors and went immediately to the business reference stacks on the second floor. Kevin sat down at a terminal and keyed in his ID number. He strolled to a rack of CD ROM disks filed nearby, searched for a moment, found the disk he was looking for and inserted the CD into a drive, waiting patiently while it loaded. Using key word search techniques, he launched a systematic search.

The CD he selected contained the university's historical records since its founding more than one hundred years earlier. In seconds, he found the records of Cabot University's development during the 1940s. Valerie dragged over a chair and watched, fascinated, as his fingers flew across the keyboard, and he scanned historical and summary financial data that was more than fifty years old.

"Bingo!" said Kevin, moments later. He pointed a finger at the color monitor. "See, Val. Here's a single reference to Saxton Controls in 1950. Now I can isolate the data on Saxton and see what specific information there is on the company."

In short order, they found a reference linking Saxton Controls to a major chemical company headquartered in New Jersey. Although the data on the company's Hillsdale division was rudimentary, clearly it had existed for at least twenty years before, during and after World War II.

"Look, Saxton Controls filed for bankruptcy in 1956," whispered Valerie, gazing intently at the computer screen. "That's why you never heard of it."

"Now I can further isolate the search on its business history," said Kevin, in his element as he keyed in some search commands. They waited while the computer searched the CD. Seconds later, the following data was displayed on the color monitor:

Saxton Controls, Inc., division of Atlas Chemical, Newark, New Jersey, incorporated in Delaware, 1935. Declared bankruptcy June 15, 1956 following loss of key government contracts. Assets liquidated, liabilities paid at rate of $0.30 per dollar owed. Divisions located in Jackson, Tenn. and Hillsdale, Penna. Hillsdale plant, manufacturer of radium-coated dials for aircraft instruments during World War II, was also subcontractor to Manhattan Project, 1942-48. Classified

**work included design and manufacture of precision
trigger mechanisms for atomic weapons. Hillsdale plant
closed 1956. Real estate sold 1960. Buildings demolished
and site cleared. Housing development constructed
1970-75. Assets of Jackson, Tenn. division transferred to
Atomic Energy Commission late 1956 in Oak Ridge,
Tenn.**

"Whoa," Kevin shouted. "Little old Saxton Controls was a nuke company during World War II! Val, they manufactured aircraft instruments using radium and they also built trigger mechanisms for atom bombs—the only thing more dangerous than that would be purifying uranium and plutonium like the government did at Hanford, Washington. This is unbelievable! No wonder we never heard of Saxton Controls. Their work during World War II was top secret, and then they went bankrupt in 1956, more than forty years ago!

"Damn! Some of those barrels we found probably contain radioactive waste! What if that shit seeped into the groundwater?" he asked, barely able to contain his excitement. "I'll bet they didn't take a lot of precautions dealing with waste, and Saxton probably generated some of the most dangerous waste materials known to man. And that crud has been stored on campus since the late 1940s!" he exclaimed.

"Shh! The reference librarian is watching us, Kevin. Let's get out of here!"

"Relax, Val. Let me print a copy of this reference," he lowered his voice and glanced at the librarian who had stood up and begun to walk toward them.

He pushed back his chair and walked toward the librarian. "I want to print a couple of references from a CD," he said calmly. "Which printer should I use?" She pointed to a laser printer near the rack of CDs. "I can take care of it for you," the librarian volunteered to help on a quiet evening.

"Thanks, I can manage," said Kevin, smiling politely.

The librarian returned to her desk.

Kevin went back to the computer and keyed a few commands on the keyboard. While the librarian watched, a laser printer on a nearby table hummed momentarily, then a single sheet of paper slid slowly from the printer. He grabbed the paper, checked be sure it was complete and shoved it into his backpack.

"Before we leave I want to review the historical records for the university from about 1940 until 1960. Maybe there's some reference to Saxton Controls, more than just the financial and company information we've found. The university's historical data is stored on another CD," Kevin explained.

He walked to the rack of disks, replaced the first disk and searched a bit further, checking the titles on the disk cases. He pulled out another CD and brought it back to the terminal. Moments later, his keyword search on Saxton Controls yielded a surprising discovery.

"Get a load of this!" Kevin's voice rose again.

"Cool it, Kevin! She's got her eye on us again."

"Look, Val. This explains everything!" He couldn't contain his excitement. He pointed to the screen.

"Read it," he commanded. Valerie leaned over Kevin's shoulder for a direct view of the document displayed on the terminal.

Arms folded, Kevin waited patiently as she read the text.

Jackson Starrett, President
Cabot College
Old Main, Suite 200
One College Avenue
Hillsdale, Pennsylvania

March 28, 1948

Mr. Richard D. Smythe, President
Saxton Controls, Inc.
River Road
Hillsdale, Pennsylvania

Dear Dick,

On behalf of Cabot College, its faculty, administration and students present and future—I want to thank you and your associates for your extraordinary gift to the Cabot College Endowment Fund. Saxton Controls' $2 million corporate pledge assures that the college will achieve its goal to become a nationally prominent center for research in the sciences. This gift places us well within reach of our $10 million endowment goal and guarantees the success of Cabot College's first major fundraising effort. With your generous support, we will be able to attract and retain a superb science and engineering faculty to our campus. In due course, the college will exert a major economic impact on the region. My heartfelt thanks to you and Saxton Controls for your support.

The Board of Trustees has authorized me to invite you to be our guest at the college's June 15, 1948 commencement exercises. On that day, we will be privileged to confer upon you an honorary degree, Doctor of Science, the first such degree bestowed by Cabot College. Your professional contributions in science and your management skills as President of Saxton Controls will be recognized during the ceremonies, which mark the Centennial year of the college's founding in 1848 as Cabot Academy.

Let me also personally thank you and the members of your Board of Directors for your warm hospitality during my recent visit to the Hillsdale facility. I enjoyed your most informative tour of operations. Of particular interest was your revelation of the vital work the Hillsdale operation performed during the war and in the years immediately following.

Very truly yours,

Jackson T. Starrett, President

P.S. Cabot College is pleased to offer storage space for the materials you mentioned during my visit to the plant. Simply transport these materials to Science Hall, rear entrance, between five and six p.m. this Friday. Mr. John Farrow, custodian, will direct the off-loading and storage in the lower level, front sub-basement of the building. We will store the barrels in that location for an indefinite period until you authorize their forwarding to your New Jersey plant. Of course, there is no charge for this accommodation.

"What does all of this mean, Kevin?" she finished reading and looked at him.

"This letter is our smoking gun, Val," he said, his voice deadly calm. "Don't you see? It proves that Cabot University allowed Saxton Controls to store those barrels on campus.

"Look," he pointed to the screen, "it even directs the company to deliver the barrels to Science Hall—notice, it's after normal working hours—and allows them to store the stuff indefinitely on the campus. And here the university thanks the company for its contribution! That proves the storage was a favor in return for a gift to the school. I suspect if we search through the archives, we'll find out how much money Saxton actually contributed to the university.

"Why the so-called temporary storage turned into fifty years in the sub-basement is still a mystery. That's not important now. What's important is that we know the name of the company that owned those barrels; we know the President specifically allowed the stuff to be stored on the campus; and given the state of disintegration of the barrels in the hole and this letter, we know the chemicals have been stored here for more than fifty years."

"I'll print this out." He selected the letter on the monitor and tapped a few strokes on the keyboard. Moments later the laser printer spit out a copy. Kevin glanced at the printout to see that it was complete, and put the sheet in his backpack.

"The mystery is about to be solved," he said quietly, his demeanor strangely calm. "Let's get out of here with the evidence." He exited the search program, removed the compact disk and returned it to the shelf. He and Valerie headed toward the library checkout counter.

"Thanks for your help with the printer," he said cheerfully to the reference librarian as they passed her desk. A student librarian made a perfunctory search of the backpack and waved them through the electronic gate. They left the library, and strolled casually across the Commons in the early evening darkness.

*   *   *   *

"Now what?" Valerie asked. The two sat on a bench facing the front entrance to Connors Hall.

"I gotta think," said Kevin. "This is really big. The pieces are coming together. Whatever else happens, we can't let the administration cover it up."

He stared at the building. With the exception of floodlights illuminating the plaza and front entrance, Connors Hall was dark. Behind them, the lights along the sidewalks across the Commons cast soft shadows in the early evening darkness.

"We have to go back inside again," he said finally.

"Why?" Valerie worried. "Why not just call campus security and tell them to check out the basement janitors' closet in Connors Hall? You won't have to identify yourself and no one can prove who found the stuff."

"No, Val," he said patiently. "Our fingerprints are all over that room, remember? We'd be dragged into any investigation. And I can't explain how we got into the building without admitting that Tony gave me a key.

He's old and Rosa's dying. He has enough problems right now; I won't drag him into this.

"Just be patient for a minute. Let me figure out how to deal with this," he reached for her hand.

They sat quietly for what seemed an eternity to Valerie. Finally Kevin rose, slung the pack over his shoulder and pulled Valerie to him. They stood motionless beneath the huge oak tree, two lovers joined in an innocent embrace. He stroked her thick blond hair, bent and kissed the curve of her neck.

"Let's go back to your apartment one more time," he whispered. They walked hand in hand across the campus and headed for Valerie's apartment.

Chapter 38

She unlocked the door, flipped the light switch and entered the living room. Kevin followed her, and with one arm around her waist, he tilted her face and kissed her deeply. His passion would no longer be denied. Shedding jeans and tops, they raced for the bedroom. He kicked the door shut as they collapsed together on the bed.

Later, Valerie propped her head with one hand and leaned over his bearded face, tracing the lines around his lips. She searched the glittering eyes of this brilliant, complex man lying beside her. He returned her gaze, his smile revealing a vulnerability and trust she had never seen before.

He wrapped his arms around her and pulled her onto his chest, their legs intertwined. "Too bad I have work to do tonight. I'd like to spend the rest of my life right here," he stroked her tousled hair and touched her mouth gently with his finger. He sighed deeply, gently rolled her over, kissed her one more time and rose from the bed. Retracing his steps into the living room, he retrieved the clothing he had shed so hurriedly an hour earlier.

Valerie caught the bikini briefs and jeans he tossed in her direction and languidly slipped them on. Barefoot and topless, she sauntered into the tiny kitchen and pulled two beers from the refrigerator.

"What happened to my bra?" she looked around the living room.

"Beats me. Check the bedroom or bathroom. Better yet, forget the bra and T-shirt, you look better this way."

She sat at the dining table and took a deep draught of beer, savoring the cool liquid. Kevin took the chair beside her, reached for his backpack and rummaged through it.

"Here, keep these printouts in a safe place." He gave her the copies of the letter from Saxton Controls and the write up describing the company's brief history.

"They'll be in my top desk drawer. No need to hide them, we can get more copies from the library," she put the papers in an unmarked manila envelope and laid it in the top drawer. She retrieved her jogging shoes, returned to the chair and laced them over her bare feet.

"What're you looking for?" she asked as Kevin continued rummaging through his pack.

"Just checking my equipment and supplies." He glanced over at her. "I could use a couple of extra towels or rags and a bottle of cleaning fluid to wipe off our fingerprints."

Valerie went into the bedroom, found her bra in a corner where it had been discarded and pulled on a clean T-shirt from the dresser. She selected three hand towels from the bathroom closet. A brief search of the cabinet beneath the kitchen sink turned up a small can of cleaning liquid. She handed the supplies to Kevin.

"Thanks. That should do it." He glanced at his watch, made a final check of the contents of his backpack, zipped it up and headed toward the door.

"Haven't you forgotten something?" she asked.

"What?"

"Me. I'm going with you, remember?"

He turned, his pack already draped over his left shoulder. "Not tonight, Val. I changed my mind. I really don't want you along tonight," he said. "I'm stretching my luck going back there a third time. If anyone gets caught, it should be me, not both of us. Besides, you may have to bail me out if I get arrested," he laughed.

"No way, Kevin. We're in this together," she reached for her keys. "We can leave my Jeep in the North Parking Lot. That way we won't have to walk home again," she said lightly.

"Nope. I'm going alone this time. I'll meet you back here in a couple of hours." His voice deepened and his black eyes glittered.

"That's final, no arguments."

"Wait just a minute, buddy," she retorted. "I thought we were a team. That means we do things together, you know? And nobody tells me what I can or cannot do," her mouth tightened into a thin, stubborn line. She walked past him and opened the door. "I haven't come this far with you to miss the finale."

He slammed the door shut, pinning her against it. They glared at each other. This willowy blond with the incredible ice blue eyes was a rich kid accustomed to having her way.

Kevin blinked first. He shook his head, resigned and pulled her into his arms. What the hell. She was right. They were in this together. Anyway, another pair of hands might actually help.

"Know what? I think we just had our first real argument, and I lost," he drew back and looked deeply into her eyes.

"Okay, you can come along," he yielded. "Just remember, Val, I'm in charge. This is my plan. Don't give me any grief when we get into the building. If you won't agree to follow my orders, you're not coming."

"Okay, okay, boss," she slapped him a high five and opened the door once again.

"And don't expect to win every argument with me in the future," he warned, getting the last word. She smiled sweetly as the door clicked behind them.

Valerie drove the mile to campus. Skirting the edge of the university, she wheeled through the unlocked gate, left upright on weekends, into the

North Parking Lot. Normally reserved for faculty and staff, the lot was only two hundred yards from Connors Hall. She braked the Cherokee and they waited silently as two female students, absorbed in conversation, crossed the blacktop in front of the Jeep, heading toward the Commons and Old Main. High above the parking area clusters of sodium vapor lamps cast a garish orange glow over the huge lot, empty except for a few scattered cars and a lone pickup truck.

"Maybe driving here wasn't such a good idea," Kevin glanced around. "When we come back, we'll be in plain view of anybody passing through here."

"We're here now. Let's get on with it," said Valerie, subdued. "Are you going to clue me in on your plan? Or are we just going to sit here all night?"

"Right. Let's go," he opened the passenger door and jumped to the blacktop.

Reaching into the back, he retrieved his backpack. Valerie waited for the chirp as the Jeep's anti-theft locking system was activated. They set off across the parking lot toward Connors Hall. Memorial Library was closed, its huge glass expanses dark on this quiet weekend. An occasional light shown from the upper floor laboratories in Starrett Science Center; otherwise the campus was completely deserted.

They walked casually to the side entrance of Connors Hall, Kevin inserted his master key and they entered the building along the familiar corridor. They retraced their steps to the basement janitor's closet and Kevin unlocked the door. The room was undisturbed from the night before.

"Now are you going to clue me in on your plan?" Valerie asked quietly.

"Yes. First, we need to eliminate most of the fingerprints from everything we might have touched. If we do it now, the final cleanup and wiping won't take long." Working efficiently, they filled a bucket with water and carefully wiped down the surfaces of file cabinets, shelves, doorknobs and the metal bars that lay on the floor. Wearing cotton work gloves, they threw the debris—broken wallboard, nails and other trash accumulated during the past two days—into a neat pile in a corner of the room.

Stopping for a moment to wipe the sweat from his forehead, Kevin regarded Valerie with a smile. Her face was smudged where she had pushed back her hair; her T-shirt was soaked with sweat, her gloves filthy. "I'm glad you're here," he said softly. She glanced up at him, tilted her head and raised an eyebrow, her blue eyes catching the overhead light.

"Me, too."

She sat back on her haunches and giggled. "I can't believe this. Here I am, scrubbing cabinets at good old Cabot U. You have no idea how much I hate to clean. Remember that trust fund my parents set up for me? I use some of the money to pay a local woman to clean my apartment. So I can spend my evenings breaking into a building and scrubbing cabinets. This is just too bizarre." She shook her head.

She sprang lightly to her feet, rag in hand and moved close to the gaping black hole, the entrance to the sub-basement. Hesitating for only a second, she jumped easily onto the earthen floor five feet below. Picking herself up, she wiped her hands down the sides of her pants and grinned defiantly up at Kevin.

"What the hell are you doing?" he hissed.

"Now it's my turn to explore. Toss me the big flashlight and a clean rag," she ordered. Disgusted, he complied.

"Wow," she exclaimed, shining the powerful beam into every corner of the earthen basement. "This place is really packed. Shouldn't we at least take an inventory of this stuff so we know how many barrels need to be disposed of?" she suggested. "If we have an accurate count, the administration won't be able to lie about how much has been stored here for so many years."

She walked along the rows, counting aloud. "Looks like twenty-five big barrels and ten smaller drums," she concluded. "There's data stenciled on the tops of some of these barrels, too, Kevin." She wiped off some of the accumulated filth. "These two barrels have different markings—maybe there's a variety of chemicals here." She pointed the flashlight onto the earthen floor around the barrels. "You were right. A lot of barrels have leaked around the bottom," she peered into the darkness, sending the beam toward the rear of the room.

"Will you come back here, Val?" Kevin demanded from the doorway above the rotted stairs. "You haven't got a clue what's in those barrels. For sure, it's toxic waste, it's probably volatile and there may even be low levels of radiation present. Please come back," he pleaded.

Hands on her hips, she returned to the bottom of the steps and looked up at him. "Tell me, Kevin, how does the university dispose of waste chemicals from Starrett Science Center? The school must have to deal with similar stuff every day."

"Promise to come back up here and I'll tell you."

"Okay, right after you tell me," she teased. He sighed and gave in.

"Right now," he began, dropping to the basement floor and swinging his long legs onto a broken step, "a truck comes from Philadelphia periodically—maybe every three months. They usually take the stuff out of the building at night, after everybody's left. They wear protective gear—you know—haz mat suits with masks. They wheel the storage drums on dollies onto the loading dock at the rear of Starrett Center, load them into a closed panel truck and off they go. I saw them haul the stuff away a couple of times when I was working late in the lab. Why do you ask?"

"Don't you see, Kevin? Tomorrow, when the janitors open the storage room and see this mess, they'll notify the facilities department. A facilities crew will simply come and cart the stuff away. You'll never know what's in these barrels," she said.

"You have a point," Kevin admitted. "If these chemicals have been stored here for years, you can bet the administration will try to cover it up. They'll call the guys from Philly to come and remove them—make a midnight disposal run. No one will see what's happening—and that will be the end of it. And the evidence will be gone."

"And you won't have a case against the university," Valerie interrupted. "You'll never be able to link whatever is in these barrels to your theory that carcinogens have leaked into the soil and created a cancer hot spot here on campus."

"Right." Hands in his pockets, Kevin stared into the dark abyss.

"You said earlier you wanted to test this stuff. Why not take a sample from one of these leaky barrels and do the analysis yourself?" Valerie's voice rose excitedly. "You're a chemist, you could figure it out. If the other barrels are removed, you still have the sample and can make the details public."

His eyes lit up.

"That just might work.

"Hold on a second. I've got a better idea. We could haul out one of these small drums and lug it over to the lab. It won't take me long to work up a preliminary analysis. I might even show it to Dr. Borovski—maybe she'll believe me if she sees the physical evidence herself."

"Great. A drum is probably better evidence than a small sample," Val agreed. "But these drums have rusted out on the bottoms. How can we get a drum out of this hole and over to your lab without it leaking all over the place, not to mention without being seen?"

Kevin didn't respond. Without warning, he crouched and then jumped down beside her.

"We'll check each drum. Maybe they're not all leaky," he said. "Help me find one in reasonably good condition."

She held the flashlight while Kevin inspected each ten-gallon drum. He tilted a few, inspecting the bottoms for leaks. He finally settled on a sturdy drum in the rear against the far wall. Tilting it on its rim, he rolled it across the earthen floor to the bottom on the rotted steps. Valerie watched silently as he carefully inspected the bottom for leaks.

"Shit, this stuff is heavy—I wouldn't think a ten gallon drum could be this tough to move," he grunted, the muscles in his arms and neck bulging with the strain. He stopped to rest and wiped the sweat from his eyes.

"How are we going to get it up those rotten steps?"

"Easy. You get out of this hole and bring me some rope from my pack."

He bent over and laced his hands together. "Put your foot in my hands." With an easy heave, he boosted her out of the sub-basement. She sprawled onto the storage room floor, picked herself up and searched through Kevin's backpack. She found the heavy cord he had purchased along with the hacksaw at the hardware store the day before. She tossed Kevin the rope and watched as he knotted the rope into multiple loops, fashioning a rough cradle for the drum. He worked quickly and expertly.

"This is a skill I learned on the farm," he related. "Maybe those years weren't a complete waste after all." Moments later the drum, securely nestled in its crude rope cradle, was ready for removal. He threw the end of the rope to Valerie.

"Brace yourself against the wall, and give me your hand," he ordered. Hanging onto the wall, she extended her hand toward him. In a few seconds, he scrambled up the rotted steps as they collapsed beneath him. He grabbed the edge of the floor and with a final lunge, landed on the storage room floor beside her.

He rolled onto his back, gasping for breath.

"Okay, let's lift the drum out of there." He reached for the rope. "I don't want to disturb this stuff any more than necessary. It may be volatile as well as toxic."

Valerie held the flashlight while Kevin, slowly and carefully, swearing occasionally, lifted the drum from the earthen floor to the tiled floor of the storage closet. Moments later he grasped the side and top of the drum and rolled it onto the floor. He collapsed across the drum, sweating and panting, muscles cramping from the strain. Valerie toweled the sweat from his neck and face, waiting patiently for him to recover.

He regarded her, a sardonic grin on his face. Reaching out, he took her in his arms and kissed her lightly on the lips. He whispered, "Do you realize what we've done?"

She pulled back, silently regarded him. "Yeah," she giggled. "I'm spending the first day of Senior Week hauling toxic waste out of a filthy hole in the basement of Connors Hall. Just think, at this very moment, I could be riding the coasters at Hershey Park with my classmates," she teased.

"Yeah, but that would be so boring compared to this. Think about it," he waved his arms around the room, "we just found a toxic waste dump so big that it'll make national headlines. I can't wait to see the look on Dr. Borovski's face when she sees this shit."

He scrambled to his feet.

"Let's get this drum over to the lab. It won't take long to do a preliminary analysis of the chemical composition—maybe I can finish it tonight."

"How are we going to haul the drum up the stairs and across the lobby?" she asked, her voice full of doubt.

"We won't go that way," Kevin decided. "We'll carry it down the hall to the elevator, take the elevator up to the first floor, then carry it down the hall and out the side door. This building—the whole campus for that matter—is deserted. The risk of being seen is small." He spoke with more assurance than he felt.

"Once we get it outside, you bring the Jeep around to the back of the building. We'll load the drum and drive over to the loading dock behind Starrett. My ID card will get us into the building and we can take the freight elevator to the fourth floor and the lab. "I can still get into Starrett and my lab until the end of June." He smiled, satisfied with his plan.

"We've got to be extremely careful handling the drum," he warned. "I have no idea how volatile this stuff is and I don't want to disturb the mixture any more than necessary." He tested the two loops in the rope cradle and tightened them, lashing the drum securely. Then he fashioned two short lengths of rope that he attached to each side. They would serve as handles.

"On the count of three," he directed, "we'll slowly lift the drum between us. I want to test this before we try to move it.

"See if you can carry half the load," he said. "Keep the drum level. We can't have the mixture sloshing around." Valerie nodded, braced herself and grabbed one rope handle.

"One, two, three." The ropes tightened around the container as they slowly raised the drum a foot off the floor. Valerie, the shorter of the two, struggled to keep the drum level.

"Good," Kevin whispered. "Now slowly set it down again. Don't drop it!"

They rested for a moment.

"Valerie, put the flashlight on that shelf," he pointed to a shelf near the light switch by the hall door. "I'll prop the door open with the backpack. Then we'll carry the drum into the hall and put it down. You sure you can handle this?"

"I can do it," she assured him. "After I got out of the loony bin at Essex, I started a weight program for women at the fitness center. I've lifted more than this drum. It's work, but if you take it slowly, I can do it."

"Good." His cocky smile projected confidence.

He opened the door. They carried the drum across the room and into the hall. They stopped and rested. Kevin retrieved his backpack and the flashlight. Without bothering to flip the light switch, he closed and locked the door to the storage room for the last time.

"Better not use the flashlight from now on," he decided, tossing it in his pack. He secured the top flap and set the pack on the hall floor against the wall. "We can see well enough by the exit light and that light over the elevator door," he nodded toward the elevator some fifty feet down the hall.

"Ready?"

"All set," she flashed him a nervous smile.

Taking a rope handle on each side, they carefully hoisted the drum and began the slow journey toward the distant elevator. Only their heavy panting and faint thumps when they rested the drum on the floor disturbed the silence.

"Only about twenty feet more," he said encouragingly.

"Piece of cake," she panted, her confidence rising as they neared the elevator.

Moments later they reached their destination. Kevin punched the up button and they listened as the elevator engaged and quietly descended. With a pneumatic sigh, the elevator came to rest and the doors slid open.

Kevin glanced back down the hall. "Wait a minute. I forgot the backpack." He jogged down the dark hall to retrieve it.

Without warning, he slipped and sprawled awkwardly on the floor.

"Damn! There's fluid on the floor. The drum is leaking! I've got this shit on my hands and pants," he yelled, his voice tinged with panic.

Running back along the dark hall, he tossed the backpack into the elevator. With a quick nod to Valerie, he grabbed the drum and together they heaved it across the threshold into the elevator. Valerie lurched across the uneven threshold and stumbled. She screamed as sharp pain shot up her leg from her foot, twisted and crushed beneath the heavy drum. The rope handle slid from her fingers and the drum tilted and sagged as Kevin lost control. The bottom edge of the drum crashed against the metal edge of the elevator floor. With a dull pop, black fluid gushed onto the floor from a four-inch gash.

Screaming with pain, Valerie tilted the drum, freeing her mangled foot. It toppled over. The hole that pierced the drum spurted black fluid, spraying their legs and sneakers. Helpless, they watched in horror as the waste liquid gushed in torrents around them and down the elevator shaft through the narrow opening between the elevator and the hall. Standing in viscous black chemical waste, they choked and gasped from the toxic fumes.

"Leave it! We gotta get out of here! It's gonna blow!" Kevin shouted.

Valerie screamed hysterically as Kevin grabbed her around the waist and lifted her over the toppled drum into the slippery hallway. "I can't walk! My foot is broken!" She stared in horror at the exposed bone in her ankle as blood flowed over her sneaker and mixed with the black toxic waste.

"Go, go!" He grabbed her around the waist. Arms around each other, they hobbled down the hall toward safety. Deep blue flames instantly enveloped the leaking drum and spread down the elevator shaft. A thin trail of expanding flame chased them down the hall. Kevin half carried Valerie, screaming with pain, to the bottom of the stairs. She grabbed the railing. Side by side, they began to climb the stairs to the lobby and safety.

They almost made it.

Chapter 39

Mike Ahearn cruised along I-80 two miles east of Hillsdale. Although the speedometer registered seventy-five miles an hour, from his perch high above the road, he was in complete control of his fully loaded 18-wheeler. The halogen lights of his huge rig offered unparalleled visibility to the edge of his high beams some three hundred yards ahead. He loved his blue and yellow tractor-trailer unit, the only home he knew.

Flicking his Fuzz-buster to the off position, he turned up the volume on the CD player mounted on the dash. The sweet sounds of Patsy Cline filled the cab and he settled back in his seat, both hands lightly controlling the huge steering wheel.

The weekend traffic out of New York City had been brutal. Now, nearly 150 miles west of the metropolitan area, he could relax. Westbound auto traffic was thinning out as Sunday night turned into Monday morning. The long haul truckers owned the highway. With luck, in a few hours he would cross the Ohio border and leave Pennsylvania behind. The Border Truckstop would be a good place to chow down and catch a few hours' rest before continuing on to Los Angeles, his final destination.

A mile east of Cabot University, an odd thump pulsed through the steering wheel. This section of I-80 was rough, abused by millions of vehicles, many of them 18-wheelers like his own. Had he not been alert, he probably would not have noticed. He decelerated slightly, rolled down the huge side window and savored the fresh night air flowing into the cab. He reached down, adjusted the volume on the CD, effectively drowning out the road noise and the deep growl of his Detroit Diesel engine. He checked his side mirror, searching for debris or the road kill he might have hit.

Seconds later an explosive flash illuminated the interior of his cab and lit the countryside in a blinding white light, transforming the warm spring night into daylight, brighter than the morning sun. Then thunder louder than any summer storm filled his cab. He lost control as an immense shock wave buffeted his fifty-three foot rig.

He reacted instinctively, his powerful arms and legs fighting to regain control of his tractor-trailer unit as huge chunks of flaming debris rained down from the night sky, pummeling the cab, littering the highway ahead. He laid down dual black skid marks as he fought to slow the truck. Tires squealing in protest, he bounced across jagged debris. Two rear tires blew with the explosive sounds of gunshots.

Unable to avoid the wreckage littering the highway, he plowed along, out of control, his rig buffeted by tornado-like winds. The huge tractor-trailer veered back and forth across the three westbound lanes as Ahearn fought to keep the rig upright. Unable to keep the unit on the westbound lanes, he tore across the grassy median strip, dirt and debris flying and ploughed into the oncoming eastbound traffic. Fighting with all the strength his two hundred fifty pounds of muscle and sinew could muster, he careened directly into the path of an equally out-of-control tractor-trailer tearing along the eastbound left lane next to the median strip.

He braced for the inevitable crash. He jerked the wheel to the right, trying to get his rig back onto the median strip just as the oncoming driver similarly tried to avoid a head-on collision. At the last second, the two giant rigs sideswiped each other, forcing Mike's rig deep into the median strip that was alive with burning debris.

Desperately, he rode it out. Hanging onto the huge steering wheel, he wrestled the rig down the middle of the median strip, tapping the brakes, fighting to keep the tractor-trailer upright, careening through the deep swale separating the east and westbound lanes.

After what seemed an eternity but in reality was less than ninety seconds, he slowed the rig and brought the monster under control. Adrenaline flowing, muscles in his arms bulging and aching, and sweating profusely he steered the slowing tractor-trailer up the gentle side of the median onto the westbound lanes of I-80.

Surrounded by devastation and flaming debris, he steered around burning vehicles—autos, pickup trucks and sport utility vehicles—blowing his air horn frantically as terrified people vacated their cars and spilled onto the highway. He finally brought his heavily loaded truck to a screeching halt.

Heart pounding through his sweat stained T-shirt, he grabbed the CB and punched the transmit key. "Holy Shit! This is Fat Man out of Fresno, California. Explosion! Explosion!" he screamed.

"On I-80 in Hillsdale, about a mile west of the Cabot University exit! My God, I almost lost my rig! I almost lost my rig!" he sobbed. "There's flaming debris and wreckage everywhere. Traffic's at a standstill; wrecked cars and long haul rigs are in flames on both sides of the road! People are scattered all over the highway, injured and dying. I see at least three bodies lying in the median strip. Get help—emergency vehicles, ambulances, fire trucks—get some cops out here!" he pleaded, his voice breaking.

The night sky lit up with multiple flashes brighter than the brightest fireworks ever displayed on the Fourth of July. Rolling shockwaves rocked the huge rig as a hailstorm of flaming debris rained down from the night sky now as bright as day.

"Somebody out there talk to me!" he screamed into the mike. He stopped transmitting, switched to receiving messages, laid his head on the steering wheel and sobbed as huge chunks of debris tore jagged holes in the aluminum sides of his trailer, crashed onto the cab and seared the grass in the median strip and along the edge of the road.

Clutching the CB mike in his huge hand, he prayed for a response. "Somebody, anybody! Please come in," he begged.

"What the hell's happening? My God, are we being bombed? I gotta get out of here," he screamed. Cranking up his cracked window, he gunned the engine and swung the huge rig onto the westbound breakdown lane. In a complete panic, relying on instincts honed over twenty years of long haul trucking, he maneuvered the tractor-trailer past burning vehicles as the injured and dying continued to crawl from their smashed cars.

Darkness descended on the horrible scene, the brilliant flashes fading, the road lit only by burning vehicles and the wildly scattered headlights of wrecked cars, flaming debris and grass fires in the median strip and the fields nearby.

"Fat Man! Fat Man! This is Coyote," an excited voice on the CB brought a measure of sanity to Mike as he steered his rig toward relative safety along the dark road ahead. "I'm about five miles west of Hillsdale, heading toward you," he yelled.

Coyote's voice out of the darkness calmed Mike, helped him to focus on driving west, away from the holocaust. "At least it's not nukes, Fat Man," the voice said reassuringly. "The nuke power station is fifteen miles up the river. I can tell you, whatever it was, those explosions lit up the sky brighter than day for miles around Hillsdale," he said.

"But it wasn't nukes, that's for sure. Whatever it was, Fat Man, it looks like the whole town of Hillsdale just blew up!

"Fat Man, what's your exact location? Gimme a report," Coyote yelled.

There was no response.

"I'm reversing direction and heading for I-81," Coyote reported. "Carrying a heavy load from Shaky City to New York. The LA bastards who pay me will dock my pay if I'm late delivering my load.

"Fat Man!" he shouted into the mike, "I'll see you in California where all we have to deal with are earthquakes, fires, mud and illegal immigration," he laughed.

"Meet me at the Shaky City Diner near the LA produce terminal a week from now. I'll treat you to the best damned meatloaf dinner you ever tasted!

"The rest of you cowboys out there better pick an alternate route. Stay away from Hillsdale! From the looks of things, there's gonna be major problems on I-80 for a long time."

Coyote slowed his rig. He pulled onto the wide breakdown lane and stopped. The tough trucker listened intently for several minutes.

"Come in, Fat Man. I'm parked about four miles west of Hillsdale. We can run west together, then cut across to I-81. Where are you, Fat Man?"

He listened for a response that never came.

"Hey, Fat Man," he transmitted, fear creeping into his voice. "You're in the middle of one helluva mess. I gotta move out. Good luck and Godspeed. Remember, Shaky City Diner in LA. Next week. You be there, it'll be my treat."

He took a deep breath. "Anybody listening in, this is Coyote," he began. "Whatever happened about four miles ahead in Hillsdale, my advice is to find alternate routes. The roads around here will be one big parking lot real soon. Turn around, get the hell off I-80 if you can."

Coyote replaced his mike on the dashboard cradle, shifted into gear and edged back onto the highway. A quarter mile ahead, he swung the tractor-trailer onto a police turnaround lane and reversed direction from the eastbound to the westbound lanes of Interstate 80. Any cops in the vicinity had much more urgent business than to worry about an illegal turn on the devastated highway.

Coyote shifted up through the gears, pushed the accelerator to the floor and headed away from the chaos, mentally mapping out a short cut route to I-81 that would allow him to reach New York City in time for his morning unloading appointment. He concentrated on the wide ribbon of concrete stretching ahead in the white glare of his high beams. Despite himself, he checked his rear view mirrors, drawn to the apocalypse unfolding behind him. A dull orange glow hung on the eastern horizon. Multiple flashes lit up the distant sky, turning the night from bright white to brilliant orange, then fading to a ribbon of light on the horizon.

He ignored the speedometer as the needle touched 85, then 90 miles an hour. Coyote rolled past a green interstate sign announcing the secondary shortcut he knew would lead him to Interstate 81 and the northeast extension of the Turnpike some seventy miles away. He swung the huge tractor-trailer unit onto the exit ramp, and made a wide left turn, heading toward Harrisburg and his alternate route around the chaos in Hillsdale.

As he accelerated rapidly away from the horror in his rear view mirrors, he transmitted the first of many messages, calling for help, warning traffic away from the small town in central Pennsylvania whose name would reverberate around the world in the days and weeks ahead.

An hour later, the lights of Harrisburg came into view. Only then did Coyote sign off his CB radio, take a deep breath and begin to relax. He slowed for a moment, debating whether to pull into the huge truck stop near the cloverleaf at the extension of the Pennsylvania Turnpike. No, he decided. Keep going. Get the hell out of here. He swung the rig toward the entrance to the Pike, stopped, picked up a toll ticket and continued on through the night.

Coyote, whose identity was never established, was cited by the state legislature, one of the anonymous heroes of the disaster that unfolded on that quiet Sunday evening in late April.

Chapter 40

They were finishing the last hand of bridge when brilliant white flashes transformed night into day, shattering the soft spring evening. Seconds later, shockwaves and thundering explosions buffeted the Atherton home, cracking the huge floor-to-ceiling panes of glass, and shattering the sliders leading to the deck overlooking the river. Momentarily stunned and blinded, the group rose as one, knocking over their chairs, staggering toward the deck. They stared in disbelief across the river toward the campus on the distant ridge.

Momentarily paralyzed, they watched in horror as the brilliantly lighted sky, which had erupted in explosive flashes, slowly darkened. It was as though they all had hallucinated identical images.

The town of Hillsdale in the distance was a picture of tranquility. Street lamps lining the residential blocks half a mile away cast tiny pinpoints of yellow light. Farther up the river, clusters of sodium vapor lamps illuminated the empty parking lots at the mall east of town.

Ruth Borovski identified the explosions' source first.

"Look!" she pointed excitedly, "Connors Hall! There on the ridge!" Her voice cracked. An ominous red glow lay low on the distant horizon. Horrified, they watched tiny licks of flame grow ever larger. In seconds, the flames burned brighter, gathering strength, changing from bright red to yellow, finally to a brilliant white, growing in intensity, fueled by an unknown source. Surrounded by shattered glass in the living room, they watched helplessly while fire engulfed the second oldest building on campus.

Suddenly, a second round of massive explosions, more intense than the first, rocked across the entire town, lighting up the sky, casting the campus buildings in stark relief. The intensity of these explosions and shock waves dwarfed the earlier blasts. Reflexively, they moved away from the shattered windows, finding safety near the fireplace. Shocked, they watched as white-hot flames soared above the campus and a wall of fire took shape along the ridge a mile away.

Dick Atherton reacted. He snatched his cell phone and punched 911.

"What's going on? This is Dr. Atherton," Dick yelled. The women looked to him for a report.

"The police say a series of explosions are centered on the campus," he reported in a remarkably calm voice. "That's an understatement."

He reached into a stand beside the sofa, pulled out a pair of small binoculars and scanned the distant ridge. "The source of the explosions is definitely Connors Hall," he confirmed. "The building looks fully enveloped, and the fire appears to be spreading toward the library. It's awfully close to the residence hall near Connors Hall."

"No! All my files and computer records are in my office!" shouted Nancy.

"I hope you kept backups here in your study. That building will be gone in a matter of minutes," Dick said grimly, his binoculars trained on the horizon.

"The second round of explosions may have been gas lines supplying the building. Whatever it was, something is feeding the fire right now. And I can see the fire engines just now going up University Avenue." The women snapped back to reality as Dick calmly reported the ghastly details of the inferno on the far horizon.

"It looks like power has been lost on the campus. University Avenue is dark now and the lights on Main Street are out, too. The whole town may be experiencing a cascading power loss," he continued, binoculars glued to his eyes.

Gingerly, Nancy stepped over the glass littering the living room and opened a shattered glass slider leading to the deck. The group made their way outside, and watched as parts of Hillsdale darkened with a major power failure. The screams of multiple sirens were clearly audible as police, ambulances and fire trucks converged on the campus.

Dick handed the binoculars to Nancy and went into the house. He returned from the master bedroom carrying his medical bag, putting his cell phone in his pocket.

"There are probably injuries," he said grimly. "Hillary, you and I should get moving. They'll need all the medical help they can get. The fire is clearly out of control. It could be a very long night."

"Right. Let me pick up my bag on the way," she said.

"Nancy, you and Ruth stay here where I'll know you're safe," he said brusquely over his shoulder. He ran through the kitchen to the garage. "I'll get back to you when I know more about what's going on."

"Be careful!" Nancy admonished futilely.

She and Ruth watched Dick and Hillary climb into the black Porsche. Nancy raised the automatic garage doors and Dick backed swiftly and expertly from the garage, spun the wheels on the black top and raced up the street. He screeched to a stop in front of Hillary's home and waited impatiently as his colleague dashed into the house and grabbed her medical bag. She hopped back into the car, slamming the door. Dick gunned the engine and raced down the hill toward the river and Market Avenue.

Despite the late hour, traffic appeared from nowhere, clogging the intersection at Market and Main Streets near the soldier's monument.

Abandoning the car, they raced up University Avenue on foot, yelling and pushing through the throngs of gawkers gathering at the scene.

Hastily erected police barricades already blocked the main gate. Fat hoses snaked past Old Main, pulsing sporadically as the water pressure dropped precipitously from system overload. They breached the police cordon on the run, waved along by campus security who recognized the two physicians.

On the Commons near Old Main, police blocked the approaches to the disaster area. More than three hundred yards from the fire, intense heat and rolling clouds of acrid smoke formed an impenetrable natural barrier. The gathering crowd, forced to retreat to a safer distance, watched helplessly as huge sheets of flame leaped high into the night sky.

Volunteer firefighters, some still clad in street clothes, joined others wearing protective gear, their backs burdened with portable oxygen supplies. Those adequately protected worked closest to the spreading conflagration. The others supported the front lines, hauling hoses into position, hooking up pumpers and providing direction.

The campus was a scene of utter chaos. The swoosh of flames and the crash of glass from shattered windows drowned out the shouted commands among the firemen. Flaming debris was propelled skyward, borne hundreds of feet into the air by the fire's intense updraft. Wreckage and debris crashed to the ground. Flying bricks, beams and steel became lethal shrapnel endangering firefighters and threatening to ignite nearby buildings.

Dick and Hillary ran toward Starrett Science Center, ignoring the flaming hell around them, jumping over hoses and dashing around firemen. A cordon of firefighters near Connors Hall dragged heavy hoses and sprayed torrents of water in a futile effort to save the burning building. A shouted order to retreat toward the library drove them back.

Defeated on one front, the firefighters concentrated on saving the library's priceless collections, the very soul of the university. Working furiously, firemen laid hoses and crawled up metal extension ladders to the roof of the library, preparing to defend the multimillion-dollar facility, a valiant but ultimately futile battle.

Dick and Hillary stopped, gasping for breath, choking on the dense smoke swirling around them. "Let's get behind Starrett and work our way across the parking lot to the residence hall," Dick shouted. He grasped Hillary's hand. Together they sprinted around the side of the science building, their bodies casting huge shadows against the orange-tinged building.

"Anyone caught inside Connors Hall didn't have a chance," he panted when they reached the far side of the science building. "Did you see the huge crater in front of Connors?" he asked Hillary.

"Yes," she shouted. "That must have been ground zero."

The two physicians slowed to a jog, struggling up the steep landscaped bank that separated Starrett Science Center's rear loading docks from the North parking lot.

"And anyone caught in the library probably is beyond help now, too," Hillary shouted. She looked at the surreal scene around them. "My God, what could have caused this devastation?"

Without warning, the huge double panes of glass that formed the library's front façade shattered with a roar. Tons of glass crashed to the ground. They looked toward the building, and then dropped instantly to the grass, knees bent and hands folded over their heads, scant protection against the glass shards and flying debris raining down. The firemen on the roof beat a hasty retreat, driven by the heat and structural failures, scrambling down ladders they had just climbed. With a mighty roar, a huge chunk of the roof collapsed into the interior of the flaming library. Dick watched in horror as a fireman disappeared into the conflagration, one of many victims of the inferno consuming Cabot University.

Beyond the collapsing library, Connors Hall continued to burn out of control, the battle to save it lost, the building's upper stories and slate roof nearing collapse. The sturdy brick walls of the old landmark glowed an ugly yellow as flames leaped hundreds of feet into the night sky. The campus resembled a war zone, the victim of a vicious firebombing.

Dick and Hillary scrambled onto the parking lot behind the library and Starrett Science Center. The vast lot was nearly empty. They ran across the hot blacktop, softened by the intense heat, past smoking hulks of what had once been three vehicles, sinking now into pools of molten, stinking black macadam, mute testimony to the fire's ferocity. They rested, panting, searching for activity around the residence hall.

Looking back toward Connors Hall, they watched helplessly as flames destroyed the proud old landmark. With a mighty roar, the heavy slate roof crashed into the interior ruins. The glowing brick walls began to weave like a flaming giant serpent, alive, bent on destruction. With a final crash, the walls fell inward, a mass of flaming rubble. Immediately, an unfamiliar acrid smoke reached them as the walls of Connors Hall settled into a ghastly heap of fiercely burning steel, wood and bricks.

The last firefighters beat a hasty retreat toward the center of the Commons, dragging their limp, waterless hoses behind them, defeated. Scores of firemen re-established the battle lines, stubbornly refusing to surrender the entire campus to the conflagration. They tried to save the library, launching torrents of water onto the fire, determined to halt its progress. Dick and Hillary watched helplessly as two fighters collapsed near the library, felled by flaming debris, killed in the line of duty.

Flaming embers and chunks of the heavy wood beams from the top floor of Connors Hall continued to rain down. Forced to the ground, the two physicians covered their heads with their arms. They described the scene later as the face of hell on earth during that unforgettable, endless night.

Dick stripped off his light jacket and pulled Hillary close to his body. He stretched the jacket over both their heads, offering minimal protection from small flaming debris. They knew full well that a random piece of debris could injure or kill them both. They struggled to their feet and retreated from the inferno, running toward the badly damaged and scorched residence hall. The building was windowless, the blast having shattered every pane in the four-story residence hall. Drapes fluttered through the black holes that used to be windows, eerily lit by the fire consuming Connors Hall.

They reached the handsome wide verandah fronting the brick residence hall, broken glass crunching beneath their feet. Bright floodlights set up on the lawn cast harsh light on the EMTs and physicians frantically treating the injured lying on the porch. Hastily rigged portable generators provided power for the floodlights and emergency medical operations. The scene was surreal, eerily reminding Dick of a war zone.

Ambulances raced across the parking lot, sirens screaming and lights flashing. Triage teams frantically conducted preliminary examinations and loaded the most seriously injured into ambulances headed for Hillsdale Hospital nearby and Essex Medical Center twelve miles away. Hillary Gardner and Dick Atherton joined the medical teams treating the injured and dying. They would not take a break until fourteen hours later.

Chapter 41

As was their custom, Chief Max Kumple, Hillsdale's only paid professional fireman, and his wife were watching Sunday evening television in their home four miles north of the campus when the first explosion occurred.

Seven minutes after the first round of explosions, Max raced up University Avenue toward the campus, siren screaming and horn blasting, a cell phone pressed to his ear, directing operations at firehouses across Hillsdale.

Kumple had never faced a disaster of this magnitude before. Even the most up-to-date training could not fully prepare him for the conflagration he and his volunteers faced that night. He fervently prayed for the strength and wisdom to deal with whatever challenges lay ahead. He slammed on the brakes at the main gate to Cabot University just as his first volunteers maneuvered three pumpers and the town's huge ladder truck into position in the driveway.

Police were already on the scene, setting up lines and holding back the gathering crowds. Standing next to the police chief was a university official, seemingly very much in charge.

"Who are you? Where's President Northrop? He should be here," Chief Kumple shouted over the chaos around them.

"I'm Tyler Hutchins, Vice-President. I'm in charge here." Dressed in a suit and tie, Hutchins thrust his fat hand toward the chief. Kumple ignored it.

"Where the hell is President Northrop?" the chief repeated, shouting to be heard above the chaos.

"He's in New York City. We're trying to reach him. Forget about Northrop! Do something! You've got to save the library," Hutchins shouted hysterically, panic in his close-set eyes, his face beet-red and sweating, his fat arms flapping helplessly. "Get some help! That's an order!" he screamed.

"Shut up, asshole," said Kumple, calmly. "You're not in charge. I'll decide what needs to be done and when. And I'm telling you that your only job is to get your boss back here pronto." He turned away, seeking his assistant chief for a preliminary report.

Porky Hutchins made a nearly fatal mistake. He charged after the chief, pounding his fists on the chief's back and grabbing his arm. Without a moment's hesitation, Max Kumple turned and with a single right uppercut, he shattered the jaw and nose of Cabot University's Vice-President of Administration and Finance. Hutchins sank to the ground, deflated like a human blimp.

229

Randy Irwin, the chief of police, jogged over to his old poker-playing buddy. "What the hell happened to him?" he glanced at the unconscious university official.

"The jackass was obstructing progress. I temporarily put him out of his misery."

"Let me brief you on our situation," the police chief managed a thin smile. "I think we've got the crowd under control, at least for now."

"You've got to move people farther back, Randy," said the fire chief. "There could be more explosions. Until I know what we're dealing with here, move everybody back."

"Done."

Police officers began moving the wooden barriers down University Avenue to Main Street. The police chief pointed to the administrator lying on the ground, unconscious and bleeding from his nose.

"What about him?"

Kumple turned to his assistant and pointed to Hutchins. "Get at least two hefty medics over here and move this turkey out of my sight."

Moments later, two volunteers rolled the corpulent body of the Vice-President onto a stretcher and carried him to the emergency medical area. An hour later, he was transferred by ambulance to Hillsdale Hospital. Later, when the wires that bound his jaws were removed, Hutchins would brag that his injury had been sustained as he heroically helped the firefighters battle to save the university.

"Now, what the hell happened here?" Kumple turned back to the police chief.

"Multiple explosions and fire originating in Connors Hall. Apparently, the building was closed and locked. We're assuming nobody was inside when it blew. That's all we know at this point. Nothing's under control right now."

Kumple turned to his assistant fire chief. "Call out every available fireman and piece of equipment within twenty-five miles," he ordered.

"We've got an inferno here," the assistant fire chief reported over the roar of the fire. "There's multiple injuries, some fatalities, no power, no water pressure on campus and the gas mains into Connors Hall have burst. I'm laying hose for hundreds of feet just to get close to the fire. We could lose the whole damn campus."

"What's the traffic status coming into town, Randy?" Kumple asked. We'll need help getting emergency vehicles through traffic on I-80 and into town."

"Don't worry about traffic. The State Police are already out on I-80. They'll get your fire engines and ambulances through to University Exit, but it may take a little time. My guys will take over from there. What else do you need now?"

"A few prayers might help." Kumple smiled grimly at his old friend and fellow church usher. "It's going to be a long night. My guys are a dedicated bunch of volunteers, not experts in fighting a disaster of this magnitude. Right now, I've got no idea when we can get this thing under control." He turned and ran through the debris littering the Commons toward the burning library.

Chapter 42

Thousands of townspeople gathered, shocked at the ferocity of the fire, witnessing the destruction of the most important economic resource in Hillsdale. Police and fire lines were quickly erected, yellow tape stretched across University Avenue and crowds were forced back to Main Street. Volunteers were deputized on the spot to handle crowd control.

Occupants of the stately homes along University Avenue near the campus were ordered to evacuate. Many refused to leave, and after initial arguments, Police Chief Randy Irwin decided not to enforce his own directive.

Through the long night, a night as warm as midsummer, Hillsdale's leading families, working by candlelight, provided food and beverages to exhausted firefighters and police. The neatly manicured lawns in front of many homes became resting places for dozens of weary firefighters, police and disaster workers.

Sobbing and in shock, a few students huddled together behind the barricades at University Avenue and Main Street. Many faculty gathered nearby, offering what meager comfort they could muster in the face of their own devastation. Together, they kept vigil through the endless night as the soul of their proud university died before their eyes.

*   *   *   *

Tony Amonte didn't stir from the bedside of his beloved Rosa even as explosions rocked their home. His conscious mind vaguely registered the sound of alarms and the wail of sirens as fire trucks pulled out of Station Number 4 two blocks away. At one point power was temporarily cut off. He pulled aside the bedroom curtain and looked into the dark street, illuminated in the dead of night by a strange orange glow. The throngs of people hurrying along the street toward the center of town at nearly midnight didn't register in his brain, numbed by the knowledge that his Rosa was dying. He would stand his solitary vigil with her until the end.

The children had been notified that afternoon and were on their way. His pain momentarily turned to anger at their absence in the final hours of their mother's life. He could not know that they were trapped in the chaos of a ten-mile traffic jam on I-80, a gridlock blocking access to the town. Only firefighting equipment and emergency vehicles were allowed through.

He reached for Rosa's frail hand, whispering the words of love he was unable to voice when she was well. He reminisced aloud about their life together, thanking her for the devotion she showered on him during forty

232

years of marriage, for the living legacy of a son and daughter who reflected the traditional values of their mother.

In her final hours Tony sat beside her, talking to her as he had done for so many years at the big old kitchen table, reminding her of the joys they had shared, praying that she heard his voice. At three o'clock, sensing the end was close at hand, Tony telephoned the parish priest. The line was busy. He redialed a second time, then a third. Busy, always busy.

He returned to Rosa's bedside, took up the vigil, desperately praying that the children would arrive in time. Rosa Amonte slipped away peacefully at dawn, with Tony at her side, unaware of the firestorm raging nearby. The Amonte children arrived home two hours later, having abandoned their cars and jogged the last few miles into town through traffic gridlock, knowing that their mother's passing was not the only tragedy unfolding early on that Monday morning.

*　*　*　*

Sheets of brilliant orange and yellow flames leaped hundreds of feet into the night sky. Spectators from afar thought the entire town of Hillsdale was consumed by the inferno. Less than an hour after the explosion, two helicopters raced out of the darkness, darting across the huge sheets of fire, defying the danger, sending live video footage to Harrisburg and Scranton television stations. A third chopper joined them shortly, as CNN began coverage from the scene.

Starkly silhouetted against the wall of flames, their call letters clearly visible, they resembled giant fireflies, swooping low, darting dangerously close to the conflagration.

Backing off the campus, they hovered above Main Street, searchlights illuminating the huge crowd below. Moments later they disappeared, to return periodically, beaming live video images across the country.

CNN and the regional stations covered the story throughout the night and the following day, dispatching choppers to film the ruins, broadcasting uninformative interviews with bewildered town officials whose guarded responses to questions about the cause of the holocaust merely fueled reporters' eagerness to sensationalize the story.

The Monday morning national news programs headlined the disaster at Cabot University. The town of Hillsdale and the university achieved instant national celebrity, its fifteen minutes of fame perverted into unwelcome notoriety as the inevitable investigations unfolded.

*　*　*　*

The senior class of Cabot University traditionally opened Senior Week festivities with a Sunday outing to Hershey Theme Park, ninety miles south of campus. As midnight approached, three chartered buses filled to capacity with boisterous, celebrating seniors became snarled in the massive traffic jam clogging the interstate highway outside Hillsdale. Climbing out of the lead bus, the driver made his way to the barricade of police vehicles, their red and blue lights flashing, a phalanx of cars blocking the highway. A state police corporal offered rudimentary details of the devastation at Cabot University.

Returning to his bus, the shaken driver spread the news to each of the other buses, climbed aboard his own vehicle and stood beside the steering wheel, barely able to speak.

"Listen up, you guys!" he shouted down the aisle. "We've got a problem and we may have to sit in this traffic for the rest of the night." He finally had the students' full attention.

"There's been a big explosion and fire—maybe more than one explosion, I guess—on the campus. The cops tell me that Connors Hall is gone, the library is destroyed by fire and they may lose more buildings. There are some fatalities—I don't know how many.

"Nobody leaves this bus until I get permission from the police to proceed. So just settle down, it's gonna be a long night."

The students grew instantly silent, stunned by the devastating news. Many had lived the past four years in the residence hall nearest Connors Hall. Only later would they appreciate the act of fate that kept them away from campus on that awful night. Had they been in their rooms that Sunday night, the toll of dead and injured would have been much higher.

*   *   *   *

President Larry Northrop, in New York City for a Monday morning meeting of the university's Board of Trustees, learned of the explosion and fire shortly after midnight when he and his wife returned to their hotel suite following a reception and dinner party for New York area alumni. A white envelope was propped against the telephone whose blinking red light signaled a message.

"Someone must be looking for me," he told his wife, opening the envelope and gesturing toward the blinking red light on the telephone. The handwritten fax message was brief. "Cabot University buildings severely damaged by multiple explosions and fire. Connors Hall and library in flames. Entire campus at risk. Please contact Fire Chief Max Kumple or the Hillsdale Police Department at once."

He lost precious moments in a futile effort to reach campus security through the university's emergency number. After several busy signals, he made an operator-assisted call and was informed that power and communications to Cabot University were temporarily severed. At his request, the New York operator rang Hillsdale's main fire station. The President was patched through to Chief Kumple at 12:30 a.m.

"Can you give me a status report, Chief? Are there any injuries?" he shouted through the noisy connection.

"Multiple explosions hit the campus before midnight—the biggest one blew a crater twenty feet deep in what used to be the plaza in front of Connors Hall. Then there were more explosions, probably fed by ruptured gas lines going into the building. Three people are confirmed dead—there'll probably be more. At least 30 people are injured, and there will be a lot more injuries, for sure."

"Have all our students been evacuated from the residence halls?" the President asked anxiously.

"Yes, sir. No problem there. Practically everybody was off campus, either down at Hershey Park or gone home for the weekend. Also, because it was late and the library was closed, only a few people were on campus when it happened."

"Can you identify those killed and injured?" Northrop asked.

"No specific names at this time, President Northrop. We're working on it. I'm sorry. I'm in the middle of total chaos here. My men say that the injured include a few students and random people who were walking across the Commons at the time of the explosions. The worst loss is some of my firefighters. Three of my men are dead, lost fighting to save the library."

"Some of my men are collapsing as we speak," Kumple reported. "Apparently, the problem is not heat or exhaustion. They're vomiting, coughing, choking. At least ten have gone down so far. We're requiring oxygen masks and protective gear for all firefighters and police within two hundred yards of the fire. Trouble is, we've exhausted our supplies. More masks and gear are being flown in from Philadelphia, but it'll take a couple of hours to get the equipment up here."

Shaken and pale, Larry sank into the sofa.

"President Northrop, can you hear me?"

"I'm right here, Chief," he shouted.

"Look, Connors Hall is lost—there was no hope of saving it," Kumple reported. "I'm sorry, but the building exploded. Right now we're trying to save the library, but we're losing that battle, too. Consider it gone," he said grimly.

"The good news is that I think that Starrett Science Center and the Engineering Center will be scorched, but we'll be able to save them. Also, the residence hall near Connors is badly damaged but we can save it. We've set up an emergency medical center there. It's safely away from the fire and the infirmary has lost power anyway."

Larry Northrop groaned.

"President Northrop, I need answers to some questions right now. There's a strange chemical odor in the air around the fire. It's very strong around Connors Hall. What the hell was stored in Connors Hall? I've got to know in order to protect my men," he shouted into the cell phone.

"Chief Kumple, Connors Hall houses the business school! The only chemicals stored anywhere on campus are in Starrett Science Center, except for some minor supplies in the maintenance building," Northrop asserted. "Has the fire actually breached Starrett, too?"

"No, sir," Kumple assured him. "We've got people on the roof, it's being hosed down and cooled. That's one building we won't lose tonight."

"Good God! What if the explosion was a bomb?" Northrop asked. "Could that be the source of the odor?"

"I don't think so. It was one hell of an explosion—actually, there were several explosions. Some of them probably caused by severed gas lines. It took a few minutes to seal off the gas. But I don't think the first explosion was a bomb. We won't know for sure until this is over."

"Also, President Northrop," the fire chief continued, "I gotta tell you I put one of your assistants out of commission—name of Hutchins," he confessed. "He was in the way, and I had to remove him. Can you designate someone to serve as your spokesman for the university?"

Larry Northrop didn't hesitate. "Yes. For now, Police Chief Irwin can speak for the university. You know him, and I trust his judgment. And don't worry about Tyler Hutchins. If he got in the way, I'm sure you handled him properly.

"I'm starting back to Hillsdale immediately," Northrop motioned to his wife to start packing. "I'll call back every hour for a report and hope to see you before dawn. Good luck and Godspeed, Chief," he said gravely.

"Thank you, sir," said Max Kumple. "Please get back here as fast as you can." The fire chief clipped the cell phone onto his belt and headed toward the inferno.

Chapter 43

Ruth and Nancy kept a vigil on the deck of the Atherton home through the long night, awestruck at the intensity of the inferno consuming the campus on the ridge a mile away. Nancy raised the binoculars to her red-rimmed eyes once again.

"The roof and walls of Connors Hall just collapsed," she reported, as ugly yellow sheets of flame flared brightly, like a miniature sunspot, its tentacles rising high into the night sky. A series of deep rumbles rolled across the river.

"It's all gone. My office, the computer labs, lecture rooms—everything. I can't believe it." Fighting back tears, Nancy was strangely enraged at the scene. In a spontaneous display of affection and sympathy, Ruth reached out and embraced her best friend and colleague. Arms around each other, they stared at the spreading destruction.

As the long night wore on and the enormity of the disaster became obvious, the neighbors slowly gathered together, supporting each other, offering comfort to Ruth and Nancy. Nancy busied herself preparing sandwiches and coffee for the unexpected visitors. Quantities of coffee were consumed while the food lay untouched.

By 4:00 a.m. the bright yellow sheets of flame slowly began to subside, finally fading to a long orange smudge on the ridge above town. At dawn the neighbors quietly returned to their homes, amid tearful hugs and unspoken sympathy.

*   *   *   *

"Sorry to wake you at this hour, but we have a major emergency at the university and I need your help." Northrop related the essentials of the disaster unfolding on campus to the chairman of Cabot University's Board of Trustees.

The chairman didn't hesitate for a moment. "Obviously, you are returning to Hillsdale at once," he said. "Let me offer my corporate jet. It will be faster than commercial air service, and it's available now.

"I'll cancel the board meeting tomorrow morning. If you think it's appropriate, I'll reschedule the meeting for a week from tomorrow. I'll join you on campus tomorrow afternoon." The chairman of Cabot University's Board of Trustees was a take-charge person, the President of a major drug company headquartered in northern New Jersey.

"If you and your wife can get to Newark International Airport in an hour, the plane will be serviced and ready to go."

"Thanks, Ron. I'm truly grateful for your assistance. I'll give you a report as soon as I evaluate the situation with my own eyes. You'll be able to tell the board members the status tomorrow before you postpone the meeting."

An hour later Larry and Jean Northrop boarded the twin engine executive jet, took seats while their luggage was stowed and waited impatiently for takeoff clearance. An agonizing forty minutes later the plane descended to five hundred feet, swept over the hills northeast of Hillsdale and made a low pass over the university. The passengers gazed in horror at the inferno below. A wall of white-hot flames pierced the night sky, leaping hundreds of feet into the air. Rolling black clouds of acrid smoke surged thousands of feet above the flames, creating a wind shear that tossed the jet about like a kite in a violent wind.

The instrument landing at Hillsdale Regional Airport through clouds of swirling smoke required all of the pilot's considerable skills. Northrop felt the landing gear lock into place only seconds before the dim runway lights appeared through the black smoke obscuring the runway.

The aircraft touched down with a soft bump and the two passengers were thrust against their seat belts as the pilot braked to a halt, then taxied briskly to the terminal. As he gathered his coat and briefcase, Northrop realized with a heavy heart that he was facing the crisis of his life. Thanking the pilot for a skillful landing in difficult conditions, he followed his wife down the plane's narrow steps.

The sky had taken on an ominous reddish glow, a false sunrise like nothing he had ever seen before. The intense heat of the fire warmed the smoke-filled air. The eerie orange glow brightened suddenly as the wind direction shifted and the smoke momentarily lifted. Two miles from the airport on the distant ridge that once held a cluster of graceful campus buildings, they caught their first clear view of the inferno consuming the campus.

A Hillsdale squad car, siren screaming, raced onto the tarmac. Within minutes, the police escorted the car through the gridlock on the airport road and they were delivered to their home on University Avenue less than a block from the main entrance to the university.

"Stay in the house, Jean," ordered Northrop. "Perhaps you can offer these men some food and drink," he gestured toward the exhausted firefighters sprawled on the lawns along University Avenue. Joined by Randy Irwin and the campus security chief, they raced up University Avenue, past fire trucks and tangled hoses to the Commons.

He arrived just in time to witness the death throes of the university's library. Firefighters, ordered to retreat to relative safety, watched helplessly as the inevitable destruction roared to a climax. Paralyzed with shock, the

President watched helplessly as the soul of his beloved university turned to ashes. With a thundering crash, the massive library roof collapsed inward. A wall of flames shot ever higher and the inferno grew more intense. The red-hot exterior walls stood guard around the flaming interior, the fiery resting place of millions of books, journals and historical artifacts.

After an interminable pause, suspended in time and forever etched in the memories of those who watched, the exterior walls collapsed with a final shuddering convulsion and roar. First, the west wall facing Connors Hall toppled and crashed into the flaming cauldron. Then the other three walls slowly, reluctantly, collapsed into the center of what once had been the intellectual core of the university. In ninety seconds the university's heart and soul became a huge pile of flaming rubble. The library was lost.

Galvanized by the loss of the library, scores of exhausted firefighters fought desperately to save Starrett Science Center. Except for Old Main, safely on the opposite side of the Commons, the science building was the principal academic unit still in danger. A brigade of firemen took up positions dangerously close to the library and hurled torrents of cooling water onto Starrett's walls and roof, determined that the science center would not die that April night.

At 6:00 a.m. on Monday, as the sun's huge orange ball appeared through the smoke and haze over the distant eastern hills, Fire Chief Max Kumple declared the Cabot University fire under control.

Chapter 44

Exhausted firefighters continued pouring water on the ruins for a week, quickly dousing the occasional hot spots that flared deep within the rubble of Connors Hall. They kept an equally watchful eye on the remains of Memorial Library. Flames flared up in random outbreaks as three million volumes and priceless artifacts lay in ruins. A thick, vile-smelling acrid smoke hung over the campus and the central business district, slowly dissipating across the town.

Miles of yellow police tape surrounded the ruins, pathetic reminders of the once beautiful buildings that had graced the campus, now huge piles of black rubble. Campus security, local police and a contingent of National Guard troops stood watch over the disaster area day and night.

For a week, thousands of spectators—shocked students and faculty, townspeople, curiosity seekers and state and federal investigators—gathered in clusters on the Commons. Stunned as the enormity of the loss began to sink in, they were first depressed, then angry. They asked each other how a fire, originating in a single empty classroom building on a quiet weekend could have wreaked such devastation. How could a fire build so quickly into an inferno? Were the local volunteer firemen so inadequately trained that they could not contain the fire? Who was to blame?

The heroism of firefighters who risked their lives to save the campus from total destruction was virtually ignored. Even the Hillsdale Chronicle was largely silent, failing to acknowledge the major contribution of the firefighters in saving the rest of the campus. Instead, editorials focused on the loss of lives and property and questioned the community's preparedness for such a catastrophe. Only later would the firefighters' fierce courage and dedication to saving Starrett Science Center and beloved Old Main receive the recognition they deserved.

Early estimates of the damage ranged upward of two hundred million dollars. No insurance proceeds could bring back the priceless artifacts displayed in the library, destroyed forever.

Starrett Science Center, its scarred and blackened exterior north wall a silent reminder of the tragedy, resumed research and development activities on a limited scale two weeks after the fire. Old Main, whose administrative records and mainframe computers were untouched, became the command center for the investigation into the causes of the fire.

* * * *

Four days after the disaster, while firefighters continued pouring water on the charred ruins, the Cabot University community learned that the human toll suffered that horrible Sunday night would rise. Without warning, more than a dozen fire fighters and police officers fell victim to a mysterious illness.

Many of the victims had been among the first volunteers to reach the scene. Initially ignoring personal safety standards, they fought desperately to save Connors Hall. Protective gear and oxygen masks were untouched, packed away in the fire trucks. Only after the overpowering odor of unidentified chemicals engulfed them did some fighters pause long enough to don the limited supply of protective gear and oxygen units.

About an hour into the long fight to save the campus, Chief Kumple belatedly recognized the danger to his men. Ordering all firefighters to don oxygen units, he desperately sought additional gear from cities as far away as Harrisburg and Philadelphia. The response was swift. Specialized protective gear and portable oxygen systems were quickly airlifted to Hillsdale, but not before local volunteers had been exposed to toxic fumes for several hours as they fought to save the campus.

Several firefighters collapsed minutes after taking up positions, choking, gasping for breath and vomiting as the fire raged around them. The emergency medical team's triage operation made a preliminary diagnosis of smoke inhalation. Those most seriously affected were treated at the scene, and then helicoptered to Essex Medical Center's intensive care unit.

In the week that followed, more firemen fell ill. Most treated themselves with the usual remedies, attributing the coughing and choking to smoke inhalation and heat exhaustion. For too long, the extent and severity of the illness went undetected by medical authorities.

The fifth fatality of the Cabot University fire was recorded when a thirty-year old Hillsdale volunteer fire fighter died shortly after being admitted to Hillsdale Hospital, having unsuccessfully treated himself with home remedies. When the newspaper reported his death, other victims finally recognized that their ailments were not isolated cases. Worse, they wondered whether the illness was linked in some way to the fumes they had inhaled near Connors Hall.

Soon, firefighters and police suffering from nausea, choking and coughing began to display more serious symptoms. Bloody diarrhea and joint pain were common complaints. Finally, scores of volunteer firefighters descended on Hillsdale Hospital and Essex Medical Center. Dehydration and complications from nausea required fluid injections. Ten people were placed in intensive care. Five more victims died two weeks after the fire.

The death toll in the Cabot University disaster quickly rose to twelve, with twenty more hospitalized in serious condition. Onlookers who had fought police lines to get closer views of the fire began to panic. In their eagerness to get a better view of the inferno had they unwittingly exposed themselves to a dangerous illness? Had the entire town been exposed to unidentified poisons carried in the acrid smoke that engulfed Hillsdale for several days?

Chapter 45

Tony Amonte lay stretched out on the old recliner in a corner of his tiny living room, a week of unread newspapers piled on the stand beside him. He had carried out the final rites for his wife, following her last wishes as best he could. With the departure of his children, there was no longer a need to maintain a stoic exterior. Finally, he confronted the loss of his beloved Rosa. Even the last few months of her illness had not prepared him for the silence, the depth of loneliness, the deep depression that engulfed him with a physical ache no medicine could assuage.

Strangely disconnected, through red-rimmed eyes he surveyed the familiar room with its inexpensive furniture, the television set opposite the sofa along the wall, the African violets on the windowsill that had thrived under Rosa's green thumb. Beyond the open screened window, the soft morning sounds of the neighborhood floated at the edge of his consciousness, distant and surreal.

He sighed deeply, shook his head, tried to rouse himself from his lethargy, desperately striving to regain a sense of reality. The old man reached for a newspaper in the stack, picked up the special edition published by the Chronicle the afternoon following the fire and forced himself to concentrate on the headlines. In the solitude of a home suddenly silent, he began to read the ugly details of the worst disaster in Hillsdale history.

He quickly scanned the graphic details of the explosion and fire, noting that its origin was Connors Hall and that the library was a heap of rubble. With mounting horror he examined the color photos beneath the stark headline. Like a moth drawn to a flame, he stared at photos of the huge crater in what had once been the plaza where students gathered in front of Connors Hall. Nowhere in the charred mountain of rubble could he detect any resemblance of the beautifully restored structure that had anchored the west side of the Commons.

Suddenly he threw the open newspaper to the floor and rushed to the kitchen telephone. Frantically he searched the directory, located a number and dialed.

"Hello," said the elderly voice at the other end of the line.

"Mrs. Ledbetter, this is Tony Amonte. I'm a friend of Kevin Parks. He lives at your place, right?"

"He has a room here, yes. But I haven't seen him for several days."

"Has he been around since the fire?"

"I don't think so—he comes and goes as he pleases, you know. Often stays away for days at a time—if I didn't know better, I'd think he has a girl friend," she giggled at the thought.

"Are you sure you haven't seen him since the fire?"

"I'm not positive," she said testily. "I just don't remember seeing him around here. I don't spy on my roomers, you know," she said. "As long as they pay the rent, they can come and go as they please."

"Thanks. Sorry to bother you." He replaced the handset in its cradle, shuffled back to the living room and slumped heavily into his chair.

Hands shaking, he pulled another newspaper from the pile and resumed reading the extensive coverage of the explosion and fire. He took little comfort from the report that authorities believed the building was empty on the night of the fire.

They didn't know he had given Kevin Parks a master key several weeks ago. They didn't know about Kevin's interest in Connors Hall. They didn't know that Kevin was obsessed with the notion that toxic wastes were stored on the campus. Was it possible? It was unthinkable, but he knew with a heavy heart that his strange young friend was gone.

Tony reviewed Kevin's last visit. It was strange that he had not shown up for Rosa's funeral. Still, the young man was such a social misfit that he had thought nothing of his absence at the time. In retrospect, he was surprised and grateful to observe Kevin's genuine warmth and tenderness toward Rosa as she lay dying.

Still, Kevin's obsessive behavior worried him. Tony had dismissed his concerns, too troubled about Rosa to worry about the fantasies of a student. In retrospect, he realized that he should not have fed Kevin's obsession. Lending him the master key to every building on the campus was a huge mistake. Now he, Tony Amonte, might be responsible for Kevin's death and could well be in very deep trouble.

Tears flowed down the deep crevices of his wrinkled cheeks. His grief for Rosa and this new concern overwhelmed him. Rosa would know how to deal with it, but she was gone.

Finally, he thought of Ruth Borovski. Kevin often mentioned her when he talked about his research. During his years as head custodian in Starrett Science Center, both she and Dr. Jacob, unlike many other senior faculty at the university, were unfailingly polite to Tony, frequently thanking him for his services, even occasionally bringing him home baked treats that he shared with the other janitors. Perhaps Dr. Borovski would know what to do.

An hour later he entered Starrett Science Center, passing easily through the heightened security, greeting by name the guards checking each person entering the building.

Ruth opened her office door in response to his tentative knock.

"Yes, may I help you?" Puzzled but courteous, she didn't recognize the wizened old man standing before her.

"I guess you don't remember me. My name is Tony Amonte. I used to be a janitor in this building. I remember you and Dr. Jacob real well. Can I come in?" he asked, his Italian accent more pronounced in his nervousness.

"Of course," she stepped back and motioned him to a chair beside her desk. "Now," she smiled, "what brings you to my door this morning?" she asked, trying to put the frail, elderly man at ease.

"It's about Kevin Parks. I need to talk to him. He visited me a couple of weeks before the fire and I haven't seen him since. I kind of wonder if he's okay. I called his rooming house and Mrs. Ledbetter hasn't seen him either. He told me that you became his research advisor after Dr. Jacob died. I'm worried about him. Maybe you know where I can find him?"

She frowned. In the chaos following the fire, she had neither seen nor even thought about Kevin. "Actually, I haven't seen him for some time," she confessed. "Our last meeting was difficult. In fact, it was very unpleasant. As his dissertation chair, I had to inform him that he is being dismissed from the university because he has not completed his doctoral research.

"Is there something I can help you with?" she asked. Why would this man care about Kevin's whereabouts?

Without warning, his face crumbled and Tony broke down, great heaving sobs filling the quiet office.

"He's dead! Oh God, I know he's dead. First, my Rosa. Now Kevin. I can't take it anymore," he sobbed incoherently, engulfed in grief.

Stunned, Ruth went to his side and awkwardly offered him a glass of water. She waited patiently for a few moments, then reached for the phone, dialed 8911 and requested medical assistance. Five minutes later, a team of university EMTs led by a uniformed security guard rushed down the hall to her office.

Tony had quieted during the seemingly interminable wait for help. He stared vacantly at the people around him, eyes focused on some distant horror, unable or unwilling to speak. As the EMTs worked on him, Ruth related her conversation with Tony and his unexpected collapse.

Tony finally roused himself and looked around the office, resisting the EMTs and refusing attempts to put him on a gurney. "You don't understand," he whispered. "Kevin Parks is dead—he's buried in the ruins of Connors Hall," he gestured vaguely out the window toward the pile of rubble at the edge of the Commons. "It's my fault. I killed him! I gave him a key to the building."

"What do you mean? Could he have been in the building during the fire?" Ruth momentarily lost her composure, horrified as the impact of Tony's tearful confession registered.

"Yes. He had this crazy notion that there are toxic wastes on the campus. He wanted to search all the buildings on campus. I figured he was a little crazy, but harmless. So I loaned him a master key to the buildings. I know I shouldn't have done that, but I figured if he looked around, didn't find anything, he would finally get it out of his system.

"My God, he must have found something. Either he blew up the building, or maybe it just exploded. Whatever. He's buried over there in the rubble." His voice rose hysterically. "Dr. Borovski, there's a body buried in Connors Hall."

He bent over and collapsed onto the floor, arms hugging his waist. He emitted a deep, low moan, the monotone moan of a person in a catatonic state. They would learn nothing more from Tony Amonte that day or for months to come.

Chapter 46

"Cabot University. Good morning, this is Officer Burns, campus security. This message is being recorded. May I help you?"

"I hope so, officer. My daughter is missing. She's a student at Cabot University, and I haven't heard from her since the fire. I've called her apartment a dozen times, day and night," said the worried voice. "Can you help me?"

"I'll try, ma'am. As you can imagine, things are pretty chaotic around here right now. Some of the residence halls still don't have telephone service. That's probably why she hasn't called you. I wouldn't worry about your daughter, she'll turn up."

"Officer, you don't understand. My daughter doesn't live on campus. I've called her apartment day and night since that horrible fire a week ago. Furthermore, my daughter is a very responsible young woman. I'm sure she would call me if she could. She is scheduled to graduate this Sunday."

"What's her name and student ID number?" Officer Burns interrupted her, rolling his eyes at the dispatcher nearby.

"Valerie M. Chapman. Her ID number is 45-6789," the voice replied. "She lives in Hillsdale Apartments—that's a complex a few blocks from school."

"We believe that all of the students—on campus and also those living in town—have been accounted for," he reassured her. "I'm checking a list of injured students right now. Hold on for a moment." He motioned to the dispatcher to hand him the stack of printouts and hurriedly scanned the pages.

Moments later he returned to the phone. "Nope. There's nobody by that name on the injured list. And all the dead have been identified. Mrs. Chapman, your daughter's probably just fine," the officer concluded confidently. "You keep trying her phone. She could be hanging out with friends.

"Or, maybe she left town for a few days," he suggested. "Not a bad idea, given the mess around here. However, if you want, I'll send someone around to check her apartment. See if we can locate her. When we find her, she'll be told to call home," the officer said soothingly.

"Would you do that right away?" the voice asked anxiously.

"Yes, ma'am. I'll send a squad car over there shortly. Give me your phone number and I'll get back to you. It may take some time to track her down," he warned. "Please be patient. And don't worry, we'll find her. I promise you, someone here at campus security will call you back when we have any news."

Part VI

The Investigation

Chapter 47

They gathered again in Old Main's auditorium on a sunny morning in late July. A television pool would provide gavel-to-gavel coverage of the upcoming hearing.

An army of technicians representing the major networks, CNN, Fox News, CNBC and C-Span set up cameras in strategic locations to provide commentary. Two pool cameras dominated a large platform built over a section of chairs in the center of the auditorium. Another camera was positioned in the front row of the balcony. A remote-controlled fixed camera sat on a tripod at the rear of the stage facing the witness table.

Roving cameramen, minicams on their shoulders, staked out positions along the wall beneath the tall windows and on both sides of the stage. A command post was set up in the transmission truck parked along the east side of Old Main. Atop the truck, a massive satellite dish, aimed toward the western horizon, provided the electronic up-link to the rest of the country and the world beyond. Network news anchors mingled with feature reporters in a corner of the large hall, chatting casually, waiting for the proceedings to begin.

A long conference table stretched across the front of the stage. Behind the table, seven high-backed leather chairs faced the empty auditorium. Several rows of folding chairs at the rear of the stage would provide seating for the commission's staff members.

Lapel microphones, one for each commission member, lay on the conference table, ready to be clipped on. Sound technicians worked their way along the table, methodically testing each mike, coordinating the sound level, assuring that even a whisper would be audible in the auditorium and transmitted to the television hookup.

Heavy cables snaked from the stage to an open window and across the lawn to the broadcast truck. Two giant television screens hung from the ceiling, ready to display the video images that would be simultaneously broadcast nationwide.

Large crowds gathered outside Old Main, poised to take their reserved seats for this opening session of the official investigation into the Cabot University explosions and fire. Today, the opening session would be broadcast live across the country. The townspeople were determined to be part of the biggest media event ever staged in Hillsdale.

At nine-thirty Old Main's doors opened, and spectators rushed up the wide granite steps to the lobby. Security guards restrained the throng pushing against the double doors leading into the auditorium. Fifteen minutes later, the doors finally opened and those with printed admission cards hustled to their assigned seats.

Newscasters began transmitting at 9:55 a.m., summarizing the tragic events that were the focus of the investigation, offering background information on the members of the Commission to Investigate the Cabot University Accident and explaining the Commission's official task. They did voice-over analyses of spectacular video footage filmed during the height of the fire that engulfed the campus. The devastation was inevitably described as having occurred on the bucolic campus of one of America's most prestigious universities.

Promptly at ten o'clock the seven members of the commission filed into the auditorium and took their seats on the stage. They were followed by a large contingent of aides, arms laden with heavy files stuffed with documents. They took assigned seats behind the commission members.

The room quieted as the chairman settled into his chair at the center of the conference table and clipped the tiny microphone onto his suit lapel. He rapped the heavy gavel smartly on the solid mahogany table.

Gazing directly into the television camera on the center platform, Jeremy Steinberg, former Governor of Pennsylvania and a retired federal judge, opened the proceedings.

"Good morning ladies and gentlemen here in Hillsdale and viewers from around the country. I call to order this first session of the Commission to Investigate the Cabot University Accident." His deep baritone voice boomed across the packed auditorium.

"First, let me explain the purpose of these hearings. This commission has been established to investigate the tragic series of explosions and subsequent fire that devastated this campus on the evening of April 28-29 of this year. Our objective is to determine the causes and consequences of this tragedy—to search for the truth, wherever it may lead us.

"The commission was established by an overwhelming vote of the legislature of the Commonwealth of Pennsylvania and has the strong support of the governor. The commission enjoys wide discretion in its work, including broad subpoena powers that authorize us to question individuals and company representatives who may have knowledge of the events surrounding this tragic accident. Investigators, scientific experts and support people have been hired to pursue every lead, to evaluate the evidence and to advise us. The commission's findings of fact, conclusions and recommendations will be forwarded simultaneously to the Board of Regents of the University of Pennsylvania System and to the state legislature. Further, the commission may (at its discretion) forward its findings to the state attorney general and to federal law enforcement officials (as appropriate) for possible criminal and/or civil prosecution.

"The legislature of the Commonwealth and the Board of Regents of the university system are to be commended for moving expeditiously to establish this commission and give it wide discretionary powers in investigating the events before, during and after this accident.

"It is well known that twenty-five innocent people perished in this accident, and nearly one hundred others were seriously injured. I regret to report that today, several months later, we cannot state with certainty that all of the victims have been identified and treated.

"Serious questions have arisen concerning the health and safety of the students, faculty and staff of this university." He peered over the half glasses perched on his aquiline nose. "Environmental health questions are grave concerns of this panel. Moreover, we intend to establish whether individuals responsible for administering state and federal occupational health and safety procedures and guidelines have complied fully with regulations concerning the disposal of toxic waste materials."

He placed his sheaf of notes flat on the table, straightened the pile neatly and peered directly into the lens of the television camera. Acutely aware that his words were being broadcast live across the nation, he played the role of chairman perfectly. Hands clasped on the table, the retired judge was a somber and imposing figure, his visage softened only by the wispy fringe of unruly white hair nestled above his ears.

"Serious charges have been widely reported in the print and television media," he continued. "A cache of highly toxic waste materials allegedly was stored on the campus of Cabot University. Indeed, if we are to give credence to the most serious allegations, one might conclude—prematurely, and without foundation, I might add—that administrators knowingly permitted highly volatile chemical wastes to be stored on this campus for nearly half a century.

"On behalf of the commission, I pledge to the faculty, staff and students of this great university, to the citizens of Hillsdale, the Commonwealth of Pennsylvania and to the appointing authorities who established this commission, we will get to the truth in these matters in due course."

He looked down at his notes, then turned to his right, a slight smile on his face.

"Permit me to introduce the distinguished members of the commission, each of whom brings unique and valuable expertise to this panel. It is a privilege to serve with such eminent colleagues—men and women whose wisdom and determination to ferret out the truth in this tragedy will be tested during the days to come."

The chairman took fifteen minutes of airtime establishing the credentials of his colleagues, detailing their expertise and diplomatically praising the wisdom of the governor and legislature that appointed them. The cameras

253

closed in on each of the four men and two women who, together with the chairman, comprised the commission. Over the next month, their faces would become familiar in virtually every household across America as the facts surrounding the tragedy at Cabot University unfolded in the harsh glare of national television.

The chairman also introduced the commission's key staff member. Greg Brown, the General Counsel, was charged with day-to-day management of the investigation. Under his leadership, the staff of more than twenty attorneys and investigators pursued every lead, assembled data culled from hundreds of interviews, developed the witness list, coordinated the commission's activities and arranged the public hearings now underway.

Continuing to set the stage and lay the ground rules, Chairman Steinberg acknowledged the senior staff members seated behind the commission and pointed out the reserved section in the front of the auditorium that was restricted to witnesses and others essential to the proceedings.

"This morning, following a short recess, I will summarize briefly the tragic events that led to the formation of this commission. I also intend to offer some details that have come to light since the explosions and fire on April 28. If we are able to maintain our schedule, the commission will call its first witness this afternoon.

"I hope our audience here in Hillsdale and around the country understand the procedures under which the commission will operate during these hearings. Please note that from time to time, it may be necessary to go into executive session. During these sessions, the commission will meet privately—cameras and microphones will not be permitted."

He looked around the room. "At this time I am declaring a fifteen minute recess." He glanced at his watch. "These proceedings will resume promptly at 10:30." The Judge unclipped his microphone, pushed back his chair and led the members from the stage. They retreated up the back stairs to the President's suite where coffee and pastry awaited.

Television newscasters filled the airtime speculating about possible revelations that might be newsworthy during this opening day of the hearings. Would new facts about the tragedy be revealed this morning? The announcers teased their audience in blatant efforts to boost their networks' ratings. They guaranteed live gavel-to-gavel coverage of events from Hillsdale, at least for today's opening sessions. Only C-Span promised live continuous coverage of the hearings.

Television cameramen and technicians relaxed as control cut away from the campus to local stations. Spectators stretched at their seats, or spilled into the wide aisles, unwilling to leave the auditorium, impatient for the proceedings to resume.

Ruth Borovski and Nancy Atherton, seated in the reserved section, rose and casually looked around the sunlit auditorium. Nancy's gaze was drawn to the high windows facing the Commons. In the distance she glimpsed the huge pile of rubble, all that remained of Connors Hall, her professional home. Even now, three months after the fire, the scene was surreal. She watched a huge bulldozer load charred debris into an enormous dump truck. The muted sounds of heavy equipment drifted through the open windows.

"Do you think the chairman will actually announce anything new this morning?" Nancy asked.

"It's possible," said Ruth.

"If it isn't confidential, tell me about your meeting yesterday with the commission staff. Aren't you scheduled to be the second witness, right after Larry Northrop testifies? That means you may be called to testify today. Do you have any idea what questions you'll be asked?"

"I had a long interview with the staff yesterday morning. They briefed me on what to expect when I testify. I didn't actually meet Judge Steinberg. Greg Brown, the General Counsel, reviewed the questions he or Steinberg will ask. They also offered guidance in how to answer their questions, how much detail to offer and how the proceedings are structured. I think they wanted to put me at ease as much as possible.

"They told me to ignore the television cameras—as if that's possible," she said. "And they warned me about the television lights. They're intensely bright and they give off a lot of heat, too."

"You'll be fine, Ruth. Relax and be yourself."

"I'm a little uneasy about testifying. Of course, I'll cooperate in any way I can. I owe it to Jacob and Kevin Parks to contribute any information that may help get to the bottom of this accident. But I don't look forward to this experience," she laughed nervously.

"It seems impossible that Jacob has been gone more than a year," Nancy said softly.

"Yes," Ruth nodded sadly. "Some days, however, it seems like only yesterday—those aren't especially good days," she confessed. "Jacob would be appalled at the devastation and the loss of so many lives. Kevin's death would be especially hard for him. Kevin was a social misfit, but he had a brilliant talent for science, the kind that Jacob said comes along once in a lifetime of teaching. He discovered that spark of genius in Kevin during his freshman chemistry class. He nurtured him and challenged him intellectually for so many years—he was responsible for encouraging him to enter the doctoral program, of course." Ruth seemed to want to talk about the past year, and Nancy listened sympathetically.

"He invested countless hours teaching Kevin, working with him in the lab, demonstrating techniques, passing along his wisdom, trying to instill the excitement of pure research. Despite his idiosyncrasies, Kevin never harmed anyone; he just wanted to be left alone with his research.

"Jacob was a father figure to Kevin. In retrospect, I genuinely believe that no one—not I, not Paul nor Anton—was more devastated by Jacob's death. Of course, that led to Kevin's obsession about cancer deaths on campus. And it triggered his clinical depression. Meantime, I ignored all the signs, ultimately dismissed his concerns out of hand," Ruth said regretfully.

"Don't blame yourself, Ruth. You managed to get him psychiatric help," Nancy reminded her.

"I hope Judge Steinberg and these hearings finally identify the cause of this disaster. If we can learn from this experience, something good may come from the loss and devastation. In any event, I'll never believe that Kevin Parks deliberately set off the explosions and fire in Connors Hall."

"I saw him only occasionally in your lab or office," Nancy said. "From what little I knew of him, he didn't strike me as some sort of mad bomber. But he certainly was weird. When you and Jacob entertained students at your home, Kevin always seemed painfully ill at ease. And I never saw him with other grad students or friends his own age. That's why I can't understand what Valerie Chapman was doing with him in Connors Hall on the night of the fire," said Nancy.

"I can't either. Their only link as far as I know was their stay in the psychiatric wing at Essex Medical Center last winter."

The television floodlights were switched on and the audience quieted as the commission and staff returned to the stage. "Ladies and gentlemen. If you will indulge me, I intend to read into the record a summary of undisputed facts that the commission staff has developed regarding the tragedy of April 28. Certain previously unannounced findings will be made public as I proceed through this rather lengthy document."

He adjusted his half glasses and began.

"On April 28 at approximately 11:30 p.m., a minor explosion occurred in the basement of Connors Hall. It was followed almost immediately by a second massive explosion centered in a sub-basement beneath the plaza in front of the building. The second explosion created a huge crater more than twenty feet deep and some fifty feet wide, destroying the plaza in front of the building and the exterior front wall of the building, exposing four floors of faculty offices, classrooms and computer laboratories. The ensuing fire completely destroyed the building, which housed the business school here at Cabot University."

He removed his glasses and pointed dramatically out the windows facing the Commons. The television cameras dutifully followed his gaze, zooming in on the huge pile of rubble that once was Connors Hall. He paused while images of the devastation were transmitted across the country.

256

"Despite the courageous efforts of firefighters from Hillsdale and many surrounding communities, the inferno also completely destroyed Memorial Library, which housed more than three million volumes and journals and severely damaged several other campus buildings. The loss of one of this country's great university libraries was compounded by the destruction of the archives housed in the library including irreplaceable historical records of Cabot University, the community of Hillsdale and the entire region. Incomplete estimates of the damage to the physical facilities currently approach $100 million. Without question, this fine university has been dealt a devastating blow."

Steinberg peered over his glasses toward the television cameras. The audience listened intently.

"However, I have some good news to report. The governor in Harrisburg has authorized me to inform you that this morning he is signing a bill appropriating the sum of $50 million in disaster relief funds for Cabot University. The funds will help rebuild and restore the buildings destroyed or damaged in the disaster. I have also been notified that Senators Johnson and Stovczek representing the Commonwealth of Pennsylvania will file a bill next week in the United States Senate earmarking an additional $30 million of federal disaster funds to support the restoration of the university."

A buzz swept the audience. The chairman smiled for the cameras and waited for the noise to subside. "Let me assure you that Cabot University, one of the premier educational institutions in this country, will not die. It will rise from the ashes of this tragedy and continue to serve the state and the country in the years ahead." The audience erupted in loud applause.

Chairman Steinberg paused once again, milking the moment for the cameras. "To continue, I remind you that the death toll in this tragedy stands at twenty-five—nine firefighters, two students and one faculty member who succumbed to a heart attack while observing the fire. Although they are not part of the official count, thirteen more people were killed in traffic accidents on Interstate 80 as a result the explosion and the flying debris that rained down on traffic a mile from the campus. Ninety-eight people were injured severely enough to require hospitalization. Ten victims remain hospitalized and on respirators today.

"An important goal of our investigation is to determine the nature and seriousness of the unidentified illness that has afflicted some individuals since the April 28 tragedy. I refer, of course, to the firefighters, bystanders and others who became ill either during the fire or in the weeks following the holocaust. Our investigation extends beyond identifying the causes of the disastrous explosion and fire that followed.

"To date, seven of the twenty-five deaths in this tragedy have been attributed specifically to this unknown illness—an illness that is characterized by severe damage to the lungs, coughing, choking, nausea, diarrhea and a skin rash.

"Unlike past tragedies—I refer to the controversy surrounding Agent Orange following the Vietnam War and to what is commonly referred to as Gulf War Syndrome—we have no intention of delaying a decade or longer before investigating these illnesses that have struck down many people in this community."

The audience buzzed. This was the first official reference to possible chemical poisoning—a rumor that began to spread immediately after the fire, a rumor never officially confirmed or denied by authorities. Steinberg paused, removed his glasses in a habitual gesture and waited patiently for the crowd to settle down.

"That brings me to a rather sensitive issue," he continued. "Immediately following the explosion and during the hours the fire raged out of control, many firefighters, police and spectators reported a strong chemical odor in the air. Some individuals experienced severe allergic reactions, including respiratory collapse. Hospitalization was required in the most serious cases. Hundreds of other residents of Hillsdale subsequently reported similar, but less severe reactions.

"In view of the fatalities attributed to this as yet unidentified ailment, the commission has scheduled expert testimony from physicians, epidemiologists and environmental specialists knowledgeable in chemical and radiation poisoning. We hope to identify the nature of the illness associated with the accident.

"The commission has reason to believe that many people afflicted in varying degrees of severity with this illness have declined treatment. I urge townspeople and others who were in this area during the fire to come forward and identify yourselves to medical authorities if you have experienced any unusual symptoms.

"You may obtain information by telephoning the following number: 888-555-4646. Or, you can send an e-mail to the commission directly at this address: commission@cabot.edu. I can assure you, your messages will be answered promptly. You will be referred to a team of physicians and assistants at the Essex Medical Center, which is coordinating these follow-up studies.

"Next, I want to summarize some of the procedures we adopted during our investigation. Immediately after the fire was brought under control, local and state authorities conducted extensive tests of the air, soil and water in the immediate area in and around the crater. I will summarize those findings this afternoon. For now, I want to review the procedures adopted in gathering the data.

"The air quality at the crater site was first measured less than two hours after the fire was brought under control on April 29. Very shortly thereafter, steps were taken to evaluate the air quality across the campus, including in the damaged buildings near the site and buildings as far as one-half mile from Connors Hall. Authorities continue to monitor air quality daily in each building on the campus.

"Air quality across the campus now is within normal limits in every measurable respect. There is no reason to fear that any toxic substances are present at this time." He waited for the crowd to quiet. "In the days ahead, expert testimony will explain the detailed methodology and results of those tests.

"Now let me review the water supply procedures," he resumed. "First, some background. Two deep wells, drilled in the 1930s, comprise the sole source of Cabot University's water supply. These wells are located behind the heating plant near Connors Hall. They tap into a large aquifer beneath the campus that would adequately meet the needs of the entire region, not just the university. The wells have been carefully maintained and appropriately improved over the years.

"State regulations and the university's own administrative procedures require periodic testing of the water supply. Unfortunately, records of some tests are incomplete. In fact, over the last ten years, it appears that the water-testing program was not rigorously carried out as required by state law and the university's own internal procedures.

President Northrop and others will be questioned on this matter when they testify before the commission. Copies of all water records in the university's possession have been provided to the commission. Independent tests by outside experts have been conducted. Experts will testify in detail on the water, soil and air quality later in these hearings.

"As reported in the local newspaper, I can confirm that the April 28 explosion severed a major water main under Connors Hall, interrupting the water supply and complicating fire fighting efforts. The loss of that water supply doubtless contributed to the destruction of Memorial Library despite the efforts of firefighters to contain the conflagration.

"Emergency water supplies were trucked to the campus for two months following the fire," he continued. "During that period, a water main was constructed between the Hillsdale reservoir and water treatment plant and the campus. The reservoir serving the town now supplies water for the university. The campus wells have not been used since the fire. Let me assure you that the Hillsdale water supply and now the Cabot University water supply are safe.

"Water samples from the university's wells continue to be tested and evaluated daily under the joint supervision of the university, the town of Hillsdale and appropriate state authorities.

"The university's buildings are heated by natural gas. It should come as no surprise to our audience to learn that the initial explosions in Connors Hall severed two major gas mains, causing more explosions and fueling the fire, hindering fire fighting efforts and contributing to the devastation. The gas supply to the campus was not halted until fifteen minutes after the explosion. Gas service was restored to the campus a couple of days after the fire was brought under control. Reliable gas service is now fully operational in campus buildings."

Steinberg glanced at his watch and straightened the sheaf of papers on the table in front of him. With a questioning nod to his colleagues seated at the long conference table, he announced, "We'll take a ninety-minute lunch recess and reconvene at 1:30."

Nancy and Ruth headed for the side exit, climbed the back stairs to the President's suite and joined the commissioners, staff members and other witnesses milling about the area. Helping themselves to the luncheon set up on a long table, they retreated to the back stairs, seated themselves and ate lunch together.

*   *   *   *

Judge Steinberg rapped his gavel and the hearing resumed promptly at 1:30. "Our first item on this afternoon's agenda is to summarize the preliminary test results of the air, soil and water quality tests. Please keep in mind that these are preliminary results. Comprehensive testing now underway will continue for some months. Moreover, this is merely a summary of our findings. Technical experts will present comprehensive testimony on these matters later."

The chairman had the undivided attention of the audience, many of whom watched the proceedings on the large television screens hung from the ceiling. Television cameras zoomed in, beaming video images across the country and print reporters scribbled on their notepads.

"First, the soil samples from the crater." He paused and took a sip of water, seemingly unaware that the gesture only heightened the drama. "The following traces of chemicals and minerals were detected in soil extracted from the bottom and sides of the crater. Radium, cyanide, trace levels of arsenic, benzene and related petroleum solvents. In short, we found a witches' brew of volatile and highly dangerous substances."

The audience erupted. Steinberg pounded his gavel in an unsuccessful effort to reestablish order. Television cameras recorded the pandemonium, alternating action shots between the commissioners on stage and the audience. The scene was beamed live across the country and endlessly repeated throughout the evening.

Print reporters rushed from the auditorium, shouting into cell phones, contacting their editors. Television anchors bolted from the room, lined up on the steps of Old Main and reported (erroneously) that the explosion on the Cabot University campus was somehow linked to the detonation of a nuclear device.

Judge Steinberg finally regained control of the proceedings. He directed the doors to the auditorium closed and guarded. Reporters and TV anchors who had hastily left the hall found themselves on the outside looking in. Frustrated, they watched the rest of the day's proceedings on a portable television set under a tree near the TV trailer. Television anchors broke in occasionally to whine that they had been ejected from the hearings.

Inside, the chairman resumed. "Let me make this very clear," he said sternly. "Further interruptions of these proceedings will not be tolerated. If necessary, I will clear this hall of spectators, reporters and television cameras," he threatened. "We will have orderly hearings or every single person not essential to these proceedings will be removed. This is my final warning." He stared pointedly toward the security guards lined up at the rear of the auditorium.

A senior aide seated behind the chairman passed him a piece of paper. He glanced down at the note, his face red, visibly angered. He put aside his notes and spoke directly into the camera.

"I've just been informed that at least one television newscaster has speculated that the explosion and fire at this university were linked to a nuclear device!" He whipped off his glasses.

"That is absolutely false!" he thundered, "The soil samples **do not** provide evidence of a nuclear detonation. That is precisely the wrong conclusion to draw from my comment. I repeat. Low levels of radium, not radiation, have been detected. Reporters who distort the facts presented in these hearings will be removed immediately. That's a promise." He glared at the news reporters seated near the front of the auditorium.

"For those who can't differentiate between radium, uranium, plutonium, or radiation, I suggest you check out the definitions on the Internet. Better yet, enroll in a basic physics course," he said sarcastically. A nervous titter fluttered through the audience.

"The inference you might wish to make is that the chemicals and other radioactive elements found in the soil suggest the possibility—I stress possibility—that volatile, highly flammable and toxic materials were stored in Connors Hall." A buzz swept across the auditorium. Instantly, campus security forces strode purposefully down the aisles, prepared to carry out the chairman's eviction order.

"Let me emphasize this point: Based on our preliminary investigation, the magnitude of the explosion provides evidence that large quantities of volatile toxic materials were stored in the building, either as liquids or perhaps as sludge. By substantial quantities, I mean hundreds, perhaps thousands of gallons of hazardous waste materials.

"Based on the analysis thus far, our experts conclude that these extremely volatile materials were disturbed in some way, perhaps by removing some of them from their original resting place. Investigators have detected trace residue of materials in the rubble near the basement elevator and shaft, which is about fifty feet from the plaza in front of Connors Hall. Our preliminary conclusion is that the waste materials exploded spontaneously, creating the enormous crater and fire that ultimately destroyed the building.

"The analysis of soil samples within the crater and in the rubble of Connors Hall will continue for some time. Also, the area within 100 yards of the site will continue to be restricted to authorized personnel for the foreseeable future." He raised his index finger toward the audience. "Violators will be charged with criminal trespass. I suggest you avoid the area unless you plan to spend some time in the county jail."

He reached for a second stack of documents.

"Let me report some preliminary findings on the air samples taken during and immediately after the fire. The air quality sampling was done by fire department personnel who were also engaged in containing the fire. Because they were focused on their fire fighting duties, the air samples were not extensive. Understandably, they were not conducted in a strictly scientific manner. Nonetheless, they provide useful corroborating evidence, and I commend the fire chief and his men for having the presence of mind to take air samples under very difficult circumstances.

"The findings from the early air samples corroborate the later soil tests taken from the crater. We have confirmed that the air near the explosion site contained traces of cyanide, benzene, arsenic, radium and other still unidentified chemicals.

"Let me emphasize that our experts have not precisely identified all of the chemical components in the peculiar odor that was widely reported during and immediately after the fire. The commission's experts continue to examine the air samples. I will report additional information when it becomes available to the commission.

"Victims who suffered the symptoms described earlier—coughing, choking, nausea, diarrhea and skin rashes—may have ingested some of the chemicals released in the intense fire. These victims are being treated for particularly lethal allergic reactions to the chemicals. Medical experts at the Centers for Disease Control continue to study the symptoms and monitor the health of victims in the aftermath of the fire.

"I am pleased to report that air quality at the site and across the campus improved rapidly after the fire was brought under control. For a period of two weeks following the fire, air samples contained decreasing but measurable traces of toxic chemicals. Air samples taken after mid-May contained no discernible traces of these chemicals."

Peering over his half glasses, he smiled faintly. "In other words, the air in and around Cabot University is now safe to breathe."

He set aside his notes, folded his hands and addressed the audience and television cameras directly.

"Was environmental contamination a factor in the tragic deaths and illness experienced as a result of the disaster?" he asked rhetorically. "This is an important ongoing concern. Environmental experts from OSHA have teamed with the CDC's medical experts to evaluate and respond to those concerns. Their findings and conclusions will be released as they become available. For now, I can only report that while it is not definitive, environmental contamination may well have been a factor in the tragic deaths here at the university.

"Let me turn now to our evaluation of the water supply." Greg Burns, the General Counsel, handed Steinberg a sheaf of documents. "I regret to report that water samples taken from the two deep wells that have served this campus for more than fifty years are, in fact, contaminated," he said somberly.

Again, the audience erupted. This time, the chairman waited patiently for the audience to absorb the news.

"Let me emphasize, there is no present danger from the contaminated water supply. The university is now served by Hillsdale's water supply, which is completely safe," the chairman said. "However, our analyses suggest that students and staff who drank water from the wells in the past may have ingested certain chemicals classified as carcinogens—cancer causing agents—by the Centers for Disease Control. Traces of benzene, radium and cyanide along with numerous trace minerals were detected in the water supply from the deep wells. Our investigation is continuing and I expect the studies to go on for some months." He passed the papers back to the General Counsel. "I have nothing further to report on this issue at the present time.

"Finally, let me conclude these remarks with a report on the deaths of two students whose remains were discovered in the rubble of Connors Hall a week after the explosion. The students—Kevin Parks, a doctoral student in chemistry, and Valerie Chapman, a senior undergraduate majoring in

European History—were positively identified by means of dental records. Their involvement in this tragedy has been the subject of enormous and highly inaccurate speculation in the local media.

"My colleagues have authorized me," he looked to his left and right as if seeking reaffirmation of their support, "to assure you that these two young people *did not*, I repeat, *did not* deliberately set off the explosion and fire that destroyed Connors Hall and Memorial Library.

"Later today President Northrop will summarize the information we have pieced together on this matter. Testimony in the days ahead will establish that these students may, in fact, be unsung heroes in this tragedy. Were it not for the persistent, indeed obsessive, actions of Mr. Parks, hazardous environmental conditions existing on this campus would not have been discovered. I defer to President Northrop to elaborate on these details." He handed the stack of papers to Greg Burns.

"This completes my preliminary remarks. We are now prepared to call our first witness."

He checked his watch and tucked his glasses into an inside jacket pocket. "Before we hear from President Northrop, we'll take a fifteen minute recess." He rose and whispered something to the General Counsel as they made their way through the side door.

Chapter 48

Judge Jeremy Steinberg rapped the gavel promptly at 3:00. With television cameras rolling, the audience quieted. They had waited months for this moment.

President Larry Northrop, accompanied by the university's outside counsel, was seated in the reserved section near the front of the auditorium. During the recess, a witness table and two chairs had been placed facing the commissioners. In the reserved section near the President, Ruth and Nancy made themselves comfortable as Northrop prepared to offer his long awaited testimony.

"Our first scheduled witness this afternoon is Dr. Lawrence Northrop, President of Cabot University. Would Dr. Northrop please come forward?"

Northrop climbed the few steps to the stage, was sworn in and seated himself at the witness table. His attorney, carrying a heavy briefcase, took the seat next to his client. Larry Northrop busied himself removing documents from his slim leather folio and arranging them in front of him.

The chairman nodded to his first witness, a welcoming smile on his face. "Good afternoon, President Northrop."

"Good afternoon, Mr. Chairman and members of the commission." The President nodded to each commissioner as the television camera behind the commissioners zoomed in for a close-up. "Allow me to introduce my attorney, Samuel Kirchner, managing partner in Kirchner, Slavin, Peabody, of Philadelphia. The firm has served as the university's legal counsel for twenty-five years." Northrop's voice was strong and confident. His calm demeanor belied the internal tension that had built up over the past two months.

"Thank you. I believe we can dispense with the introductory formalities," Steinberg responded. "The commission and, I dare say, most of the audience are familiar with your academic and professional background—your distinguished service to the university, first as a faculty member, then in various administrative posts leading to the presidency which you assumed in 1980. Is that date correct?"

"Yes," Larry nodded.

"Mr. Gregory Burns, General Counsel to the commission, will lead you through a series of questions about the events before and after the explosions and fire on April 28 and 29. Please feel free to elaborate on details as you see fit.

For the record, I might add, sir, that you have been very cooperative and forthright with the commission staff during this investigation. We appreciate your cooperation and candid responses."

Judge Steinberg motioned Greg Burns to begin.

"President Northrop, before elaborating in detail on the events that occurred here at Cabot University, I want to establish two important facts for the record." Burns paused and then read directly from the text in front of him.

"Were you aware, at any time during your tenure at the university, either as a faculty member or administrator, that highly volatile toxic waste materials were stored illegally on this campus, specifically in Connors Hall?"

"No, I was not. I learned of the existence and location of those materials in a sub-basement of the building several weeks after the disaster that nearly consumed our campus." Northrop's strong voice boomed through the auditorium. "Had I known such materials were present, I would have ordered them removed immediately in accordance with federal, state and the university's own regulations."

"To your knowledge, were any other individuals in your administration aware that waste materials were stored in Connors Hall?"

"Sir, I believe that Tyler Hutchins, Vice-President of Administration and Finance, was aware of the existence of these materials on campus. He recalled this fact just a few weeks ago."

The chairman banged his gavel in a futile attempt to restore order.

* * * *

Chairman Steinberg finally restored order after repeatedly threatening to clear the room and following a lengthy commercial break by the television pool. Larry Northrop's announcement that Porky Hutchins knew about the cache of toxic waste was sensational news, something the townspeople had suspected, but that had never been confirmed.

General Counsel Burns resumed his questioning.

"Would you summarize your knowledge of the details surrounding Mr. Hutchins' recollection of the storage of toxic waste here at the university?"

"Yes." Northrop shuffled through his papers and then began to read. "Two weeks after the fire, at my request Tyler Hutchins visited me in my office. His jaw was wired shut but he appeared to be on the road to recovery from injuries sustained the night of the fire.

"At that time, I asked Mr. Hutchins directly if he had any knowledge of toxic waste stored on campus—specifically stored in Connors Hall. Despite his injuries, he forcefully assured me he knew nothing of any cache of waste materials."

"Then how did you learn about the toxic materials in Connors Hall?" the General Counsel asked.

"Let me explain. In late June, Mr. Hutchins telephoned me and indicated he did, in fact, now recall important details about the materials. I believe his earlier memory lapse is understandable, given the injuries he sustained on the night of April 28," said Northrop.

Nancy gasped in amazement and Ruth frowned. Porky Hutchins' initial memory lapse on such an important issue was incredible, impossible to believe. And now, the President was making excuses for him. The women listened intently, their eyes trained on the giant television screen projecting a close-up of the President's face.

Northrop continued reading his prepared text.

"Let me offer some background information on Tyler Hutchins, who joined the administrative staff in 1972. During the early years, he was a close personal associate of Jackson Starrett, President of Cabot University. The Starrett Science Center is named to honor President Starrett.

Mr. Hutchins has served in a number of increasingly responsible positions. In his most recent post as Vice-President of Administration and Finance, he directed all administrative and finance functions at the university. In addition to those responsibilities, he also served as principal liaison to the state legislature. He had a major role in preparing and shepherding our budgets through the legislative process. On countless occasions he testified before the state legislature on behalf of the university. He reported directly to me. I considered him my most senior executive.

"Many of you know that Mr. Hutchins retired effective today, July 31. For the past several weeks, he has been on vacation, continuing to recuperate from his injuries. The Hillsdale Chronicle reported that he is retiring for health reasons.

"Unfounded rumors about Hutchins' actions during the early hours of the disaster have circulated in the media. I want to emphasize that reports of firefighters who allegedly observed a confrontation between my administrator and the fire chief are *false*. Mr. Hutchins has always acted in the best interests of the university. I am personally grateful for his courageous efforts on the night of April 28 and for his leadership during the early hours of the disaster prior to my return from New York City."

"What a sleaze," Nancy hissed behind her hand.

"The Hillsdale Chronicle reported that a generous pension, lifetime disability payments and a glowing commendation were inserted as an amendment to the special legislation authorizing funds for rebuilding Cabot University," Larry continued. "The commendation and retirement actions have been distorted by the media. The Chronicle published an editorial implying that Mr. Hutchins' retirement arrangement was a political payoff that rewarded one of the most disliked administrators on the campus. This is inaccurate. Mr. Hutchins has served the university with distinction for more than thirty years. He is admired and respected by faculty, staff and students. His leadership will be sorely missed."

Larry looked up from his prepared statement. "I just wanted to set the record straight on these matters," he said, without a trace of irony.

Nancy nearly laughed aloud. "Unbelievable!" she whispered to Ruth. "Larry stuck the knife into Porky after all! The Chronicle will have a field day with that testimony!"

"Thank you, President Northrop," said the chairman. He turned to Greg Burns. "Please continue with your questions."

"Let me repeat my earlier question, sir. Please relate in detail what you know about the storage of toxic materials and how you came to learn of Mr. Hutchins' involvement in this matter."

"Yes, of course.

"Following the April 28 tragedy I formed a task force to investigate the accident. The work began with an exhaustive search of our records. I want to commend the outstanding work of our staff and also thank the commission's investigative staff, numerous state and federal law enforcement officers and the United States Attorney's office for their expert assistance in this effort.

"We can now provide a fairly complete explanation of the circumstances surrounding the storage of waste materials in Connors Hall. Let me emphasize again that storage of those materials violated the university's regulations and those of state and federal environmental agencies. This information is not intended to deflect blame elsewhere, but to provide a comprehensive explanation of the tragic events of April 28-29."

Erect and poised, Larry Northrop looked every inch the distinguished college President as he read his prepared statement. He had the undivided attention of the commissioners and the audience.

"Let me digress again for just a moment" he continued. "Several years ago I approved a project to convert many of the university's priceless historical documents and important administrative records to computer media using optical scanning techniques. The original documents were displayed in the archives section of Memorial Library. They were destroyed in the fire. Although the original documents are gone, we have preserved a set of remarkably complete records on CD ROM media.

"For example, the original charter of Cabot Academy, complete alumni records, financial files and selected administrative data from 1850 to the present time have been preserved and stored in two locations—here in Old Main and at an off-campus storage site.

"After the accident," he shifted slightly in his chair, "news reports speculated that the explosions were somehow traceable to volatile toxic wastes stored in Connors Hall. Although I was not convinced that toxic wastes were involved, I authorized a complete search of our archives in an effort to dispel the rumors. Focusing on the scanned data, after three days of round-the-clock analysis, the search bore fruit."

Northrop took a sip of water and resumed. "Our search disclosed that more than fifty years ago, a private company was permitted to store what proved to be highly volatile and toxic materials on this campus. And I can confirm that these materials were stored in Connors Hall. We have a rather complete picture of the circumstances leading to the storage of those materials—when the materials arrived on campus and where they were stored. We know that due to a series of administrative lapses and errors, those materials remained unaccounted for until after the April 28 explosion."

Once more, Judge Steinberg rapped the gavel to restore order.

"From the archives preserved on computer," Northrop continued, "we learned that during World War II and until the early 1950s a company named Saxton Controls, Inc., operated a manufacturing plant east of Hillsdale on a site bordering the Susquehanna River. Saxton was a division of Capital Chemicals Corporation, one of the country's largest chemical companies, and a major early contributor to Cabot University.

"From 1941 until the end of the war, Saxton was engaged in top secret military work. At its peak, the company employed more than 300 workers, paying them unusually generous wages. Competition for jobs was intense, particularly since employment at Saxton Controls conferred automatic deferral from military service.

"Saxton Controls' security measures were extremely strong. The workers were carefully screened, many receiving the highest level of security clearance. They displayed extraordinary loyalty, doubtless aware that their work was crucial to the war effort. Given the high wages, the sense of urgency and the widespread secrecy surrounding plant operations, it's not surprising that people supported Saxton Controls and its top secret war mission. Citizens displayed an amazing willingness to guard secrets related to the war effort, somewhat in contrast to the world we live in today," he observed.

"Some of the older people in the audience today may recall the very different climate that existed during the war. It simply was unpatriotic to question the activities of a factory engaged in the war effort.

"After the war, employment levels at the plant declined markedly. Some employees were laid off; and others were transferred to the New Jersey operations of the parent company. The cloak of secrecy continued, and all former employees were forbidden to discuss their work under the threat of federal criminal penalties.

"With the return to peacetime, however, the secrecy surrounding operations at Saxton understandably led to increased speculation by local residents. Rumors arose that chemical dumping into the Susquehanna River had occurred during the war and continued into the early 1950s. In 1951, the Hillsdale Chronicle reported that large numbers of fish were mysteriously dying downstream from the plant.

"Finally in 1955, most of the plant's operations were transferred to the New Jersey headquarters of Capital Chemicals. In January 1956, the Hillsdale operation closed. Six months later Saxton Controls declared bankruptcy. The buildings eventually were torn down and a housing development was built on the land originally occupied by the plant.

"That is essentially the corporate history of Saxton Controls which we have pieced together from our own archives, from local newspaper accounts and a study of Capital Chemicals Corporation's public records between 1940 and 1956.

"Mr. Chairman, I apologize for the length of this background report. However, I believe it's important for the public to learn as much as possible about Saxton Controls and its role in the disaster here at Cabot University. I believe we will prove conclusively that Saxton Controls was the source of the chemicals that came to be stored in Connors Hall."

"Your background data on Saxton Controls is indeed interesting, President Northrop. I'm confident it is essential testimony." Glancing at his watch, Steinberg asked, "Would you like to take a short recess at this point?"

"Mr. Chairman, if possible, I would like to complete this portion of my testimony."

"As you wish. Please continue."

Northrop straightened the papers in front of him and resumed reading. "Without violating government secrecy laws, I can describe in broad outline the activities of Saxton Controls during World War II and until 1956."

A camera zoomed in on Larry Northrop's face, broadcasting the image around the country. Two television cameramen, portable cameras glued to their eyes, slowly approached the stage and recorded images of the commission members facing the President of Cabot University. Northrop savored the palpable tension in the auditorium. He took his time, sipping once more from a glass of water.

"Our investigators have learned that Saxton Controls engaged in two types of manufacturing. The company produced aircraft instrumentation that was installed in World War II bombers. It also developed and manufactured an essential part of the trigger mechanisms used to detonate nuclear devices—both atomic and hydrogen bombs."

Pandemonium erupted in the auditorium. The television cameramen panned across the audience. News anchors raced outside, pleading with their networks bosses to interrupt the late afternoon talk shows. Steinberg's repeated attempts to quell the uproar were futile. Finally, he gaveled a fifteen-minute recess. President Northrop followed the commission and staff to their familiar refuge in the second floor President's suite.

On the front steps of Old Main television commentators indulged in wild speculation, repeatedly running the tape of Northrop's sensational news. Thirty minutes later, campus security officers ordered the audience to take their seats and the hearing resumed.

Chairman Steinberg addressed the audience. "For the last time, I am warning this audience to refrain from any further outbursts," he regarded them over his glasses. "One more outburst and I'll clear this auditorium. You can all go home and watch the proceedings on television. I intend to allow President Northrop to complete his testimony today, even if it takes until midnight.

"President Northrop, we appreciate your frank and forthright testimony in these proceedings. We are ready to continue." He nodded to Greg Burns.

"President Northrop, would you please elaborate more fully on your last comment before the break?" said Burns.

"Yes. I indicated that Saxton Controls manufactured two types of products: aircraft instrumentation devices, and portions of the trigger mechanisms used in nuclear weapons."

"What can you tell us about the characteristics of each product?" Burns asked.

"Let me first describe the instrument manufacturing. The company manufactured dials—altimeters, fuel gauges and compasses—typical instruments essential to control an aircraft. During the manufacturing process, a radium-suffused paint was applied to the needles and numerals on the dials. The radium coating facilitated reading the instruments in very low light. Workers required steady hands and a fine touch to delicately paint the dials. Many of the employees in this area were female workers. They apparently were particularly competent at this precision task.

"The use of radium-suffused paint in the production process generated substantial chemical waste in addition to the radioactive risks inherent in the radium itself. Apparently, quantities of those highly toxic waste materials were dumped into the river near the plant. We have no data on which to base an estimate of the quantities. However, the early stories about dumping materials in the Susquehanna River and killing fish were doubtless accurate.

From our review of the surviving records, we believe that most of the hazardous waste was stored temporarily in fifty-five gallon barrels on the Saxton Controls property and then transported to New Jersey for disposal.

"Turning now to the production of trigger mechanisms," Northrop received a stack of documents from his attorney. "Saxton Controls received large (and apparently very profitable) government contracts during and after the war for the production of bomb triggers. Details about the production process remain classified. We have established, however, that the Hillsdale plant manufactured those trigger mechanisms over a period of at least a decade beginning in the 1940s.

"Small amounts of radioactive materials unquestionably were employed in the manufacturing process and incorporated into the finished devices. After processing in Hillsdale, the devices were shipped to the government's Hanford, Washington and Rocky Flats, Colorado bomb production facilities for final assembly.

"Our investigation indicates that both chemical and nuclear waste byproducts were generated during the manufacturing process for the triggers. I am very relieved to report that no evidence exists (at this time) to support a conclusion that nuclear wastes were indiscriminately dumped into the river. Rather, we believe that those wastes were stored in metal containers.

The ongoing investigation by state and federal environmental agencies suggests that some containers were buried in a concrete bunker at the plant site. Unfortunately, containers may still be buried beneath the housing development now located on that site. Environmental authorities are investigating that possibility. This announcement should clarify the purpose of the recent excavations reported in that area."

Judge Steinberg rapped the gavel sharply.

Larry Northrop waited for the audience to settle down. He looked up, removed his glasses and placed both hands on top of his notes. "I regret to inform you that our investigators believe that unknown quantities of the waste materials from both instrument production and the production of nuclear triggers ultimately found their way to the sub-basement of Connors Hall where they remained undisturbed for nearly half a century."

A collective gasp escaped from the audience. Steinberg raised his gavel and scowled. Larry Northrop coughed and reached for the glass of water nearby.

"Please explain to the commission and this audience why you believe that chemical and perhaps nuclear wastes were stored in Connors Hall," directed Greg Burns.

"As I mentioned earlier in my testimony, we conducted a thorough search of university records during the two decades between 1940 and 1960, focusing on the historical records scanned into our computer archives. Our search revealed a pattern of substantial contributions by Saxton Controls and its parent company, Capital Chemicals Corporation. For example, during the late 1940s and early 1950s, Cabot College received contributions well in excess of $2 million directly from Saxton Controls. Capital Chemicals contributed another $4 million between 1946 and 1952. These contributions were critically important to the development of Cabot College. In fact, they are the foundation of the university's endowment fund.

"Cabot University could not have achieved its world class reputation in science and engineering education without the financial support of those two companies. At the time, donations from Saxton and Capital Chemicals comprised more than eighty percent of the university's total endowment.

"Viewed from today's perspective, a $6 million endowment may seem insignificant. If, however, you compound that amount over a period of nearly fifty years at only 5 percent, the funds would grow to more than $60 million. Those early contributions were significant fifty years ago. Moreover, in recent years Capital Chemicals has made generous contributions and actively assisted in raising funds from other major corporations and foundations to support the university.

"During our records search we discovered a document written and signed by the President of Cabot College in 1948. Remember, we have only the scanned computer records, not the original document. The document is a letter addressed to the President of Saxton Controls and is signed by President Starrett on behalf of Cabot College. The letter acknowledges receipt by the university of a $2 million contribution from Saxton.

"I offer a copy of that letter to the commission and ask that it be made part of the permanent record of these proceedings," he rose and handed a sheet of paper to Chairman Steinberg. Returning to his chair, he continued, "With your permission, I will read a relevant portion of that letter, dated March 28, 1948." Northrop's attorney handed him a copy of the letter. The audience was silent; the only sound the faint buzz of a power mower through an open window.

"I quote President Starrett's post script to the letter."

> P. S. Cabot College is pleased to offer storage space for the materials you mentioned during my visit to the plant. Simply transport these materials to Science Hall, rear entrance, between five and six p.m. this Friday. Mr. John Farrow, custodian, will direct the off-loading and storage in the lower level, front sub-basement of the building. We will store the barrels in that location for an indefinite period until you authorize forwarding them to your New Jersey plant. Of course, there is no charge for this accommodation.

The audience sat in stunned silence.

The President continued without a pause, "This document, taken in context with the tragic events in late April, lead the entire team of investigators—university, state and federal experts—to conclude that chemical (and perhaps nuclear) waste materials were transported from Saxton Controls to this campus in 1948 and placed in a sub-basement in Science Hall, site of the now destroyed Connors Hall. Those toxic materials lay dormant, ignored and forgotten until last April 28.

"Let me summarize the subsequent events. Late that evening, two students apparently discovered and attempted to remove at least one container from its resting place. The students, Valerie Chapman and Kevin Parks, for unknown reasons, forced entry into the locked building. Whether they accidentally stumbled upon the cache of waste materials or were actively searching for it will never be known with certainty. In any event, they became the first victims of the explosions that devastated this campus.

"I understand that other witnesses will testify in more detail about the activities of Kevin Parks, a doctoral student in chemistry here at Cabot University. Mr. Chairman, you mentioned Mr. Parks and Ms. Chapman briefly in your opening remarks this afternoon. Allow me to elaborate on what we know."

"Of course, please continue," said Steinberg.

"We know that Kevin Parks apparently became obsessed with the notion that toxic materials were somehow involved in what he believed were an unusually large number of cancer deaths on the campus over the past decade. His concerns arose following the death of Professor Jacob Borovski, our distinguished professor and Mr. Parks' doctoral advisor.

He reportedly became convinced that the deaths were attributable to a so-called cancer hot spot, a cluster of cancers, which he believed were triggered by exposure to toxic materials on this campus. We cannot explain Ms. Chapman's presence in Connors Hall on the night of the explosion or the extent of her participation in Kevin Parks' search.

"The loss of these two fine students will forever be linked with the disaster on April 28. I believe that when the final chapter of this ghastly tragedy is written, they will be recognized as heroes who sacrificed their lives in a quest for answers to Mr. Parks' concerns—concerns that were dismissed by others in a position to assist them."

Northrop paused once again and sipped some water. He reached for several documents, stacked them on the table next to his prepared statement and continued to read.

"Based on our investigation over the past several months, I would like to describe the sequence of events on the night of April 28."

"Please continue," said Greg Burns.

"Investigators believe that the devastating series of explosions began with a minor explosion inside Connors Hall near the basement elevator, approximately fifty feet from the sub-basement where the toxic materials were stored. The first small explosion occurred at approximately 11:30 p.m. However, that minor explosion ignited a fire that quickly spread down the hall, through the janitor's closet to the sub-basement and the larger cache of waste materials.

"Our experts theorize (with a high degree of confidence) that a waste container probably sprung a leak as the students hauled it from the sub-basement to the elevator. A small trail of volatile materials was exposed, waiting to be ignited.

"Perhaps a minute or two later, after the fire reached the sub-basement with its large cache of drums and barrels, the volatile mixture ignited producing a second, enormous explosion. That devastating blast created the huge crater and destroyed the front of Connors Hall. The subsequent inferno that engulfed and destroyed Connors Hall and Memorial Library was fueled by severed gas lines and by the highly volatile materials.

"The two students, whose remains were found a week after the fire, were killed instantly."

Northrop was overcome with emotion, his steely composure broken. Head bowed, he clasped his hands tightly together, unable to continue. The shaken audience was utterly silent. Greg Burns waited patiently for his witness to regain control.

"The death toll has risen to twenty-five, including several firefighters," he carried on. "I'm sure the commission is aware that the losses may go higher."

"We'll take a fifteen minute recess," Steinberg interrupted and rapped his gavel. He hurried to the witness table, and together with Northrop's attorney, assisted the President from the auditorium.

Half an hour later, a calm and composed Northrop returned to the auditorium, prepared to resume his testimony.

"On behalf of the commission, I want to commend you on your forthright testimony, President Northrop," said the chairman. "I know how difficult this day has been for you. The commission and the public deeply appreciate the tireless work of you and the investigative team in reconstructing the events in this tragedy. My fellow commissioners, the university community, the town of Hillsdale—indeed the entire country—commend you for your leadership following the tragedy."

The audience erupted. This time Steinberg did nothing to quell the applause.

"Chairman Steinberg, speaking on behalf of everyone involved in this investigation, thank you for those generous words," said Northrop.

"If I may, I would like to say a few words about the two young people who died in the fire. Later witnesses will doubtless reconstruct their role in the disaster in more detail. Although we will never have a precise accounting of their last hours, I have come to believe that they were acting in the best interests of this university. I commented earlier that Mr. Parks tried repeatedly to convince two faculty members to consider seriously his theory that toxic substances contributed to the large number of cancer deaths experienced at Cabot University. Sadly, his concerns were ignored.

"I understand that the young man was hospitalized for depression. He needed help in dealing with the death a year ago of his mentor and dissertation chairman, Dr. Jacob Borovski. Ms. Chapman apparently was an acquaintance of Parks, having met him at Essex Medical Center where both were patients six months ago.

"Given that background, I hope these comments will lay to rest the speculation that has surrounded these two young people. After careful inquiry, there is no evidence—I repeat, no evidence—to support the rumor that they deliberately set the explosion and fire. Quite the contrary. All of us owe a debt of gratitude to these two students—young people who sacrificed their lives—victims of the disaster they may have inadvertently initiated.

"Thank you, President Northrop. If you feel up to further questions, I'd like to return to an earlier matter," said Greg Burns.

"Fine."

"You stated in your testimony today that you were personally unaware of the cache in Connors Hall until some time after April 28. You also indicated that Mr. Tyler Hutchins, a senior officer in your administration, knew of this secret cache of materials. Would you please elaborate on your earlier statement regarding Mr. Hutchins? Further, do you believe any other persons at the university were aware of the presence of these materials on the campus?"

"Let me respond to your second question, Mr. Burns. To my knowledge, no other persons currently employed at the university knew of the existence of those materials. Decades have passed since the letter was written and the materials were stored on campus. It's not surprising that people who might have worked on the renovation of Connors Hall have forgotten about the sub-basement and its contents.

"Answering your first question will take some time."

"I'm sure the commission and our audience are anxious to learn about Mr. Hutchins' recollections," said Burns.

Northrop smiled. "Two weeks after the fire, I questioned Vice-President Hutchins about his knowledge of hazardous materials stored in Connors Hall. He did not recall any materials stored in Connors Hall with the possible exception of some cleaning fluids used by the facilities staff. Clearly, those minor items did not cause the explosions.

"However, in a subsequent meeting about a month ago, Mr. Hutchins was able to recall some specific details surrounding the cache of toxic materials and how they came to be stored in the sub-basement of Connors Hall."

Chapter 49

"Chairman Steinberg, following Tyler Hutchins' recent admission to me, he repeated his story to the commission's investigators. They pieced together the facts I have just related plus additional information Hutchins provided in the later interview.

"According to his most complete account, one of my predecessors, Jackson Starrett, informed him of the presence of some barrels and drums of chemicals in what was then Science Hall. Starrett told Hutchins the materials were being stored at the request of Saxton Controls and were not to be disturbed. That conversation occurred around 1970, many years after the materials had arrived on campus.

"In fairness to Tyler Hutchins," he continued over the murmur of the crowd, "at the time of the fire, I believe he had forgotten the matter or perhaps thought the information was irrelevant. You'll have to ask him about that. I understand he is scheduled to appear before the commission at a later date."

"I dare say, we will look forward to Mr. Hutchins' testimony next week," said the chairman.

"Are you confident no other persons currently employed were aware of the chemicals stored in Connors Hall?"

"Yes, that's correct."

Greg Burns extracted a thick new file from his briefcase and opened it. "Turning now to the issue of cancer deaths on campus and to Kevin Parks' allegation that a so-called cancer hot spot existed at Cabot University. Did you discuss these allegations with any person or persons on campus?"

"Yes. On three occasions, faculty expressed concerns over the seemingly large number of cancer deaths on campus. The issue was first brought to my attention perhaps twenty years ago. In the space of a very short period of time—less than a year, I believe—a number of faculty and a librarian died of cancer. These people were relatively young, apparently healthy colleagues who died suddenly from very aggressive forms of cancer—most from what is referred to as "soft tissue cancers."

"At that time a small group of faculty met informally with the chairman of our Board of Trustees and later with me. They expressed concerns and requested an investigation of environmental conditions on campus. I took the request to the Board, which authorized an investigation. A confidential committee was established and a thorough investigation undertaken. The committee was never publicly acknowledged, the matter was handled in executive sessions of the Board and records of those discussions were not made public."

"Who was on that committee and what did they find?" asked Burns.

"Tyler Hutchins chaired the committee which included two members of the Board of Trustees, three senior faculty members and the Director of Buildings and Grounds. Over a period of several months tests were conducted in various laboratories and air samples were gathered in all classrooms and offices in Starrett Science Center. We now realize, of course, that we were searching the wrong building. You will have to ask Mr. Hutchins why he didn't identify and search the sub-basement in Connors Hall.

"The committee reported to the Board of Trustees that all environmental safety regulations were being followed. The Trustees received the final report and took no further action. The faculty who initially voiced their concerns were satisfied that a thorough investigation had been conducted and sought no further action."

"We were not exactly satisfied," Nancy whispered to Ruth.

"Right. Jacob was still puzzled, but there was nothing more we could do," said Ruth.

Northrop continued. "Last April, nearly a year before the explosion and fire, Dr. Jacob Borovski, a prominent faculty member, died of a particularly aggressive form of cancer. Again, Dr. Ruth Borovski and a group of concerned faculty asked for a review of all environmental procedures, including a search of the campus, to determine whether toxic materials were being properly disposed of. Last June, we closed Starrett Science Center and made an exhaustive search of the building. We found nothing.

"Again, the search was not publicized to the students, staff or the general public. I reported to the Board of Trustees that the campus was in full compliance with federal and state environmental regulations regarding the handling and disposal of toxic materials.

"Some months later—in January or February of this year, the issue arose for the third time. Dr. Nancy Atherton, a business school professor, met with me and expressed renewed concerns about the number of cancer deaths on campus. Speaking on behalf of Dr. Borovski's widow, Ruth Borovski and other individuals, she requested still another investigation.

"Professors Borovski and Atherton pointed out that some thirty-five deaths from cancer had occurred since we first examined the issue. They remained concerned that the cluster of deaths was due to a cancer hot spot. They continued to seek possible links between toxic waste problems and cancer on the campus.

"I promised to review the matter and called upon Mr. Hutchins to look into the issue once again. He objected to the most recent request, emphasizing that the search undertaken only six months earlier had proved there was not a problem and claiming it was an unnecessary burden—a poor use of limited university funds. Although he was reluctant to search Starrett Science Center again, I insisted that he conduct a brief review. A few days later, he assured me the faculty concerns were without foundation. I decided to drop the matter and I did not bring the issue before the Board of Trustees."

"Did Tyler Hutchins lead the search process each time?" Burns asked.

"Yes.

"Each time, however" his voice dropped, "we were searching the wrong building. Obviously our search yielded nothing."

"I understand that you had a final private meeting with Dr. Atherton. Is that correct?"

"Yes," said Northrop.

"What happened during that meeting with Dr. Atherton?"

"I sought to reassure her that concerns about toxic waste on campus were groundless," he whispered. "I must admit that the last meeting was somewhat acrimonious. Dr. Atherton didn't believe my assurances and seemed determined to pursue the matter further. I treated the issue as not worthy of more attention. That is a decision I will regret for the rest of my life."

Nancy and Ruth sat motionless as a television camera zoomed in on their stricken faces. There would be no winners in this investigation, only losers.

"I have no further questions of this witness," Greg Burns turned to the chairman.

"Chairman Steinberg, with your permission, I would like to read a prepared statement directly to the faculty, students and staff of Cabot University as well as to the commission on a personal matter," Larry Northrop said. He reached into his jacket pocket and withdrew a folded piece of paper.

"Much as I would like to rewrite history, the tragedy that devastated this campus in late April cannot be undone. Many people died or were injured in an accident that I could have prevented. I accept full responsibility for the disaster. Cabot University, a distinguished university, has suffered severe—perhaps irreparable—damage. Over the past thirty years, I have devoted my life to this institution—to the faculty, students and staff who have made this one of the leading universities in the United States.

"I admit publicly here today that I have failed in my most basic responsibilities as President—to preserve the legacy of the past, to nurture and challenge those who enter the university seeking knowledge and wisdom and to build an institution that will proudly and confidently meet future challenges.

"I apologize to all who tried to open my eyes, to those who looked to me for leadership and to the present and future students who will suffer from my errors. I cannot undo the mistakes of the past. I believe, however, that I can influence the future of the university."

He gazed directly into the television camera, steeling himself. He took a deep breath and continued.

"I am resigning, effective today, as President of Cabot University. Although I take this step with a heavy heart, I am utterly convinced it is the correct action—indeed, the only action—which will allow the university to move forward, to rise from the ashes of the disaster that has overwhelmed us all and to begin the long process of rebuilding, renewal and healing."

In the stunned silence that followed, he folded his statement, rose and left by the side door.

Glancing briefly across the Commons at the rubble in the distance, he strode beneath the open windows of Old Main, stepping over the heavy cables snaking through an open window from the auditorium and skirting the television truck with its satellite uplink. He brushed aside the reporters who stuck microphones and minicams in his face.

Working his way through throngs of spectators in front of Old Main, he headed down University Avenue toward the home he soon would vacate.

About the Author

Linda Kistler grew up in Pennsylvania and graduated with BS and MS degrees from Colorado State University. An accounting and management educator, she is the author of two academic books and has published more than 75 articles in academic and professional journals. A Massachusetts Certified Public Accountant, she was named Outstanding Accounting Educator in Massachusetts in 1989, has served as an Officer and Director of the Massachusetts Society of CPAs and as a member of the National Council of the American Institute of CPAs. She was Vice-Chairman of the Massachusetts State Ethics Commission from 1978 to 1981.

She is Professor Emerita and lives with her husband, Jim, in Carlisle, Massachusetts.

This is her first novel.

Printed in the United States
1311700005B/253-255